praise for

THE HAZEL WOOD

✱✱✱✱✱✱✱

"An original and imaginative fairy tale: thrilling, fascinating, and poignant in equal measure."

—*Entertainment Weekly*

"*The Hazel Wood* starts out strange and gets stranger, in the best way possible. Albert seamlessly combines contemporary realism with fantasy, blurring the edges in a way that highlights that place where stories and real life convene, where magic contains truth, and the world as it appears is false, where just about anything can happen, particularly in the pages of a good book. It's a captivating debut."

—*The New York Times Book Review*

"Insidiously beautiful, this is the opposite of escapist fantasy; it is a story about the imagination's power to loose atrocity into the (mostly) law-abiding confines of the real."

—*The Guardian*

"A darkly brilliant story of literary obsession, fairy-tale malignancy, and the measures a mother will take to spare her child."

—*The Wall Street Journal*
(Best Children's Book of the Year)

"An eerie, assured first novel. Albert occasionally entwines the haunting tales of the grandmother's book through this mesmerizing narrative, creating a fantasy as lush and twisty as ivy."

—*The Washington Post*

"A can't-miss, dark, and creepy new take on fairy tales that will have you glued to the page until the very end."

—BuzzFeed

"This extremely creepy, wondrously original, and beautifully written book conjures up a dark, bloody netherworld of fairytales and enchants and enthralls from the first sentence to the final page."   —*The Buffalo News*

"A contemporary fantasy that dwells in an atmospheric, intertwining world of terrifying circumstances; a breathtaking dive into the magic and importance of story in one's identity. 'Story is the fabric of the Hinterland,' one of the residents tells Alice. Another says, stories 'create the energy that makes this world go. They keep our stars in place.' If this is so, Albert's exquisite wordsmithing and story weaving have kept the stars aloft for a new generation of readers."   —*Shelf Awareness* (starred review)

"Alice's sharp-edged narration and Althea's terrifying fairy tales, interspersed throughout, build a tantalizing tale of secret histories and magic that carries costs and consequences. There is no happily-ever-after resolution except this: Alice's hard-won right to be in charge of her own story."   —*Publishers Weekly* (starred review)

"Highly literary, occasionally surreal, and grounded by Alice's clipped, matter-of-fact voice, *The Hazel Wood* is a dark story that readers will have trouble leaving behind. The buzz for this debut is deafening, and the fact that the film adaption is already in the works doesn't hurt."
    —*Booklist* (starred review)

"Simultaneously wondrous and horrific, dreamlike and bloody, lyrical and creepy, exquisitely haunting and casually, brutally cruel. Not everybody lives, and certainly not 'happily ever after'—but within all the grisly darkness, Alice's fierce integrity and hard-won self-knowledge shine unquenched." —*Kirkus Reviews* (starred review)

"An empowering read that will be especially popular with fans of fairy-tale retellings."
—*School Library Journal* (starred review)

"Fans of the dark supernatural will gobble this up."
—*The Bulletin of the Center for Children's Books* (starred review)

"Albert weaves a spellbinding, dark tale. The smoke-and-mirrors world of the Hazel Wood is deliciously creepy and its denizens are well-drawn."
—*VOYA* (starred review)

"It's no exaggeration to say that *The Hazel Wood* is one of the most anticipated books of the year. Fortunately this is one of those cases where the hype is justified. Readers, especially those with a fondness for dark fairy tales, won't want to miss this brilliant combination of realistic fiction and fantasy." —*BookPage*

"*The Hazel Wood* is a rich tapestry of dangerous delights, and it effortlessly balances charm, malice, beauty, and fear. The diverse characters, gritty twists and turns, vivid imagery, and captivating premise make this the perfect choice for fans of Lev Grossman, Lewis Carroll, and

Edgar Allan Poe. Chilling, atmospheric, as fresh as it is dark: the must-read of the season!"

—*Romantic Times* (RT Seal of Excellence)

"*The Hazel Wood* is thoroughly, creepily captivating, with surprises I never saw coming! Such a refreshing and beautifully written inversion of the classic fairy-tale-inspired story."

—Kristin Cashore, author of *Graceling*

"This book will be your next literary obsession. Welcome to the Hazel Wood, where bad luck is a living thing, princesses are doomed, and every page contains a wondrously terrible adventure—it's not safe inside these pages, but once you enter, you may never want to leave. *The Hazel Wood* is pure imagination candy."

—Stephanie Garber, author of *Caraval*

"Dark, spellbinding, and magical. One of the most original books I've read in years—*The Hazel Wood* is destined to be a classic."

—Kami Garcia, author of *Beautiful Creatures*

"Reader, I warn you: this book beckoned me in with delicate claws, then sank its teeth into my heart. I fear a part of me will never escape *The Hazel Wood*."

—Heidi Heilig, author of *The Girl from Everywhere*

"Elegant, ethereal, and beautifully brutal, *The Hazel Wood* is a fairy tale worth falling for. This is a dream of a book

I cannot recommend highly enough. It's like falling into a nautilus shell: every time you think you've found the end, another chamber opens. Absolutely breathtaking."

—Seanan McGuire, author of
Every Heart a Doorway

"Melissa Albert's *The Hazel Wood* is an elegant, dark fairy tale, full of the power of story. It's creepy and gorgeous, and I loved every word." —Kat Howard, author of
An Unkindness of Magicians

"Absolutely mesmerizing, magical, and inventive. Hats off to Melissa Albert!" —Karen McManus,
author of *One of Us Is Lying*

"Dark, haunting, and absolutely mesmerizing: *The Hazel Wood* grabbed me with its mysterious, upside-down fairy tales, full of thorns and sharp twists. In no time at all, I became obsessed with this book, willing to follow it anywhere—even deep into the Hinterland."

—Jodi Meadows, author of *My Lady Jane*

"*The Hazel Wood* kept me up all night. I had every light burning and the covers pulled tight around me as I fell completely into the dark and beautiful world within its pages. Terrifying, magical, and surprisingly funny, it's one of the very best books I've read in years."

—Jennifer Niven, author of *All the Bright Places*

"A winding, creepy, insidiously delicious novel. Utterly spectacular." —Melinda Salisbury, author of *The Sin Eater's Daughter*

"Full of dark, twisty corners and eerie beauty, *The Hazel Wood* is like nothing else I've read before." —Evelyn Skye, author of *The Crown's Game*

FLATIRON
BOOKS
NEW YORK

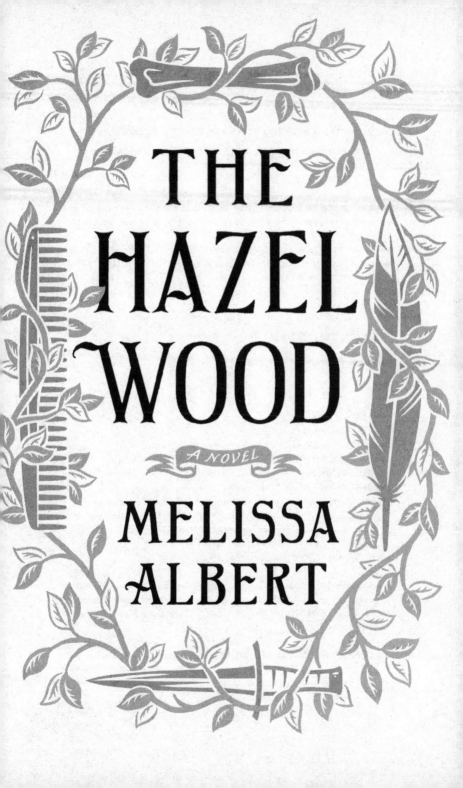

THE
HAZEL
WOOD

A NOVEL

MELISSA
ALBERT

With love and gratitude to my parents,
who never took a book out of my hands

THE HAZEL WOOD. Copyright © 2018 by Melissa Albert. All rights reserved. Printed in the United States of America. For information, address Flatiron Books, 175 Fifth Avenue, New York, N.Y. 10010.

www.flatironbooks.com

Designed by Anna Gorovoy

Illustrations by Jim Tierney

Library of Congress Cataloging-in-Publication Data

Names: Albert, Melissa, author.
Title: The Hazel Wood / Melissa Albert.
Description: First edition. | New York : Flatiron Books, 2018.
Identifiers: LCCN 2017041749 | ISBN 9781250147905 (hardcover) |
    ISBN 9781250192196 (international, sold outside the U.S., subject to
    rights availability) | ISBN 9781250147912 (ebook)
Subjects: LCSH: Imaginary places—Fiction. | GSAFD: Fantasy fiction.
Classification: LCC PS3601.L33447 H39 2018 | DDC 813/.6—dc23
LC record available at https://lccn.loc.gov/2017041749

ISBN 978-1-250-14793-6 (trade paperback)

Our books may be purchased in bulk for promotional, educational, or business use. Please contact your local bookseller or the Macmillan Corporate and Premium Sales Department at 1-800-221-7945, extension 5442, or by email at MacmillanSpecial Markets@macmillan.com.

First Flatiron Books Paperback Edition: March 2019

10 9 8 7 6 5 4 3 2 1

I went out to the hazel wood,
Because a fire was in my head.

—W. B. Yeats, "The Song
of Wandering Aengus"

~1~

Althea Proserpine is raising her daughter on fairy tales. Once upon a time she was a girl named Anna Parks, one of the legion of midcentury dreamers who came to Manhattan with their hopes tucked into a suitcase. Then she went missing. Then she came back, and achieved an odd kind of fame, glittering from some angles but dark from others. Now she's gone again, fled to a turreted house in the deep dark woods, where she lives with her five-year-old daughter and her husband, an actual royal—she just can't quit fairy tales. When I get her on the phone, her voice is as alluring as her most famous photo, the one with the ring and the cigarette. I ask if I can come talk to her in person, and her laugh is hot whiskey on ice. "You'd get lost on the way to finding me," she says. "You'd need breadcrumbs, or a spool of thread."

—"The Queen of the Hinterland," *Vanity Fair,* 1987

My mother was raised on fairy tales, but I was raised on highways. My first memory is the smell of hot pavement and the sky through the sunroof, whipping by in a river of blue. My mom tells me that's impossible—our car doesn't have a sunroof. But I can still close my eyes and see it, so I'm holding on to it.

We've crossed the country a hundred times, in our beater car that smells like French fries and stale coffee and plasticky strawberries, from the day I fed my Tinkerbell lipstick into the slats of the heater vent. We stayed in so many places, with so many people, that I never really learned the concept of stranger danger.

Which is why, when I was six years old, I got into an old blue Buick with a redheaded man I'd never met and drove with him for fourteen hours straight—plus two stops for bathroom breaks and one for pancakes—before the cops pulled us over, tipped off by a waitress who recognized my description from the radio.

By then I'd figured out the man wasn't who he said he was: a friend of my grandmother, Althea, taking me to see her. Althea was already secluded in her big house then, and I'd never met her. She had no friends, just fans, and my mother told me that's what the man was. A fan who wanted to use me to get to my grandma.

After they'd determined I hadn't been assaulted, after the redheaded man was identified as a drifter who'd stolen a car a few miles from the place we were staying in Utah, my mother decided we'd never talk about it again. She didn't want to hear it when I told her the man was kind, that he'd told me stories and had a warm laugh that made me believe, deep in my six-year-old's heart, he was actually my father come to claim me. She'd been shown the redheaded man in custody through a one-way mirror, and swore she'd never seen him before.

For a few years I'd persisted in believing he was my dad. When we left Utah after his arrest, to live for a few months in an artists' retreat outside of Tempe, I worried he wouldn't be able to find me again.

He never did. By the time I turned nine, I'd recognized my secret belief for what it was: a child's fantasy. I folded it away like I did all the things I didn't need—old toys, bedtime superstitions, clothes that didn't fit. My mom and I lived like vagrants, staying with friends till our welcome wore through at the elbows, perching in precarious places, then moving on. We didn't have the luxury of being nostalgic. We didn't have a chance to stand still. Until the year I turned seventeen, and Althea died in the Hazel Wood.

When my mother, Ella, got the letter, a shudder ran through her. That was before she opened it. The envelope was creamy green, printed with her name and the address of the place we were staying. We'd arrived the night before, and I wondered how it found us.

She pulled an ivory letter opener from the table beside her, because we were house-sitting for the kind of people who kept bits of murdered elephants around for show. With shaking hands, she slit the envelope jaggedly through its middle. Her nail polish was so red it looked like she'd cut herself.

As she shook it out, the letter caught the light, so I

could see blocks of black text through the back but couldn't read them.

Ella made a sound I didn't recognize, a gasp of complicated pain that cut my breath off clean. She held the paper so close to her face it colored her skin a faint celery green, her mouth moving as she read it through again, again. Then she crumpled the letter up and tossed it into the trash.

We weren't supposed to smoke inside that place, a cramped apartment on New York's Upper West Side that smelled like expensive French soap and wet Yorkies. But Ella pulled out a cigarette anyway, and lit it off an antique crystal lighter. She sucked in smoke like it was a milk shake, tapping the fingers of one hand against the heavy green stone she wore at the pulse of her throat.

"My mother's dead," she said on an exhale, and coughed.

The news hit me like a depth charge, a knot of pain in my stomach that kept expanding. But it had been a long time since I'd spent my hours dreaming of Althea. The news shouldn't have hurt me at all.

Ella squatted down in front of me, put her hands on my knees. Her eyes were shiny but dry. "This isn't . . . forgive me, but this isn't a bad thing. It's *not*. It could change things for us, it could—" Her voice cracked in half before she could finish. She put her head down on my knees and sobbed once. It was a desolate sound that belonged somewhere else, out there with dark roads and dead-leaf smells, not in this bright room in the middle of a loud, bright city.

When I kissed the crown of her hair it smelled like

diner coffee and the smoke twining up from her cigarette. She breathed in, out, and turned her face up to look at me.

"Do you know what this means for us?"

I stared at her, then around at the room we were sitting in: rich and stuffy and somebody else's. "Wait. Does it mean we get the Hazel Wood?"

My grandmother's estate, which I'd only seen in photos, felt like a place I remembered from some alternate, imaginary childhood. One where I rode horses and went to summer camp. It was the daydream I disappeared into when I needed a break from the endless cycle of highways and new schools and the smell of unfamiliar houses. I'd paste myself into its distant world of fountains and hedges, highballs and a pool so glittering bright you had to squint against it.

But my mother's bony hand was around my wrist, pulling me out of the Technicolor lawns of the Hazel Wood. "God, no. Never. It means we're *free*."

"Free of what?" I asked stupidly, but she didn't answer. She stood, tossing her half-smoked cigarette into the trash right on top of the letter, and walked straight-backed out of the room, like there was something she had to do.

When she was gone, I poured cold coffee on the trash can fire and pulled out the wet letter. Parts of it were eaten into ash, but I flattened the soggy remainder against my knees. The type was as dense and oddly spaced as the text on an old telegram.

The letter didn't seem new. It even smelled like it had been sent from the past. I could imagine someone typing it up on an old Selectric, like the one in the Françoise

Sagan postcard I hung up over my bed in every place we stayed. I breathed in its scent of ash and powdery perfume as I scanned what was left. There wasn't much of it: *We send our condolences,* and *Come at your earliest.*

And one marooned word in a sea of singed paper: *Alice.* My name. I couldn't read anything that came before or after it, and I saw no other reference to myself. I dropped the wet mess into the trash.

~2~

Until Althea Proserpine (born Anna Parks) died all alone on the grand estate she'd named the Hazel Wood, my mother and I had spent our lives as bad luck guests. We moved at least twice a year and sometimes more, but the bad luck always found us.

In Providence, where my mom taught art to senior citizens, the whole first floor of the house we rented flooded while we slept, on a rainless August night. A wildcat crept through a window into our trailer in Tacoma, to piss all over our stuff and eat the last of my birthday cake.

We tried to wait out a full school year in an LA guesthouse Ella rented from an earnest hippie with a trust fund, but four months in the woman's husband started suffering from symptoms of chronic fatigue. After Ella moved to the main house to help out, the ceiling fell in over the master bedroom, and the hippie sleepwalked into the swimming pool. We didn't want to start a death count, so we'd moved along.

When we traveled I kept an eagle eye on the cars behind us, like bad luck could take human form and trail you in a minivan. But bad luck was sneakier than that. You couldn't outsmart it, you could only keep going when it had you in its sights.

After Althea died, we stopped moving. Ella surprised me with a key to a place in Brooklyn, and we moved in with our pitiful store of stuff. The weeks ticked by, then the months. I remained vigilant, but our suitcases stayed under the bed. The light in our apartment was all the colors of metal—blinding platinum in the morning, gold in the afternoon, bronze from streetlights at night. I could watch the light roll and change over our walls for hours. It was mine.

But I still saw the shadow of the bad luck: a woman who trailed me through a used bookstore, whispered something obscene in my ear as she picked my phone from my pocket. Streetlights winking out over my head, one by one, as I walked down the street after midnight. The same busker showing up with his guitar on every train I rode for a week, singing "Go Ask Alice" in his spooky tenor.

"Pfft," Ella had said. "That's not bad luck, that's New York."

She'd been different since her mother's death. She smoked less, gained weight. She bought a few T-shirts that weren't black.

Then we came home one night to find our apartment windows cracked into glittering stars. Ella pressed her lips together and looked at me. I braced myself for marching orders, but she shook her head.

"New York." Her voice was hard and certain. "No more bad luck for us, Alice. You hear me? It's done."

So I went to public school. I hung Christmas lights around the plaster mantel behind our bed, and took a job at a café that turned into a bar when the sun went down. Ella started talking about things she'd never talked about before: painting our walls, buying a new sofa. College applications.

It was that last one that got us into trouble—Ella's dream of a normal life for me, one with a future. Because if you've spent your whole life running, how do you learn to stand still? How do you figure out the right way to turn your straw house into brick?

Ella did it the way we'd seen it in the movies, all those black-and-white AMC lie-fests we'd watched in motel rooms, in rented bungalows, in converted garden sheds and guesthouses and even, once, student housing.

She married up.

Sharp October sunlight sliced into my eyes as the train rattled over the bridge to Brooklyn. I had a head full of my mother's failing marriage and what felt like five cracked teeth in my mouth. I've had anger issues all my life, which Ella treated with meditation tapes, low-rent Reiki therapy she taught herself from a book, and the mouth guard I was supposed to wear but couldn't stand. During the day, I bit back every nasty thing I thought about my stepfather. At night, I took it out on my teeth.

The man my mother married, not four months after he asked her out at an event she was working as a cocktail waitress, lived on the second-to-top floor of a building off Fifth Avenue. His name was Harold, he was rich as Croesus, and he thought Lorrie Moore was a line of house paint. That was all you needed to know about Harold.

I was on my way to Salty Dog, home of the first job I'd ever lived anywhere long enough to keep. It was a café owned by a couple from Reykjavík who'd put me through a six-hour cupping seminar before I was even allowed to clean the coffee machine. It was a good job for me—I could put as much into it as I wanted. I could work hard and make perfect coffee and be friendly to everyone who came in. Or I could do it all on autopilot and talk to no one, and tips barely went down.

Today I lost myself in the comforting rhythms of the café, pulling shots and making pour-over coffees, picking up scones with silver tongs and breathing in the burnt-caramel scent of ground beans.

"Don't look now, but Guy in the Hat is here." My coworker, Lana, breathed hot in my ear. Lana was a ceramicist in her second year at Pratt who looked like David Bowie's even hotter sister and wore hideous clothes that looked good on her anyway. Today she was in a baggy orange Rebel Alliance–style jumpsuit. She smelled like Michelangelo must have—plaster dust and sweat. Somehow that looked good on her, too.

Guy in the Hat was our least favorite customer. Lana

pretended to be busy cleaning the milk steamer, so of course I had to deal with him.

"Hey, Alice," he said, making a point of reading my name tag even though he came in every day. He bopped his head to the T. Rex playing from Lana's phone. "Cool tunes. Is that the Stone Roses?"

"Oh, my god," Lana said in a stage whisper.

He stared at the menu for a good two minutes, playing the counter like a drum. Anger gathered under my skin as I waited, making it prickle. Finally, he ordered what he always did. I stuffed his biscotti into a bag, handed over a bottle of Pellegrino, and moved behind the register so he couldn't force me to do the complicated high five he'd been trying to teach me my last few shifts.

I watched him walk away, hating the short stump of his neck, the fine blond hairs on his arms, the jumpy way he snapped his fingers off the beat. My blood went high as he brushed past a seated woman, then pressed his hand to her shoulder in heavy apology.

"God, what an asshole," Lana said at full volume, watching Guy in the Hat fumble with the door on his way out. She hip-checked me. "Alice, chill. You look like you wanna strangle him. It's just Fedora Closet."

The anger receded, leaving a hot embarrassment behind. "I wasn't going to—" I began, but Lana cut me off. She was always good for that.

"Did I tell you I saw Christian naked?" She propped her chin in her hand.

Christian was our boss. He had a tiny, beautiful wife and a huge, red-faced baby that looked like a demon in a book of woodcuts. I tried but failed to think of an innocent reason for Lana to have seen him stripped.

"Are you . . . is it because you had sex with him?"

She laughed like I was far less worldly than she was, which I was but fuck you, Lana. "Can you imagine? Luisa would sic her terrifying baby on me. No, he commissioned me to do a sculpture of the family."

"Naked?"

"Yeah," she said, already losing interest in her story.

"Oh. Was he . . . was it gross?"

She shrugged, looking at something on her phone.

I had the idea, when Ella started going out with Harold, that I'd make Lana into my friend so I'd have someone of my own, but it hadn't really worked that way. She was more into having an audience than a pal.

I grabbed a rag and went out to bus, just to force Lana to make some drinks for a change. As I moved between tables, I got the prickling, shoulder-bladey feeling of someone watching me. I'm not Lana—in most situations, I go unnoticed—so it made me clumsy. I knocked over a teacup, cursed aloud, and swiped up the mess. As I did so, I cased the customers.

There was a table of women in flashing engagement rings, clustered around green teas and a single coconut donut with four forks. Two identically bearded, plaid-shirted guys at separate tables, hunched over matching Macs and unaware of each other. A woman trying to read *Jane Eyre*, side-eyeing the checked-out mom and spoon-banging toddler one table over. And a man in a Carhartt jacket and sunglasses sitting near the door. He wore a stocking cap despite the mugginess, and was nursing a cup of water.

Then three things happened: Lana dropped the plate she was holding, which landed with a crack on the checkerboard tile; the Carhartt man looked up over the tops of his sunglasses; and a shock wave of recognition rolled through me, leaving me shaking in my shoes.

We stared at each other, the man and I, and he saw me remember. As we locked eyes, I recalled things I'd forgotten: ten years ago, his car had smelled like Christmas trees. He'd ordered pancakes *and* eggs when we'd stopped for breakfast. I'd been wearing a purple corduroy jumper over a striped T-shirt and tights, and white cowboy boots with silver studs I was extremely proud of. He'd told me stories, some I recognized and some I didn't. I could never remember what they were about, after, but I remembered the feeling they gave me: the feeling you get from good poetry, *real* poetry, the kind that makes your neck tingle and your eyes tear up.

He was the man who'd spirited me away in his blue Buick, the man I'd imagined was my father. His red hair was hidden, but I knew his eyes. Then I'd been little and only knew he was a grown-up. Now I could see how young he was—twenty, twenty-five at the outside. It was ten years since I'd seen him, and he looked exactly the same: impossibly young. It was *impossible*. But I knew with certainty it was him, and that he was here because of me.

As all of this hit me, he was already standing up, grabbing his book off the table, and striding out of the café. Before the bells on the door stopped jingling, I was after him. Someone's laptop cord crossed my path, and I nearly sent the thing flying; by the time I finished apologizing and wrenched open the door, the man was out of sight. I looked up and down the quiet sidewalk, my hands itching to hold a cigarette—my mom and I had quit when we moved in with Harold.

But he was gone. After a few minutes, I went back inside.

On the table he'd left an empty cup. A balled napkin. And a feather, a comb, and a bone. The feather was dark gold, with a lacy glass-green tip. The comb was red plastic. The bone must've come from a chicken, but it had the shape of a human finger bone. It was bleached perfectly clean. The trio was laid out like a hieroglyph, a vague pi shape that impressed itself on my brain as I swept it all into my apron pocket.

"Okay, what was that?" I'd never seen Lana so curious about me before. "Girl, your . . . your lips look *white*. Did that guy do something to you?"

He kidnapped me when I was six. I think he might be a Time Lord. "Nobody. I mean, he was nobody. I was wrong, I thought I recognized him but I didn't."

"Nope. Nothing you just said is true, but fine. You're going to sit here, and I'm going to bring you some food, and you're not working anymore till you stop looking like crap. Oh, except I have to leave in twenty minutes, so hopefully you'll look better by then."

I sat down hard, my knees giving out partway. One of the engagement ring women frowned at me and tapped her cup, like we were the kind of place that did free refills. *Oh, just tempt me,* I thought, but I was too weak to get mad.

Too scared. Call it what it is, Alice. Maybe I could've talked myself into believing what I wanted so badly to believe—that he was a man I'd never seen before, who looked a little like someone I'd met briefly a decade ago. And maybe I could have forgotten about him altogether, if it weren't for the book I'd seen in his hands as he sped out the door.

I hadn't seen the book in years, but I knew what it was the instant I spied the familiar green cover.

He'd been reading *Tales from the Hinterland,* of course. Of course he had.

~3~

I was ten the first time I saw the book. Small enough for a pocket and bound in green hardback, its cover embossed in gold. Beneath its strange title, my grandmother's name, all in uppercase.

I was already the kind of girl who closed my eyes and thumped the backs of furniture looking for hidden doors, and wished on second stars to the right whenever the night was dark enough to see them. Finding a green-and-gold book with a fairy-tale name in the very bottom of an otherwise boring chest of drawers thrilled me. I'd been poking around the attic of a family we were staying with, a loaded couple with a two-year-old son who didn't mind hiring a live-in nanny with a kid of her own. We'd stayed in their spare bedroom the whole first half of my fifth-grade year, miraculously without incident, until the husband's increasing friendliness to Ella made her call it.

I'd sat cross-legged on the attic's tacky rag rug and opened the book reverently, tracing my finger down the table of contents. Of course I knew my grandmother was an author, but I'd been pretty incurious about her up to that point. I was told almost nothing about her, and assumed she wrote dry grown-up stuff I wouldn't have wanted to read anyway. But this was clearly a storybook, and it looked like the best kind, too: a book of fairy tales. There were twelve in all.

The Door That Wasn't There
Hansa the Traveler
The Clockwork Bride
Jenny and the Night Women
The Skinned Maiden
Alice-Three-Times
The House Under the Stairwell
Ilsa Waits
The Sea Cellar
The Mother and the Dagger
Twice-Killed Katherine
Death and the Woodwife

Being named Alice, of course I'd flipped straight to "Alice-Three-Times." The pages rippled like they'd once been wet, and smelled like the dusty violet candies my mother loved and I hated. I still remembered the story's first line, which was all I had time to read before Ella came in, tipped off by mother-radar, and ripped the book from my hands.

When Alice was born, her eyes were black from end to end, and the midwife didn't stay long enough to wash her.

It was so creepy it made my heart squeeze, and I was glad to see Ella. I didn't understand why her eyes were so bright, why she was breathing so hard. "This book isn't for children," she said shrilly.

I wasn't sure what to say. My mom never told me I was too young for anything. When I asked her where babies came from, she told me in Nature Channel–level detail. If her friends tried to change the topic of conversation when I walked into a room, Ella would wave away their concern. "She knows perfectly well what an overdose is," she'd say. "Don't insult her intelligence." Then, more likely than not, she'd tap her glass and tip her head toward the kitchen, where I'd dutifully shake her up a perfect martini.

Hearing her pull the age card for the first time in memory made me horribly, burningly curious. I had to read that book. *Had* to. I never saw the copy from the attic again, but I remembered the title and bided my time. I looked for it at libraries and bookshops, and on the shelves of all the people we stayed with, but I never found it. It showed up on eBay once—I used to have a Google alert set for the title—but the bidding quickly climbed beyond my price range.

So I turned to finding out more about its author instead. That's how my obsession with my grandmother, Althea Proserpine, began.

Lana left, and a guy named Norm came in to replace her. He spent the next three hours talking about a hangout he'd had with Lana that may or may not have been a date, not that he was worried about it, but what did I think and had Lana mentioned him?

I gave him noncommittal answers until finally I cracked. "Jesus Christ, Norm. This is the 'move on with your life' dance." I did a dance like I was imitating a train. "There, did that work? Lana's literally never said your name in my presence."

The injured look on his face gave me a flush of dark satisfaction. "Damn, Alice, that's cold." He took off his hat, folded the brim to make it more pretentious, and re-perched it on his head.

His silent treatment for the rest of the night gave me time to think—time to replay what I'd seen, again and again. When my shift ended, I stepped out into the night feeling skinless. The light was gone, and the houses I passed on the way to the train looked closed and clannish, like that one house you skip on Halloween. I jerked back when a man brushed too close against me on the sidewalk. His skin smelled burnt and his eyes seemed too light in the dark.

He kept walking, barely acknowledging me. I was being paranoid. Everywhere I looked for the stocking cap, the blue eyes. Nothing.

There were a handful of people waiting for the Q. I stood close enough to a woman pushing a baby in a stroller that it might've seemed like we were together. She didn't look at me, but I saw her shoulders tighten. When the train came, I got in and jumped out again at the last possible moment, like I'd seen in the movies.

But then the platform was even emptier. I put one ear-bud in and played the white noise app Ella put on my phone and made me listen to whenever I started acting like a loaded gun.

When the next train came, I practically leapt on. The scene from the café kept unfolding like a movie in my mind: the crack of the plate, the blue of his eyes, the way he'd vanished out the door with the book in his hands. But already the edges were rubbing off the memory's freshness. I could feel it degrading in my hands.

My neck hurt from holding it tight, keeping it on a swivel. The constant vigilance became a beat behind my eyes. When a guy holding a saxophone case threw open the door between cars, panic made a hot, hard starburst in my chest.

What if there was an explanation for the man's unlined face, the sense I had that he hadn't aged a day? Botox, French moisturizer, a trick of the light. My own black hole of a brain, writing an image from the past over the present.

Even so, he would still be a man who had a book that was impossible to find. Who'd told me ten years ago he knew my grandmother and was taking me to see her. What if he really had been? What if Ella had been wrong about him being a stranger?

What if Ella had been lying?

Years after I thought I'd buried it, the old obsession stirred. When the train finally rose up from underground and onto the bridge, I pulled up an article about Althea on my phone. It was once my favorite, the longest piece I could find. I even had an original copy of the magazine it ran in, which I came upon by some miracle in a used bookstore in Salem. *Vanity Fair,* September 1987, featuring a six-page spread of my grandmother on her newly bought estate, the Hazel Wood. In the photos she's as slender as the cigarette she's smoking, wearing cropped pants and red lipstick and a look that could slice through glass. My mother is a black-haired blur by her knees, a wavering shadow under the glitter of the swimming pool.

It opens like this: "Althea Proserpine is raising her daughter on fairy tales." It's an odd opening, because my mom barely figures in the rest of the article, but I guess the journalist liked the double meaning. My mom was raised hearing fairy tales, like anyone else, and she was raised on the money that came from them. Althea's estate, the Hazel Wood, was bought with fairy-tale money, too.

Before she wrote the strange, brief volume that made her name, my grandmother was a writer for women's magazines, back when the job was less "20 Sexy Things to Do with an Ice Cube" and more "How to Get That Spot out of Your Husband's White Shirt."

Until she took a trip in 1966. She doesn't name names, but she doesn't stint on telling the reporter the good stuff: she was traveling with an older man, a married editor at a men's monthly, lazing around the Continent with a group of other bored American tourists. After nine days spent drinking their liquor hot (couldn't trust the ice cubes) and writing letters to their friends at home, things went sour between her and the married man. She took off on her own. And something happened.

She doesn't say what, exactly. "I chased a new kind of story through a very old doorway," she told the journalist. "It took me a long time to find my way back." Not another word is said about what she did between 1966 and 1969, while her houseplants died and her job dried up and her New York life got mossed over and swept away.

When she returned to the States, the world had forgotten her. She felt, she said, "like a ghost moving through a museum of my old life." (She talked like a woman who knew more books than people.) She found a friend to stay with, a former Barnard classmate with a spare room, where she sat down and tapped out twelve stories on a typewriter. They were collected into a book called *Tales from the Hinterland,* and published by a tiny independent press in Greenwich Village that focused on female-penned fiction nobody read.

But somehow, my grandmother's was. Her lovely face on the back cover couldn't have hurt: level eyes, blue in color but pale gray in black-and-white. Her eyebrow is quirked, her lips lined and slightly parted. She's wearing a man's white shirt, open one button too many, and a heavy onyx ring on her right first finger. She's holding, of course, a cigarette.

The book got a few write-ups in smaller journals, and became a word-of-mouth sensation. Then a French director looking to make his first American picture optioned it for development.

The film shoot was infamous, plagued by high-profile affairs, professional squabbles, and the disappearance of two crew members in unrelated incidents. But the film itself was an art-house hit. It was rewritten as a psychological drama about a woman who wakes up in the woods with no memory of her former life; my grandmother's stories play out as dream sequences, or flashbacks. According to the reviews I could find, it bore zero resemblance to its source material.

The movie's success, partly fueled by infamy, led to several short-lived stage productions, a miniseries that never came to be, and Althea's failed stint as a TV development consultant in Los Angeles. When she got back to New York she bought the Hazel Wood, going for a song after its last owner had died under seamy circumstances in a fire that damaged part of the estate.

She'd picked up a couple of husbands along the way, the first an actor she met on the set of the movie. He left his wife for Althea, and was killed by a junkie in their apartment in the Village when Althea was pregnant with Ella. She met her second husband, a displaced descendant of Greek royalty, in LA, and took him with her to the Hazel Wood.

So yes, you could say my mother was raised, in part, on fairy tales. But death played a part. And money. Dead-husband money, fairy-tale money, too. Enough of it must've ended up in my mother's pockets to get us by despite her sketchy employment history and all the leases we've run from partway through. Staying in motion was as much a part of who we were as my mom's sharp laugh, my angry streak. Our bad luck days that abated with every move, then slipped back in like red dirt on our shoes.

But no matter how bad it got, the Hazel Wood was always at our backs. It was always the place Ella would never return to. She took care of me, and I took care of her, in a symbiotic sisterly relationship that looked cute on TV but felt fucking exhausting when you're moving for the third time in a year and don't even have a bedroom door to slam.

As I pored over the article about Althea for the nth time, it didn't read to me the way it used to. I once pictured Althea as a distant but benevolent star, a fairy godmother who watched me from far away. My fevered kid brain cooked together fairy tales and my missing grandmother and the mystery of the man who took me into a superstition I never voiced aloud. When I looked into mirrors, I secretly believed Althea could see me. When a man watched me too long through a car window or at the grocery store, I didn't see a perv, or the first harbinger of the bad luck coming: he was one of Althea's messengers. She watched me, and she loved me, and one day she would show herself to me.

But now I was reading her story with fresh eyes. She wasn't a fascinating fairy queen, she was an arrogant fantasist. Who hadn't once, from my babyhood to her death, tried to contact Ella. Ella, who had me at nineteen and hasn't had anyone but me to hold on to since.

Because that's what the article doesn't get to. Just months after it ran, Althea's second husband killed himself in the Hazel Wood. After his death, Althea closed its borders. She and Ella were shut up in there alone, living on fairy tales and god knew what else, with only each other for company. This is the part Ella really won't talk about, the fourteen years she spent rattling around in a place cut off from the world. She didn't even go to school. Who my dad is, and how she met him, is a secret so buried I've stopped asking.

My head was buzzing when I reached the apartment.

Wait. Apartment doesn't put the right image into your head. The . . . estate? Not quite, but closer.

Harold's place smelled like discreet cleaning products, my stepsister's perfume, and whatever takeout Ella ordered that night. I think Harold had some idea she would be cooking dinner for him, maybe from the dented tin box of recipes that lived in the kitchen, inherited from his mother. But he was disappointed there: Ella and I could live for weeks on cereal and popcorn and boiled edamame.

I heard the high murmur of raised voices down the hall and followed it to their closed bedroom door.

"You didn't embarrass me tonight, you embarrassed yourself."

Harold's voice ended in a hiss. I used the sounds behind the door to place them: Harold to my left, a soft shift that was Ella on the bed.

I pressed my back against the wall outside their bedroom door. *If he moves any closer.*

"You can look like trash on your own time, but tonight was about being my wife." *Wife* burned even worse than *trash*, but I stayed still, biting back the cold metal taste of rage. Ella asked me again and again to trust her. That she could handle Harold. That she loved him. That this grab at stability wasn't just for me.

Her silence was louder than Harold's voice. It's her greatest power, though she never used it on me. She'll stare at you as you try to pull your thoughts together, to say something that'll reach her, but she'll never reach back. I've watched her pull things out of people—secrets, confessions, promises to let us stay an extra month—with her silence alone. She wields it like a weapon.

"Ella." Harold's voice was suddenly desperate. I was lanced by a pity I didn't want to feel. "Ella, say something, goddammit!" I heard the rush of his clothing as he moved across the room, toward my mother on the bed.

I waited a beat and a breath, and tried to wrench open the door.

Locked.

"Mom! What's going on?"

"Jesus *Christ,* is that your daughter again?"

"Mom." I pounded the heel of my hand against the door. "Let me in."

Quiet, a creak, then Ella's voice was close. "I'm okay, baby. Go to bed."

"Open the door."

"Alice. I'm fine. We're just talking. You can help me by going to bed."

Rage was running through my blood. "He called you trash. Open the door!"

Harold threw it open, and I startled back. He was rumpled, partly undressed. His shaved head looked shadowy and his eyes were bloodshot. Harold had Captain Hook eyes—mournful and cornflower blue, with a phantom glaze of red when he was angry.

Next to him, in a dark strapless sheath and shock of wild hair, Ella looked like a black poppy. Her dress seemed designed to call attention to the tattoo climbing up her arm and almost to her throat: a psychedelic flower on a spiny stem that could've been a botanical illustration of a blossom found on Mars. I had its twin tattooed on me in mirror image—a misguided Mother's Day gift Ella had blindsided me by hating.

In the half-light of the hallway, she looked like a predator, and Harold looked like prey. The anger ebbed away.

"I didn't call her trash. I just said . . ." He ran a hand over his drooping head. "These dinners are important. They're full of potential clients, they determine the course of— Oh, for Christ's sake, why am I trying to talk to you?"

Ella leaned against the doorframe, watching him coolly. "I was wearing this the night you met me. Remember?"

"Yeah, when you were a *cocktail waitress*. Forget it, I'm not going to stand here defending myself to both of you." Harold glared at me. "I'm not a monster, Alice. Why are you always looking at me like I'm some goddamned monster?" He turned heel and retreated to the master bathroom.

"Mom."

Ella cocked her head at my tone, looked for a moment like she'd ask. Instead she sighed, long and heavy. "Go to bed, Alice. We'll talk in the morning, okay?"

She touched her forehead to mine, gently, then closed the door between us.

A dense quiet settled around my ears. It was the sound of living in a place sealed off from the rest of the city, in a vacuum of wealth.

I walked into the kitchen feeling like a thief, and foraged through cabinets in the dark.

"Is that a squirrel I hear, rummaging for nuts?"

I looked at the bag of pecans in my hand and eased it back onto the shelf. Audrey kept tabs and a running commentary on what people ate, her voice hard-edged if it was less than what she did. She sat in the unlit living room, her spume of dark hair in a topknot just visible over the back of the couch. She didn't turn as I walked closer, but she tensed.

My stepsister was a sexy, zaftig motormouth who made me feel like an awkward breadstick. She was sprawled out in cutoff sweats and a tank top, always a little under-covered even at home. I watched over her shoulder as she clicked, restlessly, on a long feed of women wearing expensive clothes, ordering things she'd barely recognize when they arrived. It made me think of someone sitting at a casino machine.

"You playing superhero again?" she asked, her voice too bright. "Did you save your mom from my evil dad?"

I dropped onto the armchair across from her. "Harold's not interesting enough to be evil. He's just not good enough."

That made her look up, eyes washed to blankness by white computer light. "You think my dad's not good enough for your mom?" She made the last two words sound like profanity. "You'd still be living out of your car if it wasn't for him. Wearing *Walmart jeans*."

I was impressed she'd heard of Walmart, and pissed at myself for telling her something true. "Hey, sometimes we lived in shacks," I said. "Or trailers. Once a garage."

She considered me. "Once I waited so long for my truffle burger it was cold when it got there," she said. "So I totally get it."

"Once our car window got broken out, and Ella replaced it with duct tape and a sled."

Audrey smiled faintly, her hand going still on her laptop. "Once my dad bought a boat and named it *The Audrey,* but he forgot to put a ballroom in so I sunk it."

"Once . . ." The image that came to me then was jagged and fast, a three-frame cut of the bad luck that chased us out of Chicago. I closed my eyes against it, then stood abruptly. "You win."

Her expression slid shut, and she smirked down at her computer. "Good night, sis," she muttered as I passed her.

"Good night, Audrey," I replied, too quiet for her to hear.

Ella and Harold's room was silent as I passed. I tried to read the silence, but it was hard through a carved oak door. I continued on to the guest room Harold had barely converted for me.

Every morning I left my eyeliner out on the sink of the bathroom attached to my room. I left books open on the bed, socks under the sheets, jeans accordion-scrunched on the floor. Every night they were gone, tucked back into the cabinet, the hamper, the bookshelf. Waking up at Harold's felt like living in *Groundhog Day.* No matter what I did, I couldn't make a mark.

I avoided my eyes while brushing my teeth, then climbed into bed with a copy of *The Blind Assassin,* because if you're not with the book you want, you might as well want the book you're with. But I couldn't focus on the words, and after a while I got up to retrieve the feather, the comb, and the bone from my dirty apron. I held them on my palm a moment before tipping them into a velvet pouch that used to hold Scrabble tiles and tucking it into my backpack.

I lay back down certain I wouldn't drift off for hours but found myself waking from a sound sleep while it was still dark. Before my eyes were fully open, I sensed my mother's presence in the room. She climbed noiselessly into bed beside me, and I loosened my grip on the covers so she could grab her share. I stayed still as she dropped a kiss on my cheek, dry-lipped and smelling of amber.

Her sigh was silvery; it tickled my ear. I held my breath till I couldn't stand it, then rolled over to face her.

"Why him?"

She went tight, like she was tensing for a blow. I hadn't hit her since I was ten, but seeing her brace made me press my hands between my knees. I expected her to beg off, to roll over, to tell me to wait till it was light and ask again. Not that she'd answer.

But she turned toward me, her eyes a faint, familiar shine. "I thought I was in love with him," she whispered. "I promise I did."

"And now?"

She settled onto her back, long fingers plucking at the comforter. "It feels good to rest. Doesn't it? It feels so good to just rest."

The roar in me, of everything that had happened—the man at the coffee shop, his book, the feather, the comb, the bone—turned down like a volume knob. Because Ella deserved this, didn't she? Peace in a city so dense and bright its lights ate bad luck like they ate darkness.

Unspoken things bloomed at the back of my throat,

then went cold. And I decided: I'd give her one more day. One more stretch of rest before telling her the same old curse had found us, in a form I didn't fully understand.

We lay quiet in the dark a while longer, and fell asleep at the same time.

~4~

I was drawn to the surface of sleep by a longing for good coffee. When I opened my eyes, Ella was gone.

The best reason to wake up early at Harold's was to get to the kitchen first. I still felt like a guest, so I preferred to slip around without being seen. A few minutes after I poured my coffee and added milk and honey to the cup, Harold walked into the kitchen in a three-piece suit all buttoned up tight, like he was making up for my having seen him so undone. Pointedly he grabbed the milk off the counter and put it back in the fridge.

"I was still using that," I said, leaning against the kitchen island and drowning a pulse of rage with a swig of hot coffee.

He side-eyed me. "Coffee stunts your growth," he said finally. "You want to look like a twelve-year-old your whole life?"

I slammed my cup down on the counter, but he was already leaving the kitchen. I felt like throwing the coffee at his retreating back, but gulped it down in one burning mouthful instead. I needed it. The redheaded man had come to me in dreams, his face looking out from steamed-over windows, his voice whispering stories over a pay-phone wire. The dreams mashed together with what I'd seen at Salty Dog until none of it felt real. Nothing but the feather, the comb, and the bone, solid in the bottom of my bag.

When Audrey's dog-whistle voice alerted me to her approach, I grabbed a granola bar from my stash in Harold's pantry and slipped out of the kitchen. I'd get my fill of her on the way to school—which Audrey she'd be was harder to predict. Maybe she'd ignore me; maybe she'd talk at me nonstop about some arcane statute of girl code one of her friends had broken. Or maybe she'd punish me for last night, for cutting our twisted bonding ritual short.

I hit the sidewalk early, an old smoker's habit. Audrey stalked out in shades at 8:35, and we climbed into Harold's black town car.

"Dad's taking off work today," she said to her cell phone, tapping away at a text the length of a Bible passage. "And you know what that means."

"I do?"

"It means," she said, then dropped her voice to a whisper, "it's imminent. D-i-v-o-r-c-e."

I let my head fall back against the car seat's gamey leather, waiting for the high of victory to hit. It didn't come. Instead, I had the perverse desire to argue.

"But they just got married. And what's his staying home have to do with it? Are they getting a divorce *right now*?"

She exhaled hard and spitty, like having to deal with me was too much to bear. "Today's the day he calls a marriage counselor. He always does that, so he can tell himself he tried. If history really wants to repeat itself, six months from now is when he leaves your mom for the counselor. But it doesn't matter who it is. Either Ella jumps first or it ends with him meeting someone else because he's an addict like that. He's predictable as an effing *book*. So don't act like I don't know what I'm talking about." She was breathing hard, staring at her phone like she wanted to kill it.

I paused, then held a hand out, pinkie up. "Don't worry, Audrey. We'll always be sisters. I pinkie-swear it."

She laughed through her nose. "Oh, yeah, we'll see each other all the time. I'll come get bedbugs at your new apartment."

"Can refrigerator boxes get bedbugs?"

"Cute." Her phone chimed, and she got back to clacking away. I got back to bathing in the thin nausea that accompanied the idea of my mom's divorce.

Ella's marriage was doomed, I knew that. Harold was the last man she should have been with. His taste in books, his rigidity, his obsession with how things looked from the outside: all of it was antithetical to who she was.

But sometimes in their early days I'd come home to

find them locked together on the couch, his tie off and her feet bare. When he kissed her on the forehead she'd turn her chin up toward him like a sunflower. Seeing it gave me a hot and cold feeling, like sweating in a winter coat. Now the air between them was fraught, but for a little while it had crackled with something quick-burning and private. Though they were never going to last, Harold was still something Ella had wanted. Not just for me: for her.

Guilt bit at me; I twitched it off my shoulders.

Audrey's phone chimed again, insistent, and something she read in the misspellings and emoji cluttering its screen made her voice harden. "Just so you know, my dad's never had a marriage last less than a year. So your mom's gold-digging skills must be super on point."

I looked at her flatly, my guilt melting down to a fine white anger. She felt the shift and her hands went nervous, jittering to a stop on her phone screen.

There was a time when I would've used words to make one clean, cold cut in her, in the place where she was softest—the rubble of acne beneath the foundation layer that ended at her chin; her father's offhand comments about the fit of her jeans; her own mother, out of touch but still plenty capable of cashing Harold's monthly checks—then gone in for the evisceration.

But I couldn't do it without hearing Ella's voice in my ear, her hands a warm weight on my shoulders. *Breathe in the light, Alice. Breathe out the anger.*

I hated that hippie shit.

"Just so *you* know," I said, nicer than I wanted to, "Ella's never dated a guy who's owned anything bigger than a motorcycle before. So she's that good at gold-digging on her first try."

Audrey made a face like my stupid retort was acceptable, then turned her attention toward using her phone's reversed camera as a makeup mirror.

The courtship of my mom and Audrey's dad, in three acts:

Act One: Harold spies Ella across the room at a cocktail party. "I thought she was one of us," he liked to say jovially. "I didn't think she was the help!" This passed for charm when you were Harold.

When the sea of people between them cleared, he'd seen she was dressed all in caterer black, holding a tray at the level of her waist. If you held them any higher, she'd told me, men had an excuse to get a good angle on your cleavage.

Harold ate a spanakopita and asked her to write her number on the napkin. Which she did. This is the part I still can't understand. Was it his Jersey accent that got her? The hair coming out the top of his shirt? My guess is it was the expensive watch glittering around his thick wrist—or, if I'm being less jaded, his eyes. They were a deep, melancholy blue, the kind that hinted at something interesting in their depths. Even if I'd never seen him deliver on the promise.

Act Two: The first date. Ella left our apartment at eight to meet Harold for a drink, and found a town car waiting for her. Drinks turned into dinner turned into a drunken two a.m. phone call letting me know she wasn't coming home till morning. This was an Ella I hadn't seen since I was nine, when she'd driven her boyfriend's motorcycle barefoot into a duck pond in the middle of a still August night. It freaked her out enough—the obsession, she'd told me later, with the idea of "What if Alice had been on the back?"—that she swore ever after to be home and mostly sober by midnight.

She'd returned from her date with Harold almost twenty-four hours after she'd left, shoeless (always a bad sign) and wearing a suit coat over her dress. I sniffed it when she wasn't looking. It smelled like the drunk finance guys who pressed too close against me in the crush of the train when I took it at the wrong time of day. I'd shaken my head. Poor Harold. Ella's going to eat you alive.

Act Three: The whirlwind courtship. Epic fifteen-course tasting menus, weekends in the Hamptons, an awkward high tea with me and Audrey. And, of course, the fateful opera date that literally began with him sending her a dress.

"I just threw up in my mouth, that's so cheesy," I'd told her.

"We can pawn it if the date's a fail," she'd shot back, smoothing it over her hips. There was a funny glitter in her eyes as she watched herself in the mirror. I thought of that later, when she came home with a twin glitter on her ring finger: a rock as big as the Ritz.

My memory of that night is tattered, a movie screen clawed to strings. The glint of the ring lodged in my eye like a shard of demon glass, and the anger overwhelmed me. I remembered Ella's drawn face as she slammed the bathroom door between us, the splintery give of its cheap wood when I kicked the bottom panel out. The slide of honeyed whiskey over my throat the next day, scalded with screaming, and the miserable heat behind my eyes when I saw Ella was still wearing the ring.

The person who married Harold six weeks later wasn't my mother. The woman who was making him miserable now? That was the Ella I recognized, coming out of deep freeze.

Harold's driver pulled up in front of Whitechapel, and my stomach did its usual roller-coaster drop. Audrey slipped her phone into her bag, hustling out of the car so quick she was absorbed into a pod of rich girls by the time my feet hit the sidewalk.

I'd spent my entire life as the new kid, and it never stopped sucking. It didn't matter if you were starting seventh grade in Podunk nowhere, or your junior year at Whitechapel, the fancy-ass Upper East Side academy Harold paid my way into. The students were the same wherever I went: clannish, judgmental, and unwilling to make an independent move.

My Monday-morning ennui was overlaid with a low-level dread. I kept expecting to see the red-haired man. He'd broken the skin that separated me from that strange, dreamlike day in my childhood, brought it close. Now that he'd shown himself, he could be anywhere: the man pretending to look at his cell phone on the corner of Eighty-Sixth Street. The jogger running with a Starbucks cup. Maybe I'd walk into class and he'd be there, disguised as a substitute teacher and reading that green book. I ran my hands down my uniform skirt and breathed.

The first half of my day was Comp, Medieval Lit, Calculus, and lunch. My performance in those classes could be rated as good, fine, bad, and terrible, respectively.

After lunch was Drama with Audrey and her gang of future Real Housewives. It was the one class she never skipped, which had something to do with the fact that our teacher was a floppy-haired former TV actor who made us call him Toby.

But she ditched today. Her absence meant that, for once, we had the right number of people to pair up for scenes at the end.

And when Toby started flinging his corduroy arms around, pairing us up at random, I had a premonition: I'd get partnered with Ellery Finch.

~5~

Everyone at Whitechapel was rich, but Finch was on another level. Back when she still thought I was impressable, Audrey had given me a Google-powered tour of her school's best and brightest—aka, richest. She'd shown me a photo of a younger, geekier Finch at a fancy event, sandwiched between a silver-fox type and a beautiful brown-skinned woman wearing a necklace Ella would've loved, which looked like a chain of throwing stars.

Finch was almost as short as me and skinny, with a crackling energy that followed him like an aura. His hair grew in every direction, and his eyes were caffeinated and quick, a brown a few shades lighter than his skin. He dressed kinda like old photos of Bob Dylan: work boots and high-waisted pants. I had no idea how he got his uniform pants to ride so high.

None of this would've mattered to me except for one thing: he knew who I was. Most people don't, and if they did, they wouldn't care. Being the estranged granddaughter of a minor, largely forgotten literary celebrity mattered to pretty much nobody, especially in a school where fundraiser auction items tended to include guitar lessons with somebody's pop-star father. It was just my luck that one of Althea Proserpine's few remaining superfans happened to go to Whitechapel, and managed to find out who I was. Finch had cornered me at my locker my first week of school.

"You're Alice Proserpine, aren't you?"

"Who told you that?"

Finch was beaming. I'd seen him around, even thought he was kind of cute, but right then I wanted to swipe the grin off his face. "Audrey. Not that she actually told me." He made a gesture down his front, as if pointing out that being short and Dylan-y was enough to explain why Audrey would sooner shop at JCPenney than be seen talking to him. It was.

"I'm Alice Crewe," I'd said quietly, looking over his shoulder. Considering Proserpine was a ridiculous last name of my grandmother's invention, my mom was cool with me going by any last name I wanted. I'd chosen mine at age eight, after reading *A Little Princess*.

He nodded. "I get it. Proserpine's a lot. I mean, I should know. Technically I'm Ellery Oliver Djan-Nelson-Abrams-Finch." He clocked my look of horror. "No, seriously. People always say, 'But what happens when two people with hyphenated last names marry each other?' Well, that's what happens. I go by Finch."

People passing by were nodding at Finch and giving me the appraising new-girl look. I should've been used to it, but I wasn't.

"Cool story, Finch," I said, with more acid than I intended.

He blinked but didn't walk away. "Your grandmother's book is like nothing I've ever read," he said in a quieter voice. It was a tone I was familiar with: the hushed voice of the true believer.

It made me prickle with discomfort, and with something else—a jealousy I didn't want to look at too closely. "I've never met her," I'd blurted, slamming my locker shut. "You probably know more about her than I do."

I wasn't sure if that was a lie or not. The bitch of it was, we probably knew the exact same stuff about Althea, from the same secondhand sources—except he'd gotten to read the book. Before he could say another word, I'd cut through the crowds and down the hall.

That should've been the last time we spoke, but Finch had a way of turning up.

First I saw him in the park, jogging in a corduroy jacket. I'd wondered if he was running from a mugger, then saw the embarrassing white sneakers and realized corduroy and denim were his exercise clothes. "Alice!" he'd yelled as he passed, his voice happy and his hair exploding around his headphones.

A week later I ran into him at a bookstore on Fifty-Seventh Street. It was like something out of a bad movie:

I'd tugged a fat, tattered copy of Yeats down from a shelf, and there he was, a book-sized slice of him in the space it left behind. He was chewing his thumbnail, reading Patti Smith.

The third time I saw him he was under an awning at a restaurant a block from Harold's, its long windows open to let summer in and a spill of rich people at tiny, marble-topped tables out. He was sitting with a man I recognized from the internet as his father and a gaunt woman with a sharp blonde bob, trailing a steak knife through crème brûlée. He caught me looking before I could turn away, and stood up like he was on strings. In three bounds he was away from the restaurant and walking beside me.

"You saved me," he said. "I was starting to levitate back there. I was starting to think, What if my entire life has been watching my stepmom take fourteen minutes to eat one bite of dessert, and all my memories of the world before that were just implanted by the Matrix? Hi, Alice."

"Hi," I said, flustered. I was on my way home from work. My shirt was covered in scone crumbs and my hair was spiked with sweat.

"You smell like a coffee bean," he said when we reached the corner. "It's awesome." He glanced back at the restaurant, his face so full of regret I almost laughed. "Okay, I better get back."

"Back to stabbing your dessert."

His smile reached his eyes then, just for a moment. A flicker of light on dark water. Then he swung around and walked back up the sidewalk.

After that he'd started waiting at my locker some

mornings, leaning against it with one foot up like something out of an eighties movie.

"Crewe," he'd say, nodding, then he'd stand there while I juggled my books. When I was done he'd pull a book off the top of my stack, walk me to class, and hand it back when we got there, like an inside joke he had with himself. Finch's approval was armor. I wasn't just Audrey's weird stepsister, I was Finch's . . . something. Charity case?

Friend?

It wouldn't be a first, exactly, but close enough. I didn't talk much to anyone. It wasn't that people didn't try—there's always somebody who wants to adopt the new girl. I'm small, with blonde hair and dark eyes that look soft and surprised until I get angry.

"Aren't you a pretty little house cat," a teacher said to me once, in a low voice nobody else could hear. It was my first week as a freshman in Nashville. His words and the way he'd looked when he said them shivered under my skin and stayed there like poison. The only way to purge it was to pour a thermos of hot coffee into the keyboard of his laptop. I never got caught, and I never stopped hating the disconnect between what I saw in the mirror and how I felt.

But it was different with Ellery Finch. I'd grown up too steeped in fairy tales and shit luck that kicked in like clockwork to believe much in coincidence. I had . . . *something* with Finch. I'd never quite decided what that might be, but there was this skin of meaning that had attached itself to him. Maybe it was the Althea connection, or the way our paths kept crossing like we were skaters spinning in a figure eight. Or maybe it was wanting to see that light in his eyes again, a possibility that made my skin flutter with heat rash.

It was weird that Audrey's seat was empty—she never ditched Drama—but I took it as the gift from the universe that it was. She had a way of identifying weak spots and sticking her fingers in them. She liked to watch me and Finch like she was watching TV.

And my premonition was right: Toby paired us up, dropping a quick wink that filled me with a hot-lava embarrassment—for myself, but also for him. Teachers who clocked their students' alliances, then tried to play matchmaker, were almost as sad as teachers who let themselves get bullied by teenage girls in Nars lip gloss.

I pretended to look for something in my bag while my face cooled, then drifted over to where Finch sat, watching me come and bending back the cover of *The Glass Menagerie*.

"Hey, Crewe."

"Finch," I replied.

"You want to read Laura, or should I?"

I hated Tennessee Williams's Laura. She reminded me too much of a fairy-tale character. Not the ones my grandmother wrote, allegedly—those women drew blood. No, she was the worst type of Grimm Brothers beauty: isolated, soft-spoken, waiting for a man to save her. She probably looked like me.

"You take Laura," I said quickly.

For the next fifteen minutes we ran lines together. He was weirdly good. Most of us didn't try, and the ones who did tried way too hard, speaking in plummy stage tones that had everything to do with the school myth that Toby was a talent scout in disguise. You should've seen Audrey chewing over Maggie the Cat.

When the bell rang, Finch put his hand out affectedly, like he was laughing at himself for doing it. That was his thing, I'd noticed: doing everything with an ironic twist. Like he was going to laugh at himself before anyone else could. Being a perpetual new kid made you an anthropologist of the American Teen, and I'd seen his type before. I'd seen every type before.

I hesitated, then shook it.

"We should meet up on purpose sometime," he said, holding on for an extra beat. "Like, outside of school. Don't you think?"

I pulled away, my mind filling like a fishbowl with reasons to say no. Ella needed me. We'd be leaving town soon anyway. The bad luck. Maybe Ella thought it was sleeping, but after last night I didn't buy it.

But Finch looked nervous. His voice had a tremor in it, a bend that gave his last word an extra syllable. His friends were watching from the door, a skinny beanpole whose name I could never remember, because it was one of the few normal names at this school—Mike? Mark?—and Astrid, a long-haired girl who looked at me with a distinctly wounded expression on her face.

"Yeah," I said. "All right."

He grinned, walking backward a few steps with his hands shoved into his pockets. He turned as one of Audrey's friends shoved by me, laughing in a way that made sure I knew she'd been listening. I ignored her and gave Finch a head start at getting gone, confusion making my hands slow and stupid as I gathered my stuff.

Is that all there is? The thought came to me on a scrap of song. The thing between us, the weird growing thing that looked like nothing head-on but sometimes glowed in the corners of my vision, like a secret. Was it just a crush, something as stupid as that? Would we get coffee now? Would he try to hold my hand?

I thought over our whole brief history—me being rude and him being funny and our quiet walks down the hall—and the idea of him wanting something more from me, something I wasn't prepared to give, closed in on me like sweaty fingers.

But there was a story I'd heard about Finch since the first time we spoke, the kind of thing you learned by osmosis going to a small school like Whitechapel. It was the first reason I'd stopped trying to drive him away, before better ones crowded in. Something about his father and the man's new wife. Something about Finch's mother and pills and a bathtub. His mom had been a little bit famous, to a certain set of people, so when she died the story was news.

It made me think of the way Finch's eyes blanked out to zero when he wasn't smiling or laughing, and the way almost nobody smiled and laughed as much as he did. And it made me wonder if we weren't a little bit alike. Behaving the way we had to to get by, while hiding a core that was a mystery even to ourselves.

~6~

After school I loitered on the sidewalk waiting for Audrey. She didn't show, and neither did the town car. I checked my phone, tapped out half a text, erased it. Every moment I stood there it became more excruciatingly possible Finch would walk out the door and see me. When the need to avoid that became too much, I started walking.

I heard the broken-box-fan sound of its engine before I saw it: a rickety yellow cab idling along beside me, with outsize fenders that made it look like a getaway car in an old movie. Actual plush dice hung from its mirror.

My heart did something funny, but the driver's hair was dark, not red. He was a boy not much older than me, reaching across to crank down the passenger window.

"Need a lift?" He looked at me from under the brim of what could only be described as a cabbie cap.

New York cab drivers never actually said that. They said, "Where you going," in a robotic voice, and if they didn't like your answer, they shook their heads and sped away.

"Nope," I said. "I'm good."

"You sure?" His brown eyes were sly. "I don't think your ride is coming."

Something about the way he said it set off alarm bells deep in the forested part of my mind. The part that tells you not to walk down a particular street at night, or to change subway cars when a certain kind of crazy gets on. "I wasn't waiting for a ride," I lied.

"Why don't you take one anyway?"

I looked straight at him, his dark, narrow face and mocking eyes, and a feeling of vertigo swept from my face to my feet. I'd never met him, but I *knew* him. I couldn't remember why or from where. It was something about the way he spoke to me, like he knew me, too, and we were having a conversation we'd had before.

I stepped back. Then kept stepping, and turned and began running down the street, my bag hanging from my fingers and bouncing against my leg. An old woman wearing fur and pearly lipstick tried to scowl at me, but Botox took all the mean out of it. I veered around a knot of tourists stopped to photograph an enormous cupcake made to look like Cookie Monster. I hit the corner and almost kept going, but a double-decker bus whooshed past, so close it blew my hair back. My stomach lurched, and a boy on the bus flipped me the bird. I'd come half a second from getting pancaked.

I walked a block on rubbery knees, feeling the way I had the time a van clipped my bike and sent me reeling into a line of parked cars. Ella had dropped her cigarette and jumped on the fallen bike, screaming at the top of her lungs as she sped after the car. Bleeding in three places, I watched her go, glad she knew I'd rather have retribution than comfort.

I got my breath back, but my mouth was dead dry. I stopped to buy a bottle of water at a newsstand and scanned the headlines while the guy made change. *Senator Under Fire in Campaign Finance Scandal. Connection Suspected in Rash of Upstate Homicides.*

The vendor's sunburnt hand slapped down on the page. "No buy, no read."

I rolled my eyes, took my water, and cut in toward the park. All at once I was desperate to get home to Ella. The cabbie, the bus, the redheaded man—I had to tell her all of it. I should've talked to her last night. Impatience made me run the final block home, everything I needed to say to her expanding like helium in my chest.

The outer door of Harold's building was slightly ajar when I reached it, and the doorman was away from his desk. The combination made me falter for a moment, which was stupid because there are a million and one cameras trained on the lobby and front sidewalk, and you can't use the elevator—a private one that goes straight to Harold's apartment—without a hollow key you insert below the panel.

My skin felt keyed up and nervy. And there was something else: the pressure-shift feeling of bad luck on the move, as familiar to me as the smell of Ella's skin. Think of a hand running over the hairs on your arm, setting all of them to rising. Think of every room you walk into being filled with the sense of someone having just left it.

Maybe Ella was already packing our stuff. I pictured her paint-spattered suitcase splayed out across Harold's high bed. Maybe we'd be out of New York by nightfall, and soon, all of this—Audrey, Harold, Finch, the Salty Dog and serving biscotti and living in an apartment that smelled like a department store—would melt together like colors going to gray on a palette. I'd remember the six a.m. feeling of opening the café, eating Chinese takeout in bed in Brooklyn, reading *Tam Lin* in Prospect Park. The highway would carry everything else away.

The elevator doors slid open onto the foyer of Harold's apartment, and I stepped out.

The first thing that hit me was the smell. A wet, almost rotten scent, with something wild curling beneath it—something green. It crawled under my skin and set my heart to hammering.

"Hello?" The apartment was oppressively silent, a quiet that pressed against my eardrums. It swallowed my voice like black water. I took a few slow steps through the entry-way, all cream-colored walls and marble floor. It was spotless.

But that stink. Where was it coming from? I pulled out my phone and called my mom. It went straight to voicemail.

I called Harold—same thing. After a minute, with misgivings, I called Audrey.

A bright string of candy-colored pop broke the quiet. Audrey's ring tone, but I had *never* seen that girl without her phone. Then I remembered I hadn't seen Audrey, period, since that morning. My mind flipped through horrible possibilities—was she dead? Was that what the smell was? Had the bad luck finally followed us up to the thirty-fifth floor? The old dread settled in my limbs.

I walked carefully through the apartment, like moving quietly would save me if someone was already inside. The rooms had an eerie, recently occupied feeling I recognized from the time a house we were staying in got burglarized. That intruder had taken all the books from the shelves and replaced them with food from the fridge. The beds had been filled with dead leaves, the mirrors cracked. Nothing valuable was gone, but a fur coat was pinned to the wall above Ella's and my bed like a dead animal, stabbed through with a carving knife.

The woman hosting us kept saying how lucky she was nothing got taken, in a bright, false voice nobody believed. The worst part was the way I couldn't stop seeing the house through the eyes of someone who shouldn't have been there. I kept imagining how it might feel to walk through someone else's space, tasting all the strange things you could do there. It made me hungry. I was less in control of myself then.

But nothing here was out of place. No meat sweating on the bookshelves, no fur coat slung up on the wall.

Except: on the kitchen island, a glass of wine fallen on its side. I moved close enough to see Ella's lipstick smudge on its rim. For a horrible, suspended moment I thought I'd find her lying on the tile floor alongside it, but there was only the wine, pooled and staining. The kitchen was the clean white heart of Harold's neurotically kept home—the wine looked like carnage.

I ran to my mom and Harold's room. I hated going in there, hated seeing the high antique bed and Ella's shape in it.

Now I threw open the door, so sure of what I'd find it took me a moment to recognize the bed was empty. Harold's bedside table was neatly stacked with copies of *The Economist* and a Kindle I knew from snooping was stocked with multivolume space epics. On Ella's side was a sweater set and slacks, laid out like mourning clothes. I ducked down quickly to check beneath the dust ruffle. Nothing.

Audrey's room looked like Sephora and Barney's had a brawl, but that was normal. No psychopath crouched in front of her underwear drawer, no rotting, leftover Blue-Print juice explained the smell. Her gum-pink phone lay abandoned on the bed, its screen bristling with texts and missed calls. *Where u at bitch.*

I saved my room for last. The smell was strongest there, a sickly braid of green and rot that felt like someone face-palming my brain. I dropped stealthily to the floor, ready to run out the nearest window if I saw anyone under the bed, but there was just a stretch of vacuumed carpet. My closet door was open, thank God, with nothing more sinister inside it than the primrose bridesmaid gown I'd worn at Ella and Harold's wedding.

Then I saw it: an envelope lying on my pillow. I made

myself take tiny steps toward it, till I could see what it said: *Alice Proserpine,* in spindly letters across the back. No address.

My stomach broke into pieces and spun like a kaleidoscope. Dimly I saw my hand reaching toward it, lifting it to my nose. Cheap ink and old paper. I felt hot, but my arms prickled with goosebumps. I ripped it open.

The page inside it was soft with use, folded in on itself. I had a sharp flare of déjà vu as I eased it open.

It was a title page I'd seen just once, years ago. "Alice-Three-Times," it said in a dense script. Inked around it was a geode pattern that made me think of ice. There was a raw edge along one side where it had been ripped from the book.

I was gripping the page so tightly I tore it. Gingerly I sat down on the bed.

"Alice-Three-Times," the story I'd never finished. It sounded like a children's game, like something girls at a slumber party said into a mirror with the lights turned off. Years ago, when I'd held my grandmother's book for the first and only time, I hoped I'd been named for her Alice, that she had something to do with me. Now I prayed she hadn't.

My mouth was dry as dirt. The redheaded man must've been here—must've done this. He had a copy of the book. He'd come back from god knows where to find me.

I had to get out of the apartment. Its walls were too

close; they were curling in over me, watchful. I tucked the title page into my bag and ran for the elevator.

The doorman was still missing from the lobby, so I couldn't ask if he'd seen Ella leaving. He tended to look at me like I'd come to deliver a pizza one night and never left, so I might not have asked him anyway.

I paced in tight circles around the lobby, keeping one eye on the street. Ella didn't answer any of my next three calls. I cursed myself for not having the numbers of any-one she might be with—her coworkers from the catering job, maybe, though they'd fallen out of touch—and tried and failed to reach Harold one more time.

When I was little I became obsessed with the idea of my mom leaving me behind when she moved. When the fear got so bad I couldn't sleep, I'd strap myself into the passenger seat of our car, so she'd be sure to remember me if she left before morning. Now I felt the sudden urge to make sure our car was still in Harold's parking garage.

Harold hadn't given Ella a key to the garage elevator yet—probably as worried she'd skip town as I used to be—but the doorman had one. I ducked behind his desk on the off chance there was an extra lying around.

His big mass of keys lay right next to a half-eaten take-out container of sushi. I turned quickly, expecting to see him coming back with chopsticks in hand, but the lobby remained empty. I held the keys against my shirtfront so they wouldn't jingle and tiptoed over to the parking garage elevator.

The first time I'd seen it I'd expected Harold's garage to be all white marble and inlaid floors. But it was like any garage I'd ever been in: echoing concrete and the wintry smell of exhaust. I could see our car from the open elevator doors, slumped among the Mercedes and BMWs. Some shitty rich kid had written *CHOAD* in the dirt on its back window.

I stared long enough to assure myself it was there, long enough for the shadows in the corners of the garage to sharpen and the taste of dust and iron to coat my tongue— the taste of bad luck. I stepped back into the elevator and stabbed at the Lobby button till the doors slid shut.

It was nearly five when I stepped onto the sidewalk, and New York was doing that perfect early evening thing where it plays itself. It makes you forget the trash piles and the twenty-dollar sandwiches and the time that guy showed you his dick on the F train, just by etching its skyline in gold and throwing the scent of sugared pecans in your face, right as someone who looks like Leonardo DiCaprio slouches by mumbling into his iPhone. Cheap trick.

Tonight it didn't work on me, because I was zinging with adrenaline, and my brain kept peeling back the corner of a strange new world I couldn't imagine living in, one where my mom was just *gone*. I was being insane. It hadn't even been an hour. But the wrongness of the envelope in my room and the dread coiling in my gut told me I was right to panic.

The title page. Was it a warning? An invitation? A clue? The person who'd left it had been inside my room. His hand had hung over my pillow a moment before dropping the envelope.

Maybe it was a taunt: *I see you, and locked doors and elevator keys aren't enough to keep me out.* But if it was a clue—if there was something in that story, some hint or message—I had to read it. And there was only one place I could think of where I might find a copy of *Tales from the Hinterland.*

I jogged the eight blocks there, because I wanted to jolt some of the spiky energy from my limbs. I knew where Ellery Finch lived because his dad was Jonathan Abrams-Finch, and richer than God, and therefore lived in a building that not only made ours look like a homeless shelter but had been written about twice in the *New York Times* style section. Not that I make a habit of reading about the lives of the rich, but Audrey does, and any mention of Mr. Abrams-Finch inspired her to loudly complain about extreme wealth being wasted on non-hot guys.

His doorman looked a lot like mine, but older. He scowled through his fancy gray mustache when he saw me.

"I'm here to see Ellery Finch," I said.

He squinted at me. "Who?"

I sighed. "Ellery Djan, um, something Abrams-Finch?"

The man sighed back at me, like I'd passed a test he was certain I'd fail. "Whose name might I give?"

"Alice Crewe. Wait—Alice Proserpine. Tell him Alice Proserpine."

The man picked up an old rotary telephone and hit a button, then I swear he started talking in a fake British accent. He apologized for my arrival and existence, letting his mustache droop with disappointment as the person on the other end agreed to come down for me.

I kept my eyes on the art deco elevator, so beautiful I wanted to cut it up into bracelets. Drama class felt miles away, but now it was creeping up on me: Finch's question. My answer. The weird thrill and curious shame of it. What would he think of my showing up here?

I schooled my expression to flatness, but when the elevator doors slid open, my vision blurred over with tears. Finch's familiar face looked like an island to a drowning swimmer.

His eyes widened and he made a move forward, maybe to put an arm around me. I put ice in my eyes and walked sideways into the elevator before he could.

"Thanks for, um. I can come up?"

"Yeah," he said. "Of course you can, Alice."

He liked saying names, I noticed. First or last or both at once. Maybe in real life it was meant to be friendly, but names were dangerous in a fairy tale. I'd wondered before if that was why Althea had changed hers to something so outlandish. A Potemkin front so good nobody would want to look behind it.

I blinked away the fairy cobwebs. This wasn't a book, this was *life*. I had to tighten my shit up. The elevator doors shushed shut, sealing us inside a tiny, opulent room. There was a low Louis Quinze–looking bench against the wall and a chandelier hanging over our heads. A chandelier. In an elevator. Finch caught me looking at it and laughed before I could.

"My stepmom's a big believer in 'you can never be too loaded or too thin or too covered in ugly diamonds.' That's a saying, right? If it wasn't before, then she made it up." He seemed nervous again. I saw it even through my self-pity and fear, and it made me feel the tiniest bit better about being there.

As did the fact that he didn't immediately demand to know why I was darkening his vintage elevator door. I'd shown up unannounced enough times in my life—with my mom, her face plastered with a smile, our suitcases tucked benignly behind our legs—to know what it looked like when someone wishes you hadn't come. Ellery Finch definitely didn't wish I hadn't come.

Harold's place was the nicest I'd ever seen till that point, but Ellery's was something else entirely. It was like a country manor straight out of a thick English book about pheasant season and eligibility. You almost expected to see Mr. Darcy skulking around a corner looking pissed.

"Nobody's home but our housekeeper," Finch said. "My stepmom's at soul bikes or whatever, and my dad's pretty much always out. It's not easy running a sweatshop empire all by yourself, you know?"

I startled at this, but he didn't even look around when he said it. I followed him across the carpet, studded with pieces of tasteful furniture that would've made Harold weep with envy. Finch must've been used to showing people around, because he took me straight to the view. It was disorienting to look out the high windows and see not the sweep of a rainy moor, but early evening advancing on Central Park. It made me forget the ugly thing he'd just said.

Finch let me look for a minute, then smiled. The nervous was back. "So. You're here."

"I'm here."

"To . . . see me. On purpose."

Oh, god. He was echoing the words he'd said when he asked me out. "No! No, I just . . ."

"I'm kidding. Sorry, I know I'm bad at it, but I just can't stop."

He waited attentively for me to speak, and suddenly I wanted to slow everything down. I had my hand on my phone, ringer turned up, but Harold's violated apartment felt very far away. Until Ella called back, I had nowhere to go. And the sooner I got what I wanted from Finch, the sooner I'd go right back to being alone. "Can I have a glass of water?" I blurted.

His eyes registered curiosity before melting into that easygoing Finch expression. The one he wore like armor. "Of course. Are you hungry?"

"Yeah," I said, even if it wasn't quite true. "I'm starving."

Finch led me into the kitchen. His housekeeper, Anna, looked like a retired Bond girl and sounded like an unretired Bond villain. She was about sixty, and clucked around Finch while making us an endless stream of tiny sugar-powdered pancakes served with tart red jam. We didn't talk much, and the friendly sounds of sizzling and the funny conversation she kept up with the batter under her breath made it so it didn't feel weird. When our hands were good and sticky with jam, she brought little finger bowls to the table, which seemed a bit much for an after-school snack. By seven p.m. she had us de-jammed and the kitchen spotless. She kissed Finch's forehead, grabbed her big Mary Poppins bag, and let herself out.

The apartment yawned around us, humming with appliances and wealth.

"So," I said. "You're probably wondering why I came over."

"Actually, I'm wondering more about the name you gave my doorman. Proserpine."

"Yeah, well. I'm hoping you can help me with something."

My voice wobbled and Finch noticed it, going focused and still.

"I really need to read my grandmother's book, and I'm hoping you have a copy."

He squinted, looking slightly let down. "Wait. You've never read it?"

"Nope. I've tried. It's hard to find."

"No kidding it's hard to find. I only got a copy because of . . . because of some family shit that went down. It was, like, the one thing I asked my dad for that Chanukah. I think he flew an intern to Greece to get it."

Relief made my eyes sting. "So you've got a copy?"

"*Had* a copy. It was stolen."

All those tiny pancakes turned to acid in my gut. "What? Like, out of your house?"

"No. Out of my *hands*. I have this friend who owns a rare book shop, and he's never seen an actual copy of *Hinterland*. I'm not an idiot, I know this is an expensive book, so I take a cab to get there instead of the subway."

Also, you're too rich to take the subway, I think but don't say.

"I've got the book all tucked away in this acid-free plastic sleeve, and once I'm in the shop, I don't even let my friend alone with the book—he's a nice old guy, I met him when I went through my first editions phase, but some things you don't let out of your sight. So he's wearing cotton gloves, turning the pages like we're in an Indiana Jones movie and they might release a demon or something, freaking out in that quiet way collectors do.

"Then the door of the shop slams open and this boy runs in. Eight or nine years old, pretty small. I grab up the book just in case, not actually thinking the kid would take it, or has any idea what it is. But the little shit ran up, sprayed something in my eyes—not mace, but like a cleaning product—and grabbed the book. I was so surprised I didn't keep a good grip on it. I ran after him, but it was too late. He got into a cab that was waiting and beat it."

I goggled at him. "Bullshit."

"Sadly, no."

"Why would he want that particular book? Why would a little kid even be in a rare bookstore?"

"I'm guessing someone paid him to steal it. For a while I wondered if my friend at the bookstore planned it, but he's a friend—that felt too paranoid. So then I thought someone might've been tracking our emails about it. Maybe specifically tracking emails that mention *Tales from the Hinterland*."

"So that's *less* paranoid?"

"Good point. In my defense, I don't really believe that. It's just . . . that book. Plenty of books are out of print, but you can still find them. *Tales from the Hinterland* should be all over libraries, rare book rooms, eBay, but it's not. Either someone's been hoarding copies, or . . ." He shrugged meaningfully. "Or something else. You can't even find scans of the stories online."

He was right. There *should* have been more—someone

should have typed the stories up, scanned them, made fan art. But there was nothing like that.

Almost nothing. I was fourteen when I found a piece of the book online, a scrap of story.

We were living in Iowa City, and my interest in Althea was my biggest secret, my *only* secret. Four years spent checking used bookstore shelves and searching out traces of her online, four years disdaining the books Ella tried to get me to read in favor of devouring fairy tales. The classic pantheon first, then broader. Weirder, darker. Tales from around the world. Always wondering how close they took me to Althea.

But it was in Iowa that my secret pitched over into betrayal: in Iowa I started communicating with Althea's fans.

Fans was a word Ella spat out like a cherry pit. And it made sense: the ones I had met—my sixth-grade English teacher, the batshit grad student who accosted us at a Fairway during our first stint in New York, the biographer who tracked Ella down and tried to get to her through me, the worst possible move he could've made—were cartoons, nutjobs with bad breath and no lives of their own.

It was different online. There I met fans who felt like me: people who'd read the book and loved it, or who couldn't find it but got hooked on Althea anyway. The *idea* of her, like a comet's tail glimpsed just before it's gone. I'd stay up getting dry-eyed and hungry, lost deep inside an internet rabbit hole, while Ella worked at a bar on the ped mall. She'd come home each night smelling of cheap beer and lighter fluid, and I'd slap her laptop shut, faking boredom.

She believed me, because we didn't lie to each other. Except when we did.

My memories of Iowa are as flat as the state. A gray spring, frat houses, bright pieces of girlness discarded in gutters—glittery slip-ons, headbands, once a pair of pink terry shorts. But one night stood out, because it was the night I jumped from message board to message board, blog to blog, finally landing on a DeviantArt page featuring excerpts of Althea's stories, painted like illuminated Bible pages.

I'd run my fingers over their pixels. They were beautiful, and more of her writing than I'd seen in one place since that day in the attic. My heart beat sideways as I clicked to enlarge a long page of "The Sea Cellar."

I started to read. I was tipsy, a little, on nasty apple wine Ella's then-boyfriend had made in his backyard press. It was sad and scuzzy being drunk alone, and the story felt like companionship—like reaching out to Althea for the thousandth time, and finally feeling her reach back.

The story opened on a young bride traveling a long way to her new husband's house, and arriving to find it all lit up, but empty. I'd read a few paragraphs—the bride, the journey, the opulent, lonely house—when the light of my laptop cam switched on.

I'd stared at its apple-green eye for two hot beats, then slammed the laptop shut.

The house was silent; a frail string of tinnitus sang a warning in my ear. I'd looked at the blanks of the windows, felt eyes on my neck and sandy fear pinning me in place.

I cracked the laptop just enough to stick my thumb

over the camera, then opened it the rest of the way. The green light was off, the browser was closed, and my internet history was wiped clean. I darted to the kitchen to grab a piece of black tape to stick over the camera, drew all the curtains, and lay in bed with the lights on, waiting for Ella to come home.

By then I was old enough to know Althea wasn't really watching me. But that was when I started to wonder if someone else was.

Ella didn't ask about the black tape, but a week later I fell asleep in front of an open thread about Althea's use of numerology, and woke to Ella's intake of breath, her smoky black hair in my face as she leaned over me to slam the laptop shut with her fist.

"What. The *fuck*. Alice."

Ella didn't talk that way to me. She talked that way to drunk freshmen trying to get served at her bar, and boyfriends who got shitty when she told them we were gone. Landlords with a knack for stopping by too often, and always when one or the other of us was in a towel.

You never told me I couldn't was the first stupid thing I wanted to say. But she hadn't had to. The taboo was baked into me. It was in everything she didn't say, the flinch in her shoulders and the way her head lowered like a boxer's when people tried to talk about Althea.

In that moment I hated her, so I said something worse.

"Why are we alone?" It was a question that had lived in me for years; I didn't think I'd dare ask it until I did. "Why are we alone if we don't have to be?"

Ella's mouth opened, soft and surprised. She sat down

slow, like her bones hurt. Then, for the first and last time in my life, she was cruel to me.

"You think she wants to be your grandma?" she said, in a voice that wasn't quite hers. "You look at her big house in that magazine you think I don't know about, and you think, Oh, if only she'd ask me to come live with her?" She shook her head. "Not a chance. Althea *doesn't want you.* So stop torturing yourself about what could be. In *this* life, it's you." She pointed at me, then stabbed her finger hard into her breastbone. "And me. Got it?"

I felt like she'd stripped me naked. In that moment, even the rising mercury of anger abandoned me. After a long, charged moment she reached for me, already crying, but I slid out of her grip and ran for the bathroom.

I was dramatic and stupid; I made up a bed with towels in the tub just to put a door between us. But by the next morning, I'd decided: she was right. I was done holding a torch for a stranger.

"I'll stop." That was all I said to Ella. She didn't say *Promise me* or *How can I trust you* or anything like that. She'd just believed me, and that time I wasn't lying. I gave Althea up like a drug, and I didn't let her back in till the day my kidnapper showed up at the café with her book in his hands.

"Alice?"

I startled, looking back at Finch. "Sorry. What did you say?"

"I asked if you heard what happened to the movie they made about it. About the stories."

"Just what was in the *Vanity Fair* piece. Disappearances, affair, all that."

"Okay, so the director died not long after it was made—you heard about that?"

"Finch? You know more than me. Just talk."

He looked sheepish. "Sorry, I'm geeking out. Okay. So yeah, he died in a single-car crash, sometime in the seventies. His stuff was auctioned off, including the original reels for the *Hinterland* film. To a rich collector, who only showed them in private screenings. Then when *she* died, she bequeathed them to the American Film Institute, but they never showed up."

"What do you mean?"

"I mean they never showed up. They got lost, or destroyed, or are still moldering in a collection somewhere, but nobody has any idea where they went. It's one of the few really lost films of that decade."

"But back to the book," I said. "Did you make copies? Photograph the pages?"

"I thought about it. Of course I did. But it didn't feel right, sharing them like that. It would've been a violation."

"A violation of *who*? Althea?"

"Of the stories," he said. "There was like a . . . a covenant, among the people who'd read them. Either you found them on your own and were deserving, or you didn't and you weren't."

His face was so serious and noble I wanted to slap it. "Or, third option, your rich dad bought them for you and you didn't have to worry about it either way."

That pissed him off—I could see it in his hands, tightening on the table's edge. But he laughed, and he made it sound easy.

"Look, losing that book was the saddest breakup I've

ever had. At least I read the stories a million times while I still had them."

"So you remember how they go?"

"Of course. I went straight home after the book was stolen and wrote their names down, too, so I'd never forget. You want me to tell you about them?"

"'Alice-Three-Times,'" I said automatically. "What does that mean? What's it about?"

"Oh, yeah, that's a creepy one," he said, then frowned. "Wait, your mom didn't name you after that story, did she?"

My eyes flicked to my phone, lying faceup and silent on the table. Not a word from her, or anyone else. "I didn't think so, but now I'm not so sure."

He looked suddenly shy again. "Can I show you something? It's something, um, I've been wanting to show you for a while. Except . . ."

"Except I was a dick when you tried to talk about Althea?"

Finch smiled but didn't deny it. "You want to see it now? It's about her."

"Yes. Definitely."

"Okay. It's upstairs, in my room."

We walked up a winding staircase to the third floor, which was all Ellery's. The carpet up there was Grover blue and felt awesomely thick through my shoes, and everything smelled better than I thought a boy's room could. To be fair, it was more of a boy's suite. The first room had a billiard/home movie theater setup, decorated with light-up beer signs I'd bet a million bucks were some interior decorator's idea of High School Boy, not Finch's.

"Please ignore the Budweiser chapel," he said, practically frog-marching me through it.

The room beyond it said Ellery Finch all over. It was a high-ceilinged study with soft recessed lighting and a wide bank of windows on one side. A beautiful behemoth of a desk sat in the center, covered in books and a laptop and a green-shaded lamp that looked like it came from a pool hall. The room was almost empty otherwise, and it would've been monkish if the three windowless walls weren't entirely given over to books.

"They're not all mine," he said. "This room used to be a creepy fake library, with all these random leather-bound reference books bought by the yard, but I've been swapping them out for the real stuff for years."

I wanted to shove him out, lock the doors, and live in the room for a month. "Bought by the yard?" I managed to say. "That's so weird."

"I know. It's a thing they do for rich people who want the effect but don't actually want to *read* the things. God forbid my dad crack a fucking book." He paused and touched his fingertips to his mouth. "Mostly it's almanacs and old censuses and stuff, but occasionally there's something good. That's what I wanted to show you, actually."

There was a door on the far side of the room that hung open a few inches. I bet it led to his bedroom, and I was almost let down I wasn't going to see it. *It'll be a vintage My Bloody Valentine poster, an unmade bed, and an Underwood typewriter,* I told myself. *What's there to see?*

Finch gently tugged a book from its place on the wall. Its green cover made my heart jump. But it was bigger than *Tales from the Hinterland,* the leather pressed and attractively cracked. He laid it carefully on the desk.

The words *My Hollywood Story* swooned across the cover in loopy print. "Check out this cheeseball," Finch said, turning to the title page. A black-and-white headshot of a Valentino type smoldered out at us from beneath a high double peak of glossy hair. He was wearing more eyeliner than Audrey after a cat-eye tutorial binge.

"Vincent Callais," Finch said. "French actor, did some American movies in the forties. He played Myrna Loy's bad boyfriend once, so that's pretty cool. His writing is hilariously terrible, but I'm a sucker for film history so I flipped through it." He opened the book to the photos at its center. "So here's poor old Vincent standing kinda near Anita Ekberg at a party . . . Oh, here you can see the netting of his toupee . . . But look—check this one out."

I leaned over the book. An elderly Vincent and his shit-eating grin sat at a restaurant table, looking greasy and overexposed. On one side of him, a blonde bunny smiled for the camera, all eyelashes and chest. On the other was a man with a perm and a boxer's build, much younger than Vince. His eyes basically had comic-book arrows coming out of them, pointing toward the blonde's chest. And next to *him,* looking like she was beamed in from another photo entirely, sat my grandmother.

My eyes flicked down to the caption. *L to R: Unknown woman, Callais, Teddy Sharpe, Althea Proserpine. 1972.*

My grandmother would've been twenty-eight then, her book a year old. I looked back at her face. Hers was the kind of liquid loveliness that held a secret: you look at it again and again, trying to catch it. That quirked brow, the lip with a nick in it, like maybe she'd fallen off her roller skates as a girl. She wore a sleeveless patterned top, and her hair was in a messy bob, dark bangs swept over her forehead. The fingers of her right hand touched her chin, absently. On her first finger, the same onyx ring she wore in her author photo. On her third, a coiled metal snake.

"She looks like you," Finch said.

Not even close. If I was a house cat, she was a lynx. "My scar's on my chin, not my lip," I said, touching the white dent I'd gotten during a particularly ugly run-in with the bad luck.

"You know what I mean. It's the eyes, I think. You look like you've got a million things going through your mind, but you're not saying them."

I hated unsolicited compliments, if that's what that was, so I kept my eyes trained on Althea. "Is there anything about her in the book?"

"Nothing. This is how I discovered her, actually, this photo. I read the entire 1970s section hoping she'd show up." He rubbed his chin with the flat of his palm, thoughtfully. "It was just . . . her face, you know? She looked like she was somebody I should know about. And that name. It's a lot of name. Finally I Googled her, which I should have done first, and found out about the book. I couldn't find it anywhere, not even reprints of the stories, just old articles and stuff. Not very long, except for the *Vanity Fair* piece. I became weirdly obsessed with reading the book, mostly because it's impossible to find."

"Is it good?"

"Good?" He thought for a moment. "*Good* isn't the

right word. It puts you in this weird headspace. I'd just gone through some family stuff when I read it. I was all messed up. Getting the book at that exact moment was just what I needed. It gave me a feeling like . . ." He stopped, narrowed his eyes at me. "Don't laugh. It made me feel the way love songs do when you're falling in love. Except in a messed-up way, 'cause that's where my head was at. There's a lot of darkness in them. I can't re-member now how much of that was in the stories and how much of it was mine. I loved them either way. I'm really sorry I can't read them again."

"So am I."

He must've heard the trouble in my voice, because his changed, too, got more serious. "Why now? You don't seem like . . . you don't seem interested much in talking about her. Your grandmother. What changed?"

I opened my mouth, and the awful confusion of it pressed in. The red-haired man, the stench, the empty apartment.

"I got home from school today," I began.

Finch waited. We looked at each other in the warm li-brary light. His eyes were brown and guileless.

"I got home, and someone had been there—someone had broken in. There was this weird smell, and I could just tell."

"A *smell*? Was there—was that it?"

"No, that's not it. Whoever it was had left something for me. On my bed."

He recoiled when I said the word *bed*. "Oh, god. What was it?"

I pulled out the envelope, flattened the title page onto

the table. He grew still, then reached for it. He touched it like it was a relic. "No way," he breathed.

"And my mom." Something in me didn't want the words said aloud, like it might make them true. "She's not there. I can't reach her. I can't reach any of them. I don't know what to do. And weird shit has been happening, stuff that'll sound stupid if I try to explain . . ."

Finch's eyes were trained on the page. He looked like he wanted to grind it up and snort it.

"Finch?"

He looked up at me and I saw the shift, when he went from geeked-out fan back to friend, I guess. "Wait, wait." He grabbed my hand, gently. He wasn't much taller than me—our eyes were almost level. "Someone broke into your apartment and left something very rare and, in context, very *creepy* in your room, and now you can't reach your mom. What if she's filling out a police report somewhere? I'm so sorry this happened to you, but I don't think you have to panic. Have you thought about calling your grand-mother? Just in case?"

I pulled my hand sharply from his. "I can't call her. She's dead."

He startled back. "What? No. I would've heard some-thing."

"Why would *you* have heard something?"

"Because there's this thing called the internet, and she's famous. Or was. Everyone gets an obituary. She can't be *dead*."

My chest burned. "I can't have you telling me my dead grandmother isn't dead right now, Finch. That's like the second or third worst thing you could pick to argue about."

"Shit. You're right, that was a stupid thing to say. This is very, very weird." He stared at me for a minute, like he was calculating something. "Okay. Okay. Your mom is fine, I'm sure there's an explanation."

"No, you're not."

"Well, no matter where they are, you shouldn't go back to your place alone. Let's go together—maybe they're already back. Or maybe I'll see something you didn't."

And there it was. Behind his gentle expression of concern, a bright curiosity. A hunger. My vow to Ella kept me away from Althea fans, rare as they were, but that didn't mean they kept away from me.

"Forget it," I said, standing suddenly. I lurched away from the table clumsily, shouldering my bag.

"What's wrong?"

"I don't talk to fans."

I thought the ice in my voice would make him shrivel, or tell me to fuck off, *I'm just trying to help you.* Instead, he looked confused. "Why?"

I opened my mouth. Closed it. If talking to a fan was a betrayal, the betrayal had happened. It was too late to turn back.

"I don't know," I said finally.

"Then how about getting over it? I don't think you have anyone else you can go to with this." He said it gently, but I felt pinpricks of shame anyway.

"That's not true. I could go stay at my friend Lana's." I probably could, too, but Lana already lived with two other sculptors and half a klezmer band in a stuffed Gowanus flat. And calling her my friend was pushing it.

"But you didn't go to Lana," he said. "You came to me."

In that moment, I wondered when the last time was that I'd made eye contact with someone for this long. Someone who wasn't Ella. I wanted so badly to not need him, but the idea of going back out into the city alone sent a feeling of cold desolation blowing through me. In my mind Harold's apartment was an alien landscape—something had passed through it, something that didn't belong. I couldn't be alone there with that feeling.

I hated needing something from someone when I had absolutely nothing to offer back. You'd think, after the upbringing I'd had, I'd at least be used to it.

"Fine," I managed, relief crashing in. "Sorry it's a school night."

Finch looked at me like I'd said something colossally stupid—which I guess I had, but it still rankled—then sprinted to his bedroom door. He slid through like he didn't want me to see inside, which made me reassess my guess at what he was hiding in there. Bikini babes on Ferraris, lots of suspicious balled-up socks?

Or, wait. That was the bad boy from a teen comedy, not a rich New York kid with a Vonnegut quote tattooed up his arm.

I had to admit, I liked Finch's tattoo.

A few minutes later, he came out in a blue zip-up, a beat leather bag I recognized from school over his shoulder. "You ready?"

I wished he didn't sound so excited, and I told him so.

"I sound excited?"

"Yeah, you do." I counted to three as I breathed in the peace, breathed out the rage, like Ella had been making me do ever since I broke a baton over a girl's head in kindergarten. It helped, a little. "This isn't an adventure, okay? This isn't an Althea Proserpine thing. My mom is missing, maybe."

"Oh." He looked down. "I really don't mean to be excited. I'm just glad to be going somewhere with you."

Are you for real? I wanted to say, but some self-preserving instinct kept the words back. I did have some control.

We traced my steps back to Harold's, where the front desk was still unmanned.

"That's another thing—I haven't seen our doorman since this morning. Weird, right?"

"Definitely weird," Finch muttered, his eyes zagging around the lobby. Now that we were in the building he was doing this thing where he walked in front of me with one hand thrown behind him, like someone was about to start shooting arrows at us.

"Can you let me . . . dude, I have to open the elevator."

He fell back, sheepish, and I applied the elevator key. Harold's elevator was a gas station bathroom compared to Finch's, I couldn't help but note.

We rode up in prickling silence. When the doors slid open, my body was tensed and humming. I was ready to scream, or gasp, or see my mom, my mouth already forming the words I'd yell at her for making me worry. But the foyer was empty.

"God, that smell," Finch whispered.

Then I saw something that sent me flying out onto the marble: Harold's briefcase, slung onto the table in the entrance hall.

All at once I felt a rush of giddy relief expanding in my chest, coupled with crushing embarrassment that

I'd made Finch come here. "Hello?" I called out. "Mom? Harold?"

Silence, then the rapid sound of approaching feet. Harold came careening around the corner, his shaved head flushed. I never thought I'd be so happy to see him.

"Harold! Where's my mo—"

The words died in my throat. Harold was holding a gun so blunt and iconic it looked like a toy, and he was pointing it square at my chest. Finch made a strangled sound in his throat, grabbed me roughly, and pulled me behind him.

"What the hell, Harold," I gasped, pushing past Finch. "It's me!"

"I know who it is," he said. His voice was high, his lips so tight there was a taut ring of white around them. I could smell him from where I stood—cologne and a sickly sweat.

My heart chugged, turning itself over like a broken-down engine. "Harold. Harold, where's my mom?"

"You looked at me like *I'm* the monster," he said.

"What?" My mouth was so dry I could hear my tongue.

"Was any of it real? Ella—did she really . . ." He made a choked sound.

All the bad luck I'd ever had was focused into one dark point, the black muzzle of the gun. "Please," I said. "Please. What did you do to her? Where is she?"

"*Do* to her? I did everything to make her happy—and you, treating me like I don't belong in my own home, like I shouldn't be allowed to touch her." The gun was drooping, like his arm was a dying stem.

You shouldn't, I thought. But it was a dim, reflexive thing; the gun still hovered at his waist. If it went off, he'd hit my knees.

"And now this," he said. "Now you bring this into my life. My daughter could've been *killed*."

"Killed?" I remembered Audrey's phone, abandoned on the bed. "Are they hurt? Ella and Audrey?"

"I'm supposed to believe you care?" He walked forward and took me roughly by the shoulder, gun still hanging from his other hand. I froze. Harold hadn't touched me since we hugged to make Ella happy at the wedding. I felt Finch go tense as Harold glared down at me with his sad blue pirate eyes. He shook me, like I was something he was checking for leaks.

"Don't *touch* me," I gasped, twisting away, right as Finch grabbed Harold's arm.

"Get away from her," he said through gritted teeth.

Harold made an anguished sound and lifted the gun. Finch and I startled back. "I loved her. I loved her so much, and she lied to me every day."

"Sir," Finch said, and his voice was strong and even. "Point the gun at the floor. We're going to turn around and leave, right now. Just please point the gun at the floor."

"We're not going anywhere," I said, my voice seesawing like the deck of a ship. "Not until he tells me where she is!"

There was a clicking of heels on tile, and Audrey pulled up behind her dad, clutching a stuffed duffel to her chest and looking drawn behind her makeup mask.

"Dad," she said. All the sharp laughter and shiny bullshit had gone out of her voice. She sounded very tired. "Put that thing down."

For a second he didn't seem to hear her. Then he dropped the gun to the table with a hard *clack* that made my back teeth hurt.

"Your mom is gone," Audrey said, in that same dead voice. "They took us, too, but they let us go. We only came back to get some stuff—we're not staying, so you can tell them that if they ask. And don't try to find us."

"Who took her? *Who?*"

Audrey's pupils were dilated, I realized, with shock or trauma. "The Hinterland," she said. "They told us they were the Hinterland."

I wanted to collapse on the tile. The adrenaline of seeing the gun was ebbing, leaving my limbs gummy and jittering, and that word—*Hinterland*. Althea again.

"What did they look like?"

Harold put his hand on the gun. "Get the fuck out."

I didn't think he would really shoot me. "Just tell me where they took her and I'll go. *Please*."

"Get the fuck out."

Finch already had me by the arm and the waist, guiding me toward the elevator. It was waiting for us and opened with a chilly *ping*. "We'll come back with cops if we have to," he said quietly. "Or someone from my dad's security team."

My eyes stayed on Harold's as the doors slid shut between us.

"No, we won't. I'll never come back here again."

~8~

Finch could've walked away forever as soon as we hit the sidewalk. He could've put me in a cab, ignoring the fact that I had nowhere to go and he knew it. He could've used his bottomless bank account to get me a hotel room for the night if he really wanted to go all out.

But he didn't do any of those things. And somewhere beneath my gratitude and my fear, I couldn't stop wondering why.

"We have to call the cops. Your stepdad could've hurt you."

I looked at my stupid silent phone and pressed my hands to my chest. It felt like a room squeezing in on itself. "Mom," I said, raggedly, to the air.

Then Finch had an arm around me again, helping me sit on a low garden wall.

"Hey. Hey. Breathe, okay? Breathe."

I took shuddering sips of air. I'd never had a panic attack, but Ella used to get them sometimes. She thought she hid them from me, but I knew.

Finch crouched in front of me. "It's okay. It's okay. Just breathe."

His words turned into an irritant, and my body coursed with a sudden fire. I pushed him aside and jumped up, my hands clenching and unclenching and cupping themselves around a phantom cigarette. I saw Ella last night in her cocktail dress, Ella's sleeping outline in the dark of my room. Ella driving and Ella laughing and Ella's level brown eyes on mine.

Ever since I was old enough for it, I was the vigilant one, always keeping an eye on the bad luck while Ella did her best to make our squats and claimed corners into a home. But I'd let my guard down. I'd let the bad luck take some unfathomable form and walk right in, and carry Ella away.

"Audrey said the Hinterland took them. What the hell does that mean?"

Finch shook his head apologetically. "I have no idea."

The street in front of Harold's apartment looked transformed. The last of the light had died. Everything was shifting shadow, the smell of old smoke, the enervating rustle of half-naked trees. Terror lapped around me and threatened to pull me under. I held it back with motion, with rising anger, with magical thinking: *If that light turns green on the count of three, my mother will walk around that corner.* It did, but she didn't.

Finch stood, too, keeping his distance as I paced. "What if—" He stopped talking, waiting for me to ask.

"Spit it out."

"You're not gonna like it."

"There's nothing here to like. Just say it." Talking was good. Talking rooted me here, under this streetlight with Finch, instead of racing outward into a wild black galaxy where I couldn't feel the tug of my mother anywhere.

"What if when she said the Hinterland, she meant the *Hinterland.*"

"Make sense, Finch. Please."

"The Hinterland. It's the place where the stories, you know, connect. They're all set in the same place."

He'd snapped into scholar mode, and it helped. The bronchitis squeeze in my chest subsided. "All fairy tales are set in the same place. Once-upon-a-time land."

"Not Althea's. There's a theory . . ."

I groaned. I'd spent enough time on her message boards, where a mix of fans and folklore scholars swapped theories about the book, to be wary. You'd think she'd be too obscure to have an internet following, but obscurity was half of her appeal. "Oh, my god. You're deep fan. You're into the theories?"

That one made it through his optimism. "Yeah, I'm deep fan," he said sharply, "and suddenly that shit's exactly what you need. You want to hear it or not?"

I was taken aback, and not in a bad way. I nodded for him to continue.

"So there's a *theory*"—he emphasized the word—"about Althea's disappearance in the sixties. That she was out somewhere collecting the stories, like Alan Lomax did with American folk music. That the Hinterland is a code name for the boonies in some northern country."

I'd heard that one. It seemed plausible, actually, which was probably why it annoyed me so much.

"So what if that's the Hinterland Audrey was talking about?" he persisted. "Maybe Althea took a story from someone who's pissed, someone who wants credit for it, and . . ."

"And now they're stalking her family, forty years later?" I finished. "Some, I don't know, Norwegian herdsman finally made his way to New York to take ancient revenge?"

The redheaded man's face flickered across my mind's eye. I should've told Finch about him, but I kept thinking of the last part of that Nelson Algren quote: "Never sleep with a woman whose troubles are worse than your own." I was about a mile from sleeping with Finch, but my troubles were becoming his anyway. I didn't want to pile on more.

He shrugged. "It's just a theory. It's got to mean something. They left a page from the book, for god's sake. Maybe it's a code."

"Look, you need to tell me about 'Alice-Three-Times,' in case there's something in it. Any clue on what I'm supposed to do next."

"Fine. But let's go somewhere we can be alone." He saw my face and smiled, tight and brief. "Alone, like, not where my dad and stepmom can hear us. One of them could actually be home by now."

We ended up at a diner on Seventy-Ninth Street, the kind of place where even a bowl of matzo ball soup costs twelve bucks. That was what Finch ordered, plus a club sandwich with extra pickles on the side. I got pancakes drowning in blueberry syrup, because that's what I ate at the diner with the red-haired man. They congealed fast on my plate, and failed to bring any repressed memories flooding back.

I kept my phone on the table between us, my heart sinking a little lower every time I looked at its mute black screen. The whole world was bending around the absence of my mother, like light ricocheting off something too dark to illuminate. I saw my face in the bowl of the extra soup spoon the waitress had laid on the table. My eyes were shocked holes.

Finch ate one pickle, put another on the edge of my saucer, and cut the last one in four and tucked each part into a wedge of his sandwich. "Okay," he said. "Here's what I remember about 'Alice-Three-Times.'"

His recounting was more detailed than I'd hoped it would be, though he kept second-guessing himself and tangling it with other tales. The basic shape of it went like this.

~9~

On a cold day in a distant kingdom, a daughter was born to a queen and king. Her eyes were shiny and black all over, and the midwife laid her in the queen's arms and fled. The queen looked into the girl's eyes, shiny-dark as beetle shells, and despised her on sight.

The girl was small and never made a sound, not even a cry the day she was born. Sure she wouldn't live, the queen refused to name her.

At first her prophecy seemed true: the months passed, and the baby failed to grow. But she didn't die, either. Two years bloomed and faded, and she was still as little as the day she was born, and just as silent, and she lived on sheep's milk because the queen refused to nurse her.

Then one morning, when the nurse went in to feed her,

she found the baby had grown in the night—she was now as big as a child of seven. Her limbs were frail as a frog's, but her eyes were still a defiant black. It was decided, then: she would live. The king pressed his wife to name her, and the queen chose a name that was small and powerless, an ill-starred name for a princess. The queen called her Alice.

Alice spoke, finally, always in full sentences. She spoke only to other children, mostly to make them cry. And once again, she stopped getting bigger. The years went by, and the royal household started to believe she'd be a child forever, playing tricks on her siblings and scaring the maids with her black, black eyes.

Until, on a morning so icy cold the breath froze on your lips if you dared to go outside, a nursemaid went to wake Alice, and found a girl of twelve sleeping in her bed. She was a creature of points and angles, a colt who could barely walk on her new legs. The servants whispered that she was a changeling, but her eyes were black as ever, and her temper the same: she didn't talk much, and she appeared places she shouldn't. The castle had trouble keeping servants, and the queen's women gossiped that the girl was to blame.

The nursemaid charged with raising Alice learned to fear the day when she'd again find a stranger in the princess's bed. On the morning she discovered a black-eyed girl of seventeen waiting for her in Alice's chamber, the woman whispered a curse and left the castle for good.

The princess was young in years but had become very beautiful, and at least looked to be of age. The king, who'd rarely spoken a word to her directly, now watched her with an acquisitive eye. He gave her gifts not meant for a daughter: A dragonfly catch for her cloak, made of red metal. A blown-glass flower that looked like a scorpion striking. The queen made a decision: it was time for Alice to marry.

Because she was the daughter of a king, in a world where these things were indulged, the girl set her suitors a task. Whoever could fill a silk purse with ice from the kingdom's distant ice caverns and carry it back to her, she'd agree to marry. If they failed, they died. Of course most of the suitors were fools. They rode a day and night to bring the ice for her little silk purse, and it melted to nothing on the way. They brought ice from a frozen stream a mile from the palace, and she tasted their treachery in its familiar, scummy tang. Or they brought diamonds, hoping ice was a metaphor, and lost their lives for the mistake.

The men who solved the puzzle were two brothers from the north, their skin nearly as pale as the ice they carried. They packed it in sawdust and carved it into bits before entering her father's hall.

When the older brother showed her it had been done, she went still. The color drained out of her face. It made him smile.

"But which one of you will she marry?" the king asked.

The brother smiled again. Everyone present was beginning to understand it wasn't a nice thing when the brother smiled. "We don't want a wife," he said. "We want a housemaid. She'll bake our bread, and clean our house, and bear the children who will serve us after she's dead."

The girl said nothing. Instead, she took her little purse of ice and tipped it down her throat. In moments, frost bloomed on her arms. Her skin went blue, her eyes iced white, and she froze solid. Her father shouted, her mother screamed, and the two brothers argued, deciding finally to take her as she was, intending to decide what to do with her on the road.

They set off that night, the two brothers and the girl, tied to a horse her father gave as her dowry. Her mother watched her go, and it was as if the sliver of ice that had lodged in her heart the day the girl was born melted away.

The brothers rode until the stars were nearly faded, then stopped to make camp. They lay their bedrolls on the ground, and lay their stiff bride under a tree. They slept.

The younger brother had terrible dreams, about a fox with holes for eyes, and a child who laughed while drowning in an ice-cold pond. As the sun bled over the horizon the next morning, he woke to find his brother dead. The man's skin bristled with frost, and his mouth and eyes were frozen open in horror. The girl was as still as ever. Her cold body didn't respond even when the remaining brother kicked it sharply with his boot.

He thought fast. He left his brother where he lay, packed up camp, and tied the girl's stonelike hands and feet with strong rope—just in case. He left her behind with his frozen brother, and rode away like the devil was after him.

As he rode he kept hearing a sound like wind through icy branches, and thumps of wet snow sliding to the ground at night. He rode faster. When his horse was covered in froth, and he was too hungry and exhausted to continue, he stopped and made camp. He sat up all night holding a knife to his chest, keeping a small fire alive. Nothing came for him in the night, and he felt foolish.

Until the sun rose and he turned and saw his horse. The animal was dead, its eyes colored over with a membrane of frost, and its mane had ice crystals in it.

The younger brother continued his journey on foot. The trees he moved through were so thick the sunlight could barely break through them, and he met no one on his way. The air he breathed tasted frozen in his throat, and chilled his eyes till they ached, though it was spring thaw all around him. It was barely dark when he lay down to rest, so tired he couldn't summon up the strength to feel afraid. When his eyes had closed, the princess came out from behind a tree hung with creeping vines. She laid her hands on his eyes and placed her mouth over his. When he was dead, she stood up tall. The ice was still in her, and her eyes swirled like cirrus clouds.

She turned. There was a scent in the air of cold lilacs, a late freeze on an early bloom. It was the smell of her mother's perfume. The black-eyed girl felt her parents' distant castle like the pulsing heartbeat of an animal she wanted to kill. She set her path back toward it.

~10~

Finch stopped talking. The diner rustled around us, spoons chiming on cup brims and plates set to tables with a smack. I felt a sharp sting and looked down: I'd ripped the cuticle on my right index finger to bloody shreds.

"Is that it?" I asked, finally.

His eyes were worried, staring over my shoulder. "No, it's just—" He half-stood, then sat again. "I thought I . . . never mind."

"What is it?" My head pulsed with a three-a.m.-black-coffee feeling, and my teeth chattered twice before I clamped my jaw shut. I jerked a look back over each shoulder but saw nothing out of the ordinary: three girls younger than us drinking coffee and wearing sunglasses at night, a table of old men in work jackets, a dark-haired woman biting into a sugar cube.

"What did you see?" I whispered.

He ran a hand through his hair, made it bigger. "Nothing. I'm on edge."

I took a last look around. Nobody looked back.

"You remembered a lot," I said.

He'd jammed another wedge of sandwich in his mouth and was chewing mechanically, his eyes darting around. "When I love a book," he said around the sandwich, "I read it more than once."

"How does the story end?"

But Finch was out of storytelling mode, his eyes still flicking past my shoulder every few seconds. "Bloody revenge, obviously."

"Revenge for what?"

"The usual. Neglectful mom, criminal dad. Shades of 'Thousandfurs,' in case I didn't make that clear."

"Coffee?" Finch and I jumped as our waitress swung by with a fresh pot.

"You're more on edge now," I said when she was gone. "Telling the story—it made you nervous."

"I've never told one of them out loud. It made me . . . it almost made me think I was seeing things." His head twitched as he checked out the table behind us: a college-aged guy and a woman in her forties, neither of them talking.

My own nerves were raw as rope, almost rubbed through. I couldn't have him breaking down, too. "Fine, no more story time. Just . . . why do you think my mom named me after that story specifically?"

"Maybe she didn't. Maybe whoever left the page is trying to mess with you. She could've named you after, I don't know, Alice in Wonderland. Or nobody at all."

He took a swig of his coffee, rolled his neck. Calm, laid-back Finch was returning, sliding into place over his skin. It bothered me that he got to see me broken and all I got was the same candy shell he showed everyone else.

"Still, maybe she did," I said, letting the story's strange rhythms play over in my mind. It was different from what I thought it would be. It rattled around in my skull, unfinished. I'd assumed Althea's work would have a strong feminist message, allegorical undertones, a clear arc of story. I'd expected Angela Carter at best, *Animal Farm* with princesses at worst. But this story had no allegiance to anything. It was winding and creepy and not even that bloody. There were no heroes, no wedding. No message.

"You know who my dad is, right?" Finch crushed oyster crackers into his soup.

"Um. Sort of." Of course I knew who his dad was.

"So my name, my full name, is Ellery Oliver Djan-Nelson-Abrams-Finch."

"Does that fit on a Scantron?"

"A what?"

"Never mind." Of course the touchy-feely grade schools Finch must've attended didn't use Scantrons. His middle school had probably graded with hearts and flowers.

"Ellery was my dad's grandfather's name, but guess where they got the Oliver."

"Oliver Twist?"

"Nope."

"Oliver Wendell Holmes?"

"I wish. But no."

"Oliver . . . Hardy?"

"My parents aren't that cool."

"Fine. I give up."

"My mom's brother. He lived in the States for a few years before I was born, when my mom was still modeling. Then he moved back to Ghana when I was a baby. My stepmother has never once called me Ellery. She *only* calls me Oliver. She likes to pretend I'm not related to my dad at all—because I don't look like him, I look like my mom. Like my uncle. She's trying, through, like, power of sicko suggestion, to imply I'm not my dad's. That I'm, like, my uncle's."

My stomach kicked like a rabbit. "Are you sure she means it that way? That'd be a pretty sick accusation."

"She's a pretty sick woman. She's trying to get pregnant right now, and she's at least forty-five. It's straight out of a fucking fairy tale—like someday she'll convince my dad I'm not even his, and her baby will inherit it all. Like I even *want* it. Like I'd *ever* want to be a man like my dad."

Finch's smiling, vaguely cloudy aspect had burned away. His face was a fierce beam of bitterness. The way he was gripping his coffee cup, I thought it might crack. I reached out to lay my hand over his before I could think.

He sat up straighter, his eyes refocusing on mine. The serene smile inched back onto his face, but now that I'd seen beneath it, I could tell it wasn't a perfect fit.

"My mom used to let me swim in fountains," I said, leaning slowly back and pulling my hand away. The memory came from nowhere; I hadn't thought about it in years. "I always wanted to jump face-first into any body of water bigger than a puddle, and most moms would never let it happen, right? Because of security guards and waterborne diseases or whatever. But what Ella would do was put on her sunglasses and sit a little ways away, while I jumped into the fountain and shrieked and partied till someone noticed. Then she'd have to pretend to be mad, but she never made me get out till the last possible second. This happened in malls, courtyards, parks. It was awesome."

"My mom punched my stepmom in the stomach once."

I choked on my water. "What? Was it at the *wedding*?"

"God, that would've been even better. I'm telling it that way next time. But no, it was right after she found out about her and my dad. Total cliché, my stepmom was my dad's personal assistant. So my mom cabs over to his office, and my stepmom's all, 'Good day, Mrs. Djan-Nelson-Abrams-Finch,' because of course she's really proper about those things, the bullshit things, and my mom hauls off and socks her in the stomach."

"Wow. Did she sue for assault?"

"Nope. According to my dad's business partner, she pretended like it didn't even happen. Once she could breathe normally again, I mean. She's a Vaseline-on-the-teeth type."

"Damn. Your mom sounds ballsy."

I stuttered to silence, remembering I had the tense wrong. Wondering if he knew I knew she was dead. But before I could feel worse, I saw something over Finch's shoulder that made my vision tunnel.

It was the boy in the cab, the one who'd offered me a lift after school. In the weirdness of everything that had happened since, I'd forgotten about him. He was slouching in a vinyl seat at the back of the restaurant, holding a coffee mug in one hand and wearing his ratty flat cap. Everything in his posture said he didn't see me, and for a second I mistrusted my racing heart.

Then he shifted slightly and winked at me, before turning his head toward the waitress.

"Finch," I said quietly, "we're going. Now." He looked at my face and nodded, dug out a few bills to throw on the table. The boy in the cap was getting his coffee refilled when we slid from the booth and back out onto Seventy-Ninth Street.

"I think there's a guy in there who's following me," I said, giving up on the idea of not sounding insane. We'd turned a sharp corner and were careening down the street, dodging clumps of tourists. For once I was glad they were there, to offer cover.

"What's he look like?"

"College age, but kinda old-timey. Like a . . . I don't know. A good-looking cabbie during Prohibition."

"Good-looking?"

His stupid question hung in the air. I was looking back over my shoulder so often, it took me a minute to realize we were weaving toward his place. Where I would, what? Spend the night? I felt a pang of self-loathing. Freeloading again, off a boy I barely knew. A boy whose eyes were the alert, shiny color of sunlight through Coke, with a kinetic energy that made him seem like he never slept.

By the time we reached his block I was seriously considering heading to Lana's. Or Salty Dog—I had a key. I could lie across two tables to sleep, sneak out before it opened the next morning.

"Look, Finch. You don't have to take me back to your—"

"Stop." His voice was so harsh that I did. But he wasn't looking at me. He grabbed the back of my jacket in his fist and pulled me toward the low wall surrounding Central Park, across and a couple of doors down from his place.

"Get down," he hissed. He was staring hard at a figure standing just beyond the spill of light beneath his awning.

At first I just saw a girl in black—black dress, black boots, a brief stretch of pale leg between them. My eyes adjusted, and I started picking out details. Her hair was a sweep of piled-up dark, with a white comic-book stripe blazing down the center. Her eyes were so light I could actually see them from where we crouched—they cast a glow. They ticked back and forth, watching the sidewalk. My skin crawled when I considered the possibility of them landing on me. When she shifted a bit in the shadows, I saw the messy scar that ran down her right temple and cupped her chin like a palm.

"Over the wall," Finch said in a rough whisper, tugging me backward toward the park. We crouched in the shadows of a juniper bush. The air was resinous on my tongue.

"Do you see that girl?" Finch asked. His eyes were glittery and weird. "That's Twice-Killed Katherine."

It took me a minute to place his words. It was the title of one of the stories in *Tales from the Hinterland*. "You mean she looks like her?"

"*Is* her. That girl is Twice-Killed Katherine." He looked at me with a face like a subway preacher, lit and fierce.

"What, like you've seen her before? This is New York. She looks like a million fashiony girls."

"You're just saying that because you haven't read it. Look at her scar. And her hair. And—oh, my god. Do you see what she's holding?"

I squinted at the thing she held to her chest but couldn't make it out.

"It's a birdcage. It's what Twice-Killed Katherine carries. *This* is it," he hissed. "*This* is the Hinterland!"

I started to respond, but the girl did something so strange and terrifying it shut both of us up for a long time.

A man in a heavy gray overcoat was walking down the street toward her, smoking a cigarette and talking into his cell phone. As he passed her, he did a subtle double-take, maybe noticing her scarred face. Before he could get too far, she opened the birdcage.

The thing that came out of it was canary-shaped, but it wasn't a canary. It was small and darting and looked like it had been hole-punched out of shadow. It unfurled its wings wider and wider, till it was the size of a hawk.

It went for the man. As Finch and I gripped hands and knelt like cowards in the park, the thing latched onto his neck. He went down noiselessly, and the creature dropped heavily onto his chest. It stretched its wings so we couldn't see exactly what it was doing. I looked back at the girl. Swallowed a scream, squeezed Finch's hand harder.

Her black-and-white hair shivered with red. Her skin turned from pale to peach, her lips curled, even her scar plumped up into unmarked skin. But the expression on her face was worse than anything. It was a kind of . . . selfish ecstasy.

The bird lifted off the man, folded itself back into a tiny wedge of nightmare, and winged toward its cage. The girl clasped the door shut and backed deeper into the shadows between streetlights.

"Is he dead?" I whispered. My voice was a skeleton leaf.

The man on the ground rose shakily to his feet. He was swimming in his coat and had the air of a person who had forgotten something. His hair was ash white. He staggered over the sidewalk like a zombie.

"Run," said Finch, and we did. We pounded through the park, pools of lamplight strobing over us and dead leaves clutching at our ankles. The air smelled silvery, with a hint of mulch, and the cold wind made my eyes stream. Sweat had pooled on my back by the time we dropped onto a bench.

"That was . . . that was not possible," I said hoarsely.

Finch's pupils were blasted wide. He looked strung out. "*That* was the Hinterland. *Fuck*."

I couldn't respond. It was my first true glimpse of the Hinterland—my first solid proof that there was something terribly real behind Althea's messed-up tales. I should've been reeling.

But I couldn't stop thinking that maybe it *wasn't* the first glimpse. All my life I thought we'd been stalked by bad luck, in the form of weather and disasters and acts of God and strange human viciousness. Maybe all this time, we were being stalked by the Hinterland.

"What she did to that man," I asked. "Does she do it in the story?"

He breathed through his open mouth a few times and fell back against the bench. "It's not how I pictured it, but yeah. It keeps her young. Or alive, maybe. It's also her re-venge."

"On the people who killed her."

"And worse. Yeah."

"So what do we do now?"

"I should call my dad. Make sure he's at home, or talk him into staying away if he isn't." But he didn't make a move toward his phone.

"Finch," I said. "Do you think . . ."

"Katherine wouldn't hurt your mom." His eyes flicked to mine. "She doesn't target women. What we need is a place to stay, get some sleep. Then we figure out what's next."

His expression mirrored what I felt—the black-hole suck of exhaustion that strikes after a trauma. When everything has changed and your messed-up brain is flying around the stars—then your body and all its needs imposes itself, cutting you off from madness.

My situation hit me hard. Homeless. Without my mom. Being stalked, by something I couldn't see the breadth of or understand. I was wrung out, and without Finch I'd be totally alone. "Thank you" was too small, "I'm sorry" so inadequate it made me cringe.

"Okay," I said. "Lead the way."

~11~

Few problems were unsolvable when you had boatloads of cash and a lifetime's worth of rich friends. Finch made some calls, and an hour after leaving the park we were ringing the bell at a townhouse in Brooklyn Heights. The boy who answered had lank indie-rocker hair that fell to his chin. I could tell he was high even before I smelled the hot-box stink surrounding him.

"Ellery Finch!" he said, but with way more syllables.

"Hey, David." Finch ducked his head, glanced at me. I'm not a smile-at-strangers type by nature, but life on the road had driven home the importance of being a gracious houseguest.

"Nice to meet you, David. I'm Alice. Thanks for putting us up."

He grinned at me for a while, then nodded. I was pretty sure he'd meant to say something, but forgot he hadn't.

David's family had the whole building to themselves. It was a converted church, exposed brick and salvaged stained-glass windows everywhere you looked. I swore I could smell candle wax and old incense breathing out of the walls.

"Glad you could take us in, D," said Finch. "Your parents are in Europe?"

"France, man. My little sister's getting in trouble in boarding school over there. She's like a crime kingpin in a uniform, man." We'd interrupted him in the middle of eating a plate of greasy microwave nachos. I found it kind of endearing, even though the cheese was probably small-batch Normandy cheddar. He offered me a bite, and I turned him down.

"The guestroom is stripped. No sheets. You and your girlfriend can have Courtney's room. Second door on the right, but you have to not mind *Doctor Who* and shit."

Finch didn't correct him on the girlfriend thing, just nodded. "Cool, man. Thanks a lot. We really appreciate it."

David made a motion like he was balling up the thanks and jump-shotting it into a trash can. "Glad to see you, glad you could come. Want a nacho?"

We declined again. The two of them shot the shit for a while, discussing people they'd gone to junior high with, before David's parents moved him to Brooklyn. I kept my eyes on the corners where shadows gathered, on the windows where the shades weren't drawn. Waiting to see a girl with a birdcage, a boy in a cap. My hand was loosely cupped around my phone, set to vibrate. Every minute

that passed without word from Ella made the chasm beneath my feet yawn wider.

I could sense Finch's fatigue, and could barely hide my
own. As soon as it was even a little bit polite, he did a
yawn and stretch. "Cool if we turn in? We have to get out
of here really early tomorrow morning."

"Yeah? You leaving town?"

Finch flicked his eyes my way. "Not . . . uh, maybe.
We'll see."

"Heading upstate, probably," I said impulsively, then
flushed. It was an idea from an alternate world, one in
which my mom was still at Harold's, and Finch and I
were really together.

"Ahh, for the leaves and shit! Apple picking, man.
Hayrides. Pumpkin carving. Scarecrows. Wax vampire
teeth, dude!"

Before he could free-associate his way toward seasonal
lattes and fisherman sweaters, Finch stood up. They did
a chest bump thing, I gave David a half-hug, and we
showed ourselves upstairs.

I checked out the darkened master bedroom as we
passed. A wide window overlooked the East River, pinpricks of lighted windows winking at me from across the
water. A fug of weed and socks and strawberry room spray
announced which room was David's, but his sister's
smelled pleasant and unpersonalized, like an expensive
hotel. When Finch fumbled on the light, we gaped at the
walls, then looked at each other and cracked up.

Before she was a boarding-school thug, Courtney was
a fangirl. Her room was papered with magazine photos,
Harry Potter posters, photos of her and her friends hanging

out in diner booths. Broadway ticket stubs marched around the sides of the mirror attached to her spindly antique vanity, and a matching bookcase was filled half with colorful paperbacks, half with DVD boxed sets. *Firefly* sat next to *Staying Fat for Sarah Byrnes*. *Supernatural* shared a shelf with *Akata Witch*. I scanned the case for *Tales from the Hinterland*, but it wasn't there.

The floor was spotless, the sleigh bed made up with swagged cream sheets, but the walls, teeming with bright celebrity teeth and yards of shiny hair, made the place feel hectic. I thought Ellery felt the same, because he turned on a side lamp and switched off the overhead. The hot riot of faces receded into gloom.

"Who gets the bed?" I asked. Nice guys like Finch don't let troubled girls like me take the floor, usually. But you never know.

He gave me a weird look. "You get the bed. Ten to one there's a trundle under there. Or a Dora the Explorer sleeping bag in the closet."

It was Betty Boop, but I still gave him credit. I washed my face and rinsed my mouth in the adjoining white-and-rose-gold bathroom, and contemplated a shower. But the idea of getting clean just to climb back into dirty clothes was too depressing. Once I was tucked into Courtney's pretty bed, I wriggled out of my uniform skirt and folded it on top of the pillow next to my head.

"Lights out?" Finch said. He was lying on top of the sleeping bag fully clothed, his hands propped behind his head.

I nodded, and he reached back to flick off the lamp. The vaporous light of old streetlamps filtered in around the window shades. Somewhere in the house, a heater whooshed to life. The feeling of settling into an unfamiliar house was a familiar one. I closed my eyes and let myself pretend, for one long minute, that it was my mother lying on the floor beside me. The pain around my heart expanded, sharp and hot as a supernova, and I rolled over to breathe into the sheets.

I knew the sounds of someone trying to hold back tears in the dark, and I knew I was making them. *If Finch tries to comfort me, I'll smother him with Courtney's Eiffel Tower pillow.*

He didn't. I counted to ten, twenty, fifty. The counting worked like Novocain, like it always did. Finally, I rolled onto my back again and stared up at the ceiling.

"There's one weird thing I haven't told you," I said into the quiet.

Finch's head tilted toward me.

"There's someone else who might be following me."

"Besides the guy at the diner?"

"Yeah." I stayed quiet a moment, trying to decide how to say it without sounding melodramatic. "When I was little, a guy, um. Took me. Abducted me. He didn't hurt me or, you know, anything. But I'm pretty sure I saw him at the café where I work."

I wasn't pretty sure, I was certain, but felt glad I hedged my bets when Finch shot up to sitting. "Holy shit. Did he do anything to you?"

"No, no way. He didn't talk to me, he didn't come near me. I just saw him. Then he ran away."

Slowly he subsided back onto his sleeping bag. "He really didn't . . . I mean, when he kidnapped you . . ."

"He never touched me. He asked me to get in his car, and I did. I was a kid. He told me stories and fed me pancakes."

Finch's response was sharp. "What stories?"

"I don't remember. I remember liking them, though. And he told me he was taking me to Althea, so." I thought of the things he'd left behind, now tucked into the bottom of my bag. The feather, the comb, the bone.

"Shit. What if he was . . . what did he look like?"

"Red hair, nice face. Smart-looking. He looked like an English teacher, but without the tweedy clothes. And he looks exactly the same now, ten years later. Like, ageless."

"Hinterland." His voice wrapped around the word like it tasted good. It set my teeth on edge, made me want to hold my secrets closer to my chest.

I was jealous of him, I realized. Jealous of the way he could love Althea—uncomplicated, a fan's adoration. Envy lodged in my chest like a chunk of green apple. "Why do you love it?" I asked. "Althea's book."

I heard him shift on the floor. It couldn't have been that comfortable down there.

"You know how fairy tales are, like, told and retold?" he said, his voice soft. "And they all fit into these certain types, and you can find a dozen versions of 'The Twelve Dancing Princesses' or 'The Juniper Tree' or whatever?"

I nodded, because I did know. I'd read them all.

"I always found that comforting. I liked formulas. I liked narrative arcs I could predict. I liked that my dad still kissed my mom when he got home, on the lips, like in a sitcom. I liked doing stuff the same way every day and reading stories I could take apart into pieces and never really being *surprised* by anything. I was anxious, I guess. I liked structure."

The rat-a-tat talk of Adult Swim bled through the floorboards. I could pick out a word here and there.

"Then my parents got divorced, and my dad and my therapist gave me loads of books about kids with divorced parents, and kids who were mad at the world, but all that anger and uncertainty made it worse. And I thought, like, boohoo, my life sucks, all that. Can't get worse. But haha, the universe was like 'Fuck that,' and she—my mom—she died. Um. She killed herself."

I knew it was coming, but the words still took a chunk out of me. I stayed very still when he said them, because I didn't know what else to do.

He breathed in and out, soft. "And my friends didn't know what to say to me, and my dad didn't know what to do with me, so it was pretty much me and books. But I didn't want the touchy-feely tragedy crap my therapist gave me to make me feel like I was less alone. I wanted that distance. I wanted that uncaring, 'here's your blood and guts and your fucked-up happy ending' fairy-tale voice. But, like, the Andrew Lang stuff wasn't cutting it for me anymore.

"Then I got my hands on Althea's book. And it was perfect. There are no lessons in it. There's just this harsh, horrible world touched with beautiful magic, where shitty things happen. And they don't happen for a reason, or in threes, or in a way that looks like justice. They're set in a place that has no rules and doesn't want any. And the author's voice—your grandmother's voice—is perfectly pitiless. She's like a war reporter who doesn't give a fuck." He breathed in like he was going to say more, then went silent.

"It was nice of your dad," I said, "to give you those other books. Even if you hated them."

He laughed, kind of. "That's your takeaway?"

"No. I just . . . I've spent so much time obsessing over Althea. Getting ready to meet her. Reading all kinds of fairy tales so I could impress her when I finally did. But she never called, and she never cared, and now she's dead." I'd never said any of this out loud, and doing it now felt like purging poison. "Some part of me has been defined by, like, her *not* being there, and now that she's gone I'm being haunted by something she created."

"You really think she created it?"

"Of course she did. What do you mean?"

He was shaking his head; he sat back up on his sleeping bag. "I told you, she was like a war reporter. She didn't write this stuff into creation—she wrote about something that was already out there. I used to think it was metaphors for something, but not anymore, not after seeing Twice-Killed Katherine." He paused. "And Alice, don't you wonder . . ."

"What?"

He flopped down again. "Never mind."

"No way. You've got to stop doing that. What were you going to say?"

When he spoke, it was almost in a whisper. "Don't you wonder if your mom's not the one they want? What if you're the target, and she's the bait?"

"Then they would've kidnapped me. It would've been easy."

"They *did* kidnap you—that man was Hinterland, you know it. Maybe it's different now that you're older. Maybe now you have to go by choice."

"Even if you were right," I said slowly, "it doesn't change anything. They want to get me to do something? They found the right way to do it. I'd follow my mom to hell if I had to. She'd do the same for me."

She would, too. Beneath the beauty and the charm and the sharp sparkle of her personality, she had a core of steel. She was like a blade wrapped in a bouquet of orchids. I hoped to god whoever took her made the mistake of underestimating her.

Finch sighed in a way I couldn't read. "Let's try to sleep. Long day tomorrow."

Questions crowded at the back of my throat. *Why are you helping me? Do you think I'll find her? Was that really Twice-Killed Katherine?* But he'd rolled away from me. A line of moonlight ran like a thin white road from the crown of his head down his back. The longer I stared at it, the more it made him look like he was splitting in two, revealing something shining beneath his skin.

I rolled over and shut my eyes tight, but it was a long time before I drifted away.

~12~

I didn't dream about Twice-Killed Katherine, like I worried I might. I dreamed about my mother. I dreamed about the day I realized we didn't move for fun, or because she was restless. That she didn't do it to ruin my life, or on a superstitious whim because she didn't like the way an old woman hovered a hand over my forehead on the bus, drawing a helix in the air before hustling off at the next stop.

I was ten, and it was our second move in less than eight months. I'd woken that morning in my trundle bed on the floor next to Ella's, feeling a tightness in my scalp. When I reached up, my fingers found the coiled bumps of braids. My hair was wrapped in a tight crown of them around my head.

But I'd fallen asleep with my hair shower damp and

falling to my shoulders in tangles. "Mom," I said, patting at my braided crown. "Why'd you do my hair?"

Ella rolled over and blinked at me sleepily. Then a look came into her eyes: fear and a spiky anger that yawned open like an aperture before slamming shut into something worse—hopelessness.

"No school today," she'd said, rolling out of bed and going straight to the closet to pull down her suitcase.

My rage that time had struck like lightning. While she was shoving our kitchen into boxes, I cut every pair of her jeans off just below the crotch, in protest over leaving town the day my fifth-grade reading teacher was bringing in Turkish Delight.

It wasn't until we were in the car, my body splayed against the seat like a shipwreck survivor in the wake of my tantrum, that I'd told her about the candy I was missing out on.

"It's not like you think it'll be," she said, the bungalow we'd spent half a year in shrinking in our rearview. "It's chalky and it smells like flowers. You'd hate it."

"You're lying," I replied, turning my head to the window.

Ella stopped the car dead, in the middle of the road. "Hey."

The heat in her voice made me turn.

"We don't lie to each other, you and me. Right?"

I shrugged and nodded. Her eyes were too intense, red in the corners like she'd rubbed them after chopping jalapeño.

And in a flash my tiny, self-centered world expanded outward: she hadn't wanted to go, either. She'd put curtains up in the bungalow, and fixed the teetering ceiling fan.

I'd held on to that revelation and saved it to think about that night, turning it over in my mind like a worry stone while Ella snored softly in the next motel bed.

It scared me, but it also coaxed me closer to her. We'd been on two sides of a divide looking across at each other. Then I realized something that seemed so simple, but changed everything. It tilted the world so she and I were side by side again. There was us, there was the world.

And there was the fear, underneath it all, that the fault for our life was mine. Ella was easy to like, with a sweet, gravelly voice that hid a sharp sense of humor and an unforgiving eye for the ridiculous, and dark hair that grew out funny so it licked down her back like flames. I was irritable, prone to fits of rage, and had been told more than once I had crazy eyes. If one of us was the bad luck magnet, I was.

That fear was what kept me quiet, kept me from asking *why*. I was terrified the reason was me.

The dream played out in living color, before fading into a thin, restless sleep. I closed my eyes on moonlight and opened them on a sunlit collage of Lin-Manuel Miranda. The floor beside me was empty, and my phone was a blank—no messages from Ella, no missed calls.

Once I had a dream in which I walked room by room through an empty house, looking for my mom. Every room felt like she'd just been in it, every hall echoed with her voice, but I never found her. Now I felt like I was living in that dream.

I swiped at my hair and mouth, checking for cowlicks or drool, and slithered into my skirt beneath the comforter. I tried and failed to replicate the hospital-cornered perfection of Courtney's made bed, before going to the bathroom to scrub at my teeth with a guest towel. My hair stuck up at odd angles, so I dunked my head under the tap.

Downstairs, Finch was tapping away at a laptop in a huge, open-plan kitchen, while David poured boiling water into a French press.

"You're up!" Finch sounded like he'd taken a hit of helium. "I found it! I found a copy of *Tales from the Hinterland*!"

I squinted at him. "Found it like you're bidding on it on eBay?"

"Found it like it's here, in New York, and we can go pick it up now."

The thrill that ran through me was as much fear as it was excitement. "No way." I dropped onto the stool next to him. "How?"

"I called every rare book dealer in town. Not for the first time, but this is the first time someone's actually *had* it."

"I hope you like weird Scandinavian health toast," David said, placing a plate of coarse brown rectangles in front of us, "because that's all we have."

I was too keyed up to eat, which made me drink more coffee than I should have, which made me even more jangled. But I didn't care, because I was about to get my hands on the book that was haunting me. Possibly literally.

And drinking coffee was a good distraction from the sinking suspicion that this was a little too easy. That our sudden good fortune could be a trap.

I was rinsing my mug in the big farmhouse sink when something dark slammed against the window. I flinched away as a massive, raggedy blackbird flapped backward, then threw itself against the glass a second time.

"Whoa!" David hustled to the window. The bird was

beating against it, a flurry of wings. "Hey! You're hurting yourself, buddy!" He slapped his palm on the glass, jerking back when the bird's motions became more frenzied.

There was something in its beak. I recognized its shape, an industrial rectangle that made my stomach lurch.

"Shit, man." David looked back at us, his face troubled. "Do you think it's blind or something? Should I—should I let it inside?"

"Don't," I said, my voice hard and quick. "Please." David frowned at me but didn't move. We watched silently as the bird charged the window with the last of its strength, before dropping out of view. The thing it had been holding snagged into a corner of the frame. I moved to the blood-smeared window and eased it open, carefully, snatching the envelope before it could come loose. My name was written across the back in a hasty scrawl.

The envelope held another soft, worn page with a freshly ripped edge. I lifted it enough to read the top.

The Door That Wasn't There
Hansa the Traveler
The Clockwork Bride

"What the hell?" breathed David over my shoulder. "That's your name on the envelope, right? Is that for *you*?"

The coffee tasted gritty and burnt on my tongue. Finch tried to meet my eyes, but I couldn't look back.

We didn't talk on the way to the subway. I felt stunned and flayed, a nerve ending exposed to cold sun. I refused to let Finch hail a cab, fearing whoever might be behind the wheel. The bookshop was a straight shot up to Harlem, but it was the kind of slow and halting train ride that makes you think something evil is set against you getting where you're going, even on days when you don't have a really, really good reason to believe that anyway.

The shop was at the end of a homey stretch of brownstones, tucked into a bottom story. The lettering on its sign reminded me of an old-fashioned candy store: *Wm. Perks' Antiq. Books &c.*, in a looping font.

"Do you think he paid his sign maker by the letter?"

They were the first words Finch had spoken since he'd touched my elbow and said, "This way," when we got off the subway. I mustered a close-lipped smile. I kept seeing the bird's flat black eyes.

Finch rang the bell beside the wrought-iron door. Half a minute later, we heard someone undoing a series of locks on the other side.

The man who opened the door looked less like an antiquarian bookseller and more like a bookie. His tie was a loud yellow, his suit an exhausted brown. He had a napkin tucked into his collar that appeared to be covered in barbecue sauce.

He squinted suspiciously at Finch—all wild hair, unzipped jacket, one restless hand stuck out for a shake. "You Ellery Finch?" he said out the side of his mouth, like he was trying to sell us drugs in Tompkins Square Park.

"I am. William Perks?" The guy agreed and finally took Finch's hand, giving it two good pumps. I held mine out, but he kissed it instead. I resisted the urge to wipe it on my wrinkled uniform skirt.

"Come in, come in. Would you believe I just got the book you're looking for this morning? I knew it wouldn't be long before the collectors started sniffing me out—it's the first one I've ever had in stock, and only the second I've seen. I'll be damned if the quality on this one isn't high, high, high."

His patter made him sound like a county-fair auctioneer, but at least he wasn't treating us like children. I'd anticipated a tidy little bookshop, lined with leather volumes and looking a bit like Finch's library, but what I got was a mind-boggling riot of bookshelves that started a few yards from the door, standing at all angles and punctuated by free-range stacks rising from the ground, in a room that smelled like paste and paper and the animal tang of vellum. And barbecue. Perks led us to a glass case in the back, full of books lying open like butterflies. Finch frowned. "Bad for the spines," he muttered.

"So I'm gonna wash my hands real good, then I'm gonna bring you what you seek." Perks put his palms together, bowed to us, and exited the room.

"Do you think he really got it this morning?" I asked Finch, low.

He shrugged. "Stranger things have happened. Like, recently."

Perks zoomed back in before I could reply. I had the idea he was as eager to sell as we were to buy.

I was right, but not for the reason I thought.

"Here she is," he said softly, slipping the book from a paper sleeve.

The sight of its embossed leather cover, dull gold on green, made my breath catch. It was the book at last, soft and inviting and perfectly sized for holding.

Perks saw my expression and laughed. "I thought you were just along for the ride. But it looks like you're the one who's buying."

"Are there any missing pages?"

The bookseller made a show of looking horrified. "Not on your life."

I relaxed, a little. "Did you really get it today?"

"I did indeed, and within the hour you all called me looking for it. You might think it's strange, but you get used to those karmic moments in the book business. Books want to be read, and by the right people. There's nothing surprising in it, not to me."

"Who sold it to you?"

"Someone who said he bought it at an estate sale. But I can't double-check everyone's story."

"What did he look like?" Ellery asked.

Say he had red hair.

Perks mulled it over. "He was young, almost as young as you. White kid, dark hair, mug on him like he'd sell you your own mother. And he was . . ." He hesitated, his eyes flicking between us.

"He was what?"

"An odd bird. A little shifty. He had that air to him, like a man out of time."

"What do you mean?"

My voice must've had a warning note in it, because Perks threw up his hands and smiled disarmingly. "It's the look these days—the train jumper look. That Brooklyn thing, girls your age must like it." He beckoned our attention back to the book. "Want to take a look?"

What I wanted was to know for sure if the boy who'd

sold him the book was the same one I'd seen outside of Whitechapel, and again in the diner. And whether it was a different copy from the one I'd seen at my café, in the hands of the red-haired man.

Perks slipped on white gloves that made him look like an off-brand Mickey Mouse. "The binding is in near mint condition." He deftly flipped the book over and back again. "No foxing on the pages. Some discoloration, of course, but that's to be expected."

As he opened the book, a scent rose from its pages, the homey must of old print and something else—something sweet. It was there and gone in an instant. Some yearning part of me wanted to believe it was Althea's perfume.

"This title's first print run was quite small, as you probably know—" Perks began. He stopped talking as the book fell open to a Polaroid photo stuck between its pages. It was flipped so we could only see the white of its backing.

He grinned. "Didn't see that before. You wouldn't believe the things you find in old books. When it's a photo, odds are ten to one it's an *arty* one, if you know what I mean. The young lady had better avert her eyes."

He flipped the photo in his Mickey hands and examined its front. Then frowned. His eyes flicked up to us, and back down to the photo. He shoved it over the counter. "What the hell is this?"

It took a moment to understand what I was seeing. The photo was of us.

Me and Finch, lying side by side in Courtney's room— me on the bed, him on the floor. Judging by the angle and the thin, spangled light, it had been taken early that morning by someone standing at our feet. We were both asleep, Ellery's arms thrown loosely over his head and mine pillowed beneath my cheek.

My blood turned to ice water. Someone had been in that room with us, watching while we slept.

Finch got his voice back first. "Sir, we have no idea how that . . ."

"I don't think so. What is this shit? You have your friend sell me this book, then you come back to buy it? Smells like day-old fish to me." Perks picked it up roughly. "Is this even a real Proserpine?"

"Please," I said, my voice unnatural in my ears. "I've never seen that photo in my life, I swear, but please just sell us the book."

Perks shook his head, spastically. "This is too fuckin' weird. Either you and the seller are in cahoots, or something else is going on, but either way you can march yourselves right outta my place."

"Look, we want to give you money." Finch pulled out his wallet, opened it. "What you told me on the phone, plus an extra grand on top. I've got a blank check, we'll wait while you cash it."

The old bookseller's face flushed a dangerous red. "I never should've bought that book in the first place, not from that shady kid. I was glad to be getting rid of it so quick, but now I don't care. You know the copy I saw, that first time?" He thrust a finger in my face. "Torched. And my buddy's car along with it. Maybe by people like you."

"But sir," Finch said. "We're trying to *buy* it."

"I'd rather take it as a loss." Perks shoved the Polaroid at Finch and jammed the book into its bag. "Get out, and don't even think about trying to come back to steal this. It'll be out of my shop in an hour. Someone else can deal with the cursed thing."

"You think it's cursed?" I said, and Perks looked at me with something close to pity.

"You seem like a nice girl," he said, shaking his head. "Why do nice girls hang around with scummy boys like this? I'll never understand it."

He wasn't that tall, and for one mad moment I thought of pushing him aside and taking the book by force. But he ushered us out onto his stoop before I got up the nerve.

"*Dammit,*" Finch said when the door had slammed behind us. "Why didn't I grab it?"

"That's exactly what I was thinking." *Someone was in the room with us last night.*

"Who the hell took this photo?" Finch stared at the crumpled Polaroid in his hand.

"No chance it was David, right?" *Someone stood over us while we slept.*

"Guy can barely put on pants. He's not up to planning this level of mindfuckery."

We were walking fast down the street, both of us looking every which way and not trying to hide it.

"They broke in, took our photo, put it into the book, then sold it to this guy . . . so he could sell it to us. Why? Why not just . . ."

"Just face you?" Finch's hair seemed to have gained another inch in the last few minutes. Clearly it expanded with stress.

"*Take* me. Like they did my mom. Why not just take me?"

"Maybe . . ." He put his palms together like Sherlock, breathed out loudly. "Maybe it's a fairy-tale thing."

"How so?"

"Maybe they can't touch you. Because you're Althea's granddaughter!" He was getting excited. "Maybe, like, since her blood runs in your veins . . ."

"I'm not a fan theory, Finch! And they took Ella. They touched Ella. She's more Althea's than I am."

I turned my head sharply. I couldn't look at him anymore. The day was overbright, thrumming with menace. I blinked at a girl across the street, wearing a long peasant skirt and walking a pot-bellied pig on a braided leash. On the other side, moving toward us, a man in a baseball cap carried a bouquet of white roses. As he got closer, I could see how they glistened with fake raindrops. An old woman watched us through the second-floor window of the nearest building, her underbite telling us to get off her lawn. The flower man had a camera in one hand. The girl looked at me as she unhitched her pig from its lead. The man lifted the camera to his eye.

They were the Hinterland. They were all, all the Hinterland.

A migraine exploded like a bottle rocket inside my skull. My knees went woozy and my teeth and knuckles ached. I smelled the dusty perfume of the book again and my vision went green, before a black crow's wing obscured my sight.

~13~

It scared me, sometimes, how little I could remember. When I looked back over my life, it melted together into one long, soft-focus shot of rain through the windshield. Focus my eyes one way, I saw drops on glass. Focus them another, and I saw the wet highway stretching out ahead. The things that stuck with me were the in-between places, not the places we landed—highways, dirt roads, truck stops. Motels with puddle-warm swimming pools clogged with leaves. An orchard we stopped at once on our way to Indianapolis, to pick apples that tasted like bananas and candy and flowers.

I remembered less from my own life than I did from the books I read. In Nashville I mainlined Francesca Lia Block.

In Maine it was *Peter Pan*, then *Peter Pan in Kensington Gardens*, then *Peter and the Starcatchers*. From the winter we spent in Chicago, while Ella worked as a custodian and apprentice costume designer at a tiny storefront theater, I remembered *The Big Sleep*, *One Thousand and One Nights*, and a cold so astonishingly complete it felt personal.

Everyone is supposed to be a combination of nature and nurture, their true selves shaped by years of friends and fights and parents and dreams and things you did too young and things you overheard that you shouldn't have and secrets you kept or couldn't and regrets and victories and quiet prides, all the packed-together detritus that becomes what you call your life.

But every time we left a place, I felt the things that happened there being wiped clean, till all that was left was Ella, our fights and our talks and our winding roads. I wrote down dates and places in the corners of my books, and lost them along the way. Maybe it was my mother whispering in my ear. *The bad luck won't follow us to the next place. You don't have to remember it this way.* Or maybe it was the clean break of it, the way we never looked back.

But I didn't think so. I thought it was just me. My mind was an old cassette tape that kept being recorded over. Only wavering ghost notes from the old music came through. I wondered, sometimes, what the original recording would sound like—what the source code of me might look like. I worried it was darker than I wanted it to be. I worried it didn't exist at all. I was like a balloon tied to Ella's wrist: If I didn't have her to tell me who I was, remind me why it mattered, I might float away.

Passing out felt like doing just that: giving up, floating into the ether. Even the pain in my head faded away.

But gravity was insistent. The world wanted me back.

A voice lapped over me in slow motion. My eyesight returned in a paisley wash of swirls and blobs, before resolving into something true. Someone crouched in front of me. The sun at their back made them into negative space. My arm felt like a bag of wet flour, but I lifted it anyway, to touch the halo of their hair. The person grew very still as I tangled my fingers into the softness by their neck.

"Mom?" I croaked.

"No. Sorry." Finch's voice was careful and small. My memory came back with it. I dropped my hand, squeezed it into a fist.

"You passed out," he said.

My back was propped against the low stone wall of a brownstone garden. The light had changed. It was hotter, more golden. After a couple of false starts, I spoke again. "What is it?"

He was looking at me with an expression I couldn't place. He looked like Ella after she ate pot brownies and took me to a show at the planetarium, his eyes all wide and reverent. He looked . . . he looked wonderstruck.

I must've been misreading it—I couldn't have looked that good passed out. I glared at him a little, and some of the shine went out of his eyes.

"You weren't out long," he said. "You didn't hit your head—you'll be fine. You just need to eat something."

"The girl," I said. "With the pig. And the boy with the camera. Where'd they go?"

He frowned slightly. "I didn't see them. I was busy with you, I guess."

The street was empty, but I still felt the presence of watching eyes.

"I caught you kinda awkward," Finch said. "You hurt your knees going down."

But the pain was good. It was something to focus on. My body had that horrible heavy post-nap feeling, where you can't tell what day it is and you could almost cry. I wanted my mom, in a way you maybe can't ever want anyone else. It was primal and sharp and it made me feel like a needle in the haystack of a cold and terrible world. *I wanted my mom.*

"We have to go. I have to get out of here."

"Okay." He lifted his hand like he was going to touch my face, then kept lifting and ran it through his hair. "We'll go as soon as you can walk. Can you walk?"

I could. A rush of pins and needles ran through my legs as I stood, and the fresh scrapes ached.

We walked. Slivers of migraine stabbed the backs of my eyes every time I looked at a surface bright with sun. Finch saw me wincing, rummaged around in his bag, and placed a battered Rangers cap on my head.

It was the sort of easy flirtatious move I saw guys make all the time, even at Whitechapel, but his fingers were gentle and the look in his eyes complicated. In the wedge of shade beneath the cap, my thoughts started to clarify. What had I actually seen on the sidewalk outside of Perks's place? A photography student. A girl with an eccentric pet. This wasn't Twice-Killed Katherine territory, this was plain paranoia.

Paranoia so quick and overwhelming I'd *passed out*. How hard would Audrey mock me if she could've seen me swooning—and being caught by Ellery Finch?

"Audrey," I said.

"What about her?"

"She stopped her dad— I mean, he wasn't going to— he wouldn't have actually *shot* me, but she stopped him. Maybe if I call I can catch her alone, make her talk to me."

I waved him away, toward the bodega we'd stopped at to get food. My phone was nearly dead, but I dialed Ella for the thousandth time once Finch was out of sight, bracing myself to hear her voicemail.

I didn't. Instead there was a long pause and a distant click, and my heart swelled into my throat. Then a nice mechanical voice told me her number had been disconnected.

I sat down hard on a Siamese pipe, pulling the brim of Finch's hat over my face. I already knew the Hinterland could sneak in while we slept, plant creepy photos in books, and send crows to do their bidding, but turning off my mother's number was so blunt, so rooted in the real world, it scared me more than anything.

Before my heart had slowed I called Audrey, so certain she'd let it go to voicemail I was briefly speechless when she answered.

"Alice?"

"Audrey. You picked up."

"Oh, my god, I can't believe my dad pulled a gun on you!" Her voice was high and fast. I pictured her face, mascaraed and alarmed between sheaves of shiny processed hair.

"Audrey, my phone is dying and I need you to tell me what happened to my mom."

"I would've called you last night, but I couldn't get away from my dad. He's been, like, embracing his gun for the last twenty-four hours. I swear he's gonna shoot himself in the balls."

I was heartened to hear her sounding like herself again, but didn't have time for it. "Audrey, please focus for a sec. My mom."

"Oh, sorry. Sorry. I'm still freaked out. We're on our way to our place in the Hamptons . . . oops, I shouldn't have told you that. We stopped for lunch, I'm in this gross bathroom. I just ate, like, a nine-hundred-calorie lobster roll. Do you think I'm in shock?"

I was holding my phone so tight I could feel ridges forming in my palm. "My mom, Audrey."

"God, I'm sorry! Okay, what happened was I went home over lunch because, well, I had to."

Audrey refuses to poop at school. Don't ask me how I know this.

"So when I got in I smelled this crazy smell—I mean, you smelled it. I thought Nadia had forgotten to take out the trash."

I made a frantic *get on with it* motion with my hand, even though she couldn't see me.

"Then I heard fighting—no big deal, considering it was practically divorce day. But then I heard Ella making this sound I'd never heard before. Like this hysterical bab-bling sound. I'm sorry, that's what it sounded like. And she kept saying, 'Please, please.' And that's when I started to think maybe she was talking to someone else."

The hairs rose on my neck. I wrapped one arm around the cold curling in my stomach.

Audrey continued, in the most subdued voice I'd ever heard her use. "I went to their room. My dad was standing there looking horrible, just totally blank—like he'd been hit in the head. And your mom was crouching on the ground. And there were two, um, two others with them."

"Two others? Two people?"

Her voice had hairline fractures in it. "Not really. I don't think. Alice, they looked like people, but I don't think they were. They were the wrong . . . they were just *wrong*. The man had face tattoos, he was kinda hot. But his feet, they were dirty and bare—disgusting. He smelled so bad I thought I'd die. And the woman, her eyes . . ." She paused. I could hear the *flick, flick* of a lighter and her sharp inhale before she spoke again. "Your mom . . . I think she *knew* them. They'd told my dad something about her—he won't tell me what it was, but it's something really bad. It made him hate her."

"Audrey, my phone's about to die. Where did they take her?"

The second she took to start speaking was excruciating. "I don't know, exactly. We were in their room, they were scaring me, and suddenly we were in a car. A nice car with tinted windows. It was like I passed out or something. The man and woman must've been in front, because it was just the three of us. My dad looked so sweaty I thought he was gonna have a heart attack, but your mom looked okay. She really did, Alice. She looked *strong*. She wasn't crying anymore, she was sitting up and looking straight ahead. When they stopped the car and let my dad and me out—in some crap neighborhood in the Bronx, it took us forever to get a cab—she smiled at me. And oh, shit, she had a message for you. I don't understand what it means, but maybe you will. Are you listening?"

"Yes. Audrey, yes, what did she say?"

"She said, 'Tell Alice to stay the hell away from the Hazel Wood.'"

I mashed the phone against my ear, like that could make me understand. "Did she say why? Did she say anything else? Did you see which direction the car went?"

I was talking so loudly a man sitting on a lawn chair across the street was giving me the stink eye. There was a second of silence, then the sound of Harold's unmistakable Jersey grumble.

"This is the women's room, Dad!" Audrey shrieked. "I'm talking to Olivia!" His voice got louder, and the phone beeped atonally in my ear as Audrey hit numbers in an effort to hang up. Finally, the call disconnected. I didn't want to get her in trouble, but I was powerless to keep myself from dialing again. It went straight to voicemail.

She wasn't crying. She looked strong. Audrey made Ella sound like a general going to her execution. Even her message to me sounded like last words.

The door to the bodega jangled, and Finch came out juggling two water bottles and a paper bag. I told him, briefly, what Audrey had said, then folded forward over my knees.

"Hey . . . hey . . ." He put a hand on my head and left it there like a hat. I squeezed my eyes shut and panted, focusing on the iron smell of my scraped skin and the little island of Finch's hand, warm through my hair.

After a minute he put his other hand on my shoulder and helped me gently upward, back against the brick wall of the bodega. "Too much blood to your head is a bad idea. Just breathe. And eat this."

The cold bagel sandwich he wrapped my hand around might as well have been a block of wood. My throat made dry insect clicks as I forced down a few bites.

"She was acting like my mom was dead," I said finally. My voice sounded so devastated it almost made me hyperventilate.

"Audrey is not the smartest girl," he said carefully. "She's not the queen of careful eyewitness testimony."

I huffed a laugh into my hands. "We have to go to the Hazel Wood."

His eyes widened. "Okay."

"I don't know what we'll find there," I warned. "I don't even know if it's still Althea's. It could just be a bunch of new rich people living there, or it could be something much worse. You don't have to go with me."

"Yeah, I do." He said it so simply. I knew he would.

That was when I remembered I had no idea where the Hazel Wood was.

"Um," I said. "Slight problem."

A flurry of cell-phoning confirmed the obvious: there was no listed address for the Hazel Wood. All I knew was that it was upstate . . . somewhere.

"Maybe it's a test," he said. "Like, only the true of heart can find their way in. That would be classic."

"The true of heart? Guess I'm out of luck."

"I'm serious. This is how we need to be thinking."

"Come on. This is real life, not a fairy tale."

He gave me what I was starting to recognize as a very Ellery Finch look, a level gaze that told me I was fooling no one. "You don't believe that any more than I do."

I didn't. In my mind, the gates of the Hazel Wood might as well have been the side of a fairy hill. If my mom were in a place where she could call me, she would have. And if she were dead—I believed this to the bottom of my being—I would know it. She couldn't die without it rending me in some way I would feel. If she were dead I'd be limping. If she were dead I'd be blind.

This meant she was either being held somewhere and kept from calling me, or she was in some faraway place that didn't have phones. I wasn't sure which was worse.

"Hey, wait a minute," Finch said. "I might've found something."

He crouched down to show me the Blogspot page pulled up on his phone, titled "Tripping Through the Dandelions." I squinted at the photo of the blogger, someone named Ness, and groaned. She was in her early twenties, and had a pretty clear style obsession with Neil Gaiman's Death. She also looked suspiciously similar to the grad student who'd accosted my mom at Fairway a while back, demanding information on Althea.

We moved to a stoop so we could read it together. His fingers were warm, sliding a moment under mine as I grabbed for one half of the screen. The post he'd pulled up was titled "Searching for the Source: Day 133."

My research into and quest to find the home of trailblazing feminist author and recluse Althea Proserpine proved fruitful on its 133rd day, as I suspected it would. 1+3+3 is 7, a meaningful number to any reader of fairy tales.

I rolled my eyes so hard I saw my brain. Then I kept reading, because, hey, we were desperate.

I have long believed the Hazel Wood is as much a state of mind as it is a place. And ever since I had the good luck of studying Althea's work under Professor Miranda Deyne, it has been clear to me that her work bubbled up from a spring fed as much by magic as by mind. I was unsurprised to learn that the Hazel Wood exists on no map, and is as estranged from Google Earth as true magic is from most university English programs today—hence the sad dearth of contemporary Proserpine scholarship.

As detailed in my post on August 11, I recently tracked down the author of Althea's well-known Vanity Fair profile. Though she moved some years ago to an assisted-living facility, she was still quite sharp. Through her daughter she revealed she was never allowed access to Althea herself, conducting her interviews instead by letter and several odd phone calls. I went in search of the piece's photographer, who was admitted to the Hazel Wood, hitting a dead end when I learned of his death overseas in 1989.

Althea's first and second known marriages ended in widowhood, and she had one daughter, Vanella Proserpine. Little is known of Althea's early life beyond that she was the only child of parents long dead. Vanella has no apparent fixed address and rejected my attempts to start a fruitful dialogue. This is unfortunate, considering what she may be able to offer to the criminally underpopulated field of Proserpine study.

I scoffed forcefully. "Ellery, I remember this chick. She's a nut!"

"A nut who might've been to the Hazel Wood. Keep reading."

I grabbed the phone and scrolled through more background and a few veiled pleas for funding, stopping short at this:

Armed only with the knowledge that the house is in upstate New York; that, according to Vanity Fair, *it's a five-hour drive from New York City and a ten-minute drive from an unnamed lake; and that it's located just outside a township of fewer than 1,000 inhabitants as of the year the profile was written, I set out to find the Hazel Wood. I was accompanied as ever by my chauffeur and fellow graduate student, Martin.*

There are recurring themes in Althea's work that are disturbing to anyone who knows of her supposed self-imprisonment at her estate: of displacement, of abandonment and assault, of a sort of supernatural identity theft, and, naturally, of incarceration. The vessel of this imprisonment changes—the body, the tower, the marriage, the cave—but close reading has led me to believe Althea was foretelling her own incarceration—not merely a spiritual but a physical one.

Yes. I have come to understand her not as recluse but as prisoner. I believe she's being held in the Hazel Wood against her will. Martin agrees, but takes a pulp-fiction perspective: he imagines her held in place by creditors, or by some original teller of the tales she has made her name on (a theory I do not subscribe to). Of course, Martin has never read the stories first-hand, nor has he sat at the knee of Professor Miranda Deyne and labored to unpack them. I believe the backstory given by Althea in the Vanity Fair *article is smoke and mirrors, just one more fairy tale told by a master of them—a master who has plugged herself into an ancient source of odd fables that feel like just one corner cut from the fabric of a much larger and stranger world.*

I believe it is a force from that very world that holds her prisoner. The true aim of my quest, which I have avoided revealing when it seemed too far from my grasp, is to reach and rescue Althea Proserpine from whoever, or whatever, it is that binds her.

Martin and I left New York City on Wednesday, driving five hours north to start, then looping around area lakes. I admit we hoped for some clue to carry us forward, knowing that, otherwise, we were looking for a tiny pea beneath an enormous mattress. We both had a powerful sense of the Hazel Wood as being surrounded by trees . . .

"Because it's called the Hazel Wood, hack!" I couldn't help yelling aloud.

We both had a powerful sense of the Hazel Wood as being surrounded by trees, and nosed Martin's Honda around many a large and isolated home in the wooded areas just beyond the state's numerous lakes. The Honda took the brunt of several canine attacks, and I'll admit I was surprised by how quickly New York's upstate homeowners are willing to pull a gun on a scholar who seeks only information, and whose independent study relies on grant money and donations. (Click here to learn more.)

On the third day—as I expected, owing to the importance of the number 3 in fairy tales—our luck changed. We stopped for breakfast at a diner owned by a woman who'd heard tell of an author who lived nearby, though she didn't recognize the name Althea Proserpine.

I scrolled through an extended rant on how unfortunate it was that every waitress and pancake-flipper in every truck stop from here to Mars haven't heard of my grandmother, who was, let's face it, a one-hit wonder whose book went out of print shortly after she went off the grid for good. Then there was this:

Our instincts told us to turn down a dirt path lined with cherry trees blooming very much out of season. When, ten minutes later, we reached a pair of tall, green-metal gates, we knew we'd found our destination: the gates were decorated with a stylized hazel tree. I ordered Martin to park the car somewhere out of sight, though we didn't see any cameras. When we exited the car, the air felt balmy—by my estimation, it was a full twenty degrees warmer than it had been when we left the diner.

We looked through the gates, but could see nothing beyond a stand of trees about thirty yards in. As we circled the estate on foot, we discovered that cunningly placed greenery around the entire perimeter kept us from seeing inside. Martin attempted in several places to scale the fence, but discovered it was impossible.

We had no breadcrumbs to mark our path out of the forest, and when I pulled up the map on my phone, it showed our location as being in the center of the Bering Sea. Martin's told him we were on the grounds of Memphis's Graceland. Was it a cosmic joke, or a sign that we were on the edge of something bigger than we imagined? Somewhere, I was sure, Althea—or her captor—was laughing at us.

Finding no way in, we had to leave the wood. I'm writing this now from my motel room, a forty-minute drive from the Hazel Wood. Tomorrow we're getting onto the grounds, by hook or by crook.

Ellery and I looked at each other with raised eyebrows.

"She's totally sleeping with Martin, right?" I said.

"In Martin's dreams."

But behind Ness's silly self-interest, there might have been something real. An ancient source, as she said, of true magical weirdness.

"The strangest part," I said, "is the fact that she stalked my grandmother to her home because she thought she had to save her."

"No, the *strangest* part is the fact that this is her last blog post."

I checked the date: January 17. Nine months ago, just before Althea died.

"How often does she usually post?"

"Every day, almost."

"Huh." I clicked on Ness's bio, looked at a bigger picture of her, and read about how she liked fairy tales, themed dinner parties, and large-scale puppetry. "Think they sicced Twice-Killed Katherine on her?" I was joking, but not.

"She's not Katherine's type, but I wouldn't be surprised. And neither would you. What are you doing?"

I'd gone back to the post and was typing into the comment box. "Asking her to contact me."

Hello. I'm someone you've tried to speak to about Althea in the past, I typed. I thought a moment. *I'm ready to speak now. Reply w/email address?*

Before I could give the phone back to Ellery, a response bubbled up, its avatar showing Ness's pale face. *Is this who I think it is?*

My heart shivered against my ribs. "Um. That was fast."

Not quite, I typed with rubbery fingers. I wasn't my mother, but I was the closest thing Ness was gonna get.

I waited one minute, two, for her response.

Are you in New York?

Yes.

A few seconds later, a Brooklyn address appeared in a new comment. I was trying to figure out what part when it disappeared again.

"Shit, shit, remember this: 475 Honore Street, 7F. Got that? 475 Honore Street, 7F."

Finch snatched his phone and plugged the address into a ride app.

My neck felt goosebumpy. "Was this woman just sitting by her Althea post waiting for me to call?"

"Looks like it."

"Isn't that strange?"

He narrowed his eyes at me. "Strange in the context of the day we're having? Not really."

He stood to wait for our car, and I tilted my head back to squint at the sun, letting the last flares of headache sear themselves like needles into my brain.

~14~

Ness lived in an ugly modern gray box at the end of a street of brownstones. I resisted the urge to look upward as we trudged toward her stoop. I didn't want to meet eyes with a snarl-haired woman through a seventh-floor window. This visit was weird enough.

Finch scanned the row of doorbells before punching the one for 7F. A few seconds later, something garbled came through the intercom box.

"What do—sa wait—?"

We looked at each other. Finch rang the bell again.

This time, the voice on the intercom was clearer. It sighed.

"What does Ilsa wait for?"

"She waits for Death," Finch said smoothly, speaking into the box.

A pause, then the nasal screech of the buzzer. Finch kept peeking at me from the corner of his eye, looking smug.

"You can say it if you want," I said. There was no elevator in sight, or even a lobby, just a narrow flight of stairs covered in sad gray carpet. Looked like we'd be huffing it to the seventh floor.

"Say what?"

"That your Hinterland knowledge got us in. I had no idea what Ilsa waited for."

He shrugged. "You could guess, though, right? When in doubt, the answer is always Death. With a capital D. That's the trick of the Hinterland."

We didn't talk again till we reached Ness's floor, conserving our energy for the climb. On the final landing, I bent over to pant and curse Whitechapel for offering Mindful Breathing and Krav Maga electives rather than compulsory PE.

"How you doin', slugger?" Finch punched my arm lightly, and I waved him off. The door in front of us creaked open, just a bit, and we startled back.

Though her face was washed clean of makeup, I recognized Ness right away. She stood wedged between the door and its frame, looking at us with unfocused eyes.

She wore black jeans and a Weasleys' Wizard Wheezes sweatshirt, stained down its front with runnels of what I hoped was coffee. Her eyes were wide and cloudy blue, her hair a nest of dark curls shot through with gray, though she seemed a little young to be graying already. I was surprised, though, by how old she did look. Her bio pic must've been taken a decade ago. Her eyes ran vacantly over Finch and settled on me. I saw her fingers tighten on the door.

"You're the one who messaged me?"

I nodded.

"Althea's . . . granddaughter, it would be? The one who threw an orange at me at the Fairway?"

"Oh. Yeah. Can I come in?"

"Just you." She stepped back from the door, with a distinct air of *It's your funeral*.

I followed, giving Finch an apologetic shrug.

"Hey, wait." He wedged himself against the doorframe. "Alice."

"It's fine, Finch."

"Is it?" His voice went low. His eyes—big, protective—made my neck go tight. This was what happened when you started to need someone: they got used to it.

"I'm good," I said tightly, and shoved him out of the way so I could close the door.

Hopefully it felt like a friendly shove.

Ness's apartment made William Perks's bookshop look like a Zen garden. The smell of it was a claustrophobic sucker punch of nag champa, old takeout, and dirty hair. Underneath it wound a base note of sage, familiar from Ella's purifying rituals.

Once I got over the reek, I started to take in the details. It was a studio, a big one. Most of the floor space was taken over by sealed-up cardboard boxes and stacks of books, and every spare surface—the dining room table, the bed, the sagging green velvet armchair—was covered in stuff. Balled-up clothes, pizza boxes, craft supplies. Lots of craft supplies. I hoped Ness was practicing art therapy; she looked like she could use it.

"You want tea?" she asked hoarsely. She looked at me sidelong, her eyes darting skittishly away when I tried to look back.

"No . . . kay," I said, twisting my response as her eyes narrowed. She turned her back and stalked over to switch on the electric kettle balanced at the edge of her minuscule kitchen counter. I wondered but didn't ask how long the water had been sitting inside it.

As we waited for it to boil, I looked for a place to sit. There was a folding chair pushed up to the table that held nothing worse than a stack of newspapers, so I went to move them onto the floor.

A headline on the top one caught my eye. *Police Launch Probe into Upstate Killings*. While Ness slapped a box of Lipton onto the counter, I sat down and began to read.

The tiny hamlet of Birch, New York, has lately been at the center of a statewide investigation, following three unsolved killings over the course of seven months . . .

"Lemon or cream?"

My head snapped up. Ness's milky blue eyes pinned mine. "Er. Sugar?" How old would the cream be? How shriveled the lemon? Sugar, at least, was safe.

As Ness turned back to jiggle an open Domino bag over my cup, something made me rip the article from the newspaper's front page and tuck it into my skirt pocket. When the tea was ready, Ness used her arm to sweep aside some of the junk on the kitchen table, and tipped the contents of a second folding chair onto the floor. She set a white-and-orange Zabar's mug in front of me and sat.

"So," she said. "What do you want?"

Not small talk, any more than she did, apparently. "I read the last post on your blog, and I'm hoping you can tell me how to find the Hazel Wood."

"Hah!" She threw back her head and yelled it, like people do in books. "Tell me three good reasons you need to go. Three is a fortuitous number in fairy tales. But you already knew that." She screwed her face up and glared at me.

"What if I gave you one really good one?"

The vacancy in Ness's blue eyes was burning off like fog. "How old do I look to you?" she said. A non sequitur.

I lifted one shoulder. If she wanted to be flattered, she was asking the wrong girl. "I don't know. Thirty . . . five?"

"I'm twenty-six years old."

I wrapped my hands tight around my mug and looked at her. The gray threads in her hair, the delicate lines around her eyes. I'd heard of people's hair going white from trauma, but this was something else.

"You got in, didn't you?" My voice was hushed. "How did you do it?"

Ness leaned forward, letting her hair fall over her face. "We got in," she said tonelessly, "because they let us in. We'd have looked forever if they hadn't. They killed Martin, but they let me live. I still don't know why." Something came into her face, the analytical light she must've once lived by. "Why didn't they kill me? Why did they let me go?"

"Who killed Martin?" I managed, leaning forward so

the table's edge pressed into my rib cage. "Was it the Hinterland?"

She peered at me, her voice settling into a pedantic singsong. "When you spend a night in a fairy hill, you come out and the world is seven years older. But when the Hazel Wood let me out, nothing had changed. Only one night had passed. Our car was still there. With Martin's . . . his coffee cup. In the holder. The coffee was still drinkable. But *I* was changed. I'd aged in a night— seven years, if I had to guess." She touched her fingers to faint crow's-feet on each side. "Just *look* at me."

I looked. It was all I could do for her.

"The point is, I wouldn't help you get into that place if you had three hundred reasons," she said fiercely.

"I told you, I only have one. They've got my mother. I have no choice. I know you think it's crazy, but I *have* to go. Anything you can tell me might help."

Ness shook her head convulsively. Then she said something in a small, singsong voice. "Look until the leaves turn red, sew the worlds up with thread. If your journey's left undone, fear the rising of the sun."

The words blew through me like a cold wind. Nursery rhymes always did that to me, even the harmless ones. This one didn't seem harmless.

"That's all I can tell you," she said. "I'm sorry."

"What did you just tell me? That wasn't anything. Why even let me come here?" A lighter clicked beneath the kindling that lived in my chest. "Why write back at all?"

She shrugged, the sharpness gone out of her eyes. Her mind was a blue sky with clouds dashing across it, clarity cut with a mental haze. She sucked in a breath and spoke all at once. "I thought it would change something. Seeing you. Wake me up again, make me care, or feel *something*. The night in the Hazel Wood was the longest night of my life. I saw things nobody should see. My friend was killed—I should be sad, right? But I'm not. I haven't felt anything since that night. I'm just *numb*. Half of me is still there, trapped in that hell. While the rest of me is here, trapped in this room."

She stood like it took the last of her strength to do it and went to the front door. I thought she'd open it, kick me out, but instead she leaned her back against it and looked at me.

"You might think you have a really good reason, but nothing could be worth this. Nothing could be worth feeling this way. I feel like a changeling wearing someone else's skin. I can't remember what I liked, or what I wanted, why I worked or left the house or did anything. It's all gone." Her voice dropped to a whisper. "I think whatever I used to be, it dropped through the binding. I wish the rest of me had gone with it."

Then she did open the door. I stood on legs I wasn't sure would support me.

"Just tell me the town," I said. "The town where your motel was. I'll figure out the rest."

Her eyes scanned mine impersonally. I sucked in a breath when I saw her pupils up close—they were faintly ovoid, like the eyes of a goat. Had they always been that way? She smirked so quick I almost didn't catch it.

"You're Althea's granddaughter," she said. "Go to the woods. If they want you to find them, you will."

~15~

Finch was waiting for me half a floor down, sitting on the stairs. He jumped up when he saw me.

"Well? Did you get the address?"

The question seemed so ridiculous I just stared at him, hearing Ness's creaky voice singing the nursery rhyme. "No. I didn't."

"Oh. Shit. So what did you get?"

"Another person telling me to stay the hell away from the Hazel Wood." As we walked down six flights, I relayed what Ness had told me. But I couldn't really get the weird bits across—the eyes, the rhyme. The words of it clung maddeningly to the tip of my tongue; I couldn't quite remember them.

"And her place was full of old newspapers and dust and crafty stuff. Just loads of unused art supplies." Suddenly the idea of them was breaking my heart. Glitter glue and sequin strings to bring back the soul of a woman who'd lost it in one seven-year night.

Finch didn't respond. When I looked back, he was biting the inside of his cheek, staring down at his shoes.

"What's wrong?" I said, nerves making my voice sharp.

"Are we still going?"

I stopped, hard, on the final landing. *"What?"* When he didn't respond right away, I charged ahead, into the thin blue light of afternoon.

On the sidewalk, I paced in place. The chilly air felt good on my skin after the close, hopeless heat of Ness's apartment. Her words had scared me, but they also made me feel relentlessly alive. I felt October sharp in my nostrils, hunger curling in my stomach, the last of that morning's caffeine jittering through my blood. The pain lodged behind my heart, that wouldn't come unstuck until Ella was standing next to me again.

"So what's up?" I asked when he joined me on the sidewalk. "Are you backing out now?"

"You misunderstand me. I'm just making sure you haven't lost your nerve." His words were lightly challenging, his eyes bright. "Your mom doesn't want you to go, Ness apparently lost herself in the woods, we have no idea where to start. I want to make sure you're not, you know. Changing your mind." He bounced on the soles of his feet, like he was about to take off.

"And what if I was?" I asked testingly. "What if I think we should turn back now?"

He mulled my words, subsiding back to earth. "Then we will. Turn back. It's your decision."

His voice was steady, and he'd said the right thing. But I didn't believe him. Something in his face made me remember not everything was about me. Maybe Finch wasn't trying to be the sidekick in my story. Maybe he was trying to start one of his own. *The Hazel Wood isn't yours,* I wanted to say. *The Hinterland neither.* Maybe I should have. But he was standing between me and being utterly alone, so I didn't.

Ella's car was trapped in Harold's garage, so Finch got us a rental, going through his dad's office to work around the fact that we were both seventeen. We drove to Target first, stocked up on granola bars and water and canisters of pistachios. I bought cheap jeans, a pack of underwear, and a black sweatshirt, and pulled them on in the bathroom. My uniform I balled up and chucked in the trash. I had a feeling my Whitechapel days were done.

Finch was waiting for me outside the bathroom, where he presented me with cop-style aviators. "Road trip classic," he said.

I slipped them on. They tinted the world a cool disco blue. "You gonna make me play car games, too?"

"Only if you're lucky."

I smiled at him but didn't reply. The strange, rubber-band intensity he'd shown outside of Ness's had abated, but I was still feeling cautious. *I'm watching you,* my eyes said when I looked at him.

Right back at you, his replied.

We sat in the Target food court while we planned our

next move, eating oil-soaked triangles of grilled cheese dipped in ketchup.

"Anna's heart would break if she could see this," Finch said, staring at his greasy hands like they were covered in blood.

"Sorry it's not Jonathan Finch–approved," I said, reflexively.

At the sound of his father's name, Finch's head stayed down and his eyes went up, holding a black weight I'd never seen in them. For a moment I felt what it must be like for a stranger to lock eyes with me.

"Sorry," I said quietly, brushing crumbs off my new jeans. "I'm just . . . we still don't know where we're even going."

"Up north, five hours away, somewhere near a lake and a tiny town." Finch recited details from the blog. "It worked for Ness."

"Whatever happened to Ness did not work for Ness."

"You know what I mean. Let's just leave the city, drive north, look for signs."

"Signs like 'This Way to the Hazel Wood'?"

"Signs like a Polaroid stuck in a book. Or a crow delivering a letter. Unless you have a better plan?" He gave the patented weapons-down smile that shouldn't have worked on me but kinda did. It almost made me forget that flash of black in his eyes.

Anyway, he was right. That was the best plan we had.

By the time we got on the road, evening was coming down. Sitting in the passenger seat looking out at a sea of brake lights on one side, headlights on the other, felt like an outtake from my life with Ella. We never left town at opportune times. It was always at odd moments, when Ella's latest job opportunity melted away like fairy gold, or the bad luck threw us one curve too many. Before dinner on a Tuesday. In the middle of the night, after a cigarette Ella swore she'd tamped out ignited a motel-room fire. I propped my temple against the cool of the glass.

"So. Wanna play a car game?"

I snorted. Ella and I had exhausted every car game known to man, and invented a dozen more.

"What? Come on, humor a New York kid. Driving anywhere is like a weird vacation for me."

He did hold the steering wheel funny, I'd noticed. At ten and two, but in this super-self-conscious way, like he was holding up a confusing shirt.

"Yeah, alright. What do you want to play?"

I expected him to say Geography or the license-plate alphabet game, but he didn't.

"Let's play Memory Palace."

I looked at him. "You made that up."

"No, my mom did. I'll go first, so I can teach you." He cleared his throat. "Okay, the first item in my memory palace is a . . . map of Amsterdam. Because Amsterdam is where I lost my, um, my virginity in a public park." He laughed self-consciously, like he was already rethinking his brag. "So, A is for Amsterdam. Now you say mine, then do a B, with a memory attached."

Did he do it on a bench? Under a bush? Just out in the middle of the grass? I bet it was in a gazebo. I'd pictured Finch having sex with some long-legged Dutch girl five different ways before I realized I was taking way too long to answer.

"Okay. A is for a map of Amsterdam, because that's where you lost your v-card." I put air quotes around the phrase with my voice. "And B is for . . . *Beloved*, because I read it when my mom and I lived in Vermont."

"Okay. A is for a map of Amsterdam because that's where I lost my . . . v-card, and I'm already regretting picking that one, B is for *Beloved*, because you read it when you lived in Vermont, and C is for, let's see, C is for crickets, because they scared the shit out of me when I was little."

I didn't make fun of him for that. Crickets were creepy. I named the three items in our memory palace, and paused. "Okay, D is for driving, because that's what I've spent most of my life doing."

"Nope. Has to be a thing. Like an object you can pick up."

"Fine," I muttered. "D is for *Dazed and Confused*, because I watched it in a motel room once."

"A movie? Because you remember watching it?"

"Yeah," I said defensively. "It's a thing, and I remember it."

"Fine, fine." After listing A through D, Finch smiled. "And E is for eggs benedict, because it's what my mom makes me when I'm sick. Made."

For a moment, we both held our breath. Then his eyes flicked to the neck of my sweatshirt, where the top of my tattoo crawled toward my collarbone. "You're up for F. F is for flower, right? I've always wanted to ask about it."

I touched the inked blossom self-consciously, remembering the look on Ella's face when I came home with it. A lost look, an anger I couldn't place. I'd felt ashamed without ever knowing why. "Yeah. Maybe when we get to T."

I did F, H, and J (falafel because Ella liked it, honey because I liked it, *Jane Eyre* because I'd read it in Tempe). Finch did G, I, and K (gingerbread because his mom used to make gingerbread mansions, icicles because freshman year he wrote an entire fantasy novel about a warhorse named Icicle, and Kit Kats because once his family lived on them for a day, when their car broke down in a snowstorm).

It was my turn again. L. I rapped out everything in our memory palace, feeling a goofy sense of satisfaction when I got it right. "Okay. L. L is for . . ."

"Don't say a food because you've eaten it or a book because you've read it," Finch said. "Give me, like, a real memory."

I felt a flush of irritation, colored with shame. "Are you saying I'm playing your car game wrong?"

"No! I just . . . I thought I could get to know you this way. Like maybe you'd share something about your past. Your family."

He said it lightly, without emphasis, but I knew what he wanted.

"You remember I've never met her, right?" I asked hotly. "Like, ever? Althea figures not at all into my life, and my mom hasn't talked to her in sixteen years."

"What about when you were little? Where you grew up? What do you remember about that?"

His eyes were on the traffic ahead, but his voice held a

sharp, acquisitive note. Like he was collecting findings on me for a book. It would've pissed me off anyway, but what made it worse was his certainty. That everyone's mind was flush with memories they could toss off casually. Half the shit I thought had happened to me happened in books. Or to Ella, in one of her stories about her early single-mom days, trying to make ends meet.

"I don't want to play your stupid game anymore," I said, turning toward the window. "And who uses a car game as an excuse to brag about having sex with some bitch in a park?"

"Some *bitch*? She was my girlfriend for eight months. It's so ugly when girls call each other that word."

"Oh, my god, Finch, go get a liberal arts degree."

In a perfect world I would've had headphones I could put on right then, and a cigarette I could smoke in his air-space, but this was not a perfect world. I settled for turning my head and staring out the window, letting all the little alphabetized memories fall from my brain like snow.

The silence in the car stretched, stretched, and finally slackened, when it became clear nobody was going to break it. *Good.*

I was staring into the scrub by the side of the road when traffic let up. Finch eased ahead at a steady clip, and the radio turned into a soothing drone as I drifted into the fugue state of the emotionally exhausted long-distance traveler. Without distraction, Ella's absence was settling back into my bones. As long as we were moving, the panic abated. Every time I saw brake lights, it kicked back to life.

Scrub turned into trees turned into a thin woods. We veered off the main road and onto something two-lane and winding. Dimly I saw a wobbling light by the side of the road ahead of us, and squinted toward it. A headlamp, on a man in ridiculous bike pants. He was jogging in place, fingers on the pulse beneath his chin. It looked silly, I smiled. Then a dark-skinned woman in a snow-colored dress materialized beside him and put her mouth to his throat.

The car flew past, road and jogger and woman hurtling into blackness behind us. "Did you see that?" I screeched. Finch jumped, the car swerving to the right.

"What?"

"That jogger—that woman—" What exactly had I seen? "Are there vampires in the Hinterland?"

His hands tightened on the wheel. "Oh, my god. Not exactly."

"Turn around."

Finch slowed and pulled a U-turn. As we retraced our path, I strained for the sight of a headlamp, or the hump of two shapes in the dim. But there was nothing to see. After five minutes of slow driving, Finch turned us around again.

"You're sure you saw something? You were kind of drifting off, right?"

I gave him a dirty look, though it was true. Had my overwhelmed mind cooked up some waking nightmare out of scary stories and the dark? I remembered the article I'd ripped out at Ness's apartment—left behind, along with my school uniform, in the Target bathroom.

"Pull over quick."

His eyes flicked to the trees, shuffling their leaves in the navy near-dark. "Wait. Let's get farther away." He drove ten more minutes, leaving the site of whatever I'd seen far behind us, then pulled the car onto the shoulder and brought his hand down on the power locks. The car ticked to quiet and night pressed close against the windows.

I searched on my phone for *deaths upstate new york*. The first hit was the article I'd seen at Ness's.

Police Launch Probe into Upstate Killings

The tiny hamlet of Birch, New York, has lately been at the center of a statewide investigation . . .

"What are you looking at?"

"Birch," I said. "Birch, New York. That's where we should go."

"Why? What did you find?"

"The jogger murders upstate."

His eyes went wide. "Hinterland?"

"I wouldn't be surprised. They've been going on for months, and they're all messed up in some way. Like, Twice-Killed Katherine messed up." I hesitated, scanning the tree line. "What did you mean, not vampires *exactly*?"

Finch faked a shudder. " 'Jenny and the Night Women.' "

I remembered the name from Althea's table of contents. "How does that one go?"

"Jenny's a spoiled brat farmer's daughter who doesn't like the word 'no.' She meets a creepy little kid in the woods who tells her how she can get back at her parents— prick their heels while they're sleeping, wash a stone in the blood, and bury it under their window. She does it, and it lets the Night Women in. Which is, you know, a pretty big mistake."

Something was sparking in my mind, an ancient, paper-flat memory trying to rise. I ran a finger over the nick in my chin. "Is there a story about—" I tried to think, but reaching for the memory was like trying to catch minnows with my fingertips.

Chicago. The raking sound of Ella's scream. Light around a door . . .

"A door," I finished. "There's a story in the book, something to do with a door. How does that one go?"

"'The Door That Wasn't There.' Why that one?"

"Just tell me."

He hesitated, ducking his head to look out at the trees. "Okay. Here's what I remember."

~16~

There was once a rich merchant who lived at the edge of the woods, in a tiny town in the Hinterland. He spent most of his time traveling but was at home long enough to give his wife two daughters, the eldest dark and the youngest golden, born one year apart.

Their father was distant and their mother was strange, often shutting herself up in her room for hours. The girls could hear her speaking to someone when they pressed their ears to the door, but only the eldest, Anya, ever heard anyone answer. The voice she heard was so thin and rustling, she could almost believe it was leaves against the window.

On a winter's day when Anya was sixteen, their mother locked herself in her room and never opened the door again. After three days the servants broke it down, and found—nothing. The door was bolted, the windows locked. Winter howled outside, but the girls' mother was gone. All she'd left behind was a bone dagger on the floor, in a puddle of blood.

Anya heard the servants whispering about it, and snuck into the room to see for herself. The stain put in her a fear of blood so intense, she took to washing out her monthly rags in the dark.

The servants sent word to the girls' father that his wife was dead, or gone, or worse, and for a long time heard no reply. Until the first warm day of spring, when he drove up in a carriage the girls had never seen.

Inside it was their new mother. She stepped down onto the cobblestones and smiled at them. She was smaller than Anya, with a heap of pale hair and blue eyes that switched coldly from one stepdaughter to the next.

For six months their father stayed home, besotted with his new wife and tolerating his daughters, who ran as wild as they'd learned to in all the years they'd raised themselves, with both parents out of sight.

Until he grew bored of the stepmother, just as he'd once grown bored of his wife—just as he'd always been bored of his daughters. He kissed the stepmother good-bye, nodded at his daughters, and was gone.

It didn't take long for the stepmother to grow impatient. She snapped at the girls, slapped them at the slightest provocation, carried scissors in her pocket to cut off hanks of their long hair when they displeased her. Every time she left the house, she locked the girls up—to keep them from misbehaving, she said. She kept them in their mother's room, where the windows were rusted shut and the dark stain on the floor taunted Anya like a vile black eye. Their mother's bed had been chopped into firewood at their father's command, all the pretty things she'd surrounded herself with locked away. They were just two girls in an empty room with a poisonous blot on the floor.

At first their stepmother stayed away for a few hours at a time. Then for whole days, then entire nights. The first time she left them locked up from dusk to dawn, Anya beat on the door and screamed till her throat and fists were raw, but no one came.

When the stepmother finally opened the door, she wrinkled her nose at the smell and gestured at the chamber pot. "Empty it," she said. Kohl and rouge melted into candy swirls on her cheeks; she wouldn't meet her stepdaughters' eyes.

Finally there came a day when she locked them in with a bowl of apples and a jug of water and never came back. The sun rose and fell, rose and fell. On the third day Anya looked out the window and saw the servants walking away from the house one by one, their belongings on their backs.

The house was empty. The apples were eaten, the water long gone. The windows stayed shut and the glass wouldn't give, even when Anya smashed at it with her boot.

That night the sisters lay together in the middle of the floor, trying to keep each other warm. Then Anya heard a sound she'd nearly forgotten. It was a sound like leaves rustling together outside the window.

It came from the bloodstain on the floor. Slowly she inched her way toward it, resting her ear just over it and holding her breath.

It was deep, deep in the night when the rustling resolved into a voice.

You will die, the voice told her.

Anya rolled back onto the floor, angry. *I know,* she replied fiercely, in her mind. *We're half-dead already.*

You will die, the voice said again. *Unless.*

And it told her how she could save herself and her sister. How she could remake the world just enough so that they could live.

It would take blood.

The next morning Anya told her sister, Lisbet, what she'd learned: they must make a door. Their mother wasn't dead, she was gone—she'd used magic to make a door, and it had taken her far, far away. Their mother's blood had spoken to Anya, and told her how to make a door of their own, to meet her.

It will take blood, she told Lisbet, but it can't be mine.

It was a lie. She wasn't bad, she was frightened. The idea of opening her own veins filled her with a sick terror that felt like falling, forward and forward without end. She ignored the bitter taste of the lie in her mouth.

She took the bone knife from the place the voice had told her she'd find it: behind a loose brick inside the cold fireplace.

It can't be mine, she said again, because I'm the sorcerer. I must make the door, and you must sacrifice the blood for it.

Lisbet nodded, but something in her eyes told Anya she knew the words were a lie.

It made her angry. When she drew the blade across her sister's wrist, the anger made her careless, and the blade bit too deep.

But Lisbet said nothing as her sister took her wrist and used it to paint a door.

She painted the sides of it first, in two continuous lines, scraping Lisbet's wrist across the stone. She lifted her as high as she could to paint a lintel over the top. When Anya eased her down and set her back on her feet, Lisbet was as white as the flesh of an apple.

Anya turned away from her sister's drained face and said the words that would make the blood into a door. Words the voice had said into her ear, three times so she'd remember.

All at once the stone wicked up the blood, and the red of it became lines of warm white light. The newly made door swung toward them, letting out a breath of warm air and a scent like clean cotton. They held hands and watched it open.

Then Lisbet moaned, and swayed, and crumpled to the ground. Her cold fingertips stretched out before her, nearly touching the door.

The door that wasn't there, and then was. The door that her lifeblood fed.

At the moment she let go her last breath, the white light shuddered and went green. The green of infected wounds, of nightmares, of the rind of mold that crawled over week-old bread. The cotton scent turned dusty and stuck in Anya's throat.

She threw herself against the door, but it was too late. It opened, inch by inch, yawning with dank air like the mouth of a cellar.

Anya didn't think her mother could be behind that door, but she had nowhere else to go. She lifted Lisbet and carried her through.

Behind it was a room like the one they'd left—but reversed. Anya's eyes went to the dark stain on the floor. It was fresh and pooling red. She ran across the room, still holding Lisbet's body, and wrenched open the bedroom door.

The hall behind it curved left instead of right, and the lanterns on the wall were gone, replaced with paintings of people Anya didn't recognize. Their eyes were burned-out holes and their mouths were wet and red. The hall hummed with that same heavy green light.

Cradling Lisbet in her arms, Anya moved through the house. It smelled of coal dust and blood. In every fireplace curled low green flames. On every table were plates of rotting meat, or blackened flowers with livid yellow pollen dripping from their hearts.

When she opened the front door she saw the sickness spread beyond the house. The branches of trees had become slender bones, and the dust of the road was crackling ashes.

I did this, she said to herself. *I killed my sister—her death made a door, and the door opened onto Death!*

It took her hours, but she dug up enough of the burnt earth to bury her younger sister. Then she set off toward town, to see if she could find anything living.

Town was a place of strange horrors. Not a body to be seen, human nor animal, just a heavy green sky that bathed the whole world in a light the color of disease, and locked doors of houses, and windows painted a blind black.

Anya saw no one. She needed neither sleep nor food nor drink, and when she ran the bone knife over her own wrist it didn't make a nick in her skin. She climbed the dense black vines spilling over the walls of a cottage, to the crumbling gray stones of its roof. She jumped off.

But she drifted to earth like an autumn leaf, touching down unharmed. There she lay, praying for an end, even though every prayer tasted as bitter as the lie that had killed her sister. It was then that the voice spoke to her again.

It had been a long time since she'd lain on the floor of her mother's bedroom letting it whisper secrets into her ear. Longer than she thought. Far away, her stepmother was dead, killed by a fever. Her father had taken a new bride. He had a son.

Can you take me back home? Anya pleaded.

You're asking the wrong question, the voice replied.

It led her through town, back to the grave she'd dug in front of her father's house. From it a black walnut tree had grown. Its rustling leaves were the only moving things in the land of Death. *Lisbet,* Anya whispered, and lay her hand on its trunk.

With a rustle like a sigh, the tree dropped three walnuts into her hands. She cracked them open one by one.

The first held a green satin dress the color of moth's wings.

The second held a pair of slippers with the black shine of petrified wood.

The third held a translucent stone the size of an eye.

When she held it up to her own, the world around her burst into life. The day was bright, the trees were blooming, and a carriage was bearing down on her. The driver couldn't see her, but the horse did—he reared up, hooves high over Anya's head.

She dropped the stone—and found herself back in the land of Death.

The stone was a window onto the land of the living.

Do with it what you will, the voice said, *but don't squander your sister's gifts.*

Anya waited until the green light had faded to murk, marking night in the land of Death. She put on the green dress and the black slippers. She combed back her heavy hair. Then she raised the stone to her eye.

She saw her home as she once knew it, when she was a girl with a mother and a father and a sister named Lisbet. She held the stone in place like a peephole as she rustled around the house's edges, peering into its windows.

She saw a beautiful woman playing the piano. Her father drinking a glass of sherry, his hair lined with white. And a boy just older than her. He was tall and narrow, growing into manhood but not yet there.

Anya's father looked at him proudly, clapped a hand to his shoulder. The boy's eye roved idly over the furniture in the room, his mother at the piano, and landed on Anya.

He stood up straight and came to the window. Anya shrank back as her father joined his son. The boy pointed at her, but her father just frowned and looked past her, shaking his head. Finally he pulled the curtains over the window.

Anya waited in the garden, in her dress the color of will-o'-the-wisps. When she lowered her arm, she stood in a place of rotting bowers and bone. When she raised the stone back to her eye, she could see the soft green of grass and the brief starlight of fireflies. She could see the boy walking toward her, his step tentative but his eyes eager.

You may ask me one question, she said. But it has to be the right one.

Who are you? he asked.

Anya said nothing.

Why can't they see you? he asked.

Anya stayed silent.

You are very beautiful, he whispered finally, reaching out to touch her. Why do you hold your hand so high?

Anya smiled at him the way she'd seen her stepmother smile. She let him bend close to her lips, closer, before dropping her arm and returning to the dead garden.

It took him many nighttime meetings to ask her the right question. By then his eyes were hollow with sleeplessness, and he looked at her with a love like hunger.

How can I get you to stay? he asked, at last.

She smiled and moved her mouth to his ear.

She told him how they could be together. How he could remake the world just enough so she could reenter the land of the living.

It would take blood.

She taught him the words to say, repeating them three times so he would remember. She pressed her bone knife into his hand. And she watched as he slid his bleeding wrist over the wall of her father's house, using it to paint a door. He swayed as he spoke the words, his face, a mirror of their father's, going pale.

The blood turned into a door that glowed with ugly green light at the seams. Anya dropped the stone from her eye as it swung open.

The boy disappeared, and the light turned into the warm golden lamplight of home. As Anya walked through the door, she could feel the faintest brush of her half-brother, stepping past her into the land of Death.

Then she was standing in her father's house, alive and alone, and Death didn't feel cheated because she'd traded a life for her own. She lifted the stone to her eye just long enough to peep through at the boy standing in her place in Death's green light, his face terrified, before putting it into her pocket.

She went to the kitchen and ate spoonfuls of honey, ripped up fistfuls of meat, and let wine run down her chin.

Then she climbed the stairs to her father's bedroom, where he lay sleeping next to his wife. She felt the bone knife twitching where it lay against her breast.

She didn't cut his throat. She cut his wife's. And she lay the stone in the dead woman's hand, where her father would be sure to find it. And lift it to his eye, to see the dead world that awaited him, and the son who would call to him, always, but whom he could never retrieve.

~17~

As Finch spoke, I stared into the woods. His voice was soft and soporific, relaying distant horrors.

The light began like a trick. He spoke about the sisters walking through their blood door, and I blinked, blinked again, but I couldn't blink it away: a thin line of white, like the trail of a sparkler pinned between tree trunks. When Finch finished the story, I put a hand to the glass.

"Do you see that?"

He leaned over, peering past me to where the ghost light wavered. "Is that another jogger?" he murmured.

As I made room for him, my elbow hit the power window button. The glass whirred down a few inches, letting in a scent like smoke and metal.

Like fire and blood.

A heady flash of déjà vu froze me in my seat. *Chicago. Ella's scream. White light.*

"Finch, drive. Drive, drive, drive!"

He slammed the car into gear and squealed onto the road. "What happened? What is it?"

Chicago. Ella's scream. White light and a smell like death. A girl's narrow fingers curling around the edge of a door.

"Nothing! I don't know. Just . . . just drive. Okay?"

He stopped asking. A few miles down the road he followed signs for a rest stop. After we parked I followed him out of the car, leaning against the pump as he bought gas, then trailing after him into the greasy warmth of a McDonald's.

"No more story time," he said lightly. "It's not doing either of us any good."

"Stop talking." I said it without heat, around a bite of cheeseburger. My mind was miles away, in the chill of a Chicago winter. The memories were coming faster now.

I'd been heel-toeing along the back of the couch like a tightrope walker. Until I fell, my chin catching the corner of our cheap glass coffee table on the way down.

There was blood. Lots of it. So much I thought I must be remembering wrong.

Then the memories fell apart into snapshots. Ella pressing a towel to my chin, using another to mop up the blood. The sudden light, the awful smell.

And the screaming. The shock of vicious cold as Ella carried me out the back door, shoeless and dripping blood in a dotted line.

We'd left everything behind. I'd needed stitches, but we didn't stop at a hospital until we reached Madison.

What had we been running from?

Back at the car, I got into the driver's seat before Finch could.

He looked in at me through the passenger window. "Are you okay to drive?"

I gave him a look, and he put his hands up. "Fine with me, I'll sleep. Google Maps says three more hours to Birch. Drive straight through and find a motel?"

"Sounds good. Let's look for something that's not too close to the woods."

The driving steadied me, gave me something to focus on, but I was still spooked. Our headlights ate up and spat out the dark as I strained to see past them, like whatever it was we were chasing might be just beyond my sight.

Around eleven, we were still an hour away. Finch was curled into an impossible ball on the passenger seat, eyes closed. Finally I saw something: the distant embers of road flares.

"Hey. Wake up."

"I am awake," he said, muffled, then lifted his head like a turtle and blinked at the road. "Is that an accident?"

"I don't know."

As we got closer, the bleached shape of a policeman swam into view, a flare in each hand. I pulled up next to him and stopped.

He ducked his head down and peered into Finch's window. He was wearing aviators nearly identical to mine. Combined with his mustache, they looked like a disguise. "You all need to turn around. Road's closed for the foreseeable."

"What happened?" I asked, peering through my windshield. I could see two cop cars and a handful of officers scattered between them. One was talking into a radio, holding it like an MC holds a microphone. Beyond them was a white SUV, half-on, half-off the road.

"Accident." His voice was clipped, a shade below civil.

I flipped off my headlights to get a better look. The SUV's doors were open, all four of them. There was a hump of something on the road beside it that made my throat go dry. But it was too small to be a person. A jacket, maybe.

"Car looks okay," I said. "Was anyone hurt?"

"Sweetheart, I'm gonna need you to turn around now."

"Sweetheart?"

The cop chewed on something, gum or the inside of his cheek. "Son, please tell your girlfriend to turn her lights back on and turn the car around, before I write her up." His voice was mechanical, the metallic eyes of his shades pointed toward Finch.

The feeling started in my cheeks, like it always did, and flooded my skin with cold fire. "You can talk to me," I said. "I'm right here. Or were you under the impression that a woman can't follow a simple command?"

"Alice." Finch put a hand on my arm, and I shook it off. It was too late to count to ten.

"Just because we're in whatever shitstain town is under your jurisdiction, it doesn't mean you get to act like I'm a baby. How dare you treat me like a fuckin' housewife!"

For a minute the cop stared at me, a muscle bouncing in his cheek. When he pulled down his shades, the eyes behind them were irritable and brown. Human. "You kiss your mother with that mouth? We're in the middle of something here, I don't have time for your shit. Turn on your headlights and go." He straightened and walked back a few paces, flares hanging at his sides.

I stayed put for a moment, unspent adrenaline sending a dying glitter through my limbs, until Finch leaned over and punched the headlights back on.

"Turn around," he said. "For fuck's sake!"

I glared at him. "What is wrong with you?"

"What's wrong with *me*?"

The feeling of knowing you're being an asshole is as bad as feeling wronged, but without the satisfaction. I turned the car around hard and fast, screeching over the grass on the opposite side of the road. "What are you talking about?" I said through gritted teeth.

"You know what I'm talking about. How privileged can you get?"

"*Me*, Ellery Djan-Finch-whatever? *I'm* privileged?"

"This isn't about money!" he exploded. "You argued with a cop because you know you *can*. It's so damned arrogant. Look at me." He gestured at the obvious; he gestured at his skin. "What do you think would've happened if I'd been the one screaming at a cop? And he didn't even give you a ticket!"

"Did you want him to give me a ticket?" I said, ignoring his point. "Should I go back and ask for one?"

He shook his head, staring out the window.

Nothing made me angrier than someone refusing to answer me. The edges of my vision fizzed into something humming and black, till I felt like I was looking at the road through a tunnel.

"Come on. Tell me what I should do. Tell me what I should've done."

"Just stop," he said tiredly. "Let's go to the nearest motel, find a reroute tomorrow."

I should've shut up, but I didn't. "Hell no. You started a conversation, now let's finish it."

"God, let it rest! You shouldn't have insulted a cop, okay? He could've dragged *me* out of the car because you were being an idiot. You think rich matters in this situation? You think a cop looks at me and sees *rich*? You're pretending you don't get it, but you do."

I did get it, I did. And the shame of it boiled into something darker. Before my brain could catch up, I jerked the wheel and turned the car off the road, sending us rattling toward the trees.

"Alice!" Finch lunged across and grabbed at the wheel, but I held it fast. The world narrowed to an oak trunk looming in my sight. Till panic clawed its way over the tide of rage, making me yank the wheel hard to the left and swerve back onto the road. We rolled over something that made the body of the car jounce hard. My head smacked the roof, and the anger burned away.

Itchy regret took its place. I'd let myself drift too close to the dark continent at the core of me, a lawless place I tried never to visit. It had been a while, but it was as familiar as the taste of medicine.

Finch sat frozen in the passenger seat. I could feel his eyes on me. I drove faster, like I could leave what I did behind.

"What. The hell. Was that?"

"I'm sorry," I croaked.

"I don't care." He said it again, sounding astonished. "I don't *care*. What the hell were you—what am I supposed to think now? How are you gonna convince me you won't try to kill us again?"

I clenched my fists around the wheel. "I won't. I wasn't. I get . . . I'm bad with people. It's stupid. I was being stupid, talking to the cop like that. It's just, disrespect makes me mad."

"It makes me mad, too. But sometimes you have to swallow it the fuck down."

"Stop," I said, lifting a hand. "I'm serious. I know that was horrible. But I can't tell you I won't drive us off the road again if you don't stop talking about it, so maybe you should take the wheel."

He settled back against the window, arms folded tightly over his chest, and said nothing. So I drove. All the way to the gravel lot of the first motel I saw: the Starlite Inn, pushed right back up against the trees. Finch glanced at them, but said nothing.

We were checked in by a man who looked exactly how the guy checking you in at a cheap motel in the middle of the woods is supposed to. I'd assumed there'd be a guest book, where I could sign funny names and maybe get Finch to look at me again, but they must only have those in old movies.

He paid for just one room, and I was grateful. At this point I didn't trust he wouldn't disappear. Go back to New York, or try to, and take a wrong turn and end up in the Hinterland.

Clingy didn't become me. I prided myself on not needing friends—I thought it meant I didn't need anybody.

Turned out it just meant I needed Ella terribly, too much. She was literally all I had.

Our room was the in-between color of despair, with a landscape painting behind each bed that was a Rorschach test for depression: if you saw a faded-out cornfield in a dusty blue frame, you were fine. But if all you could envision was whatever god-awful sweatshop must've produced it, the prognosis was not good.

"Stop staring at the ugly painting," Finch said. "You're weirding me out." He flopped down face-first on one of the beds, then immediately rolled over. "This pillow smells like the time my bunkmate peed his bed at camp. And I'm too tired to care."

I sat on the edge of the other bed. "I really am sorry."

He winced. "Don't say that."

"What? Why not?"

He threw an arm over his eyes. "Just forget it. Look, what did you see on the road, behind the cop? Not an accident, right?"

With his eyes covered, he was easier to talk to. I lay back on my own pillow. "Not an accident. I don't know why, but it felt kinda, you know. Hinterland-y. You saw the car with all its doors open?"

"I didn't see anything. There was a cop in my face, I was too busy trying to look innocent."

"You? Could you look anything *but* innocent?"

"Oh, yeah. I can be a real asshole." His voice was drifting.

"I don't buy it," I said softly. "You seem like one of the good ones."

"Shows what you know."

There was something in his voice that made me wary, and I took too long to think of a response. His breathing turned steady and slow, a contagious sound that climbed into my limbs and made them heavy as sand. I could barely lift my arm to turn off the light.

After I did, I blinked up at the ceiling and smiled: it was covered in phosphorescent stars. I let my eyes close. The sound of Ellery Finch sleeping was almost as good as having someone to reach out for in the dark.

~18~

Finch was having a nightmare.

I heard him in the next bed, making small, sorry sounds. The light that came in around the curtains was the dusty yellow of streetlamps. I couldn't tell what time it was, and my phone was plugged into Finch's charger across the room.

"Finch. Ellery."

He didn't answer. When I switched on the bedside light he flinched but didn't wake. Silently I sat up and swung my feet to the floor. I stopped there, waiting for his eyes to open.

They didn't. My body felt gritty from the motel bed, like I was swimming in the dirt of other people's bodies and just couldn't see it. I rolled my neck and watched him.

His head was thrown back and his eyes were moving beneath their lids. Usually when I looked at people too long I started seeing them as component parts: Bony noses. Eyeballs in sockets. Odd cartilage curve of ears and fingers so strange and overevolved and makeup floating just over the skin and what the hell was with *pants,* and *knees,* and how did we walk around like all of this was normal?

But Finch stayed staunchly, solidly unified. He was a boy in a bed with his neck stretched long. His mouth shaped itself around words I couldn't hear, then he moaned with such aching regret I was next to him with my hand on his shoulder before I could think.

"Hey. You're having a bad dream."

He sucked in hard through his nose. His eyes shuttered open and hooked on the ceiling, then my face. I watched the dream leave them and sense roll back in.

"Oh!" he said. In his voice were unshed tears, and I thought he might want me to look away. But he grabbed my hand and brought it to his chest and held it.

I let him. The steady pump of his heart through his shirt made me remember the heart was a muscle. Our most important one. "You were having a nightmare."

"I'm sorry. I'm sorry. Alice." He said my name like a person putting something precious down on a bed of moss.

"For what? It's just a dream."

"No, I . . ." He looked at me so intently I dropped my eyes, watched our hands rising and falling with his breath. "Alice, let's go back."

My head jerked up. His lashes were wet and his cheek

was creased. My mind shot an arrow from the first time I saw him in his uniform at Whitechapel to right now, wearing a T-shirt and boxers in this bed.

"Back to what?" I asked.

He let his head dip forward till his forehead touched mine. "There are better fairy tales," he whispered. "If the Hinterland's real, maybe all of it's real. We could look for Neverland. Or Narnia."

I hadn't cried since the night Ella announced her engagement, but I felt like crying now. "Ella's not in Neverland," I whispered back. "Or in Narnia."

"Maybe she's not in the Hazel Wood, either."

I pulled back, my skin feeling cold where it had touched his. "Maybe not. But this is what we came here to do."

"We don't have to do anything we don't want to do. There's still—we can still turn around."

"Where is this coming from?" I yanked my hand back and slammed it down on the mattress, feeling like an impotent ass when it made barely a sound. "What did you dream about?"

He shook his head. "I dreamed all of it was real."

"It is real. We both saw Twice-Killed Katherine."

"Not that. *All* of it."

"All of what?"

He kept shaking his head, looking past me. "Don't you ever feel like your life is a movie? And you're playing a part? And you waste all your time watching yourself in that movie, thinking what a good job you're doing at playing you, until you wake up and remember it's all actually real? Every person around you is fucking *real*?" His voice went fast and faster, then cracked.

"Must be nice being rich," I said, giving it an ugly edge, but I knew that wasn't it. I felt that way, too. Except I never thought I was doing a very good job in my movie.

"Everything we do has consequences," he said.

He'd caught me off guard, looking all soft and disturbed in the middle of the night. But now I was getting pissed. "This isn't an assembly on drugs, Finch. You don't need to tell me that. The *consequence* of you agreeing to drive my ass all the way to the Hazel Wood is that you will now follow through on that agreement. I have no money to give you for gas and no way to convince you to help me other than the fact that I will actually kill you if you try to drive me back to the city while we're this close to maybe finding my mother. Got it?"

We stared at each other.

"I dreamed about the Hinterland," he said.

"Yeah, I got that. But your dream has nothing to do with what we're doing." It tasted like a lie. I tried again. "It was a *dream,* not a prophecy."

"How far would you go to find her?"

"Ends of the earth."

"No farther?" He looked like he wanted me to convince him of—something.

I pressed my hands to my eyes, hard. "You feel like you're playing a part in a movie? Well, so do I. I feel like I'm playing a part in a movie where all the sets have burned down. And the script got erased. And the cameras have no film, and we're in a haunted movie lot in the bad part of town. Finch, she's not just my only family, she's my only *person.*"

When I saw acceptance break on his face, I realized

what he'd wanted me to convince him of. He wanted to know I had nothing to lose. He wanted to know, maybe, that I would die in pursuit of Ella.

Die like Ness's friend had died.

I looked at Finch, the solid boyness of him, and I knew I couldn't let him go all the way with me. Not into the black hole of the Hazel Wood. At some point in the past thirty-six hours, he'd joined the tiniest, saddest clique of people, of which Ella had previously been the only member: people I, Alice Crewe, couldn't bear to see die.

Hell is caring about other people.

I woke hours later with a feeling of fleet panic, breathing like I'd just come up from underwater. There was something in my ears, a sense of dying sound. What had woken me?

"Morning." Finch was awake and watching from the next bed, sitting up with his hands braced behind him.

I fisted the hand he'd held to his chest, remembered how he'd looked with wet lashes in the dark. But his anguish of the night before was ironed away, his veneer of chipper Finchness back in place.

"Morning. I thought I— Did you hear something?"

"Well, yeah. We've been having a conversation for the last five minutes."

"What?"

"You were talking in your sleep. I answered."

"What did I say?"

He smiled. There was something sly in it. "Nothing. Just nonsense. You know, sleep stuff."

"Finch. Tell me exactly what I said."

His amusement faltered at the ice in my voice. I wondered if he was remembering that time I nearly drove a car with him in it into a tree. "Seriously, it was silly stuff. Like you were talking about fishing and toast and crap like that. Please don't freak out."

"I hate it when people tell me not to freak out."

He swung his feet to the floor and looked at me seriously. "I'm sorry. You're right, I should've woken you up. But it was cute. You looked so mellowed out, your voice just sounded so . . . different from usual. But—"

"But you should've woken me up," I finished.

"Yeah." He stood and stretched, his T-shirt riding high over his boxers. I switched my gaze to the ceiling, eyes on the mealy yellow circles of plastic stars till he was in the shower. Why hadn't I believed him just now? What was it in his voice that told me he was lying?

Finch came out fully dressed, and I took his place in the bathroom. After showering I pulled my clothes back on over damp skin, leaving me with a clammy, half-finished feeling. I'd waited too long since my last haircut, and my wet hair brushed down past the tops of my ears. I frowned and mussed it upward. It was thick and corn-colored and wavy, and until I was fourteen it was so long I could sit on it. It was total Disney hair, catnip for every little girl with an itchy braiding finger. Ella had kept it short till I was old enough to put my foot down. And then I'd kept it long till that asshole teacher reminded me it was an invitation. *Aren't you a pretty little house cat.*

After that I hated my long hair as much as Ella did. Cutting it off helped make me invisible—no more boys reaching through all that silk to snap the strap of my training bra. No more girls asking if they could touch it, and grabbing a handful before I had time to reply.

"You ready to go?" I asked, walking back into the bedroom.

Finch had ripped open the green foil packet of ground coffee tucked beside the tiny coffeemaker on the dresser. "Yea or nay?" he asked, tipping it toward me.

I dipped my nose toward the anemic smell of packaged Folger's, and recoiled. "My bosses would go into a coma if they saw me drinking that stuff," I began, before remembering, for the first time since Ella disappeared, that I'd completely blown off Salty Dog—or was about to. I'd be missing a shift later that day. I thought of Lana, forced to deal with the worst of the regulars on her own. Would she, at least, wonder enough to call me? And how pathetic was it that the only people in New York who might miss me had to pay me to come around?

"You have bosses?" Finch replied, wrinkling his forehead in a fussy rich boy way that made me want to kill him. I tried Christian's cell phone while shoving my stuff in my bag and my feet in my sneakers. No answer. I called Lana as we walked out to the parking lot.

I could hear the music of her voice picking up as my hand dropped from my ear to my waist. Without looking, I ended the call.

"So, where do you—" Finch began, then stopped.

The rental car, parked on the pavement in front of our room, was filled with water. *Filled,* like a fish tank. The water was a silty swirl you couldn't see through.

A tight, sickly laugh bubbled out of me. It was a

reminder, clear as day: the Hinterland was with us every step of the way. We thought we were so damned clever, but wherever we went, it was because they were letting us.

Finch walked past me, hands on his head, and looked straight up at the sky.

"I hope you're not looking for rain," I said.

I thought he'd be freaked out, or aggressively calm in that Finch way I was growing accustomed to, or even pissed. But when he turned toward me he looked reverent. "The Hinterland did this."

"Yes."

"We can't go back to New York now."

"We were never going back to New York."

"No, I mean, even if we wanted to. It's like . . . we have no choice but to keep going."

"What? Yes, we do. We have a choice, and we're choosing it. This isn't fate, Finch, this is getting bullied by supernatural assholes."

Feet planted as far from the car as I could get them, leaning way forward at the waist, I opened the passenger door. A tide of water sluiced out. It lapped around my shoes, brackish and full of specks of green and gray.

"It's seawater," Finch said wonderingly, right as a fat silver fish flopped out onto the asphalt. It was wide and whiskered like a catfish, and landed on its belly. Its sides moved gently in and out. The sight of it filled me with pity—another victim of the Hinterland.

The fish was so calm, its whiskery face so ancient-looking, I wondered if it was magic, too. What would it give me, if I returned it to the ocean? What power might I be granted if I ate it?

Finch held up the room key still dangling between his fingers. "You make some horrible coffee. I'll try to get us another car."

I said a silent apology to the fish and walked away.

It turned out there was nowhere to rent a car that we could get to without a car, and no cab service for miles. Finally we threw ourselves on the mercy of the motel's desk clerk, a woman who could've been the night clerk's twin sister.

"You could try the fisherman's bus," she said. "It stops about a mile from here. It'll take you to Nike, just short of Birch." She gave us winding directions to the depot, two miles away.

"If you hurry," she added ominously, "you might catch today's bus."

Finch's and my eyes met, panicked. "Today's bus?" he asked. "Today's *only* bus?"

She shrugged and turned back to her *Redbook,* flipping lazily through photos of celebrities who were over fifty and loving it.

We hightailed it out of there, leaving the flooded car behind. Finch's bottomless wallet was coming in handy again—from an economic standpoint, he barely seemed to register the car's destruction. At least I'd had my bag with us in the room. I shoved my arm all the way to its bottom, till my fingers ran over the feather, the comb, and the bone. But I didn't pull them out.

It was good walking side by side with him, looking straight ahead. There was a strange new heat that ran through me like electricity every time our eyes met. Like our conversation the night before had tapped some hidden well of light in him, and now he was too bright to look at.

Was this what it would've been like? If Ella had never gone missing, and Finch and I had started meeting on purpose? My hand brushed against his, and I snatched it back, shoved it into my pocket.

"You tried your mom today?" he asked once we'd found our way to a wide, rutted road, where the air smelled like wet leaves and bait. If the clerk could be trusted, we'd find a filling station, a diner, and a bus stop at the end of it.

"No. Her number's out of service, remember?"

He walked a few more steps before responding. "Of course I do. I'm sorry."

"Are you okay?"

His gaze was fixed on the path ahead, but it looked like he was staring at the backs of his own eyes. "What? Yeah. Look, if we miss this bus, we're stuck at the motel all day. And night. I can't take another minute of the pee pillow, so let's hurry up."

"Have you called your parents?" I asked. "Made sure they haven't had any problems with Twice-Killed Katherine, or anything?"

"They're fine," he muttered. "Twice-Killed Katherine would choke on my stepmother if she tried anything. Too many diamonds."

There was a bitter filament in his voice that the joke couldn't hide.

"But they know where you are? Or you made up some lie, at least?"

He jerked toward me. "Don't worry about it, okay? If they notice I'm missing, which they won't, they'll think I'm staying at someone's house. Or locked in the library. Anna might notice, though." For a moment, he looked concerned, then shook his head. "Whatever. I'll deal with it if I go back. When I go back."

He snapped his mouth shut and looked at me fiercely. "*If* you go back?"

"When. When I go back."

"Not what you said."

"Freudian slip, okay? I don't want to go back, but I will. All my first editions are there. And my typewriter. And my, I don't know, my cardigans. And my— Oh, my god, my stepbrother's right. I *am* a hipster cliché."

"You have a stepbrother?"

"I do. He lives with his dad, I only have to see him twice a year. He's, like, a football player with a brain. You want to write the guy off, but then he opens his mouth and says something smart. It's irritating, actually."

The conversation was getting away from me. I couldn't ask what I really wanted to know: why was he here? To help me, or to escape? And what did it matter, anyway? The end result was the same: rich Ellery Finch, financing my way to the Hazel Wood. I'd run the cash card Harold had given me before leaving New York, just to see, and of course it had been canceled. Without Finch, I'd be scraping the bottom of my Salty Dog savings already.

Maybe sensing me formulating another question, he took off at a run. "Bus stop!" he called over his shoulder. I sped up, grudgingly, my bag bouncing against my hip. He was full of shit—the stop was nowhere in sight—but after jogging behind him for a few minutes, I saw a cabin that turned out to be the diner. Beyond it was the filling station and the lot, where a knot of old men sat on folding chairs, fishing gear and coolers scattered around them.

Finch went over and conferred with the men, flashing me a thumbs-up as he jogged back.

"Bus comes in an hour, takes us right to Nike. Good fishing, apparently. Waffles while we wait?"

The diner looked and smelled like somebody's musty living room. But the waffles were good, lacy and buttery and studded with pecans, and one of the old men gave us a beer to split when we rejoined them on the pavement. Finch was still acting tense, staring at nothing and bouncing on his toes while we waited. Finally I put a hand on his arm.

He jumped a mile. "God, your hand is freezing!"

I snatched it back. "Cold hands, cold heart."

"I don't think you have that right."

"Believe me," I said, "I do. You look like you're about to crawl out of your skin. You okay?"

"Yeah. I'm just . . . I'm good. Sorry." He looked around, then leaned in. "We're so close, you know? The car thing, that's, like, *magic*. Right?"

"Yeah. I guess it is." That strange, radiant expression was back on his face. It made my neck prickle with mistrust.

"What do you think we'll find there?" he asked. "In the Hazel Wood?"

"I don't know," I said honestly. My vision of it was like a fairy-tale collection on shuffle: Rusting gates creaking open, a castle covered in briars. Somewhere inside, Althea laid out in a glass coffin, like a sleeping beauty or a dead bride. Goosebumps rose on my arms, and I rubbed them away.

What I didn't picture was Finch coming in with me. No matter what version of the story I imagined—fitting a golden key into a lock, scaling a wall crawling with thorns—I saw myself finding my way in alone.

"How far are you planning to go with me?" I asked abruptly. "All the way to the estate? Because you don't have to."

He looked at me blankly, betrayal blooming in his eyes. "Don't play at that," he said quietly. "Just be honest if you're trying to cut me out."

"Cut you out?" I replied, just as quietly. The blood started to hum behind my eyes. "This isn't a heist, this is a search for a missing person. I don't care what else I find there, so long as I find my mom. Alive and well."

"Liar." The word twisted in his mouth, came out almost sweet. "You want to know what you said this morning, while you were sleeping?"

I did, but I didn't. I settled for cocking my head.

"You said, 'The feather, the comb, the bone.' I asked what you meant, and you repeated it. 'The feather, the comb, the bone.'"

My breath caught, and Finch leaned forward. "Wait. Do you know what that means?"

"No." It was only half untrue. "Except now I know you were lying when you told me I hadn't said anything important."

"Well, maybe it is, maybe it isn't. But it's total fairy-tale stuff. It's got to mean something. Maybe it's a clue—like, how we'll get in."

"Or else it was a dream." My fingers itched to dig to the bottom of my bag, to assure myself I still had them. The feather, the comb, the bone.

"'In bed asleep while they do dream things true.'" His voice was fervent.

"Don't quote Shakespeare to me, Whitechapel," I snapped. "And don't quote *me* to me. Especially dreaming me." Then, because I couldn't help myself: "Is there something in the book about that? The feather, the comb, and the bone?"

"If there was, would it matter?" he asked, his tone light and his gaze anything but. "If it was just a dream, I mean?"

The bus pulled in before I could answer. It was smaller than I expected, somewhere between a Greyhound and a VW, and on the side it read *Pike's Trailblazers* in army green. The driver clearly knew the fishermen but was unimpressed by us.

"You got no poles," he said. "You hiking?"

"How much?" I gave him my flat New York subway face, which worked not at all to shut him up.

"You heard about the killings up this way? A lot of them young folks, mostly hikers. I hope you're not planning on staying out on the trails after dark."

"No, sir." Finch glanced at me. "She's— I've got family up there."

"Up in Nike?"

"Up in Birch."

"You know about it, then." Satisfied, the driver closed the door and accepted Finch's cash. "Don't want to drop any city idiots up there unawares. So long as you know what to watch out for." He dropped change in Finch's palm.

"Watch out for murderers?" I snapped, still feeling jangled. "Is that what we're watching out for?"

The driver woofed a laugh through his nose and waved us past.

The ride was just under an hour, we'd been told. The old men sat in the back, like the cool kids in every grade school Ella had ever enrolled me in, and we took a seat near the front. Finch dropped into sleep almost the minute we sat down, or at least faked it. As soon as I was convinced he really was out, I dug out the feather, the comb, and the bone. They looked prosaic in daylight. Even the bone didn't look much like a finger anymore. I shoved them deep into my jean pockets, feeling better as soon as they were out of sight. I settled back and rested my eyes on the trees, watching them roll out like a tapestry.

The bus radio played the kind of country songs you can sing along to even if you've never heard them. I hummed quietly, letting my head tip back onto the seat's sticky vinyl. A slow song came on, an echoing fifties crooner that made me think of dead prom queens. The vocalist sang about swaying and kisses and stars in an eerie feminine purr, and I wondered where I'd heard the song before.

"*Look until the leaves turn red,*" he sang, as the song shifted down into a speak-sing bridge.

Sew the worlds up with thread
If your journey's left undone
Fear the rising of the sun

The words hit me like an ice cube down the back. It was the rhyme, the strange nursery rhyme Ness had recited to me. I froze, waiting to hear more, but the song ended. There was a staticky, record-player pause, and Waylon Jennings's voice poured through the speakers like whiskey. The driver bopped his sunburnt head.

It was here, I thought. The Hinterland. Here, or close enough. I looked at Finch. His lips moved a little, and I thought about waking him—or talking to him, seeing if I could lead him into a dream conversation the way he'd led me. I did neither. I recited the rhyme to myself till it was etched in my mind, watching the trees for I didn't know what. I didn't see anything but leaves.

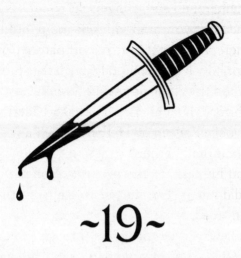

~19~

Finch woke up just as we hit Birch, sheepishly running the heel of his hand over his mouth.

"Where are we? How long have I been sleeping?" He peered out the window as the bus turned into a wide concrete lot encircling a shack-sized bait shop. "Oh. We're here." The jagged energy that had come off him in waves on our walk from the motel was back.

The old men pushed past us, sour-smelling and laughing at some granddad joke we hadn't heard. The driver gave me a hard look as I left the bus. I glared at him, wondering suddenly if he was Hinterland. If he'd done something to the radio. He wasn't, I decided. He hadn't.

Behind me, Finch held back. "What's your next stop?"

I heard him ask, as I stepped out onto the pavement. "You turning right around and going back?"

"You bet. But you can't chicken out on hiking now, son." The driver leaned forward to peer at me. "Your girlfriend doesn't look like she'd take it quietly. Just get out of those woods by dark, alright?"

Finch turned, his shoulders raised high, and wouldn't look at me as he walked down the steps.

"What was that?" I asked.

Finch stared past me, to where the old men were filing into the bait shop. He started to say something, but shrugged instead.

I turned away. If he was going through some existential fan dilemma, I wanted no part of it. I still had to figure out how to shake him before we got too close to the Hazel Wood.

Through the trees at the back of the lot, I could see the hard glitter of water. It made me thirsty. "Want to find a convenience store before we walk to Birch?" I started, turning, then cut off. Finch was standing behind me, too close, eyes wide and jaw set. I startled away from him.

"*Damn* it," I said, my heart hopscotching. "*What?*"

He smiled at me. He smiled like a dog who doesn't want to get kicked but will take it if he is. "I messed up."

Adrenaline made my stomach kick and my eyes go dry. "What do you mean?"

"We need to walk—we need to get to the highway." His voice was high and too fast as he stared at the pavement where the fisherman's bus no longer was. "Maybe we can hitch. We need to . . . if we can just get back to the city. I'll explain on the way. I should've explained last night."

"Explain what?" I planted my feet on the pavement, gripped his arm. "We're standing here till you tell me."

"I made a promise," he said. "But I don't want to keep it."

"You *need* to stop threatening not to take me to the Hazel Wood. At this point I can find it on my own."

"Not a promise to you," he said. "A promise to them."

Them. The word hit me like a blackjack. "What. The fuck. Are you talking about?" I grabbed the front of his jacket.

"I thought . . . I thought it might *help* you."

"That's not an answer."

"It is. You don't understand yet. They told me not to tell you . . ."

"Tell me what? Who told you not to tell me what?"

"I can't." He looked around nervously, a tremor in his jaw making his teeth clatter. "They're probably listening right now. We need to go."

"Just tell me. No riddles, no excuses."

He shrugged, the gesture heavy with disgust. "I wanted my life to change. I wanted for it to be real. And it is. But I don't think this is worth it."

It struck me, suddenly, that no amount of bottomless funds should've been enough to convince me to lead an Althea Proserpine fan to the Hazel Wood. It struck me, too, that I didn't know that much about Finch.

I wrestled back my rage and sudden fear, trying to make my voice reasonable. "If you don't tell me what you did, I can't help you fix it."

"Oh, no," he said, the words bottomless and bleak. "They're already here."

His eyes flicked past me, just as I registered the quiet purr of an idling car. I turned and had time to see its bright paint job and the figure at the wheel—wait, there were two of them, someone was in the passenger seat—before Finch yanked me behind him, sending a hot pain through my shoulder.

"Go," Finch said, his voice ragged. "Run!"

Off balance, I stumbled to the dirt.

The car exhaled heat like an animal from its yellow sides. It was the cab I'd seen creeping on me outside of Whitechapel. And there was its dark-haired driver, the boy from the diner. He pushed the hair from his face with a gloved hand.

His passenger stepped onto the gravel, staring at me with lantern eyes. It was Twice-Killed Katherine. She wore the same black gloves the boy did.

I froze. I knew if I moved, I would give myself away—a shake in my knees, or my voice.

"I'm sorry," Finch was saying. "I'm *sorry*. They just said to get you to the Hazel Wood. That's all! You were going anyway, you asked for my help . . ."

"Don't pretend this was for me. Since when? Since when were you working for them?"

The boy was watching us, amused. Katherine looked like she couldn't hear us at all.

"*Working* for them? No, it wasn't . . ."

"Since when?"

"Since the bookseller's," he said, small. "They talked to

me while you were passed out. They kept you . . . they kept you under a little longer."

"Thank you for your service, Ellery Finch," the dark-haired boy said. "Ready for your reward?"

"No," Finch said. His dark skin looked bloodless. "I don't want it."

"What reward?" I spat.

"What all children want," the boy said mockingly. "Entrance to fairyland."

My fault, I thought. *My fault for trusting a fan.*

Ella came to me then—the way she always looked for the good news in the shit sundae. Because maybe this wasn't all bad. Finding these people, or whatever they were, was what I wanted, wasn't it?

It was hard to remember that with Katherine's eyes crawling over my skin.

I elbowed Finch aside. "I'm looking for my mother—Ella Proserpine. I know you have her. I want her back."

"She thinks we're mother-nappers, isn't that funny?" the boy said.

Katherine sucked her teeth like an old woman. "You're sure this is her? This little *house cat*?" She lunged at me, teeth bared, and I gasped.

She stopped short, laughing. "See? Skittish as a mayfly."

But her lunge wasn't why I gasped. I did it because of what she'd called me: *house cat*. Like she knew the sticky, long-ago insult that still swam in my brain.

I felt suddenly like a child, moving through a forest of adult knees, hearing their conversations far over my head. None of this made sense, none of it had any *context*. All of them, even Finch, were treating me like a child—to be protected. To withhold information from.

For a few heartbeats, everything in the world outside my skin felt dulled and slow. I watched it all. Finch, so slumped and weary he was barely standing. The boy, his hands in his pockets but his face avid and ready. Katherine, poised near me like she would bite.

I chose Katherine.

"I'm not," I said to her, "a house cat." And I slapped her across the face.

Both of us gasped in unison. My hand where it touched her burned, and the burn spread. It was like gasoline had replaced my blood, and striking Katherine was the match.

The boy cursed, and Katherine scuttled backward, holding her cheek. I kept staring at my hand, trying to shake off the awful crawling fire. "What did you do to me?"

"Katherine, you idiot," the boy said, clipped.

She shook her head and wouldn't look at him, letting her hair fall over her face.

"What did you *do* to me?" I screamed again. I put my hands to my face to feel if I was shriveling, the way the man she'd attacked in Manhattan had shriveled. Terror made me forget what Finch had done, and I turned to him. "Did she kill me? Finch, am I dying?"

He moved to put an arm around me, then yelped and drew back. "You're so cold," he whispered. His eyes were sad and bottomless.

We were standing in the middle of the lot, where nothing moved. No cars came by, no fishermen spilled out of the bait shop. The breeze was turned down to nil; the sun hovered in the stillness like a pinned insect.

"We're doing everything out of order, aren't we?" the boy said. His voice pretended to be bored, but I heard the thin file of rage running under it. He rubbed his palms together, looking at Finch and I like we were steak.

I grabbed Finch's hand, ignoring his cry of pain at the burn of my fingers, and we ran.

We ran away from the trees, toward the highway. I had a dim idea of jumping in front of the next car when I got there. Idiotic. The world had paused like a tape deck; I couldn't even hear birdsong.

"Alice!" The Hinterland boy's voice was a savage yelp. It sounded like something that didn't come from a human throat. I couldn't help it; I turned.

He threw up his arm and . . . the ground folded like a fan. Or maybe it was the trees that moved, shivering over the pavement like a horror movie cut, distant then there, all around us.

My chest was a bellows with the air squeezed out, but I tried to run anyway. The breaths I sucked in were bitter as helicopter seeds. Trees surrounded us, and we ran over tumbled green ground. But the world wasn't working right, and suddenly we were running *toward* them, the boy and Twice-Killed Katherine, hiding behind her fading hair. She held a knife, and I was running too fast to do anything but pitch myself forward. I skidded to a stop at her feet, Finch tumbling down beside me.

The knife glinted at the level of my eyes. I opened them as wide as I could, because suddenly the worst thing that could happen was for death to take me unaware. But she didn't strike—she handed the knife to me, her gloved fingers pressing it into my palm. But careful, careful not to touch me too long. Even under the leather I could feel the way she startled back from my skin.

"Kill. Yourself," she hissed, before stepping out of range.

"What?"

The boy's mouth hung open, and I saw something terrible in his eyes. The shadows of toothy, waiting things, like all of him was hungry. "Kill yourself, Alice," he said, like it was a chant. "Kill yourself."

I had a vision of the knife's tip piercing my wrist, letting out the fire burning under my skin in a shining flood. I shook it away.

"Alice, no, no, please, oh, please." Finch was almost praying, down on the ground.

"Why would I do that?" I asked dully. The question was real. I wanted to know.

"It's you or it's both of you," Katherine said. "You or both of you. You or both of you!"

"Alice, they can't make you do anything," Finch said, his voice harsh and smoky with fear. "They can't even touch you!"

"Shut your mouth," Katherine hissed. Her foot flashed as she kicked him with the bladed side of her boot, leaving a thin line of blood running over his cheek.

Finch fell back with a cry, curling in around his wound. Katherine and the boy flanked me, standing just out of reach. No part of their skin was bare but their faces.

When my hand hit Katherine's face, it had burned me—it still burned—but it hurt her, too. Why?

"Why can't you touch me?" I asked.

Katherine sneered down at me, unmoving. The boy

was the weak link. His eyes flicked to her face and back to mine.

"Wait. You're *scared* of me, aren't you?"

"Scared?" she said, furious and low. "Of you? You're next to nothing. You're almost as bad as him." She pointed at Finch. "All you're good for now is to spill your blood and make us a damned door. Now kill yourself, or he gets it, and your mother next."

A door? I lunged at her with the knife awkward in my hand, held like I was about to slice bread. She moved lightly out of my way, kicking my hand so it sang with pain and the knife arced up and away. It clattered at the boy's feet. He picked it up and looked at Katherine.

"Kill the lamb," she said.

I saw the horrible confusion in Finch's eyes. They went dumb with animal terror as the dark-haired boy forced him to his knees. One hand peeled back Finch's chin, the other held the knife.

I had no weapon but my bare skin and Katherine's cold fire running through it, so I launched myself at the boy's uncovered face.

He recoiled from me with a shout, drawing the knife over Finch's throat in one convulsive sweep.

Fear dropped from Finch's eyes, replaced with blank shock.

The blood was a line then a smear then a red curtain falling.

"There goes our bargaining chip," Katherine said, her voice distant. "Ever heard of a bluff?"

Time slowed. Finch was a spilled cup, just before it hit

the ground. A precious something dropped into the dark beneath a subway grate. A tangled mess of infinite possibilities, countless threads, cut at the quick by silver scissors.

He was down.

I screamed, crawling forward to press my hands over his opened throat.

"Your fault, Alice," Katherine said. It was almost a whisper. She took the bloody knife and dropped it at my side. "Kill yourself."

I thought about it for a moment. I did. But Finch's eyes held mine, bright and questioning. Not dead yet, but dying.

"It's okay," I said, stupidly.

The boy who'd cut Finch's throat was pacing beside us. "Katherine?" He said it like a question before crouching to lift Finch, hoisting him over one shoulder in a fireman's carry. I cried out and reached for Finch's dangling hand, but the boy jerked him away. He lifted the knife from the dirt and twisted it in the air like a conductor's baton. The air shifted and lightened where he stabbed, peeling back from itself to reveal a rift as livid as Green River soda.

Finch's body was limp over the boy's shoulder as he stepped into the bright green gloaming. Then he was gone, and the boy with him. The last spatter of his blood hit the grass when he'd already disappeared.

I stared at the place where I'd seen Finch dying and screamed. It took a while for the sound to come. When it did, Katherine leaned over me and I screamed again, holding up palms painted in blood, trying to press them to her face.

She made a frustrated sound and flicked her hand.

Something came winging toward me: her cruel little bird, unfolding from empty air. It darted at my eyes and I threw out an arm. I felt a tug at the edge of my . . . it was hard to explain. The edge of my *self*. Like my soul was pressing against the walls of my body, ready to be sucked out like a yolk through a pierced eggshell. The sun tilted down, as if someone had thrown it off course with a baseball bat.

The last thing I heard was the rasp of Katherine's voice, so close it seemed to be coming from inside my head. "By your hand," she said, "you'll die tonight." Then I fell into a numb black sea.

~20~

Ella drove. Her face was lost in shadow, her hands lit white spiders on the wheel. She hummed a song that at first seemed tuneless, before it resolved into something that lilted and spun back on itself in an eerie round.

"Mom," I said.

She flinched. "I thought you were sleeping."

"What's that song?"

After a long pause, "A nursery rhyme. My friend taught it to me when I was little."

My mom didn't talk about her childhood, not ever. I held my breath, then dared a question. "Were you a little girl like me?"

I was very young. Six at the oldest.

"What do you mean?"

I tried to put into words what I meant. Did her insides match her outsides? Was the way my life dripped off me like water, barely leaving a mark, normal? Did the bad luck chase her, too, or had it only come around after she'd had me?

But I couldn't say any of that, because I didn't want to see her cry. She wanted me to be happy. Each new place was a fresh chance, a field of unmarked snow she gave me to run through. And maybe everyone felt this way when they moved on—that everything they'd left behind smeared together like watercolors and washed away.

I looked away from her drawn-tight face, watching our headlights slice through fog. "Books. Did you like books?"

Her shoulders dropped a little. "I did. I liked to read everything but fairy tales." She sighed, sounding older than salt and way too young to be a mother, all at once. "Hours to go, love. Get you some sleep."

My eyelids dropped like she'd anchored them with stones. I was falling asleep, or waking up, or some combination of the two. I wasn't in the car with my mother, I was somewhere else, and she was very far away. My mind clawed its way to consciousness.

"Wake up."

The sun shone red through my eyelids. I opened them a fraction and cringed. It was too bright. A gloved hand slapped my face, once, twice, three times. The third was a crack that made my ears ring, and my eyes snapped open wide.

I was in the back seat of a car, and it was night. Twice-Killed Katherine crouched over me, shining a Maglite in my face. Her teeth were small and milky blue, like baby teeth.

I could've tried to hurt her, but I didn't. Finch's death lay like a heavy stone on my chest. I saw him go in flashes, when I blinked and when I didn't. The careless slice of the knife, the wanting eyes. The relentless crumple to earth.

Katherine hung over me a moment longer, her breath stinking of week-old roses. "He'd still be alive," she whispered in my ear, "if you'd just done it." She scrambled backward like a spider, tugging me with one gloved hand.

I followed mutely. I felt every breath and the ache of my hip where I must've banged it. My mouth tasted like dead coffee and the air smelled prickling and green and my head ached like a hangover and my skin felt electrified. I was here, aching and *alive*, while Finch bled out somewhere in the Hinterland.

"What'll you do with his body?" My voice guttered and clogged.

Katherine slammed the car door, a gunshot sound I flinched from. She looked at my face like it was something she was trying to place. A puzzle piece that wouldn't fit anywhere.

"Don't waste your worry," she said. "You're here."

I looked around wildly—for the Hazel Wood, a gate, a road. Anything. All I saw were trees, pressing in around a clearing barely big enough for the car. I couldn't see where we'd come from, or how we'd get out. "I'm where?" I asked, my voice cracked. Thirst rose up in me again, more desperate this time.

"You're in the Halfway Wood," Katherine said. "And here you'll wander. Till death is preferable, and you choose it."

She grabbed my arm and flung me in a wide half-circle, like we were at a square dance. I stumbled forward a few yards and down to my knees. By the time I struggled up, she was in the cab. I lunged at the door and was thrown back as it rocketed into a wall of trees. They parted obligingly, then sealed back into place as neatly as a curtain.

I turned slowly in place, alone in a clearing in the deep dark woods.

That was when I entered a fairy tale.

~21~

The clearing I stood in was perfectly circular. I could see that once the car was gone. Something about the trees was off, and it took me a moment to place it—they didn't rustle in time with each other, or with the mild breeze that made my chapped lips tingle, but one by one. The way they shook their heads and shushed their leaves convinced me they were having a conversation.

My body shook with sorrow, with rage—rage at Finch's killers, and rage at Finch for his stupidity.

But he was dead. My body hadn't caught up with my mind.

I lurched blindly from the clearing, scraping past a stunted dogwood tree. Its heart-shaped blossoms trailed velvet tongues along my neck. I shuddered and hurried my step, trying to outrun the thought that circled my mind like a hangman's rope: What if I wandered this place for one night, like Ness, only to be ejected a day later, and seven years older?

I saw Finch's face every time I closed my eyes. The walls of my mind were painted with his blood. It stained my palms and stiffened the sleeves of my sweatshirt.

"It's okay," I whispered to myself. "It's okay." I counted to ten and did a few yoga breaths. Red ran down Finch's shirt. *I couldn't stop it I couldn't stop it I couldn't*— "*Stop* it. I couldn't stop it." I made a sound I didn't recognize, like a laugh and a wail at once, and it scared me quiet. I slapped my own face the way Ella used to when she was too tired to drive.

"It's over. Nothing to stop. It's okay, it's okay, it's okay." Nonsense words. Was this what going insane felt like? Was I really in the woods, or was I still dreaming in the back seat of my abductor's car, going somewhere even worse?

A tree flung a stinging branch of green buds across my cheek. The hurt woke me up, and for a while all I could focus on was shielding my face from branches, and trying not to trip over hidden things in the dark. The air was so close and dense among the leaves it felt like the trees were breathing on my skin.

He'd still be alive. If you'd just done it. Katherine's whisper unfolded from empty air. I slapped at it like a mosquito and sped up, welcoming the pain of a skinned knee and scratched palms, and the secret rustle of creatures that drowned out anything else.

Finally I broke free onto a creek bank. I sucked in mouthfuls of cool, wet air, propping myself against a willow tree whose branches poured themselves into the water a few yards from my feet.

I took stock of what I had. My bag was long gone, dropped in the dust of the parking lot. I still wore the cheap jeans and sweatshirt from Target, the sleeves pulled down over my hands. In my pockets, a Kit Kat wrapper and—I realized with a start—the feather, the comb, and the bone.

They felt cool in my hand and gave off an electric, intangible hum, like tuning forks. I looked around furtively and shoved them back in my pockets.

Then something wrapped itself around the bare skin between my jeans and my low-tops and yanked.

I slammed down flat, gasping, in cold mud. I spat it out and twisted till my legs were pretzeled and I could see what had me.

For a horrible, frozen second, I thought it was a corpse. It had the translucent lantern skin of a creature found in the deepest parts of the ocean. It was person-shaped, mostly, though nobody could mistake it for human. It clung to my ankle and watched me with the dull impatience of a dog waiting for its food bowl.

Terror chipped my rational mind into a furious glitter. I kicked and shrieked, aiming for the thing's horrible face. But its grip was ironclad.

When my foot hit water, plunging in all the way to the ankle, I instinctively curled my free leg up, away from the creek. The thing smiled, and tugged a little harder. My fingers found a loose stone and flung it. I missed and found another one. This time it hit with a clunk.

But not the creature. It hit the water, which a moment

ago had flowed fast and black and quiet. The creature looked around, too, one hand still wrapped around my leg.

From where my foot was submerged, a trail of thin green ice spread out like a flume, full of captured bubbles. The thing looked at me, some shallow intelligence sparking behind its eyes. It let go and slid backward, into a slushy pool surrounded by freeze. I yanked my foot free of the ice, looking around to see who had saved me. There was a rustle in the bushes on the other side of the creek, maybe. I wasn't sure.

"You still can't pass." The creature's voice was a swallowed thing full of glottal stops and touched with an unplaceable accent. It looked more like a girl now that it wasn't trying to eat me. Its muddy hair was braided, its mouth almost prim.

"Why?"

"This is my byway. I might let you wander the shore till you're dead." Its laugh was full of pin-sharp teeth.

"Or I'll walk across the ice."

The thing looked around at the meltwater already rising. Whatever strange magic had frozen it was already fading away. "You can try."

"What if I give you something?"

It froze, its fish-belly eyes suddenly interested. "Your hair? Your fingers?"

I thought of the paintings of mermaids I'd loved to look at when I was little—bird-winged women crawling over doomed ships, pensive Waterhouse girls running silver combs through their hair.

I pulled the comb from my pocket. It had been plain red plastic when I found it at the coffee shop, and again when I looked at it under the willow tree. But now it glinted like mother of pearl. I ran a fingertip over the unfamiliar carvings in its handle.

The redheaded man had left these things behind for me to find. Katherine wanted me to die in these woods, but someone else had stuffed my pockets with fairy-tale tricks. I thought of Ella, the blade in the bouquet. These woods weren't going to kill me, or drive me mad. Because I wasn't Ness. I was Ella's daughter. I was the granddaughter of Althea Proserpine.

I held the comb up so moonlight skated over its teeth. "I'll give you this if you let me cross to the other side. Unharmed. Meaning you don't get to eat or otherwise remove any part of me."

Fairy tales teach you the importance of precise communication. The thing looked disappointed by my thoroughness, but it was already reaching for the comb. When I passed it into its fingers, it slipped into the water and disappeared.

First I kneeled on the bank. I scooped up enough melt to wash the blood from my hands, reaching for a prayer, a poem, a goodbye that felt right. But all I could think of was the Vonnegut quote Finch had inked onto his skin. I never asked him when he'd gotten it, or why, and now I never would.

Everything was beautiful, and nothing hurt.

I whispered the words, rubbing at blood that looked black in the moonlight. I closed my eyes and held his face in my mind and said it one more time. And a third, because Finch would've wanted things done right in a fairy tale.

Then I stood and pressed a testing toe against the

ice. It was already spring ice, midway between freeze and slush. But the shore was so close. I took off across it at a run, sliding and nearly making it before my leg plunged through a sour spot. I felt the numb pain of frigid water and the teasing grip of the creature's fingers, then it shoved me out of the cold and sent me sprawling onto the opposite bank.

I wanted to crawl back and rinse the mud from my mouth, but I didn't dare. Instead I walked up the bank till my calves ached. It angled more and more sharply till I had to grab at bushes just to pull myself along, cursing when I gripped a handful of thorns. When I finally reached the summit, I'd cleared the tops of the tallest trees. I looked out over the whole woods, stretching to the horizon below me. The fear I'd held back with sweat, with thoughtless forward motion, settled back around my shoulders.

Then I saw it. Or part of it: in the distance, between the swaying night-green heads of the trees, a patch of something black and unmoving. A rooftop, I thought—it had to be. It had to be the Hazel Wood. I felt the phantom presence of Finch beside me, the lift of wonder he would've felt standing here.

A sudden *snick*ing reached my ears, the out-of-place preschool sound of scissors cutting through paper. I turned and saw a little girl sitting on a red-and-white checkered picnic blanket in the moonlight, cutting up the pages of an old atlas. Moonlight lit the crown of her downturned head. I wavered for a moment, wondering if I should creep quietly away, but didn't. I'd been thrust by the Hinterland into a tale. Maybe, if I let it reach its end, I would escape it.

The girl's soft little hands ripped pages from the atlas

one by one. Green maps threaded with silver rivers, castles and towns marked in ruddy ink. Nautical maps crawling with sea creatures and rippling waves, grounded at each corner by the puffing faces of the four winds. The East Wind seemed to scream as the little girl's scissors cut it into shreds. She turned the page to a yellow map that glittered. I sucked in a breath as I spied a tiny caravan crossing it, and the scissors descending to cut it in two.

"Why are you doing that?" I asked. I'd reached the edge of her blanket.

She kept her gaze on the atlas, but I could hear the scowl in her voice. It was a funny voice, froggy and boyish. "My grandmother doesn't like me talking to strangers."

I looked around for the grandmother, expecting some gorgon to launch herself at me from the other side of the hill. The girl rolled her eyes. Her face was peaky and pointed, but her eyes were beautiful, the color of the oceans she was cutting into confetti. "She's up there," she said, jabbing her scissors toward the sky.

I looked upward and saw nothing but the moon, gathering bits of cloud around itself like a shrug. For a moment I could see a face in it. Not a man's, a woman's. A beautiful, distant woman who watched me with a disapproving look.

Then the face smoothed itself away, and the moon was just a moon, a perfect orb the flat gold of a Casio watch.

"What if I introduced myself," I said, "so we won't be strangers anymore? I'm Alice."

Her scissors stopped, and she looked up. "You're Alice?" But she must've seen nothing interesting in my face, because she shrugged and tilted her head back down. *Snip snip snip.* A Queenswood labeled in looping script was sheared away from a tiny ivory castle, its ramparts bristling with spikes. "My name is Hansa."

Hansa. I knew the name—I'd read it in the contents page of *Tales from the Hinterland.*

"You're Hansa the Traveler," I said quietly, trying not to draw the attention of the moon. "Where are we?"

"You're stupid for being so much older than me," she said. Not meanly, but matter-of-factly. "You don't know we're in the Halfway Wood?"

"Not the Hinterland?"

"The Hinterland's that way." She gestured meaninglessly and flopped onto her stomach. "I'm not allowed to talk with strangers anymore."

"Why not?"

"Because I'm too trusting," she said primly. It sounded like she was quoting something an adult had told her. "And I made friends with the thief."

The thief? A character from her story, probably. I wished for the thousandth time I'd read *Tales from the Hinterland*, that I knew every inch of it the way Finch had. *No. Don't think of Finch.*

"Who's the thief?" I asked, bracing for her to tell me I was stupid again.

"She comes from that side."

"From Earth? Where I come from?"

"You really are stupid. *She* came from Earth, but it was a long time ago. She doesn't visit anymore. Now go away, please, I'm busy."

I squatted down beside her. "Hansa, one more question, okay? The thief—was her name Ness?"

"No. Her name was Vanella."

My heart went hollow. "Ella—was here? When?"

"I told you, she doesn't come anymore. You're in my light—would you leave me alone now?"

"Wait. Please. Have you seen her? Ella? Has she been here in the last couple of days? What did she steal?"

"I told you I can't talk to you," Hansa said primly, turning a page of her atlas. "Now go away before my grandmother gets angry."

"Hansa, *please*." I grabbed her shoulder—not hard, but firmly—and she hissed in pain, skittering away from me like a crab.

"Grandmother!" she screamed.

Suddenly my vision was all white fire. The moon threw its rays over me in a hot spotlight, and I screamed and swatted at my face like the moonlight was flies. I heard the prickling noise of Hansa's laughter as I staggered away.

All at once the moon's horrible spotlight switched off. I fell in the sudden dark, my eyes swimming with dots. Then I was rolling, grass slicing at my skin and crushing into a sharp perfume.

I landed at the bottom of the hill, chilled and scratched and wanting Ella so badly I could've given up right there. The green fragrance of ruined grass got into my head and gave me that high, lonesome feeling you only get at night, when you feel like the last person on Earth.

I was staring miserably into the dark when the hill in front of me cracked like an egg. A scent like the amber perfume Ella wore poured out from the glowing break in the hill; if my head hadn't been filled with green grass, it might've overwhelmed me. Before it could, I stood and ran to a cluster of bushes big enough to duck behind.

The line of light grew so viciously bright I wondered if the sun was hiding in that hill, preparing to do battle with the moon. But it faded as it widened, until I could just look at it through my fingers.

The broken hill looked violated, a wrenched-open chest cavity. Black shapes appeared in the space where it split, and became people.

Or something like people.

They moved furtively at first, stepping onto the grass like it might set off an alarm. Then one of them—a beautiful girl wearing pants and a coat that made her look like an aviatrix—somersaulted across the grass. The people with her, a mix of men and women a little younger than my mother, laughed and joined in. They didn't seem like figures you'd imagine crawling out of a hillside. Most looked like they'd gotten dressed from a Salvation Army donation box.

The aviatrix seemed to be the ringleader. She kept raising her head to sniff the air. There was something wrong with her eyes. The rest crept close to her, drawn in like down-and-outers gathered around a trash can fire.

A girl wearing an empire-waist dress over a hugely pregnant stomach threw a blanket over the grass. Everyone sat down but the aviatrix and a man dressed like Mr. Rochester. They circled each other, bowed, and brought their hands to their waists.

I was watching the start of a swordfight, I realized. Or, no—a knife fight. Their blades were short and blunt, made of a glittering metal. They moved lazily, feinting and jabbing, the rest of their party laughing and applauding impressive dodges.

If I look away, something terrible will happen.

The thought struck me out of nowhere and slid away. I kept watching, but something terrible happened anyway. While the people on the ground drank and talked and clapped, the aviatrix charged forward with a sudden vicious leap, stabbing the man in the neck. Before he could fall, she hopped back and sliced across his chest twice, marking a dark X on his shirtfront.

She stood over him, chin up and eyes down. The clapping began in earnest as the man moved weakly on the ground. Dying then dead.

Finch. The tidal horror of what I'd seen done to him came crashing back in, threatening to suck me under. The moan that rose out of me was for him.

The aviatrix looked up from cleaning her blade.

"Who's that?" she said, standing.

How had I thought her beautiful, a minute ago? Her eyes were pupil-less and perfectly round, and when she licked her lips her tongue looked sick.

"Who are you?" she asked again. "Come out where I can see you."

I stepped out from the bushes. "I'm nobody. I'm a visitor."

"From what side?"

"I . . . from Earth."

"Come closer," the aviatrix said, "so we can take a look at you."

Closer wasn't good. Closer meant I could see her face more clearly. The flat shine of her eyes and the sticky red of her mouth. The man on the ground looked less human up close.

"My, what big eyes you have," the woman said, grinning. I blinked. Was she making a joke?

"I'm looking for the Hazel Wood." I devoutly ignored the corpse on the ground. "Do you know which way I should go?" If I pretended everything was normal, maybe it would be. Classic monster-under-the-bed logic.

"You've made it as far as the Halfway Wood. You'll find your way from here. Or perhaps you won't."

Her voice was soothing. But not so soothing that I felt good about the way her followers were surrounding me. The pregnant woman closed the circle, rubbing her stomach like she'd just eaten something big.

"I'm leaving now," I said.

"Leaving? Where would you go?" asked a man with slicked blond hair, wearing a workman's coat.

"I'm . . . my name is Alice Proserpine." Hansa knew who I was—maybe they would, too. Maybe being Althea's granddaughter meant something here.

They didn't seem to hear me. Their faces were less human every second. They looked like wild animals walking on hind legs.

A sudden pain in my thigh made me gasp. I jammed my hand into my pocket and pulled out the thing stabbing at my skin.

It was the bone. As I gaped at it, it grew to the size of a sword, throbbing whitely in the moonlight.

Maybe it *was* a sword—was I supposed to fight with it? I gripped the thing clumsily, praying that wasn't what this tale needed me to do.

Then the bone began to sing.

My love he wooed me
My love he slew me
My love he buried my bones
His love he married
His love I buried
My love now wanders alone

Its voice was distinctly female, filled with such terrible sweetness I thought my heart would crack. I heard a mournful sound from far overhead, and looked up to see a wave of grief pass over the face of the moon.

The bone sang its song again, louder, and the circle of creatures around me fell back. The pregnant one scampered into the trees on all fours, the rest following behind. The aviatrix looked at me with hatred in her eyes, falling to her knees when the bone sang its song a third time.

Everyone had retreated into the woods but the aviatrix, collapsed at my feet. When the song faded, her eyes ticked to mine, brightening. Her hand went to her knife.

The bone twitched restlessly in my hand; its job wasn't done. I perched on the brink for an endless moment, then lifted it over my head. The woods shifted around me; the moon watched from her nest of clouds. I saw myself as she did, a distant girl who was a stranger. That girl knew how to fight her way out of a fairy tale. That girl brought the bone down into the aviatrix's chest.

Then I was myself again, feeling the jar of it in my hands as it went through her like a shovel through dirt, gritty. There was no blood, just her sigh, and silence. My stomach lurched, and the back of my throat tasted like a broken battery. Something hard pattered to the ground between the dead woman and my feet. It lay glittering there, carrying the smell of ozone. The moon's tears. I felt too dirty to touch them.

The bone shrank so quickly I almost dropped it, till it was the size of my littlest finger. I laid it carefully on the dead woman's chest. She already looked less than a woman. She was a golem, crumbling back into dry earth. Did that make what I'd done easier to live with? I couldn't decide.

Nobody waited for me in the trees. The aviatrix's friends had slunk off like cowards. I looked back at the hill to orient myself, then pointed my step toward the Hazel Wood.

The woods grew darker, and the air began to lighten. Around the time I realized it was getting close to dawn, I broke free into an orchard. The trees were low, planted at intervals. They reminded me of the two months Ella and I had spent living and working at an All U Can Pick apple farm.

I had a semi-suburbanite's understanding of trees—maple, birch, crabapple, oak; willow and pine are easy—but I'd stopped caring to identify what I'd walked around and under and been whipped, tugged, and scratched by hours before.

These trees were different. Their branches were made of something soft and glimmering. When I got close, I could see each trunk, branch, and leaf was cast in a thin, flexible metal.

Silver trees. They looked like Etsy jewelry on steroids. I walked slowly under their branches, glad the sun hadn't come up yet. When it did, the grove would be blinding. The silver trees gave way to gold, followed by copper, with blood-colored leaves that clattered together with a sound like bones. And I remembered the rhyme.

Look until the leaves turn red
Sew the worlds up with thread
If your journey's left undone
Fear the rising of the sun.

In the east, if this was still a world where the sun rose in the east, a wedding band of white-gold light inched over the horizon. I started to run. The trees rustled their branches as I passed, flinging down metal leaves to tangle in my hair. I felt the cheap canvas of my sneakers rubbing my heels bloody.

I ran so fast I almost pinwheeled over the edge of the ravine when I reached it. Below my feet, a fall so endless I saw clouds. Ahead, green iron gates, a hazel tree picked out across them. I caught my breath, held it.

Between me and the gates was a stretch of thin air. The sun was edging upward, the sky gathering color. My hip burned hot where the feather nestled in my pocket. I pulled it out and held it before my eyes.

It was gold edged with green, speckled haphazardly

with eyes. It shivered to attention in my palm and sent its tickling fibers coursing up my left arm. I squicked out at the sensation, itchy and warm and intimate, like someone sewing a sweater onto my body at the speed of sound. The tickle skated across my back and down my right arm. Before the sun was halfway risen, I had wings as wide as I was tall. They unfurled without my asking them to, lifting me a few inches off the ground. When I panicked, they dropped me on my ass.

The metal trees were blatantly watching now, chattering advice I couldn't understand in their rickety typewriter voices. I stood and let my shoulders relax. I listed to one side as my left wing perked to attention, then my right, and exhaled as my toes left the ground.

Setting my sights on the Hazel Wood gates, I let the wings carry me into open air.

~22~

My feet thumped crookedly to Earth. I whipped around to look for the red-leaved trees, to see if the sun had reached them yet, but a thick bank of fog had sprung up between me and the other side.

Another fairy-tale lesson learned: don't look back.

The dream I'd been living in for the past hours was fading away. I could remember everything I'd done, but it felt flat as a picture book. The mermaid, the moon. The bone that slid so easily into the aviatrix's chest. Was that really me?

I didn't want to end up like Ness, trapped in a room by memories, so I decided it wasn't. The story I'd lived through was just that: a story.

As if it agreed with me, a gust of wind blew the feathers

off my arms in one great puff. They swirled into a winged shape and flew away. My pockets were empty: I had no tricks left. Maybe that was why the Hazel Wood let me in. I reached for the gates, and they swung open without a sound.

And there it was. The grass cropped close as green velvet, racing toward the distant steps of the house. Althea's estate was pillars and white brick and gabled windows. It was a flat swimming pool set like a lucid blue brooch against the lawn, trimmed in glittering stone. It was exactly as my mind had built it, right down to the electric feeling in the air, of some wonderful thing about to unfold.

It chilled me to my marrow. Life never turns out how you imagine it will when you're young. Everything is smaller than you think, or too big. It all smells a little funny and fits like somebody else's shirt.

But this version of the Hazel Wood was perfect. It was *mine*. It was being pulled from me, from daydreams I'd thumbed over so often they were creased, and the preserved pages of *Vanity Fair*. I closed my eyes and opened them again slowly, half-expecting to see a tumbledown ruin, the truth behind the fantasy. But my vision held up.

The air smelled like crushed grass and chlorine, with the held-breath quiet of the hottest day of summer. I walked over the dewy cheek of perfectly stage-directed grass, past geometric flowerbeds and a faintly rustling fountain I was dying to drink from, but you'd have to be dumber than Persephone to drink anything in fairyland.

The house bobbed closer, gaining detail as I walked. It was perfect, from the lawn all the way to the widow's walk circling the high attic tower, where I once imagined my bedroom would be when Althea finally invited me to stay.

I hesitated at the front door. Not because I thought it would be locked, but because I had no sense of what lay beyond it. The *Vanity Fair* photographer wasn't allowed past the lawn, and my fantasies always took place out here: horseback riding, picnics. Even the daydreams about my bedroom mostly took the form of me pacing my widow's walk, surveying the swells of green. I read too much Wilkie Collins as a kid.

So whatever I found inside might be closer to the truth. Though truth, I sensed, was a relative concept here. I grabbed the doorknob, a puffing golden face shaped like the Wind sliced apart by Hansa, and turned.

The foyer I stepped into was vast, flanked on each side by a curving staircase. Stubs of unlit candles perched between each spindle. Between the flights was a pink stone fountain so big you could swim in it. Three stone women glared impassively from its center. One held a birdcage, one a translucent quartz cube, the other a dagger. Through windows taller than me came the tilted, dust-colored light of Sunday afternoon.

The scale of everything was so vast, it took me a minute to take it all in. As I did I saw bits of humanity elbowing in on the splendor: A glittery, cheap-looking cardigan hanging over a banister. A blue toy boat floating in the fountain.

And a hum, just audible over the patter of water. When I listened hard, it resolved into the secretive tones of a child singing to herself. The tune was "Hickory Dickory Dock."

I looked up and saw a little girl sitting in the bend of the left-hand staircase, watching me. When our eyes met, she went silent.

"Ella," I said, only half-believing it. But it was her; it was my mother. I recognized her from the magazine spread. She couldn't have been more than five years old. When she heard her name, she ran up the stairs and out of sight.

I followed, realizing with a start that my footsteps made no sound on the tile floor, or the marble stairs. It was instantly disorienting, like trying to talk when your ears are stuffed.

Ella swerved to the left. I followed. The hallway was so long it had to be a trick—I'd seen the house from the outside. It was big, but not like this. I jogged past one door after another, trying each one. I thought I heard a giggle behind the third, but it didn't sound like it came from a child.

The seventh door I tried opened onto a tiny room. A typewriter sat on a writing desk between two windows. Next to it, a cigarette wedged into a green glass ashtray sizzled down to a stub. An inch of ash hung from its tip. Through the window was a different day than the one I'd left, one where a gray sky pressed against winter-crisped grass.

I tiptoed to the typewriter to see what was written on the page curling out of it, in dense, irregular print.

When Alice was born, her eyes were black from end to end, and the midwife didn't stay long enough to wash her.

My neck tingled like someone was close behind me, reaching out with pinching fingers. I sprinted from the room and closed the door.

The hall had changed. Now it was a brighter place, shorter, ending in a glass-ceilinged conservatory flooded with green. Sunlight poured in over trees I recognized and some I didn't, and some I swore I'd seen just now in the woods. I walked slowly forward with my arms held out. The air was dense and damp and sweet. On a pool of grass so bright it had to be fake sat a chrome-fronted radio the color of strawberry sherbet.

I crouched down and turned on the radio. The light outside dimmed as the music came up. It was the song I'd heard on the bus, sped up into a dance tune. When I snapped it off, the light outside bounced back and swelled, till the brightness hurt my eyes. I threw a hand over them, backing out of the room and into something warm and solid.

"My god," he said, because it was a man I'd collided with. "Won't you ever leave me alone?"

It was night again. He shrank away from me in a pool of artificial torchlight. We were in an orange-lit, faux-medieval billiard room with knotty wooden walls. The man wore a rumpled tuxedo. He looked like a duke Barbara Stanwyck might've fallen in love with on a steamship crossing, before ending up with a cabin boy played by Cary Grant.

He'd dropped a very full highball glass when I bumped him. The sharp scent of gin stung my nose. In the other hand he held a gun. Not like Harold's, a blunt-nosed black thing made for violence—this gun was long and elegant as a greyhound. The man carried it propped over his shoulder like a boy playing army.

"You can see me?" I said. I wasn't sure what the rules

were here—whether I was a ghost. Whether I would die if shot by a gun.

"You're all I see. It's driving me mad. It's driven me mad!" His voice was arch, but his eyes were wet and desperate.

"Who are you?" I asked, reaching for his sleeve. "Who do you think I am?"

He stumbled back. "Get away, you foul thing. I'm getting free of you even if she can't. Your touch may be cold as the grave, but I know you come straight from hell."

He walked unsteadily through a pool of whiskey-colored light, disappearing into the darkness on the other side. From the silence came a single gunshot.

When I ran from the room, my ears popped. Listing with vertigo, I staggered down a wide, ruined hall, its tiled floor grown over with moss. Ivy grew through a shattered windowpane, and everything smelled like rot. It ended in a sitting room with water-stained walls, where a pair of striped folding chairs flanked a crushed-velvet sofa. On the table between them lay a stack of fashion magazines. Christy Turlington stared vacantly from the cover of the yellowing *Vogue Paris* on top. November 1986.

Behind me, someone knocked out "Shave and a Haircut" against the doorframe. It was Ella, looking older now. Eight, maybe. She smiled self-consciously, her lips closed over her teeth, then ran away.

"Ella," I said, but the air ate it up. When I moved a hand in front of my face, it warped a little, like I was looking at it through flawed glass.

I staggered forward, falling as I crossed the threshold.

My knees landed in the deep nap of carpet the color of old ivory. To pull myself up, I grabbed onto the silken skirts of the bed sitting just within reach.

It was a fairy-tale bed, hung to the ground with tattered curtains. Where they were sheerest, I could see the shape of someone lying motionless inside. Dripping candles in tarnished silver holders circled them, releasing a honeysuckle fragrance that filled the air like a drug.

I didn't want to see what lay on that bed. I didn't want to be in this room, or in this place. None of it fit together; it was a scrapbook of times and places and someone else's memories. Althea's, or Ella's, maybe. Was the Hazel Wood even real? Had it ever existed? Wherever I was, it wasn't a house. It was a kaleidoscope. I moved to the window, thinking I could climb out, but I wasn't on the second floor anymore—somehow I'd made it to the turret. The lawn was a taunting green sea below.

The thing in the bed made a tiny sound, a groan or a sigh, that set the hair from my scalp to the small of my back alight. I ran from the room—

And slid to a stop in a dingy yellow kitchen. A light buzzed overhead, and the stench of dill and old coffee turned my stomach. Thin spring light fell through a dirty window onto a sideboard cluttered with cups. Loneliness clung to every surface, thick as dust. On a mint-colored Formica table sat an empty mug, a water-stained copy of *Madame Bovary*, a pair of scissors. And a stack of clipped-out newspaper articles.

My hand shook as I touched the top one, splaying out the stack. *Upstate Community Rattled After Attack. Search*

for Missing Jogger Enters Second Week. Link Suspected in Up-
state Homicides. Five Victims Later, Mystery Persists in Small-
Town Murders. Remains Found, Questions Remain.

Althea had known, then. What she'd let escape, and
what they did out there.

A long scream from behind me cut the air in half. I
spun around, knocking the mug to the floor. A blue enamel
kettle shrieked and steamed on the stove, and a creaking
step sounded somewhere beyond the door.

For one electric second I considered running for the
window. Instead I stayed still, muscles jumping in my
shoulders. The step came closer, closer, then stopped outside the door.

Silence stretched till I couldn't stand it—the thick,
waiting quiet of someone listening for something. I slid
forward on the tile, put my hand on the knob, and jerked
the door open like ripping off a Band-Aid.

And stepped out into a wall of voices and music and
bodies, wrapped in a haze of wax and perfume as thick
as syrup.

I was in a ballroom, barely lit. A chandelier heavy with
half-melted candles swayed over a crush of dancers,
moving to glittery, atonal music that could've been the
soundtrack to a party in hell.

The dancers swarmed so close together they looked
like a mosh pit on a subway car, moving with the music's
headache rhythms. Bits of candlelight caught at teeth and
eyes and sweat and the shine of white wax, dripping into
their hair and hardening.

I thought I saw Ella in the swing of bodies—older

again, but not yet grown. She smiled up at her partner, too worldly, and shifted out of sight. I moved closer, trying to reach her, and the crowd pushed back.

A man with a fresh black eye danced alone, blissed on something stronger than liquor. A trio of women with bodies like fronds wound around each other in a way that looked boneless, their edges meeting and melting together in a watercolor blur. I nearly stumbled over a small figure I thought was a child, until she tilted her face toward the candlelight. The look in her eyes made me step back.

Then I saw something that stopped me cold, filling me to the knuckles with starlight.

Finch. Unmistakably, in the heart of the dancers. Finch in a white shirt, his shoulders heavy with shadows. His eyes were alight and his mouth was soft and all of him bent toward the girl he danced with. She was short and fierce and her hair ran over her back in a bright Barbie sweep.

She was *me*, me with my hair grown long, and she was looking at Finch with an expression I didn't think my face could hold.

It didn't feel like an illusion, or a dream. I smelled sweat and spilled wine and candle wax, and tasted blood as I bit through the skin of my lip. I said his name, or tried to, but the music ghosted it away.

Then the candlelight stuttered like a strobe and the crowd changed, shifted, faces sifting through pockets of shadow and light. It came to me that I was seeing a hundred terrible parties melted down into one, full of people too strange and reckless to be anything but Hinterland. Ella was gone but Finch remained, always, at the center of everything, holding me.

The house was tugging at my mind again, unspooling things I'd dreamed, tucked-away things I might've wished for, and mashing them together with the memories that breathed from the Hazel Wood's walls. My breath came short as the other me let Finch run his hands through the whole length of her heavy hair.

She lifted her face—my face—toward his. The music went shivering and slow, and all of me craned toward them as a feeling like jealousy cut its teeth on my heart. His eyes slid shut and his hair moved in an underwater drift. Even as she leaned into him I could see the glint of her open eyes, still watchful, always watchful. I leaned so far I thought I'd fall, waiting for the moment when their lips would touch.

When they did the music went to static. Someone in a half-mask and legs too long for their body grabbed my shoulder. The kiss sizzled like gunpowder in my chest; I felt too stunned to pull away.

"Join the dance or get out, daydreamer," the person said into my ear, and gave me a hard shove.

It unplugged me from the party like something ripped, sparking, from a socket in the wall, and sent me tumbling back into a long, empty hall. Ella was gone, Finch was gone, and the girl I might have been had never existed. But the party clung to me in a hazy perfume; I could still smell wax on my clothes.

Then far, far down the hall I saw a closed door with light shining out around its seams. The light was warm and it felt right, like everything else I'd seen in this house was a dream, and this was the warm human light of waking up after a nightmare. The light in the cottage you stumble on in the dark, dark woods. I ran to it, and I threw open the door, and I walked into a child's nightlight-lit bedroom.

And my heart sank, because I knew this wasn't any more real than the rest of it. It couldn't have been, because my grandmother was there waiting for me, sitting on the edge of the bed smoking a cigarette.

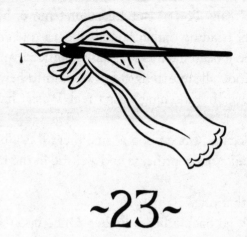

~23~

Althea looked good. She looked *real*. She wore cigarette pants and a striped boatneck shirt and, oddly, short white gloves. Like the Hazel Wood, she resembled exactly my idea of her—the level blue eyes, the elegant bones. Through the window behind her I saw snowy grounds and a strange white sky, bathing the room in a lunar glow. It made the shadows deeper. A nightlight cast a valiant circle of orange against the wall.

"Do you want to hear a story?" Althea asked.

I froze. Before I could respond, a mulish voice from the bed beat me to it. "No."

Ella lay in the shadows, arms flung over her head and one foot on the floor. She looked older again—fifteen, maybe sixteen. Too old for bedtime stories.

Althea exhaled a thin haze of blue smoke. "Oh, yes, you do."

"I really, really don't." But Ella didn't move, beyond propping her head up on her hands. She was old enough now that she looked like herself, dark and fierce and distracted. It took all my strength not to rush to her, but I knew whatever I was seeing wasn't real. Wasn't happening *now*.

Althea began. "Once upon a time there was a beautiful queen and a brave princess and a castle in the middle of a forest."

"I know that one."

"Then I'll go back a little further. Once upon a time there was a beautiful queen who thought words were stronger than anything. She used them to win love and money and gifts. She used them to carry her across the world." Althea laid out her words like a dealer lays out cards, with a distant, mesmeric precision. "And one day when she was very, very bored, she used them to convince a noblewoman to lead her into another kingdom, a place out of legend, and far beyond her own kingdom's borders."

"The Hinterland." There was a sharp edge to Ella's voice that saved it from being indifferent.

"Hush. This is my story, not yours. As I was saying, this new kingdom—the Other Kingdom—was strange and dangerous and far from home. The queen quickly grew homesick and set about trying to find a way back. It was said there were doors that could take her where she wanted to go, but they hid themselves from her. And do you know what you do when you can't find a door?" She itsy-bitsy-spidered her fingers across the air. "You build a bridge."

I stood rooted halfway between the door and the bed. Althea's voice worked on me like a shot, loosening my limbs and sharpening my vision, leaving a hot ache in my chest.

"In the Other Kingdom there were many kings and queens, each equally powerful. But the queen set out to find the kingdom's true ruler—not royalty, but someone far more important. A storyteller. A master of words. When the queen found her, she very convincingly shared her plight—she was a master of words, too—and soon the storyteller whispered the secret of escape into the queen's ear.

"But the storyteller made a mistake in trusting the queen. When she escaped from the Other Kingdom, she took something with her—something that held the walls of the world in place and kept the stars from coming down. Something she brought back to her own kingdom and shared with all of her subjects: stories. All the stories of the Other Kingdom. She told them, and told them again, and they were told and retold all over the realm."

Althea's voice was losing its soporific thrum, like the nap rubbing off velvet. Her eyes gleamed in the weird white light.

"The queen felt rich, richer than she'd ever been, until she realized what she'd done: by carrying the Other Kingdom's greatest treasure across her bridge, she'd drawn the two kingdoms tight, tight together—until they were like two hills rising side by side, then the sun and the moon in eclipse, then a hand in a glove stitched too snug."

Sew the worlds up with thread. The words sang in my head and passed away.

My grandmother's voice dropped to a whisper. "But nobody knew it except the queen. Nobody else noticed when terrible things started happening. When the queen threw festivals, demons arrived in dresses, and hid their red eyes behind masks. If she stayed in one castle too long, a darkness grew over everything and everyone around her, like briars. People from the Other Kingdom slipped through their hidden doors to mock her, for believing she'd escaped. For thinking she'd gotten away with her theft. Then one night, someone from the Other Kingdom snuck inside her castle and murdered her king."

Her voice was raw now, her head bowed low. I blinked and the room seemed to stutter; Althea was standing, and the bed she'd been sitting on was cast in deeper shadow. The glow of moonlight on snow no longer came through the window.

Althea went on. "The queen realized it wasn't the kingdoms that had changed—it was her. She didn't need to find a door, she had *become* one. A bridge, too. A place where the demons could get in. So she and her daughter ran away to a castle in the woods. The Other Kingdom followed, and over time the woods around the castle became as twisted as an oak, torn between the two kingdoms.

"But still the queen's daughter, the princess, grew up strong. She grew up fast and fleet, forever running between the Other Kingdom and that of her birth, because she couldn't remember a life that was any other way."

All the magic had gone from her telling. She spoke fast and flat. The room was changing, and Althea was, too. Her shoulders slumped; gray licked through her hair.

Without warning, her gaze swiveled toward my face. Her teeth were stained, and her eyes spun like pinwheels.

Ella was gone. The room was the same, but different. The bed was humped and tarnished, and dust lay over everything like a veil.

"You're here." Althea's whisper cracked in the middle. She was looking at me. "Is it you? Is it you, really?"

She was a ghost. Or a mirage. She *had* to be. The hunger in her voice should've made me wary, but my own hunger rose up to meet it. "It's me. It's Alice. Your, your . . ." I couldn't say it. *Granddaughter.*

"Lucky, lucky, lucky Althea," she said, low, moving closer till I could smell the sweat on her skin, the bitter almond on her breath. I froze, my heart hammering like frozen rain, and she spoke the rest of her tale into my ear.

"The Other Kingdom didn't hurt the queen's beloved daughter, because she was too clever. Clever Princess Vanella." She hissed the princess's name—my mother's name. "Until the day the princess found a baby in the Halfway Wood, left by her parents and their hunting party to sleep beneath a tree. Cherry blossoms had fallen into her bassinet. The baby squeezed them between her little fingers, staring up at the princess with her black, black eyes. The princess loved her right away. And she stole her out of her fairy tale."

My heart knew before my head. It beat tiny throbs of adrenaline, like a poison drip telling me to *run, run, before you hear something you can't forget.* I didn't run. I let her tell me the rest of our story.

"Alice-Three-Times," she spat. "You were plucked from

your story like a cherry blossom by a girl who didn't know what she did."

My mind moved like a cold computer. "I'm here to find Ella," I said stupidly. "My mother."

"Your kidnapper. That girl is nobody's mother."

For a long white moment my mind wiped clean. I couldn't even picture Ella's face. I didn't know my hand was raised till Althea stepped back, out of range.

"Look at you." Her laugh was an ugly thing. "Still feral after all these years."

I dropped my hand, wrapping my arms around myself as Ella came back to me in pieces. Bony hands and breath in the dark and the sharp line of her profile as she drove. She'd never looked like me. I'd never wondered why.

I used to picture a father somewhere, someone Ella had loved, at least for a little while. That was a lie, too.

"I don't believe you," I whispered. Another lie.

"You were her favorite story." Althea's voice grew gentler, a little. "She liked how angry you were. Like an avenging . . . well, not an angel."

"I'm a girl," I said fiercely. "I'm a person."

"You're both, and neither. You're a story, but that doesn't make you any less true."

I felt like I was watching myself from the outside, a girl with blurred edges holding herself like a child. The image stamped itself onto my brain, one of those out-of-your-skin moments that turns into memory while it's still happening. *This is the day my dead grandmother told me my mother wasn't mine. That I was a character in a story, plucked from another place.*

"She ran away from you," I told Althea, watching the

words land like a slap. "We both did. I grew up in the world. I remember it—I remember skinning my knees and reading library books and eating crap food from the gas station. Sick days watching bad TV. I remember life happening in the right order, and, and bus rides, and being lonely. I remember all of it!"

"Do you?"

I stared at her, then down at my hands, rough and chapped and un-fairy-tale-ish. I thought of the way my life faded out behind me, faint scratches on the earth washed away like footprints on dirt.

"You're crazy," I said. "And you're *dead*. And I'm here to take Ella back."

"Take her back? From who?" She smiled at me coquettishly, a ghost of what she once looked like, back when hers was a face to look at. She'd become very old since she was a woman telling her daughter a story in the dark.

"From the Hinterland," I said unsteadily. "They took her."

Althea shook her head. "I assure you, they did not. You're the one they wanted, Alice-Three-Times. She was just"—she flipped her hand—"a distraction."

Bait. Finch was right. Ella, wherever she was, had been bait.

"So where is she, then? If not here, where?" My voice rose. "I don't care if you're a ghost or a memory or a, I don't know, a hologram, but please. She's your daughter. Please tell me how to get her back."

"You think I'm a *ghost*? I haunt this old memory palace, and it haunts me, but I'm not dead." She grabbed my hand, shoved it against the sloping bread-dough skin beneath the yellowing stripes of her shirt, right where her heart would be.

A dim beat fluttered against my fingers.

Alive.

"But . . . but the letter . . ."

"It reached you? I wasn't sure it would. The death letter was to get her to bring you back." She laughed, harsh and sad. "Even that wasn't enough. So why now? What made you come back *now*?"

My heart crunched in on itself. After everything, I still wanted to think all of it had been her—that she'd sent cold fingers into the world to draw me here. Because she . . . what? Loved me? Wanted me? Stupid Alice. I liked to think I'd put my old dreams behind me, but here I was talking to one, and she made me feel five years old.

But *Ella* loved me. My mother. My kidnapper. *The Thief*, Hansa had called her.

She was still mine, maybe more now that I knew it had been a choice. My longing for her rearranged itself in my chest. It felt like a new-hatched thing, wet-feathered but fierce. I set my jaw and let it be the lifeline that would pull me from the quicksand of this hot, close room, the smell of dust and the night crawling over the windows.

"Ella was gone," I said. "They took her somewhere—somewhere in New York, maybe, I don't know. And the book—your book. It was haunting me. Twice-Killed Katherine. She . . . got me to come." I found I couldn't tell her about Finch. Seeing Althea like this would have broken his heart.

"Of course she found you. You are a walking, talking bridge to the Hinterland. Anywhere you go, the wall between the worlds grows thin. They get *through*. They do damage."

"She tried to kill me. She tried to make me cut my own wrists in the woods. Why?"

"Ah." Her eyes turned bright. "Clever Katherine. There'd be a grave cost to pay if they killed you themselves, but if you spilled your own blood in those woods? Alice-Three-Times? It would burn a door between worlds that would never fade. Their vicious holidays out there would never end."

Alice-Three-Times. The name seared and burrowed into me.

She looked at me with something approaching respect. "So you made it through the woods without a guide. Life out there hasn't rendered you completely helpless. You must be a bit like her—like Ella."

"I am," I said, biting off the words.

She sucked on the cigarette I'd forgotten she was holding. "Ella never could resist a lost lamb—especially not you in your basket, with those awful black eyes. I tried to return you myself, before they killed her getting you back." Her eyes darkened. "But Ella hated me for it, and she took you away. Far from them, far from me. Like I was a boogeyman, too."

"But they're not black. My eyes. They're brown." I said it stupid and hopeful. Like it was a loophole I could use to slip back into my real life.

"That happened after you left the Hazel Wood. It was enough to make Ella believe she did the right thing. She wrote to me, back when letters still washed up here once in a while—she said it was the Hinterland draining out of you. Saving you, giving you a real life, became her purpose. Did it work? Did you get one?" Her voice swerved sharply from desolation to hope—stunted and sad, but hope nonetheless.

I remembered the rootlessness, the travel, the cursed incidents that followed us from place to place. I felt in my back the bars of every sofa bed we ever crashed on, the heavy gaze of our hosts when we'd outstayed our welcome, and the ache of sleeping in our car for days on end, pretending I didn't know we were homeless.

I saw Ella. Gripping my arms and counting down with me from one hundred, bringing my anger back within its borders. The blanket forts she built for me in guest rooms, resigning herself to sleeping without a pillow so I could forget we were a burden for a night. The crow's-feet starting at the corners of her eyes, so out of place on a woman who never really grew up. Who chose saving me, running with me, over having a real life of her own.

"Yes," I said. "It worked. I've had a wonderful life. I *have* a wonderful life."

Althea tilted her head back, looked at me through lowered lashes. "And did she—did Ella ever talk about me?"

My first instinct was to hurt her. But I looked at the taut white knobs of her knuckles, the drawn-tight pouch of her mouth around the cigarette, and couldn't. "All the time."

"Liar," she said softly, smoke sifting through her lips. "I won't make excuses for my life, but I can tell you it wasn't my choice to lose her. She thought—I don't know what she thought. That I was the Hinterland's dogcatcher, maybe."

"Aren't you? The letter—wasn't that a trap?"

"Hmm." She stubbed her cigarette against the bed-frame, dropped the butt on the floor. "Not a very effective one."

"She thought it was over. When you died—when the letter told us you'd died. She thought we were safe."

Althea looked at me, eyes bleak. "She knew I was a bridge. She didn't know you were one, too."

It hit me like delayed pain. It had always been me. My black energy leaking into the air like blood, and the Hinterland like sharks on its trail. All the years we'd spent running, we were running from *me*.

"So they'll always find me?" I whispered. "No matter where I go?"

"They *are* you. You're all made of the same stuff." Her voice was almost sympathetic. "It's hard, isn't it, to find you're not at all the thing you thought you were?" She pointed at herself, her words poison-tipped. "Intrepid adventurer." Then at me. "Real live girl."

I wanted to argue, but I couldn't believe in a world outside of that room. "So what happens to a girl like me?" I asked dully. "If the letter had worked, if she'd brought me back. What would you have done with me?"

"But it did work after all, didn't it? It just worked slow. It made you stand still, long enough for those monsters to corral you into the Halfway Wood. But—you survived it. And you came here, to me, of your own free will. Did you not?"

The sharpened look in her eyes made me wary. "I . . . don't know. I wanted to come here. But I didn't want it like this."

"We never do, do we? When we get what we want?"

Then she peeled off her gloves and seized my hands. Her grip burned worse than Katherine's, and I gasped, trying to wrench myself free.

"This is what happens to girls like you." Her words were half curse, half plea. "She's tried so long to get you back, Alice-Three-Times. And as long as you're on the wrong side of the woods, she won't let me die."

"Who?" I could barely hear my own voice over the pain. "*Who* won't let you die?"

She ignored me, looking up like the ceiling was the sky, and a vengeful god was watching her. "I'm giving her back to you!" she cried. "Now will you let me go?"

The heat spread up over my arms and down my chest, squeezing me in its fist till my vision burst open and swung with stars. I felt the tremor in Althea's fingers, saw the wide yellows of her eyes, and her mouth shaping itself around some final words I couldn't hear. A plea, an apology. A promise, a lie.

Then I was falling end over end like Carroll's Alice, through space or water or clouds or atoms. The pain passed, and I felt *alive*, breath in my chest and blood in my muscles and nothing hurting. The room was gone, Althea was gone, and I was rushing through bracing air. When I landed with a numbing jolt, I was in the Hinterland.

~24~

I was back in the forest. But this was a forest that made the Halfway Wood feel like a Polaroid. It made the woods on Earth seem like the pencil sketches of a blind man who'd read about trees but never seen them.

In the Halfway Wood I wondered whether the trees could hear me, whether they could speak. Here they seemed practically to breathe. I'd landed with my back against a trunk as wide as a car, front to back, its bark covered in knots that suggested an implacable face. It dropped a rain of seeds into my lap. They were crescent-shaped and pinkie nail–sized, burnished the color of a harvest moon.

I looked up at the sky like I might see Althea's face there, watching me through a rip in the blue. Then I stood up and started walking. What else was there to do? I was numb. Three degrees removed from the world I'd grown up in—a world that wasn't even mine.

Finch is here. I remembered it with a feeling like jerking back from the brink of sleep. The Halfway Wood had tried to make me forget. Althea's junk drawer of a house and the woman herself, going mad in a yellow room. But Finch was *here*. He'd lived, and he'd bled out in an in-between forest, and now his corpse was cooling in a world he'd wished for.

Was he buried? Was he burned? What did a place like this do with its dead? Thoughts of him made my fingers curl and ache. I shoved them into my pockets and walked through a world where everything—everything—seemed alive.

The sun was vast and low and not so bright that I couldn't make out something happening in the fire of its surface, the tracings of a story so distant I'd never read it. Flowers furled into pellets or went lurid as I passed, sending out vapor trails of scent—cardamom, iced tea, Ella's shampoo. This new world was too strange, too lucid; it made my mind explode in a dandelion puff. Everything had a revelatory crispness, like a new day seen through the lens of a coffee-fueled all-nighter. I started reciting stuff in my head to keep my thoughts within safe borders: The track lists of my favorite albums. The names of all the Harry Potter books in order. The places we'd lived, one by one. *Chicago. Madison. Memphis. Nacogdoches. Taos.*

It kept my mind wrapped around a thin blue wire of sanity and denial. But it was slipping. Ella, I knew now, was in the place I'd left behind. And I was in an alien world, surrounded by trees whose sentient interest in my passing ranged from distant friendliness to a ruffled annoyance that made me picture a dog smelling someone else's pet on your clothes. I had Earth all over me. But underneath it, if Althea was to be believed, I was Hinterland.

I believed her. If for no other reason than how good my body felt moving through this wood. The air was crisp, almost autumnal, but everything in sight was lavishly green or flowering. The light was an ambient, suffused gold, and it did something funny to the shadows: they looked like black stamps. My own shadow gave the distinct impression of keeping up with me just to see what I'd do next; if I proved to be boring, I suspected it would ditch me.

After spending an hour pushing through low-hanging branches that either courteously shrank from my touch or pushed back, I stumbled by luck onto a path.

It was almost too picturesque, lined with berry brambles and flowers that wept fat, furry petals onto the packed dirt. They were duckling yellow and smelled like buttered toast.

I took two steps and stopped.

Birds had been singing. Three- and four-note trills I didn't recognize. A breeze had moved through all that curious green, branches had cracked, leaves had rustled, unseen animals had made their quiet way. But here the noises stopped, replaced by a focused, annihilating calm. There was a bend to the air here, an almost invisible heat that made my fingers curl and my nose itch.

It made me hungry. I was *hungry,* and my hands were so cold I felt them burning through the fabric of my pockets, chilling my thighs.

I didn't see the girl till she was almost close enough to touch. She'd stopped a few paces off the path and didn't notice me. Her profile could've been drawn in one long, economical stroke by a master, and her hair was as thick and dark as my shadow. She stood perfectly still, both hands pressed against the bark of a tree. Her mouth moved furious and silent, as if she were reading a very disturbing letter.

The air around her shivered and prismed like the heat over blacktop. *She* was what I was looking for, the hot moving point at the center of this island of charged quiet. I watched her with a feeling I couldn't name—fear or awe or recognition.

The tree trunk cracked in two between her palms. I sucked in a breath as its bark became doors, opening inward. From where I stood, just above her, I could see the top step of a silver staircase going down, and hear the sound of a party happening far away. As the girl lifted her foot and placed it on the first stair, I took a step forward.

A hand landed heavy on my shoulder, and a voice spoke in my ear. "Wouldn't do that if I were you. You don't want to come between a Story and their story."

I jerked away from the man standing next to me. He was in his early thirties, wearing wire-rimmed glasses, jeans faded almost to white, and a shabby brown bomber jacket.

And he was eating a Hershey's bar. He saw me staring at it and stepped backward, blocking it with his hand. "Dude, no. This is practically my last one. It's not like I can go buy more." His accent was American, mostly, but touched with something else. It gave a crisp edge to all his consonants.

I pushed my hands deeper into my pockets, breathing in the cool, untainted air he carried with him. "Wait a minute," I said. "You're from Earth."

He stared at me a moment, then sighed. "Oh, hell, no. You just got here? Nope, I'm not equipped to do an orientation. Wait, you didn't bring any food with you, did you? Like . . . packaged stuff?" He scanned me—sweatshirt, jeans, no bag. "Okay, that's a no."

"Orientation?" I echoed, glancing back toward the girl. She was gone, the tree trunk seamless. "And what did you say before? About a story and a story?"

"Jesus, no wonder you almost followed the Woodwife into hell. You're green, aren't you? Like, just-fell-through-a-mirror-in-Tunisia green?"

I thought about telling him I was Alice-Three-Times, seeing if he'd give me the rest of his candy bar. But I decided against it. "Is that how you got here?" I asked. "A mirror in Tunisia? Are you the only one?"

"Agh." He shoved the rest of the chocolate in his mouth, stared at me while he chewed. "Okay, I'll tell you the basic deal. The *very* basic deal, then you've got to find someone who's actually good at this. First off, of course I'm not the only one, assuming by 'only one' you mean the only jackass stupid enough to think it was a good idea to beg, borrow, or steal his way into a place without record players, bourbon, or chocolate. There are lots of refugees here. From Earth and from other places—or so I've heard. Second, *stay away from the Stories.* You'll know them when you see them. If they glow at the edges, move like they're in a trance, smell like smoke or flowers or salt, or generally look like they belong in a murder ballad, steer very, very clear. I knew a guy, a classicist from Cambridge—got in through a wishing well—who tried to save the Skinned Maiden before she got skinned. *Christ*, was that a bad idea."

"What happened?"

"Don't make me spell it out for you. Look, did you mean to get in? Because it kind of seems like you didn't."

Against his will, it seemed, he was becoming interested in me. "I didn't mean to get in. Someone pushed me," I clarified.

"Well, that's . . . that's maybe more than I want to get involved in." He looked shifty. "I don't want to be a dick, but I've got a decent thing going here. Finally. I've got a girlfriend—ex-Story, so that keeps things pretty interesting—and I was taking a walk so I could eat this without her staring at me. They think packaged food is disgusting."

He kept talking, but I didn't hear anything after *ex-Story*. "What do you mean, *ex*-Story?" I interrupted sharply. "Does that mean she used to be a, uh, a character?"

"Pretty much." His eyes flicked over my shoulder; he was getting bored of me. "Look, if you follow this path long enough you'll find a little old woman who'll ask you to do something—carry her pail, chop her wood, whatever. Just do it, and use the wish she grants you to find Janet. You understand? Don't ask to be sent home, or to be made into a princess or whatever. She can't do that much anymore; she's ex-Story, too. Tell her to send you to Janet, and she'll know who you mean."

"Old woman, Janet," I murmured. "Got it." My mind was spinning around on a hamster wheel, thinking of the implications of being ex-Story. Even from inside the Hinterland, maybe I could find a way to get free.

"That way," he said, pointing me down the path. "It might take five minutes, it might take an hour. Good travels."

"Thanks," I said, sticking out my hand.

He took it, then yelled, pulling his fingers back like I bit him.

"What? What happened?" I asked. He held his fingers to his mouth, staring at me. Staring at my hands.

"Shit," he said. "You're Story, aren't you?"

"Huh?" I looked down at my hands and gasped.

They were the blitzed white of a cheap wedding dress, so pale they were almost blue. My nails were translucent, chunks of carved ice. "What the hell!" I said, jumping backward like I could get away from them.

"I meant no disrespect, my lady!" The man bowed, walking backward. "I didn't mean to meddle. Good travels to you!"

"Wait!" I cried, and threw out one hand. He froze, like I might have the power to shoot ice rays at him. For all I knew, I did.

"I need gloves," I said.

He hesitated before shoving his hands into the pockets of his jacket, coming up with worn leather gloves. He balled them up, tossed them to me, and ran.

I caught them against my chest. They were too big and smelled like cheap chocolate, but I felt better as soon as the white of my fingers had disappeared. My heart squeezed when I remembered the story Finch told me in the diner: Alice-Three-Times swallowed ice, and it made her—*me*—into a frozen zombie. Katherine's fiery touch in the parking lot—that cold, awful feeling wasn't hers, it was mine. Her touch, the touch of the Hinterland, woke it up.

It was too much, too strange, too big to think about all at once. So I set off in the direction the man had pointed me. The path took me past a tiny hut built between two massive trees. An old man sat on a stump out front, watching me with distant eyes. He held something pressed to his ear. I nodded at him, jamming my gloved hands into my pockets.

The thing in his hand squawked, and a string of nonsense words came out. *Green scene mean. Stick quick trick. Tokyo alabaster red. King queen chick.*

"Is that a . . . is that a transistor radio?"

The man grunted, writing something down on a square of rough paper. He wrote with a Bic.

"Who are you talking to?" I tried again.

He didn't seem inclined to answer, so I turned away.

"Whoever's listening," he said to my back. "In this world or another."

"Any luck yet?"

The radio crackled again and let out a descending series of hums in a woman's voice. It sounded like a vocal exercise.

"Heard lots of things," he muttered. "But no luck."

I nodded. "Good travels," I said, because I thought it might be the greeting here. The old man stared at me strangely and went back to his radio.

The light started to change, going tawny as the sharp

shadows lengthened. Where the path petered out to a tiny foot road, I nearly collided with a tall man in black. He had a handsome, avid face covered nose to temples in thin, branching tattoos, and he smelled . . . awful. And somehow familiar.

He was a Story for sure. It came off him like a hum. I stared straight ahead, adrenaline fizzing in my fingers.

"Good travels," he said.

I nodded and tried to slip by, but he grabbed my hand. Before I could take it back, he tugged off one glove. My stomach lurched: the freeze was climbing. Unworldly white inched over my wrists.

"Hello, little Story," he said, and grinned. His teeth were thin and needle sharp.

Then I recognized it—his stink, of rot and ruin with a wild green heart. It was a scent from another lifetime. It was the sickening smell of Harold's apartment the day I'd come home to find my mother gone—here was the one who'd taken her.

Briar King. The name floated to the surface of my mind like a whisper down a phone line. The Hinterland, revealing its secrets to me. Secrets I already knew, because I was *of* it.

"You," I said.

"That's a very good start," he said. "Me?"

"You took her. Ella Proserpine. Where is she?"

He pouted at me, childish, his gaze growing dim. "Ella, Ella, Ella. I can't recall the name."

Every time his mouth formed around her name, my hands pulsed with barbed cold. "In New York, on the other side of the Halfway Wood. You took her, you left something for me—a page out of the book. *Tales from the Hinterland*."

His eyes refocused with a snap. "Oh, yes, I do remember her. Ella Proserpine, the thief. And you're the little Story girl she stole away." For just a moment, he looked troubled. "But what are you doing here? Katherine had plans for you in the Halfway Wood."

"I asked you about Ella. Where is she? What did you do to her?"

"It's hard to remember what happens out there, don't you find?" He showed his needle teeth, all at once. "Whatever I did, I assure you she liked it. That world is such a good place to have fun."

I darted forward and slammed my ice-white palm to his neck.

He gasped. Hoarfrost bloomed under my hand, crawled up his neck, snaked into his open mouth.

I wanted to see what would happen if I didn't stop. And wanting it scared me enough that I dropped my hand, breathing hard. Oh, I was cold. I was chilled through to my elbows now. I tucked them into my body like broken wings.

"What did you do to my mother?" I said it slow, so he would hear me.

The tattoos on his face had gone white; now they pulsed and juddered, warming back to black. He bared sharpened teeth at me and rolled his neck. "I can't tell you a thing, no matter what you do to me. I never remember much from out there. Though I do remember her." He shivered with pleasure. "Ella Proserpine. The blood in her *sings* to me. Her father's blood, her blood—the same. I never forget the sound, not once I've heard it."

Her father . . . Ella's father. My skin shuddered back on my bones. Ella's father died in the Village before she was born, leaving Althea a pregnant widow. Killed by a junkie, supposedly.

Or by something worse. Something shark-stupid and hungry that followed the scent of an old victim's blood, pulsing in his daughter's veins.

How much of our bad luck was him? And how much of it was the other monsters of the Hinterland, slipping in like shadows when we stayed in one place too long? I thought of the stack of newspaper clippings in Althea's sad yellow kitchen, a history of deaths kept by their accidental enabler. The Hinterland's sociopaths weren't just our bad luck, they were the curse of anyone who wandered too close to the Hazel Wood, an acid-burned wall between the worlds where terrible things crawled in.

"If you hurt my mother, I will kill you." I made my voice patient and calm. "I don't care if you're invincible here, or royalty. I'll kill you, and I'll make sure it hurts."

"She's not your mother, Alice-Three-Times," he hissed. "And I think you'd be very glad indeed if I hurt the woman who is."

Then his head twitched on his neck, the animal click of a predator scenting prey.

I followed his gaze to a point of moving green among the trees—a girl walking past us, nearly invisible in a leaf-colored dress. My stomach lurched: she stood chin up like a queen, and there was a head slung over her shoulder like a knapsack. She held it by a fistful of its bright yellow hair.

"Some of us have stories to attend to," the Briar King said. "You'll forgive me for not tending further to you."

He gave me a look that made me want to take a shower in Pine-Sol, and set off after the girl.

When he was gone I picked up the glove where he'd dropped it. Stuffed it in my pocket. Ran.

I ran like something with sharp, pointy teeth was on my trail. It took me five minutes of tearing through trees to outrun the feeling of hands grabbing at me, breath on my neck.

The Briar King. I'd touched him, but he'd touched me, too. My hands thrummed with a poisonous feeling, like I'd picked up something toxic from his skin.

When I finally stopped to breathe, bent over my knees, I realized I'd left the path behind. Before I could curse my stupidity, I looked up and saw an old woman sitting cross-legged under an apple tree.

Aside from her eyes, which were bird-black, she looked like one of the old women you see carrying mesh shopping bags full of knobby brown roots in Chinatown, right down to the pink Crocs. She eyed my bare white hand.

"Hello, child," she said.

"Hello, Grandmother," I replied, panting. I'd read enough fairy tales to know the address.

"My back aches with the weight of all my years, but I am so hungry. Would you do me a kindness and pull down an apple from that tree?"

She looked spry enough to outrun me, honestly, but I

wasn't about to argue. The tree she sat beneath winked with green apples.

"Of course, Grandmother," I said politely. The tree held its breath as I circled it, looking for a foothold. Its bark was smooth, its branches higher than my head.

"I grow weak with hunger, Granddaughter," the woman said pleasantly.

I rolled my eyes when she couldn't see me, and put one palm on the tree's trunk.

It shivered at my touch, curling its branches in like petals, then flailing them out again. A bushel's worth of apples rained down. The woman put up a pink silk parasol and waited it out. After one clocked me on the temple, I went into a hurricane crouch till they stopped.

"Thank you, Granddaughter," the old woman said dryly, as I passed her a bruised apple. She dropped the parasol and rose to her feet. Her shoes were looking less like Crocs and more like rose-colored slippers, and her track-suit unfolded into a glittering gown. Her wrinkles dropped away, leaving a face as fine-etched as a cameo.

"You were kind to me when you thought me an inconsequential old woman," she droned, like a waitress going through the specials for the last table of the night. "I will repay that kindness by granting you a wish. Only one, so choose wisely."

Despite the warnings of the Hershey's man, my mind flashed to all the wishes I might ask for. Answers, for one. A magic mirror, to find Ella. Seven-league boots. Finch, alive beside me—but I didn't think her powers stretched as far as that. So I sighed and followed his advice. "Send me to Janet."

Her face fell. "Huh. Too easy." She grabbed my shoulders, turned me around, and shoved. I stumbled forward. For a moment the world blinked around me like a camera shutter. I fell not onto grass but cobblestones.

Traveling around the Hazel Wood had given me vertigo, but this felt different. It felt exhilarating. When I looked up, I was standing in front of the red-painted door of a pretty cottage. The woods were at my back, and it was nearly night.

~25~

Without trees in the way, I could see the sky. The moon's face was clearer here, that of a beautiful woman with grief lines around her eyes and mouth. Stars tried to crowd in around her, but she kept them at a distance.

The door clicked open, letting out flickering warm light and the civilized smell of cooking meat. The woman who stood in the doorway looked farm strong and fiftyish, her hair in a fat, chest-length blonde braid pulled over one shoulder. She eyed me with open displeasure.

"Are you Janet?" I asked at the same time she yelled, "Janet, one of your strays!" Then, "Make yourself welcome." She said it grudgingly, standing away from the door.

I walked into a room so warm with food and fire I

could've cried. I nearly stretched my hands toward the blaze in the open hearth on one end of the large, plain room, before remembering and fumbling the glove onto my bare hand behind my back.

"Look at that," she said. My heart jumped, but she was inspecting the ink that showed over my collar—the top of my spiky tattoo. "How does a new arrival have a Hinterland flower on her skin?" Her voice rang with a stronger version of the clipped accent I'd heard on the Hershey's man.

"I didn't know it was a Hinterland flower." But it made sense. I'd always been fascinated by the piece of alien flora climbing my mother's arm, and never understood her horror when I had it inked on my own in tribute. Now I got it: this place was in me, of me. The tattoo meant she had to see it *on* me, too.

"Let her breathe a minute, Tam, she just got here." The woman who said it had come through a door in the back of the room. She wore overalls that were more patches than denim, and her wet, graying hair hung loose down her back.

"You're Janet."

"I am. And this is my Tam Lin. Though you can call her Ingrid." She gestured at the blonde, who'd come protectively to her side.

I nodded to show I got the reference, though I wondered what their story was, that it fit. "Someone told me you were the one to see, if I were a refugee."

"Someone was right, *if* you're a refugee. I'll admit the tattoo is surprising. You're sure you're a new arrival?" Her voice was good-natured, but her eyes were sharp. She took in the gloves I was wearing, the cheap, shiny material of my new jeans, whatever was left of the eyeliner I'd put on that morning.

"I'm sure."

Ingrid muttered a word I'd never heard before, in a voice I didn't like.

"Here." From a cabinet against the wall Janet pulled out an opaque bottle and three thin-necked glasses, laying them out on a wooden table that had had a former life as a stump. She opened the bottle and poured an inch of liquid into each. It hit the glass like vapor, then resolved into something clear and colorless. "Ingrid will like you better if we drink to our friendship first."

Janet was better at subterfuge than her girlfriend. She lifted a glass easily, but Ingrid gripped hers like it was a bomb, watching carefully to see if I would take a sip.

I'd lost my fear of fairy food since Althea told me a bedtime story in the dark, but that didn't mean I wanted to drink something that was probably brewed in a bathtub. "Is it poison?" I asked.

Janet grinned. "You've a wretched poker face, Tam. Here, look—to your health." She took a swig, pressed her lips together.

I sniffed mine—no scent—and did the same. It passed over my tongue like water, but landed in my chest like liquor. Then the taste hit. "Apple Jolly Ranchers," I said, confused. They were my favorite candy when I was little. "Or, wait. Flowers. Violet candies. No, no, it's like butterscotch sauce." I saw Ella, simmering sugar and butter in the pan. "Now it's sort of, God, it tastes like a latte." Specifically, the off-menu kind I made for myself at Salty

Dog, with honey and lavender syrup. I felt like Violet Beauregarde, babbling about what she was tasting right before she blew up like a blueberry. "What is that stuff?" I gasped.

"Truth serum, more or less." Janet smiled sympathetically at my expression. "We might've believed you without it, dear, but this keeps everyone honest."

"But you took it, too."

"We don't have many secrets between us, Tam and I. And it's more sportsmanlike this way. You look like absolute hell, I have to say. Maybe let that mess on your head grow out a bit." She clapped a hand over her mouth.

"It works quick," I said dryly.

"You're a pretty girl," she amended. "But you could do with a bath and a night's sleep."

"A year's sleep, you mean." Then I squashed my mouth shut, before all kinds of observations popped out. *You look like you should be on a crystal healing retreat in Ithaca. Did you know your house smells like fire and blood?*

"Where did you come from, and why? You can give us the short version." Ingrid's tone was clipped.

"No fair," I said. "She didn't drink any."

"Chop more firewood for us, love?" Janet said. It was only half a question.

Ingrid stood, grudgingly. "First, tell me you haven't any bad intentions here, or any plan to hurt either of us."

"I don't want to hurt you."

"Saying what you *want* is a dodge. State your intentions."

"I have no intention of hurting either of you. Or anyone else. Oh!" I grabbed at my stomach—something twisted there, as I thought about the Briar King. About the monsters who'd killed Finch and left me in the woods. "Maybe there's somebody I'd hurt," I amended, "but they're not here."

That seemed to satisfy Ingrid; she grabbed a waxy-looking coat from a peg and let herself out.

"She's protective of you," I said. "It must be nice."

Janet lifted one shoulder, dropped it. "I made my way here alone for a long while. It took some time to find my place. It took more time to become somebody worth protecting." She sat down in one of the squashy chairs before the fire, and I sat in the other.

"God, this thing smells like a wet dog," I said, and bit my lip.

She smiled faintly. "Did you or did you not arrive here today?"

"I did."

"And it's your first time here?"

I hesitated. "I can't remember ever being here."

Her raised eyebrow told me she caught the dodge. "As you may have gathered, my home is a sort of way station for new arrivals. People come here from your world—my world, once—by various means, sometimes accidental but more often on purpose. I've made it my job to welcome them, warn them, and keep track of them. The numbers get a bit dodgy, of course, what with all the things you can fall into or get eaten by. I do my best. They come from other worlds, too, but that's not my problem. There's precious little mixing between refugee groups, less than you'd think for such a small place, but . . . you look like you have a question."

"How big is it?" I blurted. "*What* is it? What's beyond it? Did you come on purpose? Is there any way to go back? And how do people become ex-Story?"

She held up a hand to stop me. "It's quite small. As small as it can be, considering its borders are shifting, un-mappable, and nearly impossible to reach. It's a kingdom of sorts, but it has many queens and many kings. As far as what's beyond it, I couldn't say. I did come here on pur-pose, God help me, and yes, there are ways back. People become ex-Story when their tales are no longer being told. Sometimes it kills them, sometimes it drives them mad, and sometimes they adjust to it nicely and assimi-late into the general population. Them I don't keep track of, though I do like to know when there's intermarriage. Their children, when they have them, tend to find their way into trouble—or into stories, which I suppose is the same thing. Now, tell me *your* story, as short or as long as you like."

I barely had time to open my mouth before I was talk-ing. Whatever she'd had me drink made the words feel like water pouring from a faucet. While I talked, I kept a dim flicker of hope in the back of my mind: that maybe, if I had enough to say, I could keep from telling her the one thing I wanted to keep a secret. At least for now, until I knew how she'd take to having a Story sitting in front of her fire. Curling my white fingers in their gloves, I told Janet about Ella, about Harold and New York and com-ing home to find her gone. I backtracked and told her about Althea's supposed death—referring to her as my mother's mother, close enough to the truth for the truth serum to bear—before jumping forward again to tell her about Ellery Finch, my night in the woods, my hours or days in the Hazel Wood. It was such a relief to speak that it took me a while to notice her face had gone ashen under the warm color of her skin.

"And I met a man on the path," I said, and faltered. Janet's hands gripped the arms of the chair, and her eyes looked past me.

She shook her head, trying to smile, then gave it up. "You said you're Althea's granddaughter. Althea Proserpine."

"You've heard of her? Have you read her book?"

"No, thankfully. Not a single copy can be found within the Hinterland's borders. I imagine you'd be thrown to the Night Women if you tried to bring one in. But I did know her—back there. On Earth. Althea was . . . hmm." Janet fumbled with something at her wrist, a narrow string of blue beads. Her fingers moved fretfully, making them flash in the firelight. "We came here together," she said finally.

"Wait, *what*?" She looked older than Ella but not nearly as old as Althea. Yet she'd been in the Hinterland for . . . "Fifty years ago you came here? With Althea?"

"*Fifty*, you said? Fifty years have passed out there?" She laughed a little frantically. "I always imagined I'd—well, maybe I knew I never would, but—I suppose it's a near certainty my parents are dead, isn't it? Fifty years, that's well into the new century, yes?"

I had a brief, dizzying desire to wow her with news of the internet but decided it mattered not at all. "Tell me about Althea," I said instead.

"Oh, how can I make it quick? How about this: she made a dark deal, and it ripped holes in the curtain that keeps the worlds apart."

"That sounds a little dramatic," said my truth-drunk tongue.

"It was pretty goddamned dramatic," she snapped. "She didn't even offer to take me back with her, the selfish bitch."

"Oh," I said softly. "She was your . . . you were together?"

"Well, don't weep for me," Janet said dismissively. "She was a day-tripper. She mainly liked me for what I could do for her. We had fun, but it never would've lasted longer than the summer."

"The summer Althea found her way into the Hinterland."

"Of course. We met at a bar in Budapest—she was a pretty American tourist who'd run away from her friends. I was an idiot who never could resist a tough girl. I told her about my fieldwork, and she decided over the course of a cheap bottle that she had to come with me." Her eyes went unfocused; she plucked the string of her bracelet like a zither.

"Your fieldwork?"

"Doors. Doors between worlds. I started out doing coursework in fairy tales—my parents were professors, my mother at a time when it was rare for a woman to make it as far as she did—but the theoretical became quite real when I found a door in a book."

"Not metaphorically speaking, I'm guessing."

"Not at all. Most books' power is in the abstract, but occasionally you'll find one with very physical abilities. It was your average fairyland door, quite disappointing if you grew up imagining fairies as air sprites or woodland types—I was stuck underground most of the time. Once I got out again, months later in real time, I was hooked. I dropped the idea of getting a degree and went *very* hands-on." Janet had the same strange Hinterland accent Ingrid did, but the more she talked about her past, the more the British in her came out.

"And you told Althea about the Hinterland door," I prompted.

"I did. That kind of knowledge was around if you could pay the right price, which I could—knowledge buys knowledge, and a pretty girl of twenty-six has other currency, too." She pursed her lips and looked prudish for a minute, daring me to judge her. When she saw I wouldn't, she continued.

"I was celebrating a very promising lead when I met Althea, and between the liquor and her loveliness, I had loose lips. God, I'm glad I sent Tam out, she'd hate to hear this." She shot a nervous glance toward the door.

"Anyway, I told her—too much. By the next morning, I already had regrets, but I couldn't put her off. But she had a . . . she seemed to have the right spirit for it. Pilgrim soul and all. It was a whirlwind, the weeks we spent planning. Buying supplies, sourcing objects we thought we'd need—cloud powders, books, waterproof boots, a very expensive magical compass that, it turned out, worked in neither this world nor the last. We fell in love, or so I thought, and she never seemed to have a doubt about the Hinterland. I should've been suspicious, I know. I'd had years to get used to the idea of leaving the world behind.

I'd cut my ties rather harshly. But she did it spontaneously. Thoughtlessly. That came clear when we got here. Painfully so."

The door creaked open, letting in cold air and the spicy smell of the Hinterland woods. Janet went quiet and watched Ingrid come in, something complicated in her eyes.

Ingrid dropped a heavy armful of split logs in front of the fireplace. "Your refugee is staying the night, then?" she asked, feeding one into the flames.

"Of course she is," Janet said sharply. "Ingrid, you're such a snob. I was a refugee myself once, you ever think of that?"

Ingrid shook her head without responding.

"That's the real problem with the Hinterland," Janet said, ostensibly to me. "Nobody here has a goddamned sense of humor. Or a god, for that matter. Maybe you need one to have the other. The sense of being at someone's mercy, so you can laugh about it." She laughed like she was giving a demonstration.

"You're tired," Ingrid said without turning around.

"Too much truth for her," Janet informed me.

I felt like I did the night I'd watched Ella get drunk on sherry and rip into Harold. It was two weeks after the wedding, and her wifey mask was starting to slip.

"You said Althea made a, um, dark deal to get out of here," I said, trying to get the conversation back on track. "What was it?"

Ingrid turned around on her knees, eyebrows up. "What are you doing talking about that one? Where's she come into it?"

"Alice is Althea's granddaughter," Janet replied regally. "And she's the one who brought her up, not me."

"A large coincidence, that is. I'm sure you hate having the excuse to talk about her." But Ingrid said it without rancor, moving to stand behind Janet and rest her hands on her shoulders.

"What was the deal?" I repeated.

"What, so you can make the same one?"

"No, so I can . . ." I winced, grabbing my stomach. When I tried to lie, the stuff I'd swallowed twisted around in there like a snake made of acid.

"Oh, just tell her," Ingrid said. "The damage is done, and she'll hear a twisted version of it if she has to ask elsewhere. Everyone hears about the Spinner, sooner or later."

"I'd rather it be later," Janet muttered. She turned her cheek into Ingrid's hand and sighed. "Things were bad here for Althea. There wasn't someone like me yet, to tell us what to do, and there were very few refugees then. We had to find our way, painfully and slowly. She ran out of whiskey first, then cigarettes, then books to read, and the poor thing *ran* on all three. Think of a bored child on holiday, but imagine that holiday is forever. Until boredom made her do something very stupid."

"What was that?"

"She started following the Stories. I don't know how she managed to do it without being killed, but she did. She talked to the characters in the margins for the bits she couldn't witness—the nursemaids, the middle sisters. She communed with dead kings and murdered wives; all those poor shades haunting the edges of things, desperate to talk. Then she'd come home and tell them to me. 'I'm a journalist,' she'd say. 'This is what I do.'" Janet scoffed. "Like she'd been doing war reporting, instead of writing about what to wear to hunt a husband."

Something broken in me ached at her words—a world ago, Finch had described Althea as writing like a war reporter. I wished I could tell him he'd been right.

"Eventually, of course, she followed the stories to their source," Janet continued. "The Story Spinner."

I heard the reverent space she put around the words, the capital S's. She said they didn't have a god here, but maybe this was something close. "Who's the Story Spinner?"

"It's in the name, isn't it? In this place, it might as well be World Builder. She's as good as. Story is the fabric of the Hinterland. Althea convinced the Spinner to make her a story she could use like a bridge. And then she just"—Janet tiptoed her fingers up the air—"climbed it right out of here."

"She climbed—what? Words? That doesn't make any sense."

Ingrid eyed me oddly, but Janet cracked a smile. "Sense," she said. "The last bastion of the struggling refugee."

"So she made her way back. Fine. But how did that—what did you say? Rip holes in the world?"

Surprisingly, it was Ingrid who replied. "It started just before I met Janet. People from that world slipping in, those from this one slipping out. At first we thought it was new stories getting started. It happens from time to time—girls get abducted by kings, mothers murder their sons. Then we wondered whether there were doors opening onto other worlds, or hells." Her Hinterland accent was clipped and compelling. It made me think of the dark shapes of icebergs, the light of a cold white sun.

"But rumor came of a place in the woods, a thin place where you could walk right out and back in again. It was discovered by a prince, a fourth son out of seven—his parents and his youngest brother were Stories, but he wasn't. He put it under guard for a while, until he and his men were killed by the Briar King. Then things got much worse."

"Worse how?"

"Stories started using the door, when they could sneak away. They like to cause trouble in your world."

"How was that Althea's fault?"

"*Tales from the Hinterland*," Janet said bitterly. "She took the stuff that makes this world run and put it into a book, a book that got printed and shipped all over her world. The stories were read, they stuck in people's brains, they got told and retold and dreamed about. New bridges were built—fragile, uncontrollable things between the worlds. Most of them were one-ways, rifts where people who loved the stories found their way through. I never understood what made the Briar King's door so stable, but now I see—it's on the other side of Althea's Hazel Wood."

"She was trying to contain it," I said, unsure why I was trying to defend her. "She thought if she stayed in one place, and shut herself off, it would be better than leading them around the world."

"If she was really so considerate, she would've killed herself," Janet said bluntly. "We've had refugees as young as ten, little girls obsessed with fairy tales, and now they're stuck living at the fringes of them."

"Couldn't the Story Spinner do something? Send them home?"

"You think she'd take that risk again? She's been too busy trying to reverse what's been done. The only people she sends through now are working for her, trying to clean up Althea's mess. A few of the lost find their way back home on that errand—they track down copies of the book and destroy them. But, intentionally or not, Althea has made herself into a lesser Spinner. My guess is she doesn't know how to control it. Every copy of her foolish book could be ash, and she would still serve as a bridge."

"I think she wanted to," I said, low. "Kill herself, I mean. That's why she wanted me back—as long as I was out there, she couldn't . . ." Then I stopped short, remembering what they didn't know about me. The words sat on my tongue, burned my stomach when I swallowed them down.

"Wanted you back? What do you mean, she wanted you *back*?" Janet eyed me, sharp as a terrier.

"She . . ." I clutched my stomach. "It's none of your business!"

"Yes, it is. Answer me, and the pain will stop: who are you?"

My stomach stopped burning the instant I pulled off the gloves, laying them flat across my knees. They looked like the hands of a corpse, but flexing, eerie, alive. Ingrid gasped so hard it was funny and moved in front of Janet. Janet just looked at me like I was Christmas and the Fourth of July wrapped up in one.

"My god. You're not anybody's granddaughter, you're

the prodigal returned. No wonder she pushed you back through!"

"You know who I am?"

"Everyone knows who you are. You're almost as bad as Althea—you're like a seam ripper moving around out there, letting the beasties through. Not that they manage out there long. None of the Stories can, but you." Her eyes were alert; I could practically see her brain ticking. Suddenly I could see her at twenty-six, beautiful and quick and squeezing people for information on the doors between the worlds. "Alice-Three-Times. How did you do it?"

"I didn't do anything. My . . . Ella. Althea's daughter. She took me when I was a baby, from the Halfway Wood. Then she just ran with me. We moved a lot—bad things happened when we stood still. What do you mean, I'm a seam ripper?"

"Ella Proserpine. I remember hearing about her, even before she took you. Poor thing grew up wild in the Halfway Wood, in and out between worlds. She's probably half mad by now." Her eyes widened as she took in my expression. "Oh. What an idiot I am. All these years later—she must be like a mother to you."

"She *is* my mother." It was painful to think of Ella now—the narrow shape of her, always too skinny, the delicate face and ant-black hair inherited from a dead man. Her life in three sharp pieces, two of them nearly unknowable: The broken puzzle of the Hazel Wood. The perilous fringes of the Hinterland. And an escape that was its own kind of trap—a fugitive's life on the road.

"Yes. Of course. She would've had to be, to do this for

you. To take you away and *keep* you away—how curious." Janet's eyes were distant. "Do you know your story? 'Alice-Three-Times'?"

"Part of it."

"The leaps. In your age. Did they happen out there?"

Ella kept a stack of Polaroids in a fireproof metal box in our car's glove compartment. Me stone-faced at age two, solemn at eight, glowering at fourteen. Me in the ocean, me on a bike, me with my fingers dipped in sugar water, reaching for a butterfly.

I shook my head. "No. I just grew up."

Janet bit her nail, looking about nineteen. "So she pulled you onto another clock, and held you there. Maybe that's it." She sat up and held her fingers out straight, hovering them just over mine. "Tam, bring us a bowl of water. Alice, can I touch your hands?"

I nodded, and she brought her fingers lightly down on mine. She winced and drew them back. When Ingrid brought the water in a shallow clay dish, Janet told me to dip my fingers in.

I did. Nothing happened.

"Tell me again about Althea," Janet said. "You say she was absent all your life?"

"Absent is a strong way to put it. I just . . . never met her."

"Hmm. That boy you told me about. Ellery Finch."

A beat. "What about him?"

"He was killed in front of you." Her voice was cool. "And you did nothing to stop it. Could you have stopped it?"

The liquor was still working on me, and it made the

words come before I could think. "I could have. I'm Alice-Three-Times, aren't I? I think I could have."

The words glittered in the air like gnats. I brought one wet hand to my mouth.

"I'm sorry," Janet said, and she really looked it. "That was a stupid question. And 'truth serum' wasn't the most precise way to put it. It's more like—it works on what you think you know, not what's necessarily *true* . . ."

Her sympathy closed in on me like smoke. "Don't try to make me feel better about this. And don't talk to me like I'm a child!" My voice went hard, and the water where my right hand still sat ran with ribbons of crackling freeze, hardening all the way up the sides of the bowl.

"Dammit!" I pulled my fingers out, rubbing them raw against new ice. Ingrid looked at me with frank awe, like I was a household saint. The patron saint of cold drinks, maybe.

"*Dammit,*" I said again. "How am I supposed to shower?"

"You have bigger problems, I think." Janet studied me, her eyes faraway. "Alice, roll up your sleeves."

I pushed them back tentatively, then quicker as horror flooded my heart, finally ripping the sweatshirt off over my head.

My arms were death-white to the shoulders. They looked like mannequin limbs, like deep-water creatures, like nothing that belonged to me.

I thought of the Briar King, gasping as my cold swept through him. What would happen when it climbed higher? Toward my throat? Into my lungs? My breath came short and fast.

Janet moved behind me, placed a comforting hand on my neck, where hopefully my skin still looked like skin. "Don't panic. If anything, it'll make it spread quicker."

"The Spinner will know what to do," Ingrid said. Her shoulders were hunched respectfully; I was worried she might try to genuflect in my direction.

"Maybe so. Alice, you'll go to the Spinner in the morning."

"Go where?"

"Hard to say. But if the Spinner wants to speak with you, it'll happen."

I had a horrific image of a giant spider in a sticky web. "Wait. The Spinner is *human*, right?"

Janet wiggled her hand in the air. "Eh. Again, hard to say."

"I'm sorry." I said it to Ingrid. Fear had chased the anger away, and now I just felt meek. "For bringing this into your home."

"That's good," Janet said comfortingly. "That means your mind is still your own."

Then she patted me and stepped away, her voice going brisk. "Enough stories for tonight. And enough Stories. The best thing you can do now is eat something and try to get some sleep. And wash yourself. You're riper than cheese."

I didn't think that was the truth serum talking. It was just the truth.

~26~

Ellery Finch was in my dreams that night, alive then dead, and trying desperately to tell me something. Plumes of red smoke unrolled from his tongue when he opened his mouth. Twice-Killed Katherine whispered in my ear, and the green ground of the Hinterland rose up to meet me. I slammed into waking on a worn-out sleeping bag in front of the fire.

The first thing I did was sit up straight and peel off my shirt. The white had inched up my shoulders some, but it hadn't reached my neck. I could still hide it away. I stood gingerly, as if moving too quickly might cause the freeze to spill over into my chest. Soon enough it would, I guessed, no matter how carefully I moved. When I pressed two fingers gently to my sternum it made my heart feel like it had brain freeze.

I could hear the companionable sounds of Janet and Ingrid in the next room, making food and talking low, laughing. Ingrid stepped lively when she saw me, handing me a mug of something that looked like coffee but smelled and tasted like kasha. She watched me like I might freeze her heart in her chest, or spit up diamonds.

Janet's instructions for finding the Spinner were frustratingly vague. "Let it be known that you're in this world, and the Spinner will find you," she said. "It's very likely the Spinner already knows."

The dodgy pronouns still had me convinced I was walking right into Ron Weasley's worst nightmare. "So I walk around yelling, *'It's me, Alice! I'm back!'*?"

"Don't be ridiculous." Ingrid startled at Janet's tone, watching me like I might take offense. "You just . . . let your sense of this world take over. It doesn't matter where you've spent your life, you are *of* this place. Stop thinking of yourself as a tourist."

She gave me a clean tunic thing to replace my ripped, disgusting sweatshirt, but I refused to part with my jeans. Just slipping them back on made me feel more human. More *Earth* human. When I finally left the cottage, giving Janet a grateful hug that made Ingrid very nervous, they lingered in the doorway like they were sending me off to school.

I walked toward the trees, shifting and whispering in the rinsed morning light. When I got close their whispering resolved, for a moment, into words.

Not this way.

I stopped short. A sweet release started in my limbs, the feeling a tree must get in spring, when its sap unfreezes and starts to run. When I blinked, I could see faces in the bark—funny ones, wizened ones, lovely ones. I blinked again and it passed, but the *feeling* remained. Following some inner compass, I turned away from the woods, walking back toward the cottage, then past it.

I didn't know from acres, but Janet and Ingrid's cottage backed onto enough cleared land that it took me at least ten minutes to cross it. It was covered in rambling vegetable gardens, an orchard of fruit trees, outbuildings, and long stretches of meadow where goats ripped at grass or watched me with their oblong eyes. I got the feeling they could talk to me if they chose, but they had nothing to say.

At the end of the property was a low white fence, and beyond that a dirt road. I hopped the fence and turned left. A girl in cutoffs passed me on a bicycle. When I turned to watch her go, she was watching me, too, peering back over her shoulder.

The road ambled along between stands of green. I tried to clear my mind and hold on to the feeling that had put me on this path, with mixed luck. I was always shit at meditation, no matter how often Ella made me try it. I smelled salt on the air and almost turned toward it— somewhere, not too far away, was a fairy-tale sea. But the Hinterland sense humming through me said it wasn't the place I needed to go.

Once, through the trees, I saw a woman who looked like a sleepwalker, beautiful and wearing a blood-colored dress. Her hooded eyes met mine with interest, and she gave a tiny tilt of her head. It filled me with a stupid pleasure. *It's just like one Prius driver nodding to another,* I told myself, but it was more than that. Something had changed since yesterday—I wasn't lost. When the ground suddenly dipped, tipping my step down into a bowl of grass dotted with creamy pink blossoms, I felt like I'd seen it before. And when I came upon a boy all in white lying fast asleep, curled around a silver mirror, I felt like I'd been expecting him. The air around him was thick with magic, shimmering like a mirage over a hot black road. I tiptoed around his body and back up the other side.

I passed a few cottages, an army-green all-weather tent, and a lean-to made of flowering branches. Beneath it sheltered two long-haired children, who watched me pass with hopeless eyes. I hurried my step, thinking they were Stories, but once they were out of sight I wasn't so sure. When I saw a Tudor-style tavern on a patch of overgrown grass, I couldn't tell if it was curiosity or instinct that made me stop.

Judging by the sun, it wasn't even noon yet, but the place was nearly full. When I walked in, less than half the heads bothered turning.

It was, without a doubt, a refugee bar. The crowd looked like the backpackers at a European hostel crossed with the cast of Medieval Times. I saw Converse sneakers and backpacks, peasant skirts and blue jeans. A girl wearing a tunic similar to mine was holding an ancient flip phone in her hand, rubbing a thumb over it like it was a good-luck charm.

The bartender was a massive man wearing a dashiki and an impressive brown beard. When I bellied up to the bar, he was whistling a Beatles song.

"Hi," he said. "What'll it be?" His accent was French, I thought. With a touch of Hinterland laid over it.

"What do you have?"

He eyed me hungrily. "New arrival, is it?" His voice carried, and I sensed a ripple of interest in the room. "For you, I've got coffee, *real* coffee, but only if you can pay."

My hands went automatically to my pockets, empty.

"Not in money," he said. "In information."

"About what?" I asked guardedly.

He arched a dark brow and leaned over the bar. This man looked like a Story, but the air around him was thin and breathable, and he smelled like nothing but hops and sweat. "About the world, of course. Ours."

I had my gloves on and my sleeves pulled down low. "What do you want to know?"

"To start, what year you're from. Then you get a drink on the house for every post-1972 song you can sing from start to finish. A free meal for each if you let me record you."

"Leave her be." A second bartender straightened up from where she'd been crouched behind the bar. "New house rule: no accosting new arrivals till their second time in the bar."

She smiled at me. Her hair was yellow, and she wore an honest-to-God dirndl that pushed her breasts up. She looked like the St. Pauli girl.

"First drink's on the house, newbie," she said.

"But no coffee," the bearded guy protested. "That's only for trades."

"Fine. Tea okay?" She turned and started pouring before I could respond. The tea was a thin brew the color of

Mountain Dew. It smelled like pine needles but tasted pleasantly mild.

"Thanks," I said, trying to peel my eyes off her hoisted chest. The other bartender did not make the same effort. He watched as she hopped over the bar and started gathering mugs and plates from the rickety tables, then spoke to me under his breath.

"Seriously, though. What year is it?"

I told him, and his mouth drew down at the corners. "Oh," he said bravely. "Well. Did you bring any books with you?"

The other bartender overheard him and rolled her eyes, disappearing through a door behind the bar.

So I told him the plot of Harry Potter. And *The Golden Compass*. He plied me with free cups of a buttery yellow beer that tasted exactly like kiwis, and I sang rustily for his recorder—"Smells Like Teen Spirit," "Landslide," "Billie Jean." The recorder looked like something Alexander Graham Bell might've used, a jerry-rigged contraption of tubes, exposed wiring, and a skinny arm scribbling over a soft metal plate.

He saw me looking. "I don't know how it works," he confessed, flipping it over to show me its empty insides. "It shouldn't."

By then a small crowd had gathered around us, including a bronze-skinned woman with a drowsy, just-woken air to her, whom I read immediately as ex-Story. She was accompanied by a boy of about fifteen, wearing hip plastic glasses. An old man in an antique suit sipped endless mugs of bright green tea and listened to my singing attentively, flashing a parchment-colored smile. There were two barefoot dudes who looked like they'd stumbled in straight from Burning Man and put me on edge. They wore twinned expressions of total peace, but the whites of their eyes were shot through with red. The flora might be different here, but *some*thing growing nearby could make you high.

People drifted in and out, and the bartender—his name was Alain, and I had it wrong, he was Swiss—served me a plate of flatbread and stew spiced with something that caught at my throat. The shadows grew long over the bar, until finally he sighed and grabbed a leather satchel from the floor.

"I'm off," he said. "You're back to Janet's tonight?" I'd told him where I came from, though not what I was after. He and everyone else in the bar seemed to know Janet.

I shrugged noncommittally and stretched, reaching inward for the otherworldly sense that drove me here. It twitched to life, half-drowned by liquor and talk and human connection. I'd kept my gloves on, and it almost let me forget I didn't belong with these people. Unless I could figure out how to become ex-Story, this wasn't my Hinterland. These weren't my kind.

And if I couldn't figure it out?

I could stay. The thought ghosted up from the part of my brain that plugged into the Hinterland like it was a mainframe. It carried with it a hard beat of fear, but beneath it, something else: surrender. After a life of running, always running. Meditating and counting and clinging to Ella's hands in an effort to stay afloat on an oceanic anger.

I could do it, I thought. If I let myself believe Ella wasn't back there waiting for me.

But if I let myself believe that, I would drown for good.

After Alain left, the blonde bartender put stubby candles out on the tables, like she was in a Brooklyn restaurant preparing for dinner service. But as I watched her, I realized there was more to it. Something was happening around her hands, some trick of the light. As she moved from table to table, putting the candles down, she flicked her fingers in complicated patterns, like she was signing or weaving or moving them into place for cat's cradle. One by one, the people at the tables got up and left without a word, grabbing their stuff, dropping money, and slipping out into the night.

When the last one left, she sighed and pulled the clip from her hair, massaging her scalp as it fell to her shoulders. She had fairy princess hair, like mine would be if I let it grow out.

She slipped onto the barstool next to mine and tapped the back of my glove with one finger. "Hello, Alice-Three-Times."

Her voice was throaty and low, and even through the gloves her touch sent a line of pale fire from my fingertips to my shoulders.

I pulled them off, stretched my fingers so the bones cracked. "I've been looking for you, I think."

She laughed. "I've been looking for you longer."

I *saw* her now that she wasn't masquerading as a bartender. I felt her tight-packed energy, so fierce it almost distorted the air around her. Her eyes were too close to mine, too focused, two blue saucers that ate up light. I didn't let myself look away.

"What did you do, to make them all leave? Was it magic?"

"Nothing so unpredictable as that. I just . . . tweaked the narrative. Made it the right time for them to go."

"So you control everyone here? Not just the Stories?"

The Story Spinner pushed up on her elbows, pulled herself a pint of something bubbly from across the bar. "I don't have to control anyone, least of all the Stories. Once I set them going, they're like clockwork. A self-contained engine." She looked at me dryly. "Well. Usually. What I do is keep the threads untangled, keep the realms separate, make sure the stories have room to unfold. But *you*"—she pointed a finger gun at me; I wondered for an aimless moment whether the Hinterland had guns—"are the hitch in the clockwork. Is it too much to hope that you came back to finish your story?"

This, I realized, was Althea's *she*. The one who wouldn't let Althea die, who let her go once and regretted it. She wouldn't make the same mistake twice.

"Can I? Finish it, I mean? If that's all you need me to do before I go, then I'll do it." I didn't know what I was promising, or what it might mean, but what she said made it sound finite. Like maybe I could make a deal.

Her eyes took the measure of me, a quick water-blue assessment that made me feel like a bolt of cloth or a coffee cup. Just for a moment, before they dropped like mercury into soft sympathy.

Don't trust her, then. Though that was already clear.

"When you finish a story," she said patiently, "it begins again. Until I stop telling it. And while they're being told, stories create the energy that makes this world go. They keep our stars in place. They make our grass grow."

"Are *you* a Story? Or an ex-Story?"

"I'm not from here. I'm not from there, either," she added, before I could ask.

A third place, then. The idea plucked at the edges of my brain. I imagined a whole universe of worlds floating in an unfathomable vastness, like lentils scattered through ashes. It was such a lonely vision it made my chest ache.

"Are you going to let me go home?" I whispered.

"Oh, Alice." The regret in her voice sounded real. "Look at yourself—at your hands. It'll reach your mind soon, you know. It'll reach your heart. They've been waiting a very long time for you to come back—the queen, the king. And stasis is worse than stories, they say." She laughed, like what she'd said was funny.

"You say stories run until you stop telling them," I said wildly. "Can't you just decide, then? To stop telling mine—to let me go?"

"What about the Hinterland makes you think I'm *nice*?" She drank half her beer down, leaned in. "I did a favor for a woman once—a spinner in her own way, I have a soft spot for my kind—and look where it got me. Rules exist for a reason. But. *But*." She held up a finger. "You can't finish your story, but you can change it. *Technically* speaking, you can. You can choose another ending, and destabilize it from the inside. If you fail to close the loop, finish it right, the story might let you go. In theory."

"I can do that," I said quickly. "I'll do that. I could go home, if I manage to do that?"

She rested her chin on her hand, eyes hooked on me

like I was an experiment. "It's a big if. But yes, perhaps you could. If that's the new ending you chose."

"How do I do it? Where do I start?"

"Where do all these things start? *Once upon a time.* And you just . . . go from there."

Something struck me—Finch had never finished telling me my story. "But what if I don't know how it ends? 'Alice-Three-Times,' I mean?"

"Maybe your odds will be better that way. Or, more likely, the ending will find you. And then you'll begin again. Even if you did manage to break it, and leave this place behind, don't forget—time works differently than you think it does. There's no guaranteeing you'll recognize the world you're trying to return to."

I flashed on an image of hovercars and robot politicians, Ella long dead and myself a relic of a time known only in books. "There's *some* chance I'll get back to my own time, isn't there?" I asked, pathetically. "Even if it's slight?"

The Spinner looked at me like she knew exactly how my story would end—in more ways than one—but was just curious enough to see it unfold for herself. She swallowed the last of her drink, throat working in a python pulse, and stood. "Come with me."

~27~

I followed, leaving my gloves on the bar. I knew without looking that the freeze was spreading; I could feel an itchy flutter over the skin of my neck.

She led me behind the bar and through the swinging doors. If I'd thought about it, I would've expected them to open onto a back room like the one at Salty Dog—boxes, coats, maybe a messy desk.

But they led straight out onto a cobblestone street. It was empty, lit by the moon peering between rooftops. Across the way was a shop window warm with candles, their flames making the toys behind the glass glimmer. There were puppets and instruments and a lake of blue tin, crossed in tidy arcs by tiny tin skaters. Masks, hoops, a carnival doll in aged lace with a face of polished wood. At the center of it all stood a model castle that looked like a wedding cake. I could see movement in its tiny windows. I took a step closer, and the Spinner stopped me with a hand.

"Don't get too excited. That's not your story."

As I turned away, something moved in the darkness beyond the window display—a shape too long and slender to be human. I shrank back, following the Spinner.

Propped against the wall of the bar were two bicycles. She climbed on one and I took the other—a vintage beast, heavy as hell with soft, underfilled tires.

"Go quiet," said the Spinner, her whisper carrying back to me, "and don't interfere."

It was a good warning. The village we rode through was sleeping, but it was filled with wakeful things.

We rode past a house that hung too close over the road, as if it had outgrown its lot. Three women moved like mist around its eaves, reaching up to tap their fingernails against its windows. One looked around at me, her eyes pale marbles, and I pedaled faster. A few streets down, a small figure in a nightgown lay on the very edge of a rooftop, arms reaching toward the moon and one foot hanging down to kick at nothing. I saw her for a moment and wondered if she was Hansa.

At the village's edge sat its largest, loveliest house, backed by a long, torchlit garden. In it a boy paced and held his head and spoke to the air. I could see the barest shimmer in it, could almost make out who or what he spoke to, before we wheeled past into dark.

The road that carried us out of town was glittering red dirt. The moon hit it at funny angles, throwing spangled bits of light into my eyes.

"Stay on the path," the Spinner said, "no matter what we see in the woods."

Her voice had changed. She was still a figure on a blue bicycle, but her speech was low and rough, and the shape of her had swelled.

She grinned back at me, white teeth in a hard, unfamiliar face. "Best not to go through the woods looking like a tavern wench. Too tempting for some of the stupider Stories."

I kept my eyes on her back awhile, watching for another change, but the woods were distracting. The trees woke up as they scented the Spinner. They thrashed their branches, filling the air with their thick, resinous breath. It got into my nose and under my skin and made me question my reasons for following this stranger through the fairy-tale woods.

For Ella, I reminded myself. To finish my story.

But she couldn't have felt further away.

The road changed to white stone and narrowed, snaking like a necklace through the boiling heads of the trees. I was slicked with sweat and stuck all over with leaves that bleached pale as they fell. None of them landed on the Spinner.

A sudden metronome beat rose from the swirl of trees and night. It filled my chest like a heartbeat and threw off the rhythm of my breath.

"What *is* that?"

The Spinner braked just off the road. I stopped beside

her and looked at the side of her face. The blue eyes were the same, but her features were heavy and blunt.

"Don't watch me, watch the road."

Down the path of white stones just wide enough to hold them came a caravan. In front and following behind, men in military dress on high black horses. Between them, two horses carrying a litter. I winced to see them sag under its weight, then breathed in hard when I saw what was inside it.

A woman so pretty it felt like a trick. Her head was shaved and she wore no jewelry; there was nothing to protect you from her face. I looked at it from one angle, then another, watching it change like a hologram. The ice climbed my throat with reaching fingers.

I couldn't breathe, and the metronome tick was maddening. It came from the woman in the litter. A woman in bridal white, ticking like a clock. Her beautiful bare head turned in a dozen quick beats, and her eyes fixed on mine.

The Spinner moved between us, wrapped warm hands around my throat. The ice receded under her fingers till I could breathe again. "Not yet, Alice-Three-Times," she whispered.

I sucked in icicle air. *Not yet?*

When the Spinner moved away, the caravan had passed.

"Not yet?" I said. "What does that mean, not *yet*?"

"It means the only way out is through. Through the woods, through the story, through the pain. Did you think you'd get what you want for *free*?"

I fell back, chastened. "Can you at least tell me where we're going?"

"I told you. 'Once upon a time.'"

I slipped on loose white stones, rolling my bike's dead weight back onto the road. "What does that even—and why on bikes? Wouldn't horses be faster?"

"Horses are unpredictable," said the Spinner. "Even for me. They tend to turn into Stories halfway there." She turned and pointed a finger at me, her face irritable and as human as I'd seen it. "*Never* trust a Hinterland horse."

We rode on. My legs grew tired, then numb, then tired again, as we pedaled for a long quiet space that felt endless. Once I saw a face watching me from between branches. It was there and gone so suddenly, its eyes so sensitive and sad, it took me a moment to register it wasn't a human's face but a bear's, standing on its hind legs watching the road.

At the darkest part of night, when the moon had waned to a sliver, the veil of trees to our right fell away, revealing a lake. The water was flat as a level and dense as mercury, welling like a bead against its banks. Here and there something glimmered under its surface—tracings of green or purple sparks; a hard arc of bubbles that could've been white skirts, or a drifting mass of fins. Pale palms pressing up, as if against the underside of ice. The cold in me spread down, seeping past my thighs, making my stomach churn and my knees pop with every pedal. Finally the water ended and a line of trees began, covered with glossy black blossoms.

Just before dawn, I heard the crackle of firelight among them, and smelled smoke. Then came music—a wild, sad music that slipped away like a fading dream every time my mind tried to catch it. I slowed down to hear it, to try to place the instrument.

Not an instrument, a voice. A sweeping voice with a bracing range that made even the trees go quiet. I tilted my head back to watch the sky.

Then the Spinner was there, rolling her eyes, singing "Yellow Submarine" at the top of her lungs and slapping me hard. "Pedal!" she yelled between verses. "Have some pride in your pedigree! You're not some idiot refugee, you're Alice-Three-Times!"

I followed her, anger thudding dull behind my eyes. Once we'd left it far enough behind, the music crept from my body like a sugar high, leaving me shaky.

At the end of night the forest ended sharp as a knife, the road turning from a narrow chain to a broad white ribbon. The last of the moon slipped away and the sun bellied up, the two shouldering past each other for one radiant moment that seared brighter than fireworks and filled me with a rush of joy.

Until the Spinner turned us toward the castle.

Home.

The word swam up from the same neglected place inside of me that knew the name of the Briar King, and recognized the contours of this world in the way I'd know the breadth of my own body in the dark.

It looked like an abandoned toy. The road wound toward it, and it grew up from the road, made of the same white stone. It was a rambling thicket of turrets and dull windows and decorative outcroppings. At their center was a narrow tower slashed with murder holes. The whole thing wore a shroud of fog that breathed and twisted under its own weather.

I planted my heels hard in the road, tasting bile at the back of my throat. "I'm not going in there."

The Spinner laughed, and I startled back. She'd changed again. Her face was a soft circle, her hair cropped shorter than mine. She was dressed like a knight.

"And yet," she said, hand on the hilt of a narrow sword, "there's no way out without first going in. Once upon a time, Alice-Three-Times."

Her final words had an extra resonance to them, a blur. Like they wore a mask to hide their true intentions.

Don't trust her. But my heart was slowing, and the thought found no purchase.

The fog drifted and spun, moving like steam over tea. A black shadow hovered around me, a migraine aura narrowing in on the spiky shape of the castle. We were walking our bikes toward it, not riding, and I couldn't remember when I'd stopped pedaling. My mind felt curiously blank.

The Spinner's back wheel made a chewed-up, motorcycle sound. I leaned to yank out the playing card stuck in its spokes.

Twice-Killed Katherine's face looked up at me—two of them, in flipped mirror image like a queen card. In the top she looked freshly fed; at the bottom she was gaunt, her hair run through with a frail skunk stripe.

The Spinner snatched it away, tore it in two. "Refugees," she muttered. "They have funny ideas about fun."

The sight of Katherine's feral face shoved me back into

myself. The shadow receded, and I could see the orange wash of sunrise on white stone, the overgrown curves of gardens stretching behind the castle. My hands sticking out of my tunic sleeves like scarecrow limbs made of ice.

"Ella," I whispered. "Mom."

The Spinner cocked her head. "Nothing goes into the story but you," she said. "Right now you've got your other life all over you—they'll smell it on your skin." She gave me a smile that should've been beguiling but made my shoulders rise protectively. "They'll be jealous. The quickest way to end this is to begin it, and that's no way to start, is it?"

The condescension in her voice almost made me buckle. *The quickest way to end this*, like she believed I could. But she didn't. She never had. That wasn't why she'd led me here.

She was a jailer taking me back to my cell, and I was letting her. Based on the idiot notion that somewhere inside it was a key.

The castle grew larger as we moved closer, giving me a dizzy, shrinking feeling. The shapes of it sharpened, but everything else was flattening: the scent of green and pollen and rain, the smoky taste of morning. Birdsong and breeze went tinny, like I was hearing them through bad speakers, then cut off short as we stepped into the castle courtyard.

I sniffed in hard, let air run over my tongue—tasteless. The castle was a dead place.

"Not dead," the Spinner said. "Just stopped. Missing a gear."

I startled. "How did you—"

She shook her head, impatient. "The quicker it begins, the quicker it ends."

The clockwork bride in her litter had eyes like the Spinner's, I realized. If the Spinner created everything, had she made some of us in her own image? She could wear any face, but she couldn't get rid of those eyes.

I blinked and saw my hand pushing open the door to the Hazel Wood. Then here, now, pushing at the tall stone doors of the castle.

~28~

The first thing I heard was the music. A hectic, two-bar tangle, played over and over again. We entered a hall so high and vast it felt like a gym, its gilded corners softened by mossy masses that had to be birds' nests. A U-shaped table in the center of the room was lined with people. People eating, laughing, whispering to each other, stabbing at their meat. In the center of the room was the source of the awful music: a man in dirty green with a head of dark curls, holding a violin. He sawed at it savagely, in a jerky motion that looked painful.

I froze, and the Spinner stuck hard fingertips in my back. "We are the scariest things in this castle."

So I crept forward like I was moving through water, waiting every moment for the violinist to turn, to stop playing his horrible song. But he didn't. Nobody at the table took notice of us, the Spinner in her armor and me in my jeans. The wrongness of their movements crawled over my skin, and in a sudden, horrible flash, I realized why.

They were *stuck*. All of them. They were moving like butterflies stabbed through with a pin, enacting their last shiver of freedom.

The musician's tormented playing of the same wild notes. The woman in a heavy headdress, lifting a knife to her mouth, then lowering it, then again. The man who threw his head back and laughed, a gusty sound scraping dryly over a throat that must be bloody-raw. Slowly I circled the musician till I could see his eyes. His head was cast down over his instrument, his hair a curtain between us, but they met mine, straining up in their sockets so I could see their dark blue anguish.

I did this. My leaving—it did this. I broke free of the musician's gaze with a feeling like gauze unsticking. But now I saw them: all over the room, eyes running over me like searchlights. Dozens of moving points of misery and fear and appeal, as they ate, talked, laughed, a murmur that rose beneath the violin's twisted notes in a madhouse swell.

I felt myself sinking, and the Spinner buoyed me up, her mouth amused.

"Leave them," she murmured. "They've been alright without you for seventeen years—what's another minute or two?"

Seventeen years. Seventeen years in this rictus. Finally I was grateful time worked differently here. Maybe it felt faster to them, like time passing in a dream.

I shrugged her off. "You could help them," I hissed. "You could make them . . . make them *sleep*, at least."

"Nobody can fix a broken machine if they don't have the parts," she said, and led me into a passageway whose floor prickled with rushes. Here and there they rustled with tiny things moving in circumscribed paths.

The walls of the passage were hung with tapestries that tugged at my mind like stories left unread: A girl standing on a dock at the edge of a subterranean lake, an empty boat waiting in the water. A woman with a cut-glass face dancing with a man whose eyes were hidden. A little girl I recognized, standing at the prow of a ship.

Against a shadowy corner a man stood bracing himself, forever caught in the act of undoing his belt. In a hell-hot kitchen, a trio of women with burst-red faces made a chorus of ugly music: clank of spoon, thump of dough, eerie scrape of knife over whetstone.

At the center of a room filled with instruments, a child threaded her fingers around the strings of a harp, under the eye of a woman sipping, endlessly, from a teacup. A maid leaned against the wall in another dark hallway, her face wet with ancient tears.

In the castle's center was a perfectly round courtyard, where snow fell on small figures moving in shudder step: an arm rearing back with a snowball, a slip and a thump on hidden ice. The same shrill cry of hilarity as a snowball hit its mark, which sounded in repetition like the shriek of a dying animal.

I knew I was being corralled toward something, not just by the Spinner but by the bob of the compass hidden in my chest, tugging me toward the heart of the castle, to the foot of a winding staircase of stone.

"Almost there," the Spinner breathed.

The only way out is through. I climbed. We rose and rose, past landings and tapestries and people stuck in a long record skip: A little boy crying out as a cat bit his finger, the cat rearing in a painful strike. A man and a woman wrapped in a rolling embrace on a lonely landing.

The stairs narrowed into a tight seashell whorl as we climbed into a room that appeared in pieces as we rose. A stripe of cold fireplace, a woman's goose-pimpled legs where her skirts rode up. A wall unsoftened by tapestries, the bed where a second woman lay with her hair gathered around her like a cloak.

The room was dim. It smelled like a blown-out match and the close breath of the women—one whey-faced on the bed, her belly an oceanic swell and her hands squeezed into angry balls. Her breath was caught in a staccato beat; she'd been arrested at the crest of a wave of labor pain. A midwife with a blunt face hung over her, making a noise that was meant to be soothing.

My legs were almost too heavy to heave over the landing. I knew if I lifted the hems of my jeans I'd see skin gone to white.

"When you were ripped away they crawled back to their starting places," the Spinner said. "And there they've waited." Her eyes slid over the two women like they were furniture. They slid over me. She breathed out long and slow, her face changing into something I forgot with every blink.

She rolled up her sleeves—she had sleeves again, not armor—and opened her mouth.

"Why did you make me?" I asked her, before she could speak. I felt like a convict standing on a gallows with a noose around my neck, asking after the nature of God. "Why like this? Can I really end my story? Were you ever going to let me go?"

"Let you go?" Her voice was honey on razor blades. "Go to *what*? This is your purpose—the start of your story. This is what you were made to do."

"So you lied. I can't really change anything."

She smiled at me, a tender smile that sent fear jackrabbiting through my blood. "You won't want to, Alice. Can't you see that yet? The Stories are perfect. The Stories are *worlds*. I made a whole world just for you, and in it you get to do what nobody gets to: you get to live, and live, and live. And everything will come out the way it's meant to, no matter what. I made it that way."

"But how is that living?" I whispered.

Something passed over her face, a look of soft indulgence. "You've lived more than most already. You burn so brightly, Alice-Three-Times. So much anger, so much ice. A story wouldn't have waited like this for just anyone."

"But I'll be dying, too. That's the end of my story, isn't it?"

"That's what you're worried about? Dying's not so hard, Alice-Three-Times. You've done it before."

I went for the stairs. I wouldn't get far—my legs felt like logs and my breath came out in white clouds. But I wanted my last act as a free person to be one Ella would be proud of. Ella, who bought my freedom with seventeen fugitive years, all so I could throw it away on a gamble.

I was right: I didn't get far. I barely had time to turn before the Spinner yanked me back around. She touched my cheek and the ice rose to meet her, shivering through me and up to her fingers in waves.

It shouldn't have hurt. If I was just the stuff of stories, the ice sealing my throat shut shouldn't have burned like fire and the pain of going breathless shouldn't have felt endless and the fear rising off my skin shouldn't have smelled like a cornered animal. The pain was so massive it pressed out reason. I couldn't even whimper.

The Spinner spoke into my ear. "When Alice was born, her eyes were black from end to end."

I went blind. My body shuttered in like a telescope and I lost track of my limbs and where my head was and found myself suddenly *bodiless,* just an awful yawp of cold and dark, and a focused rage that should've eaten me up like a cinder.

I was imploding and I had nothing to scream with and my mind was melted plastic and my last clear thought was of the Spinner's sociopathic blue eyes, etched into the cold glass of my fading consciousness. Then I was nothing in the dark.

~29~

The dark was vast and pendulous. It rippled from the edges of me. Everything was echo and pulse, float and stretch, sleep and wake and a distant hunger. Something waited in my hummingbird heart: potential. A distant rage. I nipped at it like sugar water. Then a whoosh and a wrenching in my core, and the velvet dark ripped open. There was cold and terror and chilling white light.

The first thing I saw was a face, red cheeks and watery blue eyes. Not my mother's. I'd lived beneath her heartbeat, light and restless, for too long not to know this face didn't belong to that heart. The blue eyes raked over me, registering fear and something else—satisfaction. Though I didn't have the words for that yet. Two rough hands lifted and turned me.

The next face I saw matched the heartbeat I'd rested my cheek against for nine months, as I stretched and unfurled and grew myself from the inside out. A wide mouth, damp ropes of blonde hair. Eyes the hot brown of wet fur. She twisted her hands in bloody sheets. She looked at me and turned away. My mother.

But that word plucked at something else in my rapt, nascent baby brain. *Mother.* I saw someone else, a girl with unruly black hair and long fingers. She tangled them with mine and spoke into the angry pulse at my temple. *Count to ten, Alice.*

The tendrils of the story grew up and over me, like briars pulling a tower down. And I forgot.

It was so easy after that to let the story happen to me. I was a princess. I lived in a castle. I had eyes so black they drank the light. My siblings were scared of me; they ran like rabbits when they heard the bouncing of my silver ball. My father was a head of dark hair as he left the room, a booming voice that terrified the maids. My mother was a placid fairy queen at the far end of a table, plucking at the strings of a lute or the threads of some useless embroidery.

I grew up. I grew in jumps. The older brother who teased me one day, when I was only seven, got his the next, when I woke up taller than him. My bones stretched in the night. It was excruciating. It felt like stars had crawled into my joints and exploded.

But everything else felt so good, so free. I never knew how hard I'd worked to keep the darkness at bay—I remembered, distantly, that I'd done this before, under other circumstances. Lived, grown up. When I thought too hard about it, something silvery and webbed flickered over my sight. When I stopped thinking, my vision went clear.

There were other hints that there was something more to my life. Some secret that lay just beside it, ready to crack open like an egg. Sometimes at night I heard a shower of rocks at my window, like fingertips tapping. Sometimes I saw a face that was almost familiar, in a place where none should be—in the woods, or looking up at me from the frozen yard. If I peered too long the glittering sparks flared up and my head ached, so I stopped looking.

It felt good to be cruel. I let it wash over me like a warm black bath. My mother never punished me—she made her servants do it. Every stripe they laid on my back I paid out on my mother's other children. She didn't treat me like her own; she treated me like a cuckoo. I think she almost believed I wasn't hers. She hated that we had the same silly hair.

I was fascinated by ice from the first time I tried it. Cream and honey and lavender syrup stirred into chipped ice, after a banquet dinner celebrating one of my father's bloody victories. It slid into my stomach and lit a tiny fire. After that, in the cold months, I'd go outside and suck on icicles, eat snow. In the summer I'd hide in shadowy places, unmoving. My siblings felt safer then.

They weren't safe in winter. I played tricks on them, put nasty things in their beds and ruined their chances at balls. After my little brother broke my hand mirror I led him deep into the woods on an icy night, promising him we were looking for erldeer. I left him alone in a clearing and trekked back alone. He returned home hours after me, led by a stranger who'd found him in the woods. He didn't dare tell what I'd done.

When I came down to breakfast one morning in a woman's body, as shaky on my new legs as a fawn, my father looked me in the eyes for the first time. He looked down my body and up again. He smiled in a way that made me afraid.

Soon after that, my mother announced it was time to marry me off. She didn't do it to save me, but to deny him. She did it with the air of a woman withholding a toy from a hated child.

I didn't care from which direction safety came. By then I knew the king wasn't really my father—a contingent of men had spent a few weeks at the palace some months before I was born. They lived in the ice caves at the very edges of the Hinterland, and answered to a warrior queen. Rumors say she was briefly the king's mistress. My mother got her revenge with the man who gave me my ice-chip eyes.

When my eligibility was announced, I knew I could be frivolous. A princess can set rules for her suitors, even a blackhearted girl like me. It was high summer when I told my father I'd marry the man who brought me a velvet purse full of ice from the distant caves. It wasn't sentiment that drove me, it was curiosity.

No, it was something else—instinct. I felt, not for the first time, the influence of some unseen force in my life, some hand that wasn't my own. That feeling was what once made me throw my brother's toy cart into the fire. The way he tugged it carefully along with its little wooden handle put me in mind too much of myself.

The suitors came. They presented me with ice, but not from the caves. I knew by sight, by touch and taste, the ice dug out of sawdust in a barn, the ice from a frozen creek, from the glacier atop a mountain. Summer became winter, and nobody had gotten it right.

The brothers who finally won me were both tall, with hair the color of a fox's pelt, but the similarities ended there. The older brother was broad-chested, hard as flint, with a flat brown glare. He had a dirty face when he presented himself to my father. The younger one stood behind him, looking down. He was lean and favored one leg. He looked like someone I could break.

They came at the raw edge of spring. Where other men had gone down on one knee to present me with their gift, the older brother slung it into my lap. I knew before I opened the bag he was the man I would have to marry.

The ice was beautiful. It danced with the phantom green lights the skies over the caves were said to hold, and was cut into delicate cubes. I looked at the first brother's heavy hands, then the narrow fingers of the second. He was the one who'd done the cutting. He kept his head down, like he was ashamed of himself. I couldn't see his face.

The first brother spoke his intentions out loud—they meant to make me a servant, not a wife. I could see on my parents' faces that they didn't care, so long as I was won fairly. They couldn't save me from this. Wouldn't.

So I swallowed the ice.

It left a burning trail down my throat and hit my stomach like blue fire. It coiled there, and it sent its vines into my arms, my legs. It froze the last bit of life out of my deadened heart and slowed the workings of my mind. I had a quick mind, and there was just enough time to feel fear lance through me before my thoughts turned into cold honey.

I heard my mother's distant scream, my father's shout. I watched everything through a latticework of frozen tears: the brothers arguing, the eldest hefting me over his shoulder like I was a bag of grain. My littlest sister sank her teeth into my hand before I was carried away, and reeled backward, coughing.

The brothers tied me to the back of the horse that was my dowry. I saw nothing but the curtain of my own hair and the puffs of my breath freezing whitely on the air.

Someone followed us out of the castle yard. Down the muddy road, into the trees. Someone who made my head throb and sparks sizzle over my sight. I heard their tread like an echo to the brothers'. I was frozen, trussed, on my way to a life of servitude, but the follower—that was what filled me with fear.

When the brothers stopped to make camp, they left me on the horse—tied, upright, unmoving. As if from the bottom of a well, I heard the older brother's laughter, the crackling of a fire. Much later, hands untied me from the horse, laid me flat beneath a tree.

When they were asleep, the ice that sat like frozen coals in my stomach shifted. The freeze came slowly undone. My lips and eyes thawed, my fingers pricked, and I started to shake. When I felt strong again, I slid free of my ropes and walked over to the older brother. He was even uglier in sleep, his face twisted by cruel dreams. I hung over his sleeping body and fitted my lips to his. I blew my ice into him, along with my hate. He went with a shocked flutter and a rotten-tasting sigh, his heart frozen before he could struggle.

I returned to the horse and listened for the follower. I listened even in the frozen half-sleep I couldn't fight back, which came over me the moment I was still.

The hours passed, the light turned silver, and the younger brother's shout broke the air when he found his brother dead.

His boots stomped over the thawing ground. Some deep, moving part of me braced itself for a kick that didn't come.

Instead, the brother crouched and blew warm breath onto my eyes.

As fast as they thawed, they froze over again, but I managed to shift them in their sockets. For the first time since they'd taken me, I was looking at the man's face. At his dirty red hair.

"Hello, Alice," he whispered.

I stared and stared, recognition crashing into me. My words came out in a hiss, and my fingers moved feebly in the air over my chest.

"Try," he whispered, so quiet it was almost a breath. "Remember."

He was a man I'd seen twice before he'd come with his brother to present me with ice, but I couldn't remember how or where. Not family, not servant, not soldier. *Who was he?* I saw the dusty blue side of a carriage, a hoop fallen on grass.

That wasn't quite right.

I saw a rusty blue Buick, the Hula-Hoop I'd been spinning doggedly over my hips when he pulled up beside me.

"Hi," he'd said.

I'd ignored him, annoyed he made my hoop fall.

"I'm a friend of your grandmother's," he told me. "The writer, Althea Proserpine. She wants to meet you. Will you come with me to see her?"

My head snapped up. "Does she have horses?"

"Lots of them. And a swimming pool. She wants very much for you to visit, Alice."

I'd let the hoop roll to a halt and climbed into his car. I clicked the heels of my white cowboy boots together like Dorothy, for luck, and we were off.

The memory crashed through the delicate webbing that kept my world together. I shivered and thawed on the grass, sending off meltwater and seized with visions. A woman in white denim overalls studded with cigarette burns. The sound of her quiet cursing, waking me to a sea of brake lights stretched out on the road ahead. *Go back to sleep, Alice.*

Her name. What was her name? The memories boiled up—Christmas lights on a whitewashed wall, slipping my legs out from beneath hers in early morning. The smell of coffee beans, cheap macaroni, burning sage. The sour crunch of my ankle when I jumped from a crabapple tree and she wasn't quick enough to catch me. The feeling of her beside me in the world, the invisible searchlight that stretched between us.

"Ella," I wheezed from my frozen throat.

The man didn't hear me; he dipped his ear closer. "Do you remember me?"

"Blue Buick."

He grinned. "We're changing it already," he whispered.

"It's almost broken. I needed you to come back here, so you could help me break it."

"Why . . ."

"Because I'm not a page in a book," he said, cradling my head.

Then he screamed, a high rabbit sound that boiled the last of the ice from my blood.

He fell onto me, pinning me to the ground. I was still weak, and it took longer than it should've to get free. It took an age. When I finally struggled out from under him, I saw the ax in his back. Behind him stood his brother, humped and frozen and watching me out of dead eyes. All around us the air thrilled with silver sparks, so bright I squeezed my eyes shut. I could still see them against the hot red of my eyelids: a glowing tapestry of threads. Tiny, even brighter flickers of light ran like spiders around the hole we'd snagged in it: a hole the shape of the redheaded brother who'd tried to change our story. I winched my eyes open and saw the raw threads being snipped and stitched back into place by invisible fingers.

A handful of tiny, spidery points of light jumped toward me. I shrieked and scrambled back, my movements dulled by cold. One of the lights reached my temple, burning through it like a fleck of ash thrown off by a bonfire. First I felt it on my skin, then *under* it, burrowing there and re-arranging my brain.

"Ella," I gasped, holding her in my mind's eye. Her brown eyes, her long blonde hair . . . *no*! That wasn't her, that was the other mother. The one who made my cruelty grow like a vine.

More of the sparkling things jumped at me, as the

redheaded man moved limply on the ground. His brother fell back to earth, dead again once he'd done what the story needed him to do.

"Spinner," I whispered. I remembered her now, how I'd followed her like a lost dog into the twisted heart of the Hinterland. Into the story I meant to break free of, long, long ago. Because this wasn't a life I'd been living, it was a *story*.

When it was far too late, she'd told me there was no way out. But she hadn't told me it was because the story fought back if you tried. The spider-sparks still worked in the air, moving the weaving back to rights. They pulled the ax from the younger brother's back, they sizzled into my brain, they put him on his feet and closed up the rip in his flesh.

He couldn't die, I realized. Until it was part of the story. It would be me who would kill him, as I had his brother. Because in this story, I was the monster.

But was that really me? Horror hardened my skin. It sent the cruel little sparks bouncing off it like fire off a forge. I held on to that tenacious spike of fear and rage. I couldn't let my story end this way.

The redheaded man stood, but barely. His eyes were wild; he leaned over his knees and vomited up a thin yellow bile.

"We have to go," he panted. "Before . . ."

Before it happened again. I moved between him and the corpse on the ground. If I was a monster, at least I could be a helpful one.

"Get on the horse," I said. It came out slurred, like I was on Novocain.

I grabbed the ax from where it lay next to the dead man. The threads glittered to life, an angry matrix that flexed around my fingers on the handle, biting at my skin with a pain that started out irritating and turned to agony.

"Get on the horse," I said, turning my face from the sizzle of my skin. "Now!"

Still gasping, the younger brother heaved himself onto my dowry. On the ground, his brother jerked, then rose, lurching, his movements close enough to human to make the differences horrifying.

I wrapped my burning hands tight around the ax handle. The corpse watched me through eyes like frozen forget-me-nots, and lunged.

I smelled sweat and ice and something rank and unplaceable, before swinging wildly. The ax thudded into his shoulder with the sick sound of a boot on mud.

He looked down at it, then up. I swore he smiled at me, his teeth small and gray, before folding his hands around my throat.

Can you really die in a story?

Maybe not.

But you can die in a whole world built for it, full of cruel queens and black-eyed princesses and men with hands meant for violence. At least for a little while. My vision opened and closed like a butterfly's wings and my head fell forward. The corpse laughed again, till I arched up and fixed my lips on his.

I blew. Not ice this time. I blew out ice's opposite: the heat and the rage of being away from Ella. Trapped here. Forced into the role of murderer by a distant storyteller with no horse in the race. I did it because a girl doing nothing in a fairy tale ends up dead or worse, but a girl who makes a decision usually gets rewarded.

My reward was this: the taste of metal and sweat on lips like two cold maggots. His hands slackening on my neck. Dropping to his sides. He made the horrible grinding sound of a motor failing and fell to the ground. I angled my head to the side and pulled the ax from his chest.

When I turned I felt like I was wearing twenty tons of iced-over armor. I moved, shivering, toward the horse. It shied away from me, from the insect onslaught of sparks surrounding me. The redheaded brother leaned down and covered its eye with one hand, whispering soft things into its ear.

The fabric of the world was fully visible now, a glittering weave that snagged around us both. I hefted the ax and swung it through the threads suspended between me and the horse, but nothing changed.

"God*dammit!*" I screamed. I fell to my knees and started crawling. The horse, surrounded by the glittering, shivering source code of the world, did what I'd have liked to do: reared back in holy terror and ran.

The brother thumped hard to the earth, keening as the wind was knocked out of him. The sparks sizzled, faded away. It was just him again. Me. The dead man on the ground. I felt something begin in my stomach—the ice, gathering itself.

The air in front of us shuddered like bad TV, and— there was a horse. Empty air, then a horse to fill it. Same animal, but wearing blinders this time.

"No," said the brother, brokenly. "It can't be."

It could. It was. *Ella Ella Ellaellaellalalala*. I said the name till it turned to an aching syllable soup in my head. What did it mean? When I stopped thinking too hard about it, the bright pain behind my eyes went away.

There's no way out. Not from the inside.

The cold was spreading through me like kudzu. Its fingers crawled up my throat; soon they would reach my black eyes. The sparkling air had faded to gray. I couldn't remember why the man beside me was crying.

I slumped to the ground, anticipating the bite of rope around my wrists.

And all at once, the air lit up like a Christmas tree. Two shapes were moving fast toward us, setting the grid of the world alight.

A young man and an older woman. On . . . bicycles. They were on bicycles, one red and one green.

"Get her feet!" the boy yelled. His voice was cracked and strange, like he spoke around burrs caught in his throat. He had dark skin, a cloud of dark hair, and eyes as bright and steady as an animal's.

A hot thump of recognition cut through the curling cold.

He was the one who'd been following me. Not just today, but all my life. In the yard, in the woods. In my father's hall, once, before he was dragged away. The somebody who always set my head to aching, woke the sparks waiting at the corners of my sight.

Then he was next to me, grabbing my wrists. His touch drew my senses to the surface. I fought against him instinctively, and against the woman he was with—gray hair, blue tunic—who tried to hold my feet.

"Alice. Goddammit, *Alice*." The boy ducked out of the

way as I pulled a hand free and swiped at his chin with my nails.

Then I knew him. I went stiff so suddenly they dropped me. "Finch."

"Yep. No time to catch up, we've got to break you out of this thing."

I had something to say to him. He was somebody I could almost remember—somebody important. I saw blood and trees and a ceiling full of stars.

"But . . . you were dead. Weren't you?" When he dipped his head to hear me, I saw the blurred scar across his throat, a narrow brown rope.

"Not quite. If you can . . . can you stand up? That'll be easier than dragging you. But I'll drag you if I have to. If you forget who you are."

"Finch, it won't let me go."

"We've had time to look into these things, and it *will*," said the woman, her voice severe.

I gaped at her. "Janet?"

She smiled, slightly, and nodded toward the redheaded brother crouching speechless on the ground. "Friend or foe?"

"Friend. I think. Yes, friend."

Janet helped him to his feet, and still he didn't speak. The glittering veins of the world had receded; they weren't close and hot and blinding, they smoldered at a polite distance.

"What are you doing here?" I asked.

"I did some field research," Janet said triumphantly. "Every ex-Story I spoke to says the stories broke one of two ways: they were wound down by the Spinner, or picked apart by an inciting incident. And that inciting incident always had to do with a refugee wandering in at the wrong time. From there we extrapolated—" She stopped short, looking at me and Finch. "Oh. But you weren't asking me, were you?"

"Your eyes are black all over," he said. His crooked, raspy voice was so changed I couldn't tell how he meant it. He touched his fingers to my chin and hissed.

"God, you're like . . . well, like ice. Obviously. But we don't have time for this, get on the bike."

He was different from how I remembered him, in the dim memory rising from my wrung-out brain. This boy was thick through the shoulders. His hair was shorter than it used to be, and his arms were flecked with scars—silvery nicks and burns and raised patches of rough tissue. His eyes were what I remembered best, but they looked so tired.

I hiked my skirts and straddled Janet's bike seat while the brother took Finch's. As they pedaled away with two Stories weighing down their wheels, I looked back over my shoulder. The horse that shouldn't have been there went up in a shower of sparks.

We lit out toward the grid of sizzling light. I braced myself, ready for a galactic ripping or the blinding pain of riding a bike through a wall of fire.

But the wall receded as we moved. It stayed ahead of us and beyond our reach, its light just south of blinding. Janet huffed as she pedaled, her wheels slipping in spring mud. We wheeled past a stretch of trees, a run of scraggling bushes, a tree like a weeping willow in bud. We passed them again: trees, bushes, willow. And again, until I realized the woods were repeating themselves on a loop.

We were being given a chance to turn around. Every other minute, the same blue-breasted bird showed itself on the branches of the flowering willow, singing a chastising four-note song.

"Janet," Finch called back, warningly.

"I see it."

"Stop!" I cried.

Janet skidded to a halt.

I slipped from the bike, walked a few unsteady steps, and turned. "Don't follow me."

I left them behind to walk toward the sparking wall. It was endless, a net hung down from the cool Hinterland sun. It stayed in place, allowing me to meet it. I kept going till I couldn't keep my eyes open, then stood there bathing in the light it cast.

What would Althea do? The woman who'd built a bridge between two worlds, then brought them together like a hand in a glove?

I thought of her in the dark with her daughter, years ago and a world away, telling a story. I thought of the words she wrote down tripping over tongues and across continents, slicing fissures in the walls of the world.

"Once upon a time," I whispered, "there was a girl who got away."

The light burned a little less brightly through my lids. Maybe.

"Once upon a time there was a girl who changed her fate," I said, louder. The words ran together like beads on a string. Like a story, or a bridge I could climb—up, up, up, like a nursery-rhyme spider.

"She grew up like a fugitive, because her life belonged to another place." I held my fingertips out, feeling the ice of them meet the wall's fine, hot fizzing. "She remembered her real mother, far away on an Earth made of particles and elements and, and, and *reason*. Not stories. And she ripped a hole in the world so she could find her way home.

"And she lived happily ever after in a place far, far from the Hinterland," I said. I begged. "And the freeze left her skin. And she found her real mother in the world where she had left her."

Slowly, slowly, I opened my eyes.

There was a hole snagged in the wall. The air around it glittered like the last wandering traces of a firework. It was just the right size for a girl. I put my hand out behind me and beckoned.

The spokes of two rusty bicycles clicked closer, but the wall stayed in place. I kept my hand extended until Finch's fingers closed around mine, warm and sure. I led him, ducking, through the hole I'd made, Janet and the fairy-tale brother just behind.

When I stepped beyond the borders of the story, I felt it in my teeth and my belly button and the roots of my hair. Behind me the brother groaned, stumbling heavily against Janet. Finch put an arm around me, and his heat neutralized my cold.

We stood at the edge of a shallow valley filled to the knee with fog.

I sucked in air that tasted like rain and barbecue. Not

too far away, a little girl moved through mist that reached almost to her neck. Beside her, a man in a white T-shirt laughed, lifting her onto his shoulders. She wore beat-up Rollerblades.

My whole body was cramped and half-asleep. The sun was hot; I was hungry. My nose itched like I was allergic to something, and I stank. Finch did, too. His smell and mine were rank and human in a way that made me weak with longing. The brother staggered forward, his eyes round. He kept looking back toward the trees we'd left behind, then at his hands.

I sank down to the grass and cried. As I did, I swore I could feel the shiny black washing out of my eyes.

"You saved me," I said when I could speak again.

"I tried," Finch said. "But I think maybe you finished the job."

I shook my head, thinking of the horse blinking into view from empty air. "No. It was too . . . I lived for years in that thing. In that story." The whole stretch of it spun before my eyes like a carousel. The cold queen, the absent king, my own dark appetites. "For how long?"

"I don't know how long we've been here," Finch said softly. "Time doesn't work right, so nobody bothers keeping track."

"How are you alive?"

"The guy who cut my throat—he was on his way back to his own story—he dropped me pretty close to a refugee village. Left me to die. It was close, but they patched me up. Healing took some time."

"And Janet?"

"We learned quickly we had a mutual acquaintance,"

she said. "We found out what happened to you, and we decided—well, we thought we might help you along a bit. It was his idea." She looked at Finch, and the motherly pride in her eyes made my heart bob like a buoy.

"You were there," I said. "Through all of it. You were—always on the edges, trying to get me to notice you."

Finch laughed. "Dang, Alice. I knew you'd see me eventually." His laugh had changed—it was a man's laugh, rumbling under the rubble of his throat. It made me shy.

"Hey!"

The man in the white T-shirt had noticed us; he was waving from the sea of mist. He carried his daughter into one of the cottages squatting on the rising side of the valley, then jogged toward us. But not too close.

"Good travels to you," he said cautiously.

"Do you have water?" Janet asked. "Food? They could use it." She gestured at me and the redheaded brother.

The man's face cleared, and he smiled. "I'm ex-Story, too," he said.

"How'd you—" I began.

"The clothes. And the smell. Like burnt hair and, you know—" He plucked at the air with his fingertips. "That magic smell." He was handsome. Twenty years ago he might've been somebody's prince. Or somebody's poisoner. The Hinterland didn't tell nice tales.

He brought us a bucket of water, and I sucked down cups of it till my stomach ballooned. The redheaded brother didn't speak until he'd done the same. He kept smacking his lips, letting the water run over his chin.

"I can taste it," he said. "It's sweet and it's . . . dusty. Like stone. Can you taste it?"

I knew what he meant. Everything I'd ever eaten or drunk in the story paled next to the electric flavor of this river water. "Yeah. I can taste it."

He looked at his hands again, trailing his fingers through the air like he was on something. "Look at this. It's all me, doing this. It's mine." He looked up at me sharply, suddenly fearful. "It's over now, isn't it? No more story? No more dying?"

I could see Janet hovering over my shoulder, aching to dart in and start asking questions. I ignored her, ignored Finch. I looked at the man who had followed me to another world, to coax me home with gifts that carried me through the Halfway Wood.

His eyes were hazel, and broad freckles dusted his cheeks. It was the details that could drive you crazy—did the Spinner really create him just so? Did she decide on that wedge of darker brown in his left eye? Did she engineer my love of honey?

"Why did you take me?" I asked. I tried to say it gently.

He smiled faintly, his gaze going inward. "I did it for her. For the thief."

"The thief? You mean . . . Ella?"

He poured a cupful of water over his hair, tilting his face toward the pale sun. "Before she stole you, she wanted to steal me."

Oh. Fourteen years my mother spent alone with Althea in the Hazel Wood. But not all alone, not with the Halfway Wood so close.

"But if you . . . if you loved her. Why did you want to take me away from her?"

"I wanted to *help* her. And you. And, yes, myself. You

were never going to be free, not until we broke it. I'm right, aren't I? You were never really free?"

I shook my head. I felt stunned and hollow, looking at this stranger my mother might have loved. I would never reach the bottom of what Ella gave up for me. I would never know all the secrets of the life she left behind to run with me. "So what now?" I asked hoarsely. "Are you going back through the woods? To find her?"

He smiled at me, the kind of smile that cost something. He looked young enough to be a college student. My stupid, yearning heart dipped as I remembered dreaming, long ago, that he was my father.

"I've lived too many lives since I loved her," he said. "I've died too many deaths. It doesn't just . . . it leaves an echo."

It leaves an echo. Would it be the same for me? There'd been moments even before the story, wild, piercing moments, when the Hinterland sang high in my blood and I wondered—should I stay here? If, a world away, Ella might already be gone? Maybe I belonged in this place, where my bones grew in the night and my eyes were black ponds and my cells were made of the same strange stuff that made up the trees and the water and the earth.

But now I was feeling an itch under my skin. Somewhere far away, on some other clock, the days were counting down on my mother's life. Whether seven years had passed or seventy, I had to get to wherever she was. She deserved to see me this way—as an ex-Story, not just a stolen one.

I turned away from the red-haired brother. "Which way to the border?"

The handsome man had backed up politely while we

spoke, pretending not to hear us. Now his face closed like a fist, and he pointed in a general way toward the land stretching beyond the valley.

"I don't know what could be waiting there for you," he said. "But good travels to you all the same."

I turned to Finch. "It's time. Let's go home."

His face was soft and sorry. Janet touched the red-headed brother's sleeve; she led him gently away.

"Alice," said Finch.

It dawned on me, what I already should have known. "You're not coming, are you?"

He sighed and took my arm, walking with me into the fog. It swirled around our knees, our hips, higher. It had a gentle, flexible give, like wet petals against my skin.

No matter how much time had passed in this world or the other, Finch had changed. He'd grown up. At the fringes of my story, in a brutal make-believe world. But that wouldn't have been his whole life. He must've been living with more of the displaced all this time. I pictured him at the refugee bar, falling in love with some Earth girl. In my mind she had a smile without shadows in it, and perfect jeans.

I was feeling more human all the time.

"I'm not going back," he said, answering my question minutes after I'd asked it.

"Why not?"

"Because this was always what I wanted. Not quite the way I got it, of course. It shouldn't have been like that. Alice, it shouldn't have been blood money." He sounded suddenly, comfortingly unsure.

"I know. You've made up for that, don't you think?"

"I hope so," he said seriously. "But that wasn't what this was about. I wanted to see something through to the very end. And I've been living here all this time, in this world. It isn't all bad. It's beautiful. And strange. And bigger than you'd think. Alice, there's a whole ocean. And ice caves—oh, you know that. I heard there are pools in the mountains that are a thousand feet deep, and clear as glass."

"Fairy-tale shit."

"Yeah." He laughed. "Fairy-tale shit."

"And there's a girl?"

He smiled. It was so kind I almost died of embarrassment. "There might be. But believe me when I say I wouldn't leave the whole world behind just for a girl."

"Yeah. You would." I meant it, too. He'd grown into the sort of man who would do more than that for someone he loved.

He'd done a whole hell of a lot for me.

"So what do I do now?"

"Now you find the Spinner. It shouldn't be hard—she'll be on the move since the story broke. Cleaning up messes, looking for you."

I'm just one big fucking mess, aren't I. That's what I wanted to say. But didn't. Finch deserved better than my self-pity. It felt like he'd become too old for it.

Janet was grilling the redheaded brother on his first escape and my abduction when we returned. "You taught yourself to drive a car and it didn't kill you," she said comfortingly. "You'll do fine without a story. Who needs a story?"

He kept nodding, jittery with cold feet. I got it—life was a big thing to live without a map.

Janet turned her flinty eyes on us. "You off to find your own country?"

"Come with me?" I said impulsively, knowing she'd turn me down.

It still hurt a little when she did, however gently. This was a journey I'd have to take alone.

I hugged Janet, and I shook the brother's hand. Then I stood in front of Finch. He wrapped his arms around me, and the last burning ember of ice in me melted to nothing.

I was hungry, and so tired the ground moved like waves beneath my feet. But I didn't trust myself to stop now, to rest. I climbed onto Janet's red bicycle and set out for the edge of the world.

~30~

The land beyond the valley was uneven, grass littered with rocky bits where my wheel caught and turned. The sky was a mottled blue, the sunlight strange. I rode for a time alongside a stream that flowed but made no sound. I passed a quarry and crossed a bridge barely wider than a car, stretching over a ravine so deep I couldn't see the bottom. The earth and sky looked unfinished here, sketches from a restless pen. The air was thick and silent. I wheeled through a tunnel of firs that moved their branches and smelled, disorientingly, like rain on hot pavement. Past them was a dirt road with endless flat plains on either side. Far, far away I saw a glittering line at the horizon. The ocean? I sniffed but smelled no salt.

I rode till the water in my stomach stopped sloshing

and I was thirsty again. When I got close enough to see the water more clearly, I realized it was a desert of sparkling sand. At the edge of it sat the Story Spinner, looking like she had the first time I saw her. She wore a baby-doll dress and leggings and sat next to a sprawled-out blue bicycle. She was drinking something from a plastic thermos, and didn't raise her eyes till I was right in front of her.

She squinted up, head cocked to one side. "You broke your story. It's not worth being told now."

"It was never my story," I said. "It was yours."

"Not here looking for revenge, I hope?"

The idea made me tired, a fatigue with no bottom. I shook my head.

"Good." She stood, brushing sand off her leggings. "I can't make any promises about what you'll find back there," she said. "Time works—"

"Differently than I think it does. I know." I stumbled off the bike, my knees woozy and buckling, and stood in front of her.

Was there a right way to say goodbye to my maker? My captor? The woman who'd funneled me back into my sad and endless story as easily as a wasp led out through an open window?

She smiled at my confusion and gave a two-fingered salute, like a girl in an old movie.

No goodbye needed, I guessed. I turned away from her, knowing her eyes would be the last thing I remembered when all other memories of this place had flattened into photographs.

I stepped onto glittering sand, just over the border of the Hinterland.

The sand was hot as embers. The heat scalded my feet, then scaled my body, hurting worse than the spider sparks. I took a breath in to scream, but the pain was already passing. The sand was glittering white, then dun, then grassy, then just grass. When I looked up I saw an acre of overgrown lawn, running up to the edges of a slumping, tumbledown house. The Hazel Wood.

A terror clawed up out of the tiny part of me that wasn't too tired to feel. How many years did it take for a place to fall apart like this? From a distance it was picturesque, but as I walked closer I could see its destruction. The great house looked like it had grown up from the ground, and the ground was trying to take it back. Vines grew through cracked windowpanes, and grass crawled over the steps. The swimming pool looked like a frog pond and smelled worse.

When I reached the steps, I lifted the skirts of my princess dress and kicked off the shreds of my slippers. I walked up to the door and knocked.

I waited a long time, but nobody answered. The door was locked, and while I could've climbed through a window, there wasn't any point. The Hazel Wood's warped clock had finally run down. If Althea was lucky, she was dead.

She wasn't who I needed to find.

The Hazel Wood's gates let me out into a normal wood. No ravine, no grove of glittering trees. I walked barefoot to the road, feeling every pebble, every acorn and piece of trash. The first few cars slowed down to look at me in my ragged dress, my hair that fell almost to the tops of my thighs. But none of them stopped. I tried to glean clues about how much time had passed from the make of the cars, without luck. No hovercraft, at least.

Finally a minivan drove by me, stopped, and backed up. In the driver's seat sat an old woman wearing a rain bonnet over frosted hair. She rolled down the passenger window and peered at me.

"Now why on earth would you wear a dress that lovely into the woods?"

I was out of practice, talking to people. No words came. I tried to smile reassuringly. *Don't be afraid of me, old woman.* It probably looked terrifying. I had, until very recently, been a literal fairy-tale monster.

She sniffed. "You don't need to *snarl* at me. Either you've gotten lost during a costume party or your story is much more interesting than that, but either way—"

"I don't have a story," I said. My voice sounded like a rusty hinge.

"Well. Do you need a ride or not?"

I shook my head, then nodded, then walked slowly around the ugly hulk of the car to let myself in. The dashboard lights blinked like insect eyes, and the air inside smelled like nothing that should exist on heaven or earth. New car smell, I remembered. *Keep it together, Alice.*

"Thank you," I mumbled, about five minutes too late.

"Good lord, you stink," she said. "Have you been kidnapped? Did you just escape? Should I be taking you to the police?"

"What year is it?" I burst out.

Her eyes widened. "You poor child. You really don't know?"

She told me, and I closed my eyes against her words.

Two years. Two years had passed since I walked into the Hazel Wood. It was better and worse than it could've been; relief and terror warred in my chest and made me shake. Once I started, I couldn't stop. The panic folded over me like a hand, and I gave in.

When I was little I tried to walk across one of the parallel bars on the playground like it was a tightrope, till I slipped and fell onto it stomach first. The wind was knocked out of me, and all I could do was keen, a horrible sound that sent the other kids scattering.

That was what I sounded like now. I couldn't breathe, and I couldn't stop. Next to the messy specter of my coming undone, the woman's driving peaked to frantic. She pressed her body toward her window and called someone on her phone. An eternity passed before the car screeched into a diner parking lot, where an ambulance was waiting.

When the paramedics opened my door and laid their hands on me, I went silent. They startled back before grabbing me again, helping me out onto the gravel.

"Can you tell me your name?" one of them asked kindly. He looked like a skinny Harold.

"Ella Proserpine," I said desperately.

"Okay, Ella, can you walk with me, please? Try to unlock your knees."

"No, Ella is my mother. I'm Alice," I said. "Alice Crewe. Alice Proserpine. I'm Alice-Three-Times."

The paramedics exchanged a glance over my head and half-carried me into the ambulance.

Somehow, I fell asleep on the way. When I woke up I was wearing a clean blue hospital gown. I flinched away from a terrible smell, woke up the rest of the way, and realized it was me. I was fully convinced another two years had passed since I'd last been awake.

I filled my lungs, ready to scream out fresh panic, then saw her sitting in a hospital chair. Her head was flopped onto her chest, a fresh starburst of gray running through the dark strands of her hair. She wore a black hoodie, black jeans, and the cracked red cowboy boots she'd had since forever.

My mother. Ella Proserpine.

~31~

I sat up, let a wave of dizziness pass, swung my feet to the floor. I could feel my muscles running over each other in funny, fucked-up ways, but the cool of the linoleum took the worst of the hot throb out of my soles.

"Ella," I whispered. "Mom."

She lifted her head suddenly, breathing in hard through her nose. She smiled when she saw me, then gasped, her eyes spilling over with tears. She stood and wrapped her arms around me, and held me till it hurt.

When we'd cried enough, and studied each other's faces, and I'd counted her new crow's-feet and gray hairs and decided I could live with losing two years, she asked me. "You know, don't you?" Her eyes were nervous, scanning my face.

"Know what?"

"Who I am—what I did. How I'm not really your, not your . . ."

"You are." I said it like a vow. I repeated it till she believed me.

A long time after that, once the doctors had come in to examine me, and Ella chased off a policeman who wanted to take a statement, and I ripped like a wild dog through the contents of a hospital tray and half a vending machine, she told me her side of the story.

The Hinterland had taken her from Harold's and put her in a dingy, empty studio apartment in the Bronx. No phone, no fire escape, no neighbors, no way to pry open the windows or door. After three days she was nearly starved and all screamed out when she tried the front door for the thousandth time.

It opened. Nobody was guarding it, and nobody stopped her as she walked down four flights of stairs and emerged, trembling, onto the sidewalk. She made her way back to Harold's, but the doorman called the cops on her. A friend from her old catering job gave her some clothes and some cash—her credit card was canceled, and the old card she'd used before Harold was attached to an almost empty account. She sold the jewelry she was wearing and followed the same path as Finch and me: renting a car and heading to the Hazel Wood.

But the Halfway Wood wouldn't let her in. She lived in a motel at first, before finding a place above a hairdresser's in Birch, of all places. She worked at a diner, hiking the woods looking for an entrance on her days off. Months passed without luck or hope, until the day I walked out of the woods and gave the paramedics her name before I told them mine.

She never saw any sign of the Hinterland, in the woods or out of them. Her bad luck days had ended after I disappeared—not that she'd put it that way. But she mourned being locked out of the Halfway Wood, I could tell. "Maybe I'm too old now," she said. "Maybe that's how it works."

"It's not Peter Pan," I said firmly. "It's *freedom*."

She looked at my eyes and smiled. "All the ice is out of you," she said. "Even that little bit I could see way down at the bottom. My angry girl."

She never made me feel like she missed it, but I could tell she did, a little. I was slower to anger now, more circumspect. I didn't live like each day was a fuse to burn through and forget.

We cooked up a paper-thin amnesia story for the police, my face was in the news for a while, and I was told the county would be in touch when they had a lead on what, exactly, had happened to me.

I was home for a couple of weeks when Ella told me the rest of her story: She hadn't found the Hinterland in her wanderings, but she'd found the Hazel Wood. Not the dreamlike place I'd walked through, but a tumbledown mansion full of cat shit and broken windows. She'd let herself in and found Althea in her writing room, a few days' dead.

Her hands shook only a little when she told me. "When I thought she was dead the first time, I thought it was over—the bad luck. I thought it was her all that time, sending the Hinterland to bring you back. I didn't think it was . . ."

Me. She didn't think it was *me*, the dark magic in me tugging it along behind us like a fish on a hook.

"I've learned my lesson," she'd continued. "Don't take a letter's word for it when it comes to death. And don't run away from your inheritance."

It turned out the Hazel Wood was ours, as I'd once wished it to be. Ella sold it to a woman looking to start a writers' retreat, and bought us a condo in our old neighborhood in Brooklyn.

She got another job waiting tables, and I stocked shelves for a food co-op when I wasn't floating around pretending to think about going back to school. On paper I was nineteen, and Ella didn't want to push me.

But the empty days, all in one place—they made me restless. I walked for hours, from Brooklyn to Manhattan and back again, or down to Coney Island. I started rereading the books I'd loved when I was younger, all those paperbacks picked up in musty shops, off stoops, from library shelves, then shed like leaves on the road.

When I reread *Boy, Snow, Bird* I remembered Iowa City, living with Ella in a cramped prefab a few blocks from a frat house. *Howl's Moving Castle* was the converted barn in Madison where we camped out for three lonely months after the terrifying end to our time in Chicago. As I read the words I felt memories reasserting themselves like letters drawn onto misted glass. On a frozen day in February I carried a pair of tallboys onto the Long Island Ferry and read *Wise Child* as we chugged through the water. I closed my eyes and remembered the red flowers that grew around our guesthouse in LA when I was ten. Then I opened them and put my tongue out to catch New York snowflakes. They tasted sick and gritty, like chemical rain.

I went to bed in my own room, but night after night I found myself waking up next to Ella, her hands in my hair. I'd shaved the whole brambly mess off when I got out of the hospital, and it was growing back wispy and darker. More like hers.

"Shh," she'd whisper, the way she always had. "It's over. It's over now."

I saw Audrey once on the High Line. She'd changed her style. Out with the bronzer and the flat-ironed hair, in with precise red lipstick and a pea coat with a Peter Pan collar. I liked it. She looked like Amy Winehouse dressed as Jackie O.

We sat on a deck chair in the sun and shared a cigarette, a French brand with a box that looked like pop art. Because she was Audrey she didn't ask right away about Ella, or whether I was okay, or what the hell had happened to us since her dad pulled a gun on me and tossed me out into a long, cold night full of things worse than muggers.

I loved her for it.

She smiled when I coughed on the fancy imported smoke, watching me from behind Fendi shades. "Not so tough now, are you?"

I seized onto this piece of intelligence—what I'd looked like from the outside, two years ago. "Was I tough? When you knew me?"

"You were scary as fuck. You know that. You looked

like a haunted china doll." She peered at me over the tops of her sunglasses, eyes lined like Isis. "Now you seem a little . . . I don't know. Lost?"

"How's Harold?" I asked, changing the subject.

"Oh, he's fine. In love again. As always. How's Ella?"

I paused, letting the cigarette burn down between my fingers. How *was* Ella?

"Resolved," I said, finally. "All that shit with the . . . all that scary shit. It's resolved."

"Good," Audrey said, with a note of finality. She plucked the cigarette from my fingers and took a last drag, then pinched it out and put it into her pocket. She gave me a hug that was all elbows, then walked away without looking back.

I knew I shouldn't, but I couldn't help walking by Ellery Finch's building, staring up at the windows. Of course he'd disappeared, too, the same time as me, but his father must've written him off as a runaway. As far as I could find, he hadn't even made the papers. Maybe they'd hired a private investigator. Or maybe they really had cared as little as he thought. But I doubted it. I didn't know how you couldn't care for Ellery Finch.

I had dreams about him sometimes. In my dreams we did things together that we never did in life—walked through parks, held hands in bookshops. I woke up from a dream in which we'd waded in water up to our knees with the realization that I could picture him now without seeing his near-murder in the trees. It had played and replayed till it burned itself away.

I would've gone on like that forever, I think, using paperbacks to shake old memories loose and roaming around as if permanently sun-stunned. But when I'd been home for just over a year, I ran into Janet and Ingrid drinking iced coffee outside an East Village café.

My vision went full dolly zoom, and I stopped so fast a woman ran her stroller up onto the backs of my heels. I got out of the way, muttering apologies but refusing to peel my eyes from Janet's face. I walked toward her with my arms stretched out like a zombie's, like she might get away.

She seemed happy to see me, but mildly so. Like it was a pleasant surprise, not a seismic shift in reality as she understood it.

"You look much better without the frostbite," she said, standing up and taking my hands. Ingrid nodded coolly from beneath the brim of a Mets cap.

"How did you . . . what did you . . . ?"

"Shh. Sit. Eat something. Ingrid?" Her accent was more British than I remembered it. Less . . . Hinterlandy.

Reluctantly, Ingrid handed over a square of oily cake wrapped in parchment. It slid like wet sand down my throat, but it did make me feel better.

"How did you get here?" I asked when I could talk again.

Janet reached her fingers down her front and pulled out a flat purse on a strap, like the money belts old ladies wear when they vacation in big cities. Which, I guess, is what they were. But she didn't pull out a stack of traveler's checks—she pulled out a flat booklet.

It was green leather stamped in gold. *PASSPORT*, it said across the top, and *Hinterland*. In between, a flower like the one on my arm. I held it gingerly, like it might evaporate, and opened it. There was a flurry of stamps inside, some with dates that made sense, and some that didn't. The stamps were of doors, mostly, but one was a ship, one a train, another a stylized boot. The place-names were unfamiliar, so odd they slipped from my mind before I could understand them.

I smiled wider than I had in weeks. "More doors. You found them."

"Not by myself," Janet said modestly. "There was some mixing of refugee groups near the end. Some of them knew a few tricks I didn't—more than you'd think relies on having the right paperwork."

"Near the end? Of what?"

She tugged the passport from my grip and slipped it back into her purse, tucked the purse away. "Well. Things haven't been so up to snuff in the Hinterland these days. I'm afraid we started a bit of a trend. One broken story begets another—you weren't the only doomed princess to want a happier end."

"Wait. I was doomed? What was my end supposed to be? I never knew."

"I think it's best if you keep not knowing, don't you? Wouldn't want to make any self-fulfilling prophecies. Anyway, the place doesn't run the same without those stories ticking away. Things are getting a little . . . fuzzy."

"I nearly fell through a thin place," Ingrid put in.

"Right," Janet said. "She was knee deep in the ground, nothing but black and stars under her feet, and the damned story kept trying to weave her out of the world. But we got her out all right, didn't we?"

Ingrid made a face like it wasn't *that* all right.

"Finch—did he come back with you?"

Janet's face went soft. "He didn't. That boy has other worlds to explore. We're not always born to the right one, are we?"

I didn't know how badly I wanted to see him again till I learned, one more time, I never would.

"I don't know who I am without it," I said impulsively. I said it like an ugly secret.

"Without the Hinterland? You weren't back in it so long, were you?"

"Without the *ice*."

"Ah. Well, you aren't the first ex-Story to feel that way. It's like half of you got sucked out with a straw, isn't it?"

It was. It was exactly like that. "What should I do?" I asked desperately.

She touched my cheek, then wrote something down for me on the back of a napkin. An address, a date, a time.

That was how I ended up in a nag champa–scented psychic's parlor on Thirty-Sixth Street. The psychic wasn't in—she didn't start work till noon, and it was ten a.m. on a Sunday—but the room was half-filled with people who had singular faces. Cruel features, or lovely ones, delicately drawn. More than one of us had feral Manson eyes, rose-red lips, chapped mouths bitten till they were bloody. I estimated two-thirds of the room wore nicotine patches, and nearly everyone had ink on whatever skin was visible. Tattoos of remembrance, bits of Hinterland flora or the outline of a dagger or a teardrop or a cup. Or a door.

And all of us had something empty in our eyes. Something eager to be filled. There were some fully human refugees there who'd lived in the Hinterland too long to know what to do with themselves back on Earth, but most of us were ex-Story. When their world fell apart—our world—they came here.

Every week, the Hinterland's refugees gathered in the psychic's parlor to talk. Drink coffee. Settle grievances. It was a last stop before prison or an institution for lots of them. The violent ones, the Briar Kings, were already gone. Faded into the crowd, burying themselves where they could do the most damage, or dead. When a world dies, it doesn't go with a whimper. I felt like an outsider there, too, but then we all did. I'd sat at enough misfit lunch tables in my life to know the feeling. We were each our own island, gathered together into one messed-up archipelago.

I stocked oats and pecans and lucuma powder at the co-op, and tried to stay in my own bed the whole night. I read books that helped pave over the chinks and canyons in my memory, and let Ella comb henna through my hair. On Sundays I drank bad coffee and listened to the refugees' stories, and they started to fill me up. My memories became denser. I was building a scaffolding out of them to hang a real life on.

With a girl whose fairy tale had been so dark I didn't see how she could be anything less than a sociopath, I made a pact: we'd go to school. Her for the first time, me again. By then the group had someone at work forging documents for anyone who needed them. My friend became Sophia Snow, a fairy-tale name I tried to talk her out of. I went with Alice Proserpine, and moved my birthday two years up. I wanted to be seventeen on the record.

The doors to the Hinterland were closed, the world

winked out. The ice was out of me. The Spinner's world had set Finch loose, too. At night, when I couldn't sleep, I pictured him journeying through starry spaces and dusty doors, strange universes he could sift through like coffee beans.

Sometimes after those restless nights, I wake up early in the morning, woozy with dark dreams. I check my reflection in the mirror. I slide on sunglasses before Ella wakes up, and I go walking. I drink scalding tea and ride the ferry and breathe hard into my hands. When I come home again, my eyes are brown, and faultless, and you could almost, almost say they look like my mother's. Ella Proserpine's.

ACKNOWLEDGMENTS

Thank you first to Faye Bender, magnificent agent and tirelessly patient partner in explaining how all this stuff works, and then making it happen like a wizard. My friends and family have grown weary of my saying, "Man, I love Faye," so I'll just leave it here for posterity: Man, I love Faye.

To Sarah Dotts Barley, my book's perfect love match: Thank you for making the editorial process an exciting, energizing, ridiculously fun one, free of dread. I couldn't have asked for a better advocate and second brain for the book, or a happier home for it than Flatiron/Macmillan. Big thanks also to Amy Einhorn, Liz Keenan, Emily Walters, Patricia Cave, Nancy Trypuc, Robert Allen and the audiobook team, Anna Gorovoy, Keith Hayes, Lena

Shekhter, and Molly Fonseca. For the gorgeous cover, illustrations, and endpapers (endpapers!), thank you to Jim Tierney.

Thank you to Mary Pender-Coplan, amazing film agent, and to the agents who helped this book find homes around the world: Lora Fountain (and Léo Tortchinski); Ia Atterholm; Sebastian Ritscher, Nicole Meillaud, and Annelie Geissler at Mohrbooks; Milena Kaplarević, Ana Milenkovic, and Nada Cipranic at Prava i Prevodi; Gray Tan and Clare Chi at Grayhawk Agency; and Kohei Hattori at The English Agency. Thank you also to Ryan Doherty at Sony Pictures Entertainment, and to Lucy Fisher, Lucas Wiesendanger, and Charlie Morrison at Red Wagon Entertainment.

To my parents, Steve and Diane Albert. Thank you for everything, including a childhood so loved and secure I was free to lose myself in fictional worlds, to the ultimately happy detriment of my social life, eyesight, and standing at the Cook Memorial Library. I love you very much.

To Bryan, my childhood partner in crime. To Amy, my playmate then, my BFF now.

To my badass beta readers, brilliant writers all: Jeanmarie Anaya, Natalie Zutter, and Jennifer Kawecki. To Emma Chastain, whose insightful, hilarious, true writing inspires me, for offering early encouragement. To Molly Schoemann-McCann, one of the funniest writers I know, for reading the first ten pages of the book and telling me it was the one to finish. To Joel Cunningham, a great SFF advocate, for general genre brilliance, support, and loving portal fiction.

To the Quidditch Bitches, Tara Sonin, Annie Stone,

Sarah Jane Abbott, Kamilla Benko, and Ellie Campisano, for your feedback, your support, your writing I can't wait to read every time we meet—and for being people I just want to hang out with, ultimately leading to me writing more words. To Kim Graff and Phil Stamper, for writing dates that socially pressured me to write more words instead of sitting at home eating watermelon.

Thanks to Dahlia Adler and the B&N Teen team, for your passion and advocacy for YA literature, and for consistently blowing up my to-read list.

To my sensitivity readers, Dylan Stasa and Mariah Barker (Gryffindor and Hufflepuff, respectively), for your smart and generous feedback, and for liking the Harry Potter references.

And, finally, to Michael, extraordinarily handsome husband who also happens to be the funny, wonderful love of my life. Thank you.

TURN THE PAGE FOR

TWO FOUND STORIES

FROM ALTHEA PROSERPINE'S

TALES FROM THE HINTERLAND.

READ AT YOUR OWN RISK.

Jenny and the Night Women

A rich farmer and his wife, heartbroken because they could not bear a child, prayed for the gods to give them one, but there were no gods to hear. And so, because they knew the way of things in their part of the world, they got their child through different means. In spring, the wife swallowed the pink-and-white bloom of an apple blossom. So eager was she to do it that she didn't notice, at the flower's heart, the creep of brown—it had half rotted with rain. By summer, the blossom had ripened and unfurled, turning to fruit in her belly. In autumn, the woman felt sick to her soul. She retched and retched and vomited up an apple. It was red and crisp and delicious, its juice sweet as wine and its skin firm like the skin of a drum.

She ate the fruit with ferocious appetite, swallowing the

core along with the flesh. At the fruit's heart was a circle of soft brown, just as if a worm had burrowed in. But the wife didn't notice the rot, and she didn't taste it, and she felt nothing but joy as her belly swelled and ripened.

In the course of time she bore a child, a pink and white and beautiful child, with a core of hidden decay. Because they'd waited so long and so longingly, the farmer and his wife spoiled the girl. They named her Jenny, and there was nothing she wanted that she didn't get. Day by day, year by year, she grew prettier and prettier, and worse and worse. By the time Jenny turned twelve, even her father could see it.

"She's a grown girl and a farmer's daughter," he told his wife. "Not a princess. Beautiful or not, who will marry a farmer's daughter who thinks she's royalty?"

Reluctantly, Jenny's mother agreed. They would no longer obey her every whim.

The next morning, Jenny wanted cake for breakfast. Remembering her promise to her husband, her mother refused. Jenny looked at her a long moment, then ate her bread and jam.

That afternoon, Jenny asked for one of the kittens the barn cat had birthed. Her mother told her no: they'd been promised away. Jenny narrowed her eyes and said nothing.

That evening they were hurrying back home through town, where they'd traded eggs for salt, when Jenny spied a glassblower selling his wares. She demanded her mother buy her a glass flower.

"No," her mother said. "You have enough pretty things, and you break most of them."

Jenny screamed. She tugged her golden hair, and stamped

the heel off one of her soft leather boots. But her mother wouldn't budge. "You'll have to wear broken shoes," she said grimly.

Furious, Jenny slapped her mother across the face. Quick as a thought, her mother slapped her back.

Jenny had never in her life been struck. Holding her cheek, crooked in her broken boot, she ran past the edge of town and into the trees.

Soon her mother's cries were beyond hearing. At first Jenny was warmed by the thought of her mother's regret. Then Jenny was angry with her mother, for disobeying her and forcing her to run away. Then she grew frightened, as the forest's familiar edges gave way to something wild and unknown.

The sun was down and both Jenny's boots long abandoned when she saw a glimmer of light through the trees. The glimmer became a flickering orange glow. It made Jenny's mouth go dry with desire, for food and a fire to warm her hands by. She wasn't afraid of who she might meet there, so certain was she that everyone she met would love her.

Her certainty dimmed when she saw the person sitting on a fallen log beside the fire, staring into its heart: a girl with tangled hair to her waist, wearing a red kerchief and a rough brown dress.

"Go on your way or sit beside me, but choose one," the girl said, staring into the fire. Her voice was old and deep, like she'd borrowed it from another person.

Jenny came forward on dirty feet, one hand tugging at her hair. She tilted her head sweetly, imagining how the firelight must be playing over the beauty of her face.

"Please," she said. "Won't you help me? I'm cold and hungry and lost in the woods."

The girl only looked at her. "Stupid of you to lose yourself, wasn't it?"

"It was my mother's fault," Jenny snapped.

And she told the girl of her mother's crimes, inventing a few besides. By the end of her tale the girl was shaking her head.

"Your mother deserves to be taught a lesson. Your father, too, for allowing her to treat you this way."

There was an edge to the girl's voice, teasing and unkind. Jenny sensed it and recoiled—she was rotten in her middle, that was true, but she wasn't yet rotted through. There was a part of her that listened to the girl's words, and heard what was beneath them, too: a dark mischief that promised a hard ending.

But the girl by the fire was clever. She saw Jenny pull away, and she changed tack. "Someone as pretty as you," she said, "should be treated like a princess."

"*Beautiful*," Jenny corrected her. "And *queen*. Someone as beautiful as me should be treated like a queen."

"Yes. You should play a trick on your parents. You should teach them a lesson. That they mustn't underestimate you, or learn to say no. Once they start, they'll never stop."

That was a horrible thought. Jenny remembered all the pretty things her father gave her, then imagined them gone. She saw herself wearing dresses with tears in them, and walking around barefoot because she'd lost her shoes in the woods. The visions were so sad her eyes filled with tears.

The girl was smiling now. One of her front teeth was dark with decay, and the other overlapped it, as if to hide it from view.

"I won't let them do this to you," she said. "I'll tell you, my Jenny, what you must do."

And she said words that sounded like an incantation, in a funny, trilling voice that buzzed over Jenny's ear. "Take a needle," she said.

"Take a stone
and Prick their heels thrice.
Bloody the stone
and Bury it low
and Let the Night Women come.

"You'll bury it beneath their window," she said, "to invite the Night Women in."

The buzz of the girl's chant was caught in Jenny's ear. It rattled there like a dying fly. "Who are the Night Women?" she asked.

"They're beautiful," said the girl. "Just like you. And they always give you exactly what you desire. And now," she continued, "go along home. Your parents will punish you terribly when you return, I'm sure, and it will be worse if you wait."

She pointed Jenny toward a path the girl hadn't noticed before, promising it would lead her back to town. Jenny left her sitting by the fire in her old brown dress, smiling her brown-and-white smile.

The walk back was quicker than she thought it would be; she'd been just outside town all along. The first thing she saw when she broke through the trees was her mother, wringing her hands, and her father, holding a lantern. When they saw her they fell on her with embraces and tears of relief. At once Jenny forgot the girl in the woods, with her crooked teeth and her strange commands.

Frightened at having lost her, her parents were obedient again. Jenny asked, and Jenny received. Her father took her back to the glassblower and bought her a whole bouquet of translucent red roses. Her mother bought her a pair of satin boots with fifteen buttons apiece, to replace the ones she'd lost.

This went on for a little while. But soon her parents forgot the fear of almost losing Jenny.

A little while after she returned from the woods, Jenny asked for a beautiful doll with blue glass eyes the exact shade of her own. Her mother reminded her she had too many toys already.

When her father's friends came over to drink beer and laugh at jokes Jenny didn't understand, she was made to stay in her room, instead of paraded out in a new dress, her hair combed to shining.

The next morning, her mother refused to let Jenny take the last of the fresh cream to dump into her bathwater, slapping her hand when she reached for the jug.

Her fingers stinging and her eyes damp with rage, Jenny remembered the little girl in the woods. She forgot the brown tooth and the old voice and the hard, curious mischief in her eyes. She remembered, instead, the warmth of the fire, the girl calling her beautiful. She heard the words the girl had said, remembering them now as curious and funny.

So Jenny took a needle. Jenny took a stone. Jenny waited until her parents were asleep, and let herself into their room. Their faces were in darkness, but moonlight poured over their legs. It was easy to pull up the coverlet to reveal their feet, and to prick the hardest parts of their heels, where they wouldn't feel it. As she smeared their blood over the flat gray stone she'd found in the garden, the very last hidden bit of her that wasn't rotten yet gave a shudder.

Who are *the Night Women?* she wondered. *And who was that little girl in the trees?*

She smothered the thought, carrying the bloodied stone out into the night. As she dug up the earth outside her parents' window, burying the stone beneath it, the last bit of goodness at her center blackened and curled. She was rotten clean through.

Jenny lay awake in the dark of her bedroom, wondering what would happen when the Night Women came. She listened to the wind rattling the windows, the tap of branches on the glass. Slowly, slowly, the rattle became voices, distant and low and rich as wine. The tapping became the steady drumming of fingernails.

Scratch, scratch.

She sat up in bed.

The shatter *thump* of glass breaking.

She pulled the covers to her face, hiding all but her beautiful blue eyes. The rattling voices were closer now; they were musical and sweet. Someone laughed. Then a moan, quick and cut off in the middle. Her mother's?

She strained to hear the sounds, listening, not daring to breathe, and then—

The voices receded, became rattling again. The finger-nails were branches. Nothing more.

She settled back in bed, almost relieved, almost disappointed.

But something waited for her in the anteroom between awake and dreaming. Something was rummaging around in her mind. Someone's narrow, tickling fingers sifted through her thoughts, turning them over to see their ugly white bellies.

Go to sleep, she told herself, already half dreaming. Perhaps the thing with fingers couldn't follow her into the deep.

But it could, and it did. By the time the sun rose, Jenny, sleeping Jenny, had no more secrets.

She woke feeling slow and cold and hollow. Before the sun was fully up, Jenny's mother opened her daughter's bedroom door. She was smiling. Her hair was braided back, and she wore the lovely green dress she saved for weddings. In her hands was a breakfast tray covered with good-smelling things, and she laid it across Jenny's lap.

"For you, my love," she said, kissing her daughter's forehead.

Jenny's father, behind her, smiled. "Only the nicest things for my beautiful girl." There was a thin line of sweat above his lip. His foot would not stop tapping.

Jenny ate the breakfast. It was everything she liked, all of it hot and sweet and delicious. It was so good she could almost ignore the feeling of unease in her stomach.

It wasn't until the final bite that she understood what felt so wrong.

It was her mother. Usually she smelled of butter and vanilla and the wildflowers she put in her bath, and the something below all that that was just *her*. It was the first and truest scent Jenny knew. But when she'd leaned in to kiss Jenny, she hadn't smelled like any of those things. She hadn't smelled like anything at all.

Jenny's father bought her a horse. She'd always wanted one, but he'd said she was too young, she'd have to wait until she was fifteen. Now she was twelve years old and had a beautiful piebald mare, with a soft brown mane and a saddle of glistening leather.

"We love you, Jenny. So much." He held the reins in his fist, smiling proudly down at her. The horse shied away from her father's touch, as if his fingers were fleas.

Jenny loved her horse. Her mother and father watched as she learned to ride, their faces lit with pride. Her father hadn't been out among his farmhands for days. He preferred to sit beside her mother and watch Jenny ride. Watch Jenny eat. Watch Jenny play with the new toys he carried home for her, beautiful things of glass and metal and wood wrapped in rustling blue paper.

But Jenny's horse was her favorite gift of all. The animal was gentle and patient, and loving it might've healed the rot at her core, in time. But a week after he led it home for her, her father moved toward the horse to tighten its saddle. The animal jerked away from his touch. As he reached for it again, insistent, the animal reared up, throwing Jenny into the dirt, and ran toward the fields.

The sound of her mother's scream was not right. Even through the pain of landing hard on her back, the air knocked out of her and her eyes filled with tears, Jenny was chilled by the sound of that scream.

Her mother ran to Jenny, but her father ran past her, after the horse.

When he returned, he was favoring one shoulder, and his shirt was slick with blood.

"That animal will not hurt you again," he said, and darted his head down to kiss Jenny.

Jenny screamed and screamed, and her parents paced outside her door. Finally the sound of her mother's crying became too much to bear.

"Jenny, Jenny," she wept, when her daughter finally opened the door. "What can we do for you? What can we give to you? Please, tell us, what will make you happy?"

Her parents' faces, side by side, were paler than they'd been. Her father looked narrow in his shirt, and her mother's mouth stood out redly against her skin.

Looking at them gave Jenny the stuffed-sick feeling of having eaten too much sugared cream. "Leave me alone," she said unsteadily. "I will be happy if you leave me alone."

Her mother's face twisted, but she nodded and went away.

She came back, deep in the night. She sat by Jenny's

bedside and stroked her daughter's hair. Silently her fingers worried all the knots from it. Her scentless breath touched Jenny's cheek, while Jenny tried to make herself silent and small. She lifted one eyelid, just enough to peek.

Her mother was smiling again, always smiling. It was a smile so wide and radiant her face could hardly hold it. She looked like someone had grabbed the sides of her mouth and tugged.

Jenny squeezed her eyes shut and went back to sleep.

Always at night now she heard the whispering, the fingernails on glass and the sweet, low laughter. One day she saw her mother pulling a boot over her bare foot and gasped: the foot looked like a dead thing, purple and black with bruises and crusted with blood. She eased her boot on, wincing, then turned and saw her daughter. The wince dropped from her face, replaced by a bright smile. "My love," she said, holding out a hand.

Jenny turned her face, hurrying away. When she came too close, her mother stroked her cheek. She kissed her forehead, held her hands, buried her nose in her hair. Jenny twitched and shuddered and twisted away, but her mother's smile never wavered. As her husband grew thinner, Jenny's mother thickened. Her body sweetened, it swelled like a tick. Perhaps a baby was dreaming inside it, in the place where Jenny once rooted.

Her mother seemed to think so. She rubbed her stomach, her nails long and curling. "I am growing you the loveliest gift," she said. "You'll be so pleased, when I give it to you. Kiss my cheek, and I will give you chocolate. I will give you toys. I will give you all the pretty things that girls deserve."

Her belly was round as an apple now. And where was Jenny's father? She hadn't seen him in days. If he'd gone to town, he'd be back by now, with an armful of dolls. His fields were empty, and his chair, and his side of her mother's bed. If he wasn't there, who was it her mother whispered with when Jenny heard whispering in the night?

The same ones, perhaps, whose fingernails tapped on the glass.

Jenny, Jenny, were you always so foolish?

Not anymore, she decided. Never again. That night she let her mother kiss her cheeks and her eyelids and her chin, enduring the awful blank of her touch. She ate the sugary foods that were fed to her, that melted on her tongue like sweet air. She let the woman comb all the tangles from her hair.

Then she closed her bedroom door, gently. By moonlight she packed three dresses, five handkerchiefs, and the four gold coins hidden under her bed. All her dolls and stuffed kittens and glass roses she left behind.

She thought she'd sneak out by the window. But the rustling had already begun, the *tap-tapping* on the glass. Her mother's bedroom was just beside her own, and something was already there at her window.

Jenny opened her bedroom door, quiet. She crept through the dark house, its empty rooms, smelling of baked things and dust.

Her mother waited for her by the door. Moonlight threw

the swollen shadow of her belly across the floor. Her fingers stroked and stroked it.

"Are you going away, my Jenny? Were you going to leave me? If I'd lost you, I'd never have been happy again." Her voice was woeful, but her smile was bright. And her tongue—had it always been so long, so wet and red?

"But I didn't lose you," she went on. "And I never will. You are my daughter. Beautiful as the sun, and more deserving. I want you close, my Jenny. As close as you can come."

"I don't want to," Jenny whispered.

The woman's fingers on her belly tapped and tapped. "My Jenny always wants. Come closer, so I can whisper of all the things she'll get."

Jenny felt her feet root to the floor, felt her body become pliant and soft. She felt herself changing, becoming, altering in a way she couldn't see.

The mother inched forward on long bare feet, black with bruises. She rubbed her belly and the thing that lay inside it, ready to become something, too. She smiled at the girl and licked her lips. Her smile was wide, then wider, a grin, then a gash, then an unpeeling.

Jenny was sweeter than you'd think. It's always that way with rotten things. When the mother was done, she laid down for the last time in her life. Her body made an awful sound as it fell away from the thing her stomach carried, like a peel from a fruit.

The thing she'd birthed stretched. It untucked. It was shaped like a shadow that warped and ran and bent in odd places. With a shudder and a sigh, it gathered itself into the narrow form of a woman. Beautiful, with fingernails made to scratch at windows. Jenny's blood on the floor was red as candy, and the mother's gathered in black pools, reflecting moonlight like the glass eyes of a doll. The Night Woman was wet with it as she let herself out into the open air, to greet her sisters.

Ilsa Waits

Ilsa was six the first time she saw Death's face, and she never forgot him. From that day on, Ilsa carried a knife.

She lived in the heart of the Hinterland woods, in a village where the sun rarely shone. The people there were hide-tough and wily; they were used to tricking the land into providing them food, the woods into letting them live. Ilsa had six older brothers, and she outlived every one. One was taken by dream sickness, one by bad milk. One went mad in winter and froze, and one took his life with a knife. One fell from a tree branch and broke his neck, and the last faded away before dying of a broken heart.

The villagers said Ilsa had no heart to break. She was invisible to Death, they whispered. She'd made a deal with him, trading her brothers for her own safety and for her inheritance: a tract of land big enough for a house and garden. A slender crop of dusk cherries and black melon. A cow whose milk couldn't be trusted. And a mad old mother to keep alive, year after year. Ilsa was a girl made for bad luck, they said. After she burned the body of her sixth brother, the villagers turned their backs on her.

But Ilsa had a secret that kept her from despair. His name was Thom. He lived on the other side of the village, and she loved him almost as much as he loved her.

First their love was secret because they were young. Then it was secret because love had no place in a home marked by Death. With every loss it became harder to tell, to become engaged, to marry, until the two decided they couldn't wait any longer: they would go away to live where they would and marry when they wanted, somewhere else in the great, wild span of the Hinterland.

The night before they planned to leave, Ilsa lay beside her mother in their cold cottage. But she felt something else with her in the dark: a terrible, familiar something that didn't speak to announce itself or warn her before it went away. The taste of honey and herbs coated her tongue, sweet as life and bitter as loss. A four-note crying song whistled around her head. Then it left her, a narrow channel of icy air whistling to the east, where her beloved lay sleeping in his mother's house.

She ran there in bare feet, but it was too late. A bright nosegay of red blossoms shaped like fingers hung over the door, signifying that sickness had come to stay. She peered through the windows and saw Thom lying ill, just through the windows but beyond her reach.

When news spread of his sickness, the few who knew

about him and Ilsa whispered that she had caused it, that once again she was drawing Death close to do her bidding.

But, while it was true Ilsa had once met Death, they'd made no compact. She'd seen him easing the last breath from her father's body and had guarded against him ever since: a copper knife in her boot, a narrow heartwood hairpin tucked against her temple. Death was wily, too, and six times he'd eluded her. She'd heard the tread of his boot and smelled the grave dirt on his breath, but she never again saw his face.

And now Death was coming for Thom. On the third night he lay dying, Ilsa walked through the village in a blood-colored dress, her feet bare and dusted in her sixth brother's ashes. In one hand she carried her copper knife, in the other the fresh-killed body of a songbird. She hummed cremation songs under her breath and left a narrow trail of sparrow's blood on the dirt.

The villagers watched her come, and some ran ahead of her. When she reached Thom's house, his mother was waiting for her in the doorway holding a hatchet.

When she saw Ilsa standing there like a specter, like a dirty blood-bride, like a trap set for Death, she let the hatchet fall from her shoulder and let Ilsa in.

Thom lay in the middle of the cottage's one room. His hands were full of earth to bind him. Pools of moonlight on water lay at his head and feet to confuse Death. But Ilsa had tried those tricks already, and Death had melted through them like wet sugar the moment her head was turned.

Tonight, she would not turn her head. Tonight she would catch Death and lead him away.

The house was empty. Death had already come for Thom's father, and marriage for his sisters. His mother prowled around the house with her hatchet, and Ilsa was alone.

She washed the earth from Thom's hands with the hem of her skirt. She drank the rest of the water and let it spill down her front, to make a mockery of Death. She dropped the sparrow to the ground and crushed its bones with her foot.

When Death slipped in, it was between one breath and the next.

There was Ilsa, Thom's shallow breaths, and moonlight.

Then the girl, the dying man, the moonlight, and a shape in a narrow-cut coat, his boots made of a fine tanned leather that wasn't animal.

Ilsa believed she'd remembered his face, but she was wrong.

There were the pale eyes, the dark skin, the hair that wasn't any color she could place. The smile slow-growing and the teeth hooked on lip and the wide hands almost lost in the unlit spaces of the cottage. But she'd forgotten the quick life in his face, the scent of faraway and long ago, the sense of distance and open skies and hot sun and wide water and places she could only fathom the edges of.

When he held out his hand, she dropped her knife and took it.

His grip was hot and dry as dust. He led her to a carved red door where before there'd been only beams, and stood back.

Open it, he said. Or don't. But know I haven't bewitched you.

Ilsa felt it was true: her mind and body were her own. So she opened the door.

On the other side was a hallway of cool white stone. Ilsa forgot the village and the dead and the dying the moment her cracked feet crossed over.

She followed Death though passages filled with the rushing sound of water, and halls where pillars alternated with air, up and up to the place where a king lay on a bed draped in black. The king was young, his eyes were bloodshot, and he was all alone.

Kings cannot escape me, Death said, and used his fingers to sieve the final breath from the king's mouth. It took the form of a steady blue flame, which Death tucked into the canteen that hung around his neck.

Then he took Ilsa's hand and jumped with her, through the window behind the king's bed.

They landed light as leaves in a night garden that smelled like lavender. An old woman lay under the waving leaves of a piper plant, her eyes soft and an arm curled over her chest. Death wound the last rattling bit of life through her teeth like a lock of bronze hair and dropped it into his canteen.

The innocent cannot hide from me, Death said. There was a dark joy in his voice.

At the end of the garden was a pond. Ilsa followed Death into its waters. When they were submerged to their necks the world spun like a hoop and sent them crawling out onto another shore, of a green island that sat like a mossy stone in the heart of the Hinterland sea.

A blue-eyed woman in traveling clothes stood at their arrival, drawing her sword. Death twitched his fingers like he was coaxing a cat, and the woman's life fled her throat on a tide of glittering sand. This time he seemed to marvel at it—a red wisp, like a twist of blown glass—before tucking it into his canteen.

Those who hide cannot escape me, Death whispered. His breath crackled like cremation fire.

All night he led Ilsa from place to place, bleeding the life from men who cowered and women who wept, children who watched him with eyes made of stone and sickness, and babies whose life's last light looked like glints of sun on water. When he was done his head hung low with the weight of his canteen.

Ilsa saw sand and sea. She saw stone and sky. She saw palaces of ice and brick and marble and villages like her own, trapped in the trees. Cave pools attended to by silent women, and a well where a boy scooped up buckets of golden mist. When the sun threw its first light over Death's dark hands, he drew them back. He stood beside Ilsa, in a cottage kitchen where a man whose last breath was the color of a wren's feather lay lifeless over a cookpot.

There was a door in the wall, a carved red door Ilsa remembered from a life long ago, in a rude cottage where a man whose face she'd forgotten would die by morning.

No. She threw herself in front of it. She'd come to understand, sometime in the night, that Death had changed her again, breath by breath. She couldn't go back to what she'd been.

You can't, she said. She couldn't manage more.

But the door behind her faded into red smoke, and she slipped through, back to the close air of Thom's cottage.

A gift for you, Death said, gesturing behind her. His smile mocked her. For being my companion for a night.

Then he was gone, leaving behind a scent of salt and wind.

And Ilsa, alone in her red dress.

Behind her, Thom stirred. Around her, the village breathed, full of bodies that held a secret just behind the lips: a twist of colored smoke or mist or flame, faded or glittering like starlight, ever ready to be plucked by Death's fingers and tucked into his canteen.

Thom called her name. His voice was beloved once, but now it grated over her ear. Ilsa turned so he could see her outlined in the day's first light. When he spoke her name again it was a question, one she answered by walking from the cottage on dirty feet, caked with the mud, salt, and sand of the whole of the Hinterland.

Death passed over her beloved: that was the gift he gave her. But it was no longer the gift she wanted.

After that night, Ilsa followed the rumor of Death from house to house. She waited by bedsides, beneath windows, at the edges of accidents. But wherever she went, Death stayed away. He would not snatch a life when Ilsa was close.

The villagers changed their minds about her. Miracle worker, they called her. Destroyer of Death. But her night with Death had turned her into something else. Something stranger. When people spoke or wept or laughed or whispered, she could see it flash behind their teeth: their life's last light. Ilsa could see in the dull green flame that lapped behind a woman's molars how she would live and how she would die. She read a lifetime of lies and secrets in the snowy wisp circling a child's tongue. A baby watched her over its mother's shoulder, a tendril of silver singing over its gums.

In a cold haze Ilsa reached for it, tried to pluck it free.

The child screamed, and the mother turned, a knife already in her hand. She slashed out at Ilsa's face, and the baby's glittering life-light swam free of her fingers.

After that the villagers didn't call Ilsa anything. Her mother put a blanket, a knife, and a skin of water in a pack and closed her door to her last living child. Thom called out to Ilsa as she left the village, but she walked past him without looking back.

The whole wide world was ahead of her, Death's fingers combing through it like wind, culling its little life-lights. If he refused to return to her, she would go to him.

That first night, Ilsa slept in her cloak by the side of the road. She thought she'd walk until she found a place where the trees gave way to sky or the earth to water. But she would've died before morning if a twig hadn't cracked beneath the boot of the man leaning over her, holding a knife to her throat. She opened her eyes and went without thought for his life-light. It was a dull yellow throb over his tongue; it came away like a pebble in her fingers. The man's eyes went wide and stayed that way, as he slumped over her in the leaves.

The light was heavy in Ilsa's fingers. She rolled it from hand to hand, remembering the way Death carried all the Hinterland's lost lives in a canteen.

She took her drained waterskin and tipped in the little light. Then she lay awake the rest of the night, waiting for Death to come claim it.

He never did. When the sun rose, she rolled up her blanket and kept walking. Once she'd made herself a red-clad trap for Death, and he'd come. Now she would make herself something even more alluring: a rival.

First Ilsa tried to make sure they deserved it. She found low men who waited behind taverns with knives. Woman who whipped their dogs and their children, men fat on gold who stepped on the backs of the lean to get more of it. She saw the world: the sand, the stone, the mountains, the sea. The skin she carried around her neck grew heavy with life-lights, but never heavy enough to tempt Death.

She started to slip. She killed a man for speaking an unkind word to his wife, waiting until he slept to coax free the little light—a purer color than she'd imagined, it made her pause—then failing to resist the faint blue beat of his wife's. She wouldn't take the lives of children, she told herself, until she saw one with a dirty face that made her think of her third brother. The sight filled her with a hot, hard pain that felt like longing, and she peeled away his piercing copper light.

Her brothers wouldn't have recognized her in her long black coat, her knuckles scabbed and her hair streaked with clay-white strands. Her own life-light was the only one she couldn't see. If she could've she'd know it had been the color of sun through alder leaves once. Now it was the color of dirt dried hard on a dead man's boots.

Ilsa couldn't sleep the night she killed the boy. She finally drifted off with her back against the wall of a tavern, and woke with a man standing over her.

No, no, no, he said, when her hand went to her knife.

I've been watching you. I can do more for you than become another life on a string.

Ilsa's heart quickened. This was a messenger, perhaps, of Death. She looked carefully at the man, searching for his life-light. But his face was a scooped-out shell. She saw nothing in it: no future, no past.

Ilsa hadn't been frightened in a long time. Not since she'd made herself the thing that was feared.

Who are you, old man?

He smiled. I'm one like you, he said. A searcher. But I found what I was looking for long ago.

And? What was that?

His smile was not a kind one. Ilsa was too hungry to notice. I found this, he said, folding something into her hand.

She looked at what he'd given her: a cut-glass vial the size of an acorn. Inside it, liquid as thick and black as her hair.

Ilsa had seen the four corners of the Hinterland and the spaces between. She'd stolen the violet life-light of a despot king. She'd walked down a staircase into the sea. She'd watched the Moon lift a girl off her feet, sizzling her bones to stardust and placing her in the sky. But she couldn't envision where the contents of the vial might take her. And even if it were poison, she told herself, she'd meet Death at last.

When she looked up, the man had gone on his way. Without hesitation, Ilsa drank from the vial. The liquid slid thick over her tongue, heavy with the taste of sorrow. It peeled back the living world, turning all of its movement and color to smoke.

She stood for a moment, lost. But in that smoke was a golden pulse, a fine thread of light. It beat just there, beside her hand. She touched it, and it jerked back, hovering beyond her reach. She took a step, then another, following it through the gray fog of the vanished world.

Her boots tumbled and turned over unseen grass, pebbles, and dirt, as she followed the golden thread through the mist. Soon a pond appeared at her feet, shining like quartz in the gloom. She followed the golden thread into the water, deeper and deeper, until the pond closed over her head, the mud slipped out from beneath her feet, and she dropped lightly to the agate floor of the land of the dead.

The realm was a silent one. Ilsa walked through hematite forests, past lakes of frozen fire. She walked beneath the cut-crystal leaves of a grove of hazel trees, where spirits spied on her from behind tourmaline trunks. The waterskin around her neck, sloshing with its burden of souls, grew heavier as she approached Death's palace.

It was an ugly place, a crouching animal bristling with spires. The shining thread led right to its iron doors, where it ended at a ruby knocker shaped like a ring of the red flowers that meant sickness. Her shoulders ached with the weight of the waterskin, so heavy she wasn't sure she could carry it. She heaved herself onto Death's doorstep. Ilsa knocked.

Ilsa waited.

A figure that looked no more substantial than the shades in the trees answered the door. It stepped back, beckoning to her to enter.

She followed its silent tread, her boots echoing on the

green-banded floors of the palace. They moved through cold marble halls, toward the distant hum of a party.

Finally they stepped into a chamber larger than any Ilsa had seen, with walls covered in soft moss and a ceiling freckled with stars. Music wound through the air like black flags, twining around the limbs of a floor full of dancers. At the far end of the hall Death sat easy on his throne, eyes burning in his face like pale planets.

You've found me at last, he said to Ilsa.

At the sound of his voice, the dancers went still and the music died. The waterskin around Ilsa's neck felt heavier still. The faces of the guests turned toward her as one, and she felt a terror that started in her fingers and spread like wildfire.

She knew every face, because she'd killed each one: the man she'd slain in the forest stood just there, holding a glass of something red to his lips. The child whose light she'd thieved for no reason stared at her from atop a table. Their faces were empty without their life-lights, their mouths filled with darkness. Ilsa took a step back, then fell to her knees, heavy with the weight of the lives she carried.

She would die, she knew, if she couldn't run. The weight of the waterskin would strangle her, or the shades gathered against her would. With shaking fingers, she tugged desperately at the skin around her neck.

The rope holding it snapped, and it tipped on its side as it fell, all the lights it carried spilling out. They spun over the floor, massing into a dark and glittering fog. It illuminated the faces of the dead before it swallowed them.

When the fog cleared away, the dead had changed. Their life-lights flickered from their faces like ugly stars.

Ilsa gripped her copper knife in shaking fingers, but Death held up a hand, staying the crowd where it stood.

What will her punishment be? he asked.

The sea of living dead rustled with dark ideas, words that wrapped themselves around Ilsa's imagination and stripped the blood from her cheeks.

No, Death said. The punishment will fit the crime. He slid through the crowd like a cool black knife, and tipped Ilsa's chin in his long fingers. A theft for a theft.

She thought of the man who had given her the vial. *I'm one like you*, he'd said. She remembered the emptiness in him, that had terrified her.

But the thing Death pulled from her wasn't her life-light. It was the thing that hid behind it, like a moon in eclipse, too hidden even for Ilsa to find.

It took the form of a fingertip-point of frosted black glass. When it was gone Ilsa felt a hardening come over her: she felt impervious, untouched.

Death rolled the stolen thing in his wide palm. This is your death, he said. You wouldn't wait for it—you wouldn't wait for me—so you've lost the right to it. He popped it into a blank space between his molars for safekeeping.

You wanted to defeat Death, he said, and now you have. May you enjoy your long walk through the land of the living.

You may find Ilsa, sometimes, on the back bench of a tavern, or sitting on a stone overlooking the sea. When she looks at you, you'll sense the black hole in her, the nameless, missing something that makes you afraid. Her face will fade in time, until the moment of your passing. And there she'll be, hovering just over Death's shoulder, hoping to hitch a ride alongside your spirit back to the land of forgetting.

JOURNEY

BEHIND THE SCENES OF

THE HAZEL WOOD

An Interview with Melissa Albert

Where did the idea for *The Hazel Wood* come from?

The idea began with an image, of a fairy-tale character who'd slipped free from their story and showed up in the real world. From there, other elements fell into place: the reclusive author with a dark secret, the uncanny bad luck chasing my heroine from place to place. Books I took inspiration from in writing it include Lev Grossman's Magicians Trilogy, with its wonderful mix of high fantasy tropes and a lived-in contemporary world; the hard-boiled voice and epic metaphors of Raymond Chandler's Philip Marlowe books; the delirious fantasy worlds created by Catherynne Valente; and, of course, all the fairy tales I read obsessively as a kid.

When did you start writing? Have you always been a storyteller?

My mom likes to talk about how, at age three or four, I'd bring her a crayon and paper and dictate stories to her—mostly about scary animals I met in the woods (I had an apparent terror of peacocks), and all of them ending with my coming safely home, where she was waiting with dinner. From there I leveled up to writing short stories about mermaids and fairies, Bruce Coville and Francesca Lia Block fanfic, and I painstakingly mapped Choose Your Own Adventure books. Outside of a brief stint in my early twenties, when I veered into arts writing and reporting, I kept writing fiction for fun. But 2011 is when I started taking the idea of novel writing seriously, after discovering and falling head over heels for contemporary young adult literature. I'd always loved lit fic, but something about the glorious, plotty head rush of great YA books like *Daughter of Smoke & Bone* and *Akata Witch* and *Feed* made me want to write one of my own.

This is your first published book! How does that make you feel?

Like most writers (or so I like to think), I have a graveyard of partly finished novels on my laptop, except it's more of a zombie graveyard because I never know what's actually dead and what I'll want to go back to. I'm thrilled *The Hazel Wood* is the book that has become my debut, because it combines so many of my obsessions, fictional and otherwise: contemporary fantasy, fairy tales, portals, New York

City, book nerdery, a string of uncanny events that combine into a far weirder whole. It's a book I'm proud to see my name on, and it's a kick—if a slightly "everyone can see me naked" one—to watch it head out into the world.

What is one thing readers might be surprised to learn about you?

I'm nothing like my heroine, Alice. At all. She's fiercer than me, and fearless about telling people exactly what she thinks of them (at times perhaps too fearless). I, on the other hand, still worry about people whose feelings I hurt in the '90s.

Can you tell us anything about what you're writing next?

I'm working on a buffet of things at the moment, in that excited, slightly nerve-racking state of not knowing which one I want to deep dive into. But every one of them involves magic.

During all of the interviews you've done, what question have you never been asked about your writing or your book that you wish you'd been asked—and what's the answer?

I've gotten the opportunity to interview some incredible authors through my work with *Time Out* and Barnes & Noble, and the questions I always love to ask are (1) What's the first piece of fiction you ever wrote, because the answers are often hilarious (and sometimes illuminating), and (2) What does your process look like, in case someone really has this writing game figured out and can give me some tips. I talked a bit about the first above, and as for the second I find myself thinking a lot about George Saunders's gorgeous insights on the inherent mystery of it all, this process by which artists, in the "pursuit of specificity," work "outside the realm of strict logic." For me that translates into figuring it out as I go, being pleasantly surprised (or elated) when something I dropped on page seven fits by happy accident with what I want to do on page two hundred, and doing my best to avoid the most obvious paths.

If readers want to find other books in a similar vein as *The Hazel Wood*, what would you recommend?

I would send you directly to Lev Grossman's the Magicians Trilogy, which roots a brilliant, depressive young man's very funny coming-of-age in a deeply specific, gorgeously rich dual fantasy world; J. M. Barrie's *Peter Pan*, which is weirder, darker, and more mind-bogglingly wonderful than you can imagine if you've only encountered Peter via Disney; Helen Oyeyemi's *Boy, Snow, Bird*, perhaps the best and wisest fairy-tale retelling I've read; and Catherynne Valente's brain-melting *Deathless*, *Radiance*, and Fairyland books, the reading of which is the closest a square like me ever comes to getting high.

A Discussion Guide

1. Consider Alice's narration. How would you describe Alice? What did you take away from Alice's experiences? What do you feel Alice has gained by the end of the novel?

2. What were some of the references you caught to classic children's literature in the novel? Were any of your own favorites mentioned? How do you think these references influence the story?

3. How are Finch and Alice different? How are they similar? Why do you think they bond so intensely when they're thrown together?

4. When did you first expect that the stories and characters from Althea's book might be real?

5. Ella keeps the truth of Alice's childhood a secret from her. What do you think of this choice? If you were Ella, would you have taken Alice from her story? Would you have told her the truth? When?

6. How would you describe the Spinner?

7. How did you feel when you finished the novel? Were you surprised? Satisfied?

8. What five words would you use to describe *The Hazel Wood*?

9. Would you want to read Althea's stories in *Tales from the Hinterland*?

© Laura Etheredge

Melissa Albert is a web editor and the founding editor of the B&N Teen Blog. She has written for *McSweeney's*, *Time Out Chicago*, and more. Melissa grew up in Illinois and lives in Brooklyn, New York. Find her on Twitter at @mimi_albert.

www.HazelWoodBook.com

*Can you ever truly
escape the Hazel Wood?*

THE
NIGHT
COUNTRY

MELISSA ALBERT

COMING FALL 2019

FLATIRON
BOOKS